The Clock T

We g n
the m e,
under a
strang f
destiny .
the sak for all we
had sha I knew then that we could not part without some ceremony to mark the occasion. It was in that split second that the idea of a vow occurred to me. A vow to bind the three of us in life and in death, which none could break – more binding than the marriage oath, more solemn than a baptism. Without pausing to think, I put it to them, finishing by saying: "It'll be a promise to last ten years. Binding us to go to the other's aid if called – no matter how far the journey, how long the gap between or how great the dangers. And at the end of that time we'll meet here again, at the orphanage, under this clock tower, to give some of what we've earned to our successors."

The Clock Tower

JEANNE MONTAGUE

G

Gainsborough Press

This edition published in 1996 by Gainsborough Press
An imprint of Leopard
20 Vauxhall Bridge Road, London SW1V 2SA

First published in Great Britain by
Century Publishing Co. Ltd 1983
Arrow edition 1986

Phototypeset by Input Typesetting Ltd, London
Printed and bound in Great Britain by
Cox & Wyman Ltd, Reading, Berkshire

ISBN 0 752 90365 9

To my mother, Winifred Alix,
with love and thanks

BOOK ONE

Nancy

I met Murder on the way –
He had a mask like Castlereagh –
Very smooth he looked, yet grim:
Seven Bloodhounds followed him:

The Mask of Anarchy, SHELLEY

A savage place! as holy and enchanted
As e'er beneath a warning moon was haunted
By woman wailing for her demon-lover!

Kubla Khan, COLERIDGE

Prologue

The sun was a fiery disc burning through an overcast sky which, dust-heavy, was like bronze gauze. The day was hotter than it had seemed indoors, or perhaps I was starting a fever again. My face flamed and I could feel the sting of sweat running down it before I had covered many yards. I stopped to rest, realising that I had been almost running, pressing my hands to the pain in my side and screwing up my eyes against the glare.

The arid landscape appeared to swell and shrink in time with my own heartbeats, and there was a ringing in my ears. The throbbing in my temples, never absent for long lately, surged intolerably inside my skull and stabbed through to the back of my neck. My heart was pounding faster, and I opened my mouth, breathing hard in an effort to control myself. The hot wind failed to dry the moisture from my face – terrible wind – the *samoom* which, so the old people said, brought madness to many. It was devil-driven from the desert, pungent with the odour of hot sand.

I went on, moving more and more slowly despite my efforts. It was like one of those bad dreams when one's feet seem weighted through one struggles to flee from some dark, unnamable thing. I must reach the town. Fear was driving me, fear and love and my damnable curiosity which would not accept an apparently rational explanation for the dreadful events of the past weeks. Greater still than the risk I was now taking was the fear of remaining in the house.

I was being followed. I knew it. Wanly, I realised that my disguise was woefully inadequate. Only a fool would have supposed that an Arab burnous would hide the fact that I was a white woman. Misery imprisoned and invaded me as that caul of reddish cloud did the sickly sun.

I had never walked this distance before. Usually I rode in a carriage. Only sheer, terrified necessity had forced me to attempt it. Marshalling my fading courage, I descended towards the cluttered, dirty streets, jostled by the crowd, pressing close to the adobe walls to avoid the mules and bad-tempered camels. I shot a glance over my shoulder and my blood stood still. That black-robed figure which had been dogging me had paused by a sweetmeat stall. I had failed to shake him off. A dreadly, paralysing coldness crept down my spine. I remained there motionless, breathless, fighting to regain my self-control. I was ashamed of such cowardice. Where was my bravery now? I, who had never been timid in my life until I came to this accursed country.

No matter what transpired, I must complete my mission. The coffee house must be located, that place I had once visited under carefree circumstances. I fostered the frail hope that the owner might be co-operative or open to a bribe. I had learned through bitter experience that everyone here was venal. Information could be bought, if one paid a high enough price. I was certain of it. It was the only thing I could be sure of in this dark tangle of confusion which was making me doubt my own sanity.

With a tremendous exertion of will, I plunged into the labyrinth of twisting alleys and, at last, recognised one or two landmarks. I came to a pathway which ran along the walls of a shrine. The weird light bounced off white walls, sliced across by inky shadows like gaping wounds. People passed under the arch leading to the bazaar. Above, the livid sky outlined the dome whose tilework was detailed in blue and gold. Colours to ravish the eye and bewitch the senses. Even now, they cast a hypnotic spell on me. I fought against it. I must keep my wits about me. My pursuer was still there, remorseless as death. I dodged into the bazaar.

It was then that I saw Nell. I could not believe my eyes. There she stood, haggling with a Syrian merchant over the price of a length of silk. Somehow, her sudden appearance in such a place and at such a time exaggerated my already dizzying feeling of unreality. Nell, like some visitation from the past. I knew her at once although it had been years since we last met. She was grown-up now and extremely elegant, wearing an expensive-looking dress, a huge hat on her piled-up fair hair. Very much the European lady tourist, shining like a jewel amidst the turbans and yashmaks. I forgot everything else, overcome by surprise and the wild surge of hope that rushed through me. A single ray of light, dancing with dust motes and circling flies, slanted from a latticed window high up on the wall, illumining her, my angel of deliverance.

She looked so endearingly familiar that I shook off the nightmare in which I was trapped. "Nell!" I shouted recklessly, while heads turned in my direction. "Nell – it's me!"

She glanced up. Our eyes met and her expression of astonishment was almost comical. For the first time in I don't know how long, I felt myself smiling. "Nancy!" she gasped, throwing down the merchandise and running towards me with hands outstretched. "My God! It can't be! What on earth are you doing here?"

I seized her gloved hand and drew her into an angle of the wall away from those inquisitive stares. "Hush, keep your voice down. It's a long story and I haven't time to explain," I burst out, then heard my voice faltering, choking: "Nell – oh, Nell – I'm so glad to see you. You've no idea – it's been terrible – terrible!" I could speak no more for a moment, close to tears.

Her eyes were wide with alarm, those eyes which were of a blue so intense that it verged on purple. "I don't understand," she began, adding: "Why are you wearing that silly outfit? Is this some sort of a joke?"

I gripped her feverishly. "Joke! I wish it were. You must help me. I'm in trouble . . . please believe me . . ."

"My dear girl, what is it?" A variety of emotions chased across her features and she put her arm about me. I leaned against her, awash with relief at having found an ally. This was only a momentary indulgence. I dragged myself away. Time was of the essence.

I was trembling in every limb and the bazaar spun sickeningly. My hand encountered the wall behind me and I steadied myself. This was certainly not the time to faint, but it was as if every glittering, overloaded stall there was rushing in on me. I hated that crowded market-place where foreign tongues babbled endlessly, and flies, sand, beggars and filth abounded.

"I'm sorry," I faltered. "Forgive me for alarming you."

Her voice restored me – that crisp voice which had always had a slightly acid ring to it. She was still cool, almost aloof, even now when she must have been nearly as shaken as I. "Are you ill, Nancy?"

I shook my head. "No – at least I don't think I am, though others say different."

"Then what's going on?" Her eyes ran down over me and a trace of her old, well-remembered mockery returned. "Have you gone native? Turned Muslim? What would Old Mother Bowell say?"

"No – nothing like that. I can't tell you – not here – not now. Where are you staying? I must see you again – privately – somewhere we can talk. Don't look at me as if I'm mad! I'm not mad – I'm not!"

"Calm down, dear," she said and there was a warmth in her tone which was an entirely new quality. Yes, she was different, there was no doubt of it. Time had done its work with her as it had with me. "I don't think for a moment that you're mad, but I wish you'd tell me why you're so upset."

"Listen, Nell . . . we made a promise once. D'you remember? Now I'm going to hold you to it. Are you staying in a hotel? Can I come there?" I was speaking fast, the words tripping my tongue.

She lost some of her poise and hesitated before saying: "Of course I remember, I'd be a poor sort of friend if I didn't. I'm at the Stanley Hotel. I suppose Charles won't object if we meet there."

My mind was not functioning properly. I must have gazed at her stupidly. "Charles?"

"My husband. Oh, yes, I'm a respectable married woman now." She gave a light rather forced little laugh. "Mrs Charles de Grendon."

She was not happy. I sensed this strongly. These days I had become acutely aware of the atmosphere surrounding others. It was as if a top layer of skin had been flayed away, leaving me helplessly vulnerable to their pain. There was an air about Nell which filled me with foreboding. "You are married?" I repeated slowly.

She was very bright about it, putting on a brave show. "Yes, indeed. Everyone thinks we're the perfect couple. Charles is charming and so handsome, but he is rather possessive. He may not approve of a friend of mine turning up out of the blue."

"He can't complain if it's a woman, surely?" My spirits, which had risen at the sight of her, began to sink again.

"You don't know Charles," she replied with a wry smile.

"But you've got to help me. I'm in danger – dreadful danger," I insisted. I was fighting for my very life.

Her eyes lifted to mine and she must have read the desperation there. Her brows winged down in a worried frown, yet she shook her head, still dubious. "Danger? What danger? Are you threatened by someone?"

"Yes, Nell. I don't know who – not yet – but if you don't help me, anything can happen – anything," I whispered, darting a quick glance about us. As I did so,

I saw the hooded man again. He was half hidden in a doorway, his features obscured, but I felt his eyes watching. "I must go. It's too dangerous here. The Stanley Hotel, you said? Good. I'll see you tomorrow afternoon. Keep faith with me. I need you desperately. I swear that I'm telling the truth."

It was terribly hard to leave her, but I did it, mingling with the throng, unsure of which direction to take while the heat, the jumbled odours of spices, sweaty bodies, human and animal excrement, rose like a miasma about me. I noticed that people were beginning to leave the bazaar, hurrying home, glancing skywards, for the wind was rising again. Every instinct within me was screaming to go too, but my stubborness insisted that I carry on with my search. My nerves were strung to such a pitch that I gave a cry and swung round, fingers clenched around the hilt of my dagger, when a beggar tugged at my burnous.

"May Allah give you good health," he whined, holding out his bowl.

He was a most repulsively deformed creature. I tried to pull away but he clung on the harder. I stared at him suspiciously. Was he one of them? Had he been ordered to delay me? Perhaps not – perhaps he really thought I was an Arab. By now I was familiar with the formal greetings exchanged by even the most humble and had acquired a smattering of the language. "To your kindness, I am well," I muttered. I had the presence of mind to deepen my voice to a masculine pitch.

He grinned, displaying rotting teeth. One of his eyes was diseased, and he had an incredibly dirty turban wound round his head. I winced at the rank odour seeping from his rags. "*Effendi* – for the sake of Allah! Oh, ye charitable! I am seeking from thee a cake of bread. My supper must be thy gift."

I dropped a coin into his bowl, keeping my face averted, my hood shadowing my face. "Allah will sustain thee. He will help, content and enrich thee," I responded and tried to turn away. He gripped my robe persistently.

"*Salaam*," he said, eyeing the money then leering up at me. "May your shadow never grow less, Merciful One. I receive this bounty from thy hand, though thou art not a Believer."

I froze at this implication, reading knowledge in his eyes. He was blocking my path. The alley was deserted, dark too, with that unnatural daytime darkness which precedes a sand-storm. He glanced up at the lowering sky glimpsed between the rooftops. "The genies will ride the wind, *sitt*," he said, abandoning the pretence of taking me to be a man. "Go home. Seek the shelter of thy master's house."

A feeling of utter helplessness and futility swept over me. He knew all about me. How foolish I had been to imagine that any purpose could be served by my entering the native quarters. Of course I had been watched. Of course I had been followed. Nell was my only hope now, and I thanked God for leading me to her. Yet some streak of obstinacy, some foolhardy pride in my nature would not admit defeat.

"Get out of my way!" I commanded, though my knees were shaking so much that I could hardly stand. "Direct me to the street of the *kahwehs*."

He wagged his head from side to side sorrowfully, as if regretting my folly. "Thou must not enter there, *sitt*."

"Indeed I must." My voice was sharp with fear and the darkness thickened around me, almost tangible. The wind tore down the alley with the roar of waves trapped in a cavern. Sand whipped up in clouds, filling my nostrils, grating between my teeth, blinding my vision.

The beggar had to shout to be heard above the howling gale. "Go home, *sitt*," he repeated, pulling his tattered cloak over his head, crouching against that buffeting; grotesque, not quite human. One of his misshapen hands reached towards me in the gloom. "Go home, and take this with thee."

My fingers closed on metal. I raised my eyes to where he had been, but he had melted away like a midnight phantom. The alley was empty of all save myself, the wind, and the thing in my hand. I held it close to my face, trying to see it. It was a talisman, or so I thought at first glance, then, as I looked more closely, I shuddered and flung it away. It spun off like an arc of bloody flame in that unearthly light. I still seemed to see the symbols that had been crudely cut into it. This was no good-luck charm which I had taken so unwittingly. It was a curse.

With a cry of horror I turned and ran. I whimpered aloud in shrill terror and despair like a hurt dog as I stumbled back the way I had come. It was useless to fight any more. I should never find my way to the *kahweh* and even if I had it would have been to no avail. I should have been met by bland, polite faces and a pack of wily lies. Now there was only Nell. I would give her my journal. It would be safer with her. Written in it was everything which had happened, and there was someone who would move heaven and hell to prevent its contents coming to light.

By a miracle I found myself on the road back to Ramleh. My breath burned my throat. I could hardly see for dust. The *samoom* blotted out every other sound – roaring, howling, as if indeed the devils rode it. I was frantic with fear and it seemed that I was being beaten by huge black wings, demonic laughter screaming in my ears. With my head bowed and my arms protecting my face, I fought my way on. My journal! I must get my journal and take it to Nell!

I crawled up the hill. Below, above and around me, the dust swirled like fog, eerie shapes appearing and dissolving. The palm trees bent and groaned before the onslaught, their fronds distorted into spears. The clouds parted and I saw a distant dome and a minaret rising like monsters from a brownish sea. Then they vanished as the dust met and mingled again, darkness closing about me, wrapping me in a stifling embrace, the wind demons yelling in lunatic triumph. My palm burned as if branded by that metal disc which had been designed to attract the forces of evil and which was sent to me by someone who wished me ill.

I flung out my arms in a vain attempt to thrust that thick, suffocating blackness away. I was screaming, my voice joining those of the elements which jeered and mocked in response. I felt them sealing my eyes, crushing the last vestige of control from my brain. Then my hands encountered something cold and solid. Gates towered over me. The great iron gates of El Tarifa. I wrapped my arms round them, sobbing, and it was at that moment that the wind died abruptly. I had come back, but this brought poor comfort. Wherever I went in this dreadful city, I should find no sanctuary, and this place was the most hostile of all.

Nell. I clung to the thought of her like a desperate mariner clings to a lifeline. Her swift action was the only thing which could save me now.

Chapter 1

"So, Nancy, I hope I find you in a suitably chastened frame of mind," Mrs Bowell said, her mouth opening and closing like a rat trap. She was a severe woman and I had never seen her smile, not at us, at any rate. Oh, she pasted a grin on her doughy features on Sundays when she cornered the vicar, or when ladies and gentlemen of the orphanage committee called, but after they had gone, she reverted to type, hard-faced, unbending. She was stupid, captious and fault-finding, unremitting in her intention to save the souls and punish the bodies of the two hundred parentless girls in her charge.

"Yes, ma'am," I replied, standing before her, head held high though I felt faint with hunger and my flesh ached from the thrashing I had received.

I hated her. All night long from my bed of damp sacking in the coal-hole, I had prayed that she might die. For more than ten years she had persecuted me. Old Mother Bowell, we called her behind her back. When I say "we", I mean Rebecca, Nell and myself. I did not take much notice of the other inmates – I had my two bosom friends and they were everything to me, a feeling which I think they returned in full. None of us had any relations. We were quite alone in the world, so we had become a close-knit family in ourselves, and tried to sustain and comfort each other in that bleak building situated on a cliff above the winding Avon Gorge in the city of Bristol.

Mrs Bowell was seated behind her flat ugly table in that equally unattractive room. It was a place of dread where we were chastised or lectured. I shall always remember its odour – the very same smell which clung to her plain, rusty-black dress, an unlovely garment which clothed her tightly corseted body. The creaking of her stays had, more than once, reduced us three to helpless, dangerous giggles. This was her workaday outfit with a high collar buttoned beneath her several chins, the bodice a suit of armour, the skirt sweeping down to the floor, rustling like a bat's wings at her every movement. She wore a stiffly starched white apron, and a small linen cap on her greying hair which she strained back from a centre parting and secured in a bun at the back. A gross, plain, evil-tempered woman who should no more have been allowed anywhere near children than a monstrous wild sow. Round her ample middle she had a black leather belt and from this swung a heavy bunch of keys – the keys of our prison – the Cardwell Asylum for Exposed and Deserted Young Children.

This smell which I speak of was a combination of carbolic and antiseptic. It clung to the brown serge curtains and seeped up from the highly polished bottle-green linoleum. A coal fire smouldered in the iron grate, pewter-coloured by the daily application of blacking and elbow-grease. The dull flames lit the brass tongs, poker and shovel and glinted on the rim of the mesh guard. After years of buffing similar objects, I viewed them with dislike. There was the mournful patter of rain against the window panes for it was a wet summer, typically English – the summer of 1900. The coming of the new century had been an exciting event, and we had been as thrilled as anyone, anticipating great things, but it had proved to be just another in a long chain of disappointments. Nothing changed for us – our lives continued to be as grey and cheerless as before.

The orphanage had been founded by Sir George Cardwell who, in the eighteenth century, had decided to expend a portion of the vast fortune amassed through the exploitation of his factory workers and the profit from the slave trade by opening this home for foundlings.

No doubt he was a very clever man who lulled his conscience, was praised for his beneficence and satisfied his vanity by the sight of a regiment of homeless boys and girls wearing his uniform and a badge emblazoned with the initials G.C. It was like a brand forever reminding them, and those who came after, that it was due to his generosity that they were fed, clothed and educated.

Though he had been dead for over a century, Mrs Bowell always spoke of him in those hushed tones reserved for the sickrooms or church. His descendents continued to give financial support and took a spurious interest in the orphans. I did not give a damn for him or them, most rebelliously ungrateful. They were a bunch of snobbish, canting hypocrites.

Mrs Bowell continued to fix me with a black, baleful eye. "It's as well that you will be leaving soon, my girl," she commented heavily, adding with a disapproving sniff: "Particularly after last night's shocking Bbehavioour-

Nothing would have iinduced me to stay there, even had I been able. I could not wait to shake the dust of the place from my feet. I swore to myself that I'd never enter it again, no matter what! Trust her to harp on about my conduct, even though I had ben so savagely punished for causing a near riot in the dormitory. Nell and Rebecca had suffered too. It had not really been our fault, but scapegoats had to be found and, as usual, we had borne the brunt of Mrs Bowell's wrath.

It had happened after dark. Miss Winifred West, known as Silly Winnie by the girls, had settled us down and extinguished the gaslamps, leaving one glowing in the corridor outside, its dim, jaundiced beam filtering through the fanlight. No one went straight to sleep. There was the usual whispering, chattering and muffled giggles from the twenty identical iron bedsteads. As soon as the door closed behind that kindly, ineffectual spinster who had the thankless task of teaching us English, my bed creaked as Rebecca and Nell slipped in beside me. This had become a nightly habit. It was here that we exchanged the warmth and comfort so lacking in our affection-starved lives. Here we talked of forbidden topics, alarmed and curious at the changes taking place in our adolescent bodies.

We compared notes, kept in total ignorance by those in charge, compelled to gather haphazard and mostly inaccurate information on the basic facts of life. Rebecca was the eldest, and it was she who had come to the rescue on that awful morning some months before when I had discovered blood staining my undergarments. I thought I was going to die, sick with the grinding pains in my stomach. She knew all about it, telling me solemnly that it was the "curse", the punishment placed on Eve by God, because she had tempted Adam to eat the fruit of the Tree of Knowledge. Through gritted teeth, writhing in agony and fear, I muttered that our foolish mother of the human race should have left the damned apple where it was! More than ever I envied boys who possessed the freedom for which I longed and were not forced to endure this shameful misery.

Yet, in a strange way, I was proud of this evidence that I was maturing, I did not like the idea of having babies though, and was highly embarrassed about the whole process, unable to look upon it as a perfectly natural thing, my viewpoint warped by the religious bigotry hammered into me from infancy. There was something so primitive, so animal about this function. The other girls joked about it but to me it was just an additional humiliation. I suppose I should have grown hardened to being humiliated, never knowing anything else, but there was a fierce spirit in me which rebelled violently against any reminder of my lowly status. I could not, *would* not, buckle down and accept my lot and this attitude landed me in constant trouble.

I loathed the drab brown uniform. Charity girls had their necks covered by white tippets when other youngsters had them bare. Our hair was hidden under odd-shaped caps, resembling cottage-loaves, and the style had not changed since Sir George's day. It was instantly recognisable. We stuck out like a sore thumb wherever we went, our youthful sensitivity open to ridicule. We were ordered to look modest and chaste at all times. No personal ornaments were allowed. Lack of such frivolities was intended to promote self-forgetfulness and a dedication to a prayerful life. Rebecca found this particularly hard, hungering for pretty clothes and jewellery. On one occasion she sinned by wearing a cheap little ring which she had picked up from the gutter. Mrs Bowell pounced on her in the classroom, shouting:

"What animal besides a charity girl wears a ring?"

Connie Wilton, Rebecca's sworn enemy and Mrs Bowell's toady, came up with the prompt reply: "A pig, ma'am!"

Mrs Bowell expressed approval. "Quite right, Connie. Go up."

We wore brown Holland pinafores for working in, and white ones for Sunday best. Each child was known by the number pinned on her shoulder. Our underwear consisted of patched hand-me-downs, and we knitted our black woollen stockings. Until we reached fourteen, our hair was as close-cropped as the boys who lived in a different building. This was deemed essential to keep heads free from lice, a further mark of Cain. I had never become reconciled to the cries of: "Charity! Charity!" chanted at us by other children. It always reduced me to boiling fury, making me break from the crocodile and lash out at those jeering tormentors, bloodying noses and starting a furore for which I was invariably beaten later.

On the night in question, Rebecca and Nell huddled close to me and I relaxed, fondling Rebecca's curls. She had been permitted to grow her hair for a year now, but she grumbled that it was a mixed blessing, adding to the jealousy which most of the girls already felt towards her. Her locks were blue-black and shiny, already flowing about her shoulders. I petted her, whispering that they envied her because she was so beautiful.

" 'Handsome is as handsome does'," mocked Nell, aping Mrs Bowell. "Wonder what Handsome does that's so dreadful," she added in her own voice, then dropped it an octave or two, warning: "You'll come to a bad end, my girl, always singing and dancing and prinking in mirrors? Where's your modesty? Where's your humility? Why don't you drag along with bowed head?"

"Stuff!" retorted Rebecca. "Those rules were made up by the old and ugly. I don't intend to abide by 'em. Thank God I'm leaving this bloody place soon!"

I knew that Nell was joking, so did Rebecca. We were both intensely proud of our friend's good looks, and spent every moment of our free time talking or sitting together, talking and talking. Not that we were given much opportunity. Mrs Bowell was fond of saying "the devil finds work for idle hands to do!" and she stretched her ingenuity to devise means of frustrating Satan. Nell had voiced the opinion that Old Mother Bowell must have more than just a nodding acquaintance with the devil as she seemed to know so much about him.

Bedtime was our refuge, the high spot of our day, when we were able to be lavish with our caresses, unconsciously seeking that tactile rapport so essential to our needs. Sadly, we had been rigidly denied such expression of feeling that it was inevitable that our avid hunger for love and our growing awareness of bodily urges made our gestures of affection more intense now. Our innocence blinded us to the fact that this might be misunderstood, smeared, dirtied and dragged down.

Naturally, we talked of boys. They were a mystery. The only contact we had with those in the orphanage was the piles of socks we had to darn for them and the shirts we were forced to sew. They in return, cobbled our heavy, lace-up boots. We saw them from afar, filing into church on Sunday and, once a year, uniformed and well-scrubbed, we all joined in the thanksgiving service in memory of Sir George. So, denied masculine company, it became an absorbing topic.

"Have you ever been kissed by a boy?" whispered Rebecca, winding her soft arms about my neck, her warm breath fanning my cheek, her skin smelling faintly of soap.

I was indignant. " 'Course not, silly. How could I? We live like bloody nuns here. But I've wondered about it. What d'you think it feels like?"

"Horrid, if he had whiskers and bad breath like Mr Bowell," put in Nell. "He's a randy old pig. Bet he'd like to try it."

We stifled our laughter, convulsed at the idea of Mr Bowell as a suitor. He was a pompous person, completely dominated by his wife and equally zealous in carrying out her maxim of "spare the rod and spoil the child". Balding and corpulent, he was too fond of the bottle. We girls had learned to keep out of his reach for he was also too free with his hands, when his wife was not looking. Indeed, a most unattractive candidate for kisses with his field of freckles under the unhealthy-looking skin of his face whose outlines were lost amidst jowls which drooped from his side-whiskers like a rooster's wattles.

"I've been talking to Peggy," Rebecca went on, an excited edge to her voice. "And she told me that the gardener's boy caught her in the outhouse the other day and kissed her."

We were agog for further revelations. Peggy was the skivvy who slaved all day in the vast, gloomy subterranean kitchen under the eagle eye of Mrs Starkey, the cook. She was eighteen and a mine of information. I suspected that she embroidered the stories of her lurid aventures to impress us.

"You don't want to believe everything she tells you," scoffed Nell. "She's a bloomin' liar."

"Go on, tell us more," I urged, curiosity aroused.

"She said it wasn't as good as when she went out with that soldier bloke, who's always hanging around the back door, a-courting her," Rebecca answered, adopting a worldly-wise casualness. "Just a peck, you know – as if he didn't know what to do. It was different with the soldier – he stuck his tongue in her mouth, so she said – and then he told her he'd buy her a bonnet from Rendal's shop if she'd let him take her drawers down."

There was a moment of stunned silence as we mulled over this extraordinary statement. Our drawers were sacred garments, to be anchored firmly in place at all times. We only removed them at bedtime when sedately shrouded in our enveloping nightgowns. In my eyes the scruffy, snub-nosed maid of all work suddenly acquired the glamour of a Scarlet Woman, though I was not too sure what this meant.

Then, curiosity inching through my astonishment: "What did he want to do that for?" I asked, gazing at the white blur of Rebecca's face in the gloom.

Before she could reply, another voice struck across this very private conversation. It belonged to Connie Wilton who occupied the next bed. "So he could do dirty things to her, stupid!" she announced scornfully. "And Becky Smale should know all about that, seeing as how her mother was a whore!"

Rebecca pulled away from me, half crouching, glaring at Connie. "What d'you mean? You don't know nothing about my mother!"

" 'Course I do! It's as plain as the nose on your face. You're a bloody foreigner, ain't you? A Dago girl, and they're all filthy whores!" Connie brayed triumphantly, and her cronies joined in the sport, yelling insults.

" 'Cor, just look at her! She's an Eye-talian bitch! She ought to be selling ice cream! Hokey-pokey, a penny a lump, the more you eat, the more you pump! Ice cream – ice cream – all hot!"

"That's a bloody lie!" Rebecca shouted. She was trembling with rage. I knew how much she hated the fat, spotty Connie. "I'm as English as you! At least I'm not a slimy creep – teacher's pet!"

"Just 'cause I do my work and Mrs Bowell likes me," Connie sneered in a maddeningly superior way, sitting on the side of her bed, that nasty little traitor, ever eager to run off and tell tales. "You're not English! You're a Dago pig! Pig! Pig! Ugly pig! Your name should be 'Smelly', not Smale. Becky Smelly! Becky Smelly!"

"That's right, Connie," echoed her friend, Betsy Culverhouse, raw-boned and angular, without a single redeeming feature. "All dirty foreigners stink!"

"Bet her dad had a barrel organ," chimed in Annie Snow, another objectionable tattle-tale. "She'd make a good monkey, dancing on the top. You know how she loves to show off!"

"Bastard – bastard – Dago bastard!" chanted the rest, more joining in this cruel baiting.

"We're all bastards," I said suddenly, my voice cutting across the noise, silencing them. I stood at Rebecca's side and was glad that I was so tall, my head well above theirs, my fists bunched, ready to fight. "Why the hell d'you think we live in this dead-and-alive hole?"

"Speak for yourself. I'm not a bastard," shouted Nell, a small, fair girl who had always seemed a cut above the others, maybe not physically superior, yet everyone feared her lashing tongue. "I can remember my father. He brought me here when I was five."

"That's even worse," said Connie crushingly. "He didn't want you. He gave you away."

"You bitch!" Rebecca snarled, making a lunge at her, but Connie moved fast for one so plump, a neat feint born of long practice at dodging blows.

"And you're a stuck-up cow!" she yelled from the far side of the bed. "Always mooning after Nancy and that daft Nell. What d'you get up to in bed together, eh? Pawing at each other – messing about! I'll tell Mrs Bowell of you, so I will! Dirty Dago – or perhaps you're a gypsy, that's even dirtier! You've got to be something foreign with that kinky black hair and those horrible, slanty yellow eyes! Gypsy brat! Gypsy brat! Got any clothes pegs to sell? And where's your ma, eh? Down on Broad Quay, chasing the sailors!"

That did it. Rebecca could just about control her temper at insults directed at herself, but any slur on her mother drove her mad. She had never known her, of course, but I guessed that she had enshrined her in her heart – as we all did our mothers – and could not bear to hear her name fouled by a spiteful creature like Connie. She sprang at her, caught hold of a fistful of dun-coloured hair and gave it a savage wrench. Connie screamed, and Rebecca rammed her knee between hers so that she lost balance and they fell to the floor with Rebecca on top. They were well versed in fighting; the orphanage was a hotbed of trouble, and its primly self-satisfied board of governors would have been shocked to the core had they known a quarter of what took place within its walls. Rebecca knelt on Connie's chest while she kicked and squirmed, her nightdress riding up about her thick, white thighs. Then, with both hands locked on Connie's hair, Rebecca banged her head on the floor repeatedly.

Satisfied to see her pulping Connie, I launched myself on Betsy, battering her with my fists. Bedlam reigned. The other girls were leaping up and down on the beds in frenzied excitement. Some were for us but the majority supported Connie and her faction. We had been lone wolves for too long to be popular, and our attitude to authority alarmed them. They lived in mortal terror of Mrs Bowell. Then the door crashed open and she stood there like an avenging archangel. A flustered Mr Bowell was turning up the gaslamps while she descended on us. Her heavy tread shook the floor. I heard the hiss as her cane shot upwards and felt its burning cut on my shoulders and arms.

"What is going on?" she thundered, her face dark with anger.

I flung up my arms to protect my face from those whistling cuts. Rebecca had released Connie who began to blubber loudly, clinging to Mrs Bowell's skirt. "Becky hit me, ma'am! Oh, don't let her hurt me!"

"You wicked, wicked girl!" roared Mrs Bowell, eyes starting out of her head, directing her fury to Rebecca, each word implemented by a stroke of the switch. "Ungrateful, ungodly slut!"

"Connie started it!" I shouted, wild with indignation.

Mrs Bowell rounded on me, the cane like a live thing in her expert hand. Rebecca had not flinched beneath the blows and neither did I. We had made a pact never to let her reduce us to tears, so we defied her while she continued to upbraid us, the switch taking its toll on our defenceless bodies.

"I don't want to hear your lies!" she stormed, her bosom heaving, beads of sweat glistening on her upper lip.

"Becky was swearing, ma'am," Connie sobbed, grovelling at her feet. "Awful words – I told her to stop – then she hit me."

"You'll wash your mouth out with soapy water, Becky Smale," snapped Mrs Bowell, but this did not content Connie.

"Nancy was saying them too, ma'am – and Nell – but Nancy was the worst." There was a triumphant light in her mean little eyes.

"No doubt," said Mrs Bowell ominously, glaring at me. "She's more trouble than the other two put together. Mr Bowell," she addressed her husband over her shoulder without bothering to look at him, "take this creature and lock her in the cellar. A night there should give her time to reflect on the error of her ways."

He leapt to attention. "Yes, my love – certainly she must be severely punished," he stuttered and came towards me, laying his damp, blunt-fingered hand on my arm.

I shook him off. "Don't touch me!"

"He will do his duty as befits someone positioned by the Almighty to act as your guardian," she bellowed, reaching down to pat Connie's bowed head for she was howling with renewed vigour.

It was on the tip of my tongue to shout that her husband's attentions to the girls were very far from paternal, but I knew that this would only lead to further trouble. Uppermost in my mind was the desire to save Rebecca and Nell, so: "I'll take my punishment," I said icily, "but leave my friends out of this. It was my fight, not theirs."

This was too much for Nell. "Connie is the culprit – the spineless little sneak!" she cried, defiance in every line of her body, chin up proudly, unafraid and filled with the kind of contempt which stamped her as far superior to the Bowells in every respect.

"Shut your mouth!" raged Mrs Bowell, having no weapon but that of the blustering bully when crossing swords with Nell's sharp wits. "Connie's a good girl. I know you think you're mighty clever, miss, but I'll take her word against yours any day."

"She's lying, ma'am," insisted the loathsome Connie and I vowed that I would murder her if I got the chance. She was looking up at Mrs Bowell with swimming eyes, clinging to the hands of the stout, black-clad figure looming over her. "They were all in it – whispering things . . ."

"What things? What were they saying?" Mrs Bowell shook her impatiently. "Speak up, Connie. Don't be frightened. I'm determined to get to the bottom of this."

Connie hung her head. "I don't like to say, ma'am . . . they were talking about dirty things – things that no Christian girl would even think about – they whispered of men and women . . . and what they do together to make babies," she said in a low voice, blushing, hesitant, as if her maidenly modesty was offended.

Mrs Bowell's face turned an unpleasant puce shade. "Is this true, Nancy?" she demanded, slapping the cane against her skirt as if itching to use it again. What could I say? She was determined to make an example of us so arguing seemed useless. I did not answer, staring at her with naked hatred in my eyes. She struck me across the cheek with her open palm. "I'll not tolerate dumb insolence!" she yelled.

That stinging slap goaded a response. "What if it is? It's only natural that we want to know, and Connie talks dirtier than anyone else!" The indignant gasp from Connie did not halt me. I was in full spate now. "Oh, yes she does, and it's no use her denying it. She's man-mad! That's why she hates Rebecca so – 'cause she's pretty – and no bloke in his right mind would ever look at Connie's ugly mug! She called her a Dago – a gypsy brat!"

A sneer lifted Mrs Bowell's lips as she ran her eyes slowly down over Rebecca who tossed back her head with that mulish expression on her face which always spelled trouble. "Well, perhaps Connie was right," she jeered. "Who knows what gutter she came from? Or you for that matter. But I've struggled to turn you into clean-living Christians, and I get no thanks for my pains." Her anger was mounting now; she was out of her depth and she knew it. "To think that you've been corrupting these innocent lambs by talking filth! Yes, filth! I despair of the three of you, I really do! I'll teach you a lesson you'll not forget. You'll never meet again while you are under this roof. D'you hear me? You'll be separated now, and for the rest of your time here."

She thrust her face close to mine as she mouthed the words – the shining, sweaty face that I had hated for so long. I gave her a slow, insulting stare, taking in that thin-lipped mouth which had hurled abuse at me daily, those pudgy hands which slapped and pinched sensitive skin so relentlessly, down over that blowsy body.

"Go to hell!" I hissed.

She gave an outraged gasp, and for one glorious moment I thought that she was about to have an apoplectic fit and fall, foaming, to the floor. I had longed to say that to her for years. Mr Bowell was spluttering, and poor Miss West seemed to shrink into herself. It was odd to see her in her grey flannel dressing gown, her mousy hair loosened about her shoulders. The sympathy in her eyes was undisguised, but it was useless. She had never been able to stand up to the Bowells. The other girls were petrified, as round-eyed as owls.

mrs Bowell recovered her powers of speech. Her face was ashen, and pinched about the nostrils. A terrible calm seemed to have settled over her, and the effect was more awe-inspiring than if she had raved at me. "You have a foul mouth, Nancy," she said quietly. "Such arrogance in one so young. I fear for your immortal soul, child. Even that ugly red hair of yours marks you out as spawn of the devil. But, despite all, I will still wrestle with him to save you. Such wicked pride shall yield to the power of the Lord. Miss West, be so kind as to bring me the whip."

The silence could have been cut with a knife. We were used to being caned, but the whip was an instrument of dread, reserved for the most heinous of crimes. I could only once recall it being used on a girl who had stolen bread from the kitchen, driven by hunger. She had died shortly after her thrashing, though it had been hushed up. I could feel the palms of my hands beginning to sweat. "I'll kill you if you lay one finger on me!" I shouted hoarsely as Miss West returned, reluctantly handing over the whip.

My threat was ignored. Mr Bowell threw himself on me. I was enveloped in a bearhug, my arms tightly clamped against my sides. I had not thought him to be so strong. His grip was like a vice as he crushed my ribs. He was panting, enjoying himself. Such close contact was most degrading for I was naked beneath my night-gown. It was only the work of seconds for him to rope my wrists and tether me to the foot of my bed in such a way that I was forced to lean over the hard rail. I felt his hand at the back of my neck. There was a wrench as my garment ripped, and a rush of cold air on my bare back. His hand lingered on my skin.

Mrs Bowell rolled back her sleeves and made a few practice cuts through the air. Then there was no sound in the room except for the swish of the whip and the impact as it met my flesh. The pain was like a giant explosion, a scorching, searing invasion of my body right down to the bone, blow following blow till agony obliterated everything, turning all sensation into one huge scream. But that cry was only in my head. I did not voice it, biting down on my lower lip till the blood salted my tongue. I was too proud, too angry to yell, tasting the bitter gall of injustice which filled my whole being and corroded my soul.

Mrs Bowell's face swam mistily above me and her voice seemed to come through thick woollen cloth. "I'll teach you to defy me!"

When her husband cut me loose I would have fallen but was supported by his arm. Then I was frog-marched out of the room and down through the house to the basement. There Mrs Bowell gave me a hard shove in the small of the back and precipitated me into the dark bowels of the cellar. I stumbled, missed my footing and fell down the stone steps. The door thudded behind me.

I spent a wretched night there, only half conscious, with no company in the inky blackness save the scampering, squeaking rats. In the morning I was hauled out, and after a cup of water and a stale crust, was marched off to church. There I glimpsed Nell and Rebecca and, like myself, they shared the disgrace of wearing their dirty, weekday clothes. We felt like lepers, the worst kind of outcasts, which was Mrs Bowell's intention. The vicar must have been told of our misdeeds for his sermon included a long tirade on the deadly sin of pride. We had to hide our faces in the grubby brown aprons of daily use, instead of those of pristine white like our meek, dutiful peers. Connie sat smugly in the front pew between the Bowells.

Now Mrs Bowell cleared her throat, bringing me back to the present, with its acute misery of lacerated skin and hunger. "I have arranged for you to be transferred to another dormitory. You will still eat in the dining hall, but you will be at the far end of the table where I sit. During lessons, you'll go to the back of the class. There will be plenty of work for you in the wash-house. At no time will you meet Nell or Becky. Do you understand?"

"Yes, ma'am," I said obediently, for my back was a mass of bruises and I had no wish to taste the whip again, yet I was already planning ways to outwit her.

She dismissed me curtly and, true to her word, the edict was put into practice immediately. It was a lonely time for me, bereft of my friends. The most revolting chores were reserved for me, and I guessed that Nell and Rebecca were being equally badly treated. I saw them from a distance only, and then a great surge of misery would well up in me, bringing the hot tears to my eyes. I read unity in their resolute faces. We might be parted and punished but we would win through in the end.

As the days dragged on, I became desperate. Rebecca was due to leave in August, around her fifteenth birthday, and I had to see her before she left. Peggy proved a staunch ally, always happy to steal a march on the Bowells. In her simple philosophy rules were there to be flouted. Rebecca had been put to work in the kitchen with her, and this was close to the steamy wash-house where I slaved over the big copper and wooden tubs, armed with scrubbing-board and brush. One day, as Peggy whisked through, she pressed a slip of paper into my hand. My arms were wet to the elbows, but I managed to stuff it into my pocket, then begged permission to visit the privy, taking a quick sprint through the drizzle. There, amidst the cobwebs and smells, I leaned my back against the door and read my note. It was from Rebecca, begging me to meet her under the clock tower after lights out. Nell would be there too.

I was well aware of the danger and the fate awaiting me if I was caught, but this added spice to the challenge. Nothing would have stopped me going. It was essential that I preserve a perfectly normal exterior to avoid arousing suspicion, so I was as sullen as ever. Supper in the long dining hall was the worst ordeal for I was certain that Mrs Bowell was watching me with narrowed eyes as she ladled out the watery soup from an enormous tureen. I wondered uneasily if I had betrayed myself. It would be typical of her to say nothing, letting us think that all was well, and then suddenly pounce. Nothing happened however, and as we filed out to go to bed, I met Rebecca's eye and she winked.

It was a night of summer storm following a humid, wet day. I was glad of the racket from the heavens; any noise I might make would be drowned. I lay flat on my back on the lumpy flock mattress, watching the play of light from the corridor making queer patterns on the ceiling. Ever since that fatal night, the girls had settled down quickly, quiet as mice. Supervision had been doubled. Each shuddered at the thought of the whip. Mrs Bowell had made her point.

After a while, I knew by the even breathing from all sides that they slept, but I did not stir until I heard the clock strike eleven. The floor was cold to my naked feet but I was used to this. It was not thought necessary to provide us with slippers. I had no legitimate excuse for rising. Each girl was given a chamber pot for nocturnal calls of nature. It had been my unsavoury duty of late to empty the slops every morning. We had to be very ill indeed to be allowed to fetch a drink. My usually nimble brain failed to invent a watertight excuse for leaving the dormitory. There was no help for it. I must take my chance and simply pray that I did not meet anyone.

Hardly daring to breathe, I took my cloak from the back of the chair near my bed, put it on over my nightdress, padded to the door and opened it a crack. The quietness yawned up from the maw of the house through the dead air, collecting almost solidly on the gloomy landing. A fork of lightning blasted the corridor for a second with blue-white frosting, then thunder cracked overhead. I sped away to where the stairwell curved down into pitch blackness.

In the kitchen the range still glowed, throwing scarlet bars across the flagstones. It was warm there and I wanted to linger, but this could not be. Out in the scullery the tiles struck damp to my bare feet. I froze as something moved, a shadowy form in the dimness, but it was only the cat who had left his nook by the hearth and followed me, eager to be off into the wild, wet garden. He rubbed himself around my legs, back arched, thrumming with ecstasy as I drew a finger across that ticklish feline place beneath his chin. I dared not let him escape or Mrs Starkey would raise an uproar next morning. I might as well have saved myself the effort for he was most determined. I struggled with the bolt which slid back with a sound like a pistol shot. I cursed and wondered why it was that at night all noises are magnified, trifles which go unnoticed by day. The door swung open and the tabby catapulted between my feet, disappearing about his courting.

Darkness was like a solid wall, the trees rustling and dripping, heavy with the rain which came sluicing down. The wind thrashed the bushes, flapped at my cloak and whipped the tattered clouds across the tormented sky. Once again lightning showed me the way and thunder rattled. My feet encountered the sharpness of the gravel path. Beyond lay the quadrangle. The surface glimmered, dotted with puddles, inches deep. I splashed through them and the hem of my nightdress was soggy around my ankles. Its condition, and that of my cloak, would have to be accounted for later. I would face that when it came.

I was the first at the trysting place, hurrying to the clock tower, staring up at it. We had often met there in the past, a favourite rendezvous. It brooded over me in the darkness, a square, turreted edifice adorned with gargoyles acting as waterspouts on the gutterings. I mounted its broad shallow steps, seeking shelter under the arch of the doorway. I waited for a while, shivering with cold, peering through the curtain of rain. A shape materialised out of it.

"Nancy – Nancy!" Rebecca cried with a catch in her voice, flinging herself into my arms.

I could not see her clearly, hanging on to her, my fingers tracing over her face and streaming, tangled hair. Before we could break apart, Nell was there too, being hugged in turn. Nell, usually so controlled – now she was crying. We all were. We could break our own rule for once and cry now that we were together. "Oh, your back – your poor back!" she began, then her voice hardened. "God, I'd give my eye-teeth to use that whip on her! The old bitch!"

"It's almost healed, Nell," I assured her. "But what about you?"

We talked in hushed voices, and they told me their own tales of misery and ill treatment, heedless of the rain. Every moment was precious, and Rebecca said: "I'm leaving tomorrow."

"Where will you go? What will you do?" I was very anxious for her. We had often daydreamed of what we would do when we left. She was determined to go on the stage and we had already decided on a name for her. Nell had thought of it of course, bookish, clever Nell. No longer would she be Becky Smale. Oh, no, she would leave that hated title at the orphanage. From now on she would be known as Rebecca Costello. Looking into that lovely, wayward face, I read there a grim determination to stop at nothing to gain her ambition. It alarmed me and I feared for her.

"I've to see Old Ma Bowell in the morning. I expect she's found me a place as a slavey with some damned God-fearing family, but I'll be hanged if I'll take it!" she said angrily, her golden eyes sparking. "I'm off to the Hiring Fair at Chipping Sodbury. It'll be a step in the right direction. I'll write to you when I get fixed up."

"Don't leave it too long," I begged, holding her slim, cold fingers in mine. "I'll be off myself come the New Year."

"Damn it, does that mean that I'll have to manage the repulsive Bowells all by myself?" grumbled Nell. "I shan't be fifteen till October twelvemonth. I call that damned unfair."

I gave her an extra hug, saluting her courage. She was covering it well, but must be devastated at the thought of being left there. We fell silent, staring into the uncertain future. I sensed a tense excitement in Rebecca, always the optimist, single-minded about becoming rich and famous. I wanted to travel and Nell had a talent for writing, but now the stark reality of life outside the orphanage walls reduced us to three frightened girls, little more than children. We had hated it there but it was the only home we had ever known.

"We'll have to go soon," whispered Rebecca. "Connie is always spying. Mrs Bowell has told her to watch us."

"Mr B. is still up," said Nell. "He's in the stable."

"Oh, Lor' – then we'd better be careful," I warned, staring across the square towards the stableyard. Through the rods of rain I could see a tiny glimmer of light.

"Don't worry," Nell replied, a thread of laughter in her voice. "I made sure there was a full bottle of brandy there."

"What have you been up to?" I asked sharply, knowing her capable of devious trickery.

"They made me work in the cellar, clearing it out," she said with a shudder, "I hate it. You know how frightened I am of spiders, and there are huge ones down there – great big hairy brutes, but Old Mother Bowell wouldn't let me off. Mr B. came sidling up to me the other day. No, he didn't try to paw me, just said that if I smuggled out an extra bottle or two, he'd see that things were made a bit easier for me. You know how he likes his drop of tipple, but she don't approve. We shan't have any trouble with him tonight. I heard him singing to himself, happy as a pig in shit – and he's forgotten to lock the side door."

We giggled, then sobered, drawing closer in the moments of parting, and as we stood there, under the old clock tower in the rain, a strange feeling possessed me – a sense of destiny and foreboding rolled into one. For the sake of all we had suffered – for all we had shared – I knew then that we could not part without some ceremony to mark the occasion. It was in that split second that the idea of a vow occurred to me. A vow to bind the three of us in life and in death, which none could break – more binding than the marriage oath, more solmen than a baptism. Without pausing to think, I put it to them, finishing by saying. "It'll be a promise to last ten years. Binding us to go to the other's aid if called – no matter how far the journey, how long the gap between or how great the dangers. And at the end of that time we'll meet here again, at the orphanage, under this clock tower, to give some of what we've earned to our successors."

They did not like it at first, I knew that. Something ominous, urgent in my voice made them fear the solemnity of the undertaking. Then Nell, cool, rather amused, said: "But dear old Nancy, of course I'd come to your rescue if you got yourself in some dreadful mess. You don't have to make me swear horribly like Hamlet's ghostly father. What on earth d'you think is going to happen?"

Rebecca fidgeted, uncomfortably aware that I had already flown to her defence and thereby suffered a terrible beating. Then at last she said nervously: "Oh, come on, let's swear, and get it over with. It's quite a comforting thought in a way."

Nell cast her an ironic look. "What's it to be, then? Mingling of blood? The sacrifice of Silly Winnie at dawn on a blood-stained prehistoric stone? Come, Nancy, this is your brainwave. What are we to swear?"

But I knew Nell too well to be upset by her sarcasm. I calmly took each of them by the hand and with what was perhaps unconscious blasphemy said: "Repeat after me, I swear by Almighty God . . ." And so the fatal vow was taken. A ten-year binding oath that would lead each of us into stranger paths than even I, with my fleeting premonitions, could have divined.

Then Rebecca, more to lighten our sombre mood than anything, I think, suggested that we each keep a journal. "We could record what happens to us along the way, and later exchange them, sharing each other's adventures."

"I'm not sure that I'd want to read yours – they're sure to be scandalous!" quipped Nell.

"I hope so!" returned the incorrigible Rebecca, almost jigging with excitement. "Oh, come on, Nell. Don't be stuffy. You'd be good at it. I don't much care for writing, but I'd do it for you and Nancy."

It wasn't exactly my forte either, but I agreed, seeing the sense of this suggestion. It was impossible to think clearly of anything in that sad hour of parting. Apprehension shivered down my spine. The thunder still muttered in the distance, like a drum-roll of doom. Then we were kissing and weeping and saying goodbye. My friends slipped away like wraiths into the darkness, leaving me alone on the steps. God only knew what would befall us before we met again. Perhaps we never would meet. I might have looked my last on them. I watched them through my tears, and then they were gone from sight, swallowed up by the wet night.

Chapter 2

When Rebecca left, it was as if part of myself went with her. I still had Nell, that sharp-tongued comrade. Whereas Rebecca and I had been orphanage inmates from birth, Nell was different. She had known a life apart from this, abandoned there by her father when a little girl, but able to remember him. It must have been very terrible for her, waiting for him to return and claim her as he had promised. He never came. Once upon a time she had talked of him, but as the years passed, this ceased. It was as if she had formed a protective shell about herself, fair, pretty, deceptively fragile-looking, using her intellect as a defensive weapon which she wielded without mercy. Like Rebecca, she had proved herself my equal in temper and rebelliousness, though in a less obvious manner.

Contrary to my vows on the subject, I found as the time approached for my own departure, that I was forced into the position of considering various offers of employment provided by Mrs Bowell. The winter had closed in, and it was essential that I go straight from the home to a secure post. Had it been summer still, a few nights spent in the open, though hazardous for a young girl, would not have threatened my very life. The frosts and snows of January would most certainly have done so.

I reluctantly obeyed when I was ordered to put on my Sunday dress and go to her room one morning shortly after my birthday. My boots were polished, my linen was clean and my thick red hair was contained more or less tidily under my cap. As I put it on I saw my face in the small mirror. How sullen was the droop of my mouth. How wary the light in my eyes. I had no confidence at all in my appearance, too tall, too gawky, as Mrs Bowell was fond of telling me, and I positively hated my carroty hair.

I fought to still my inner trembling as I waited outside her door. Peggy had told me that I was to expect an interview with a man of the cloth who was seeking a servant. This had done nothing to lift my spirits. I had had quite enough of vicars and suchlike, allies of the orphanage authorities, and the idea of working for one of them depressed me beyond utterance. I could hear the subdued murmur of voices within, recognising Mrs Bowell's "visitors" tone. I tapped on the door and she trilled for me to enter.

She was seated by the fire, a tray of tea things on a sofa-table and, in the wing-chair opposite, was a small, snowy-haired gentleman dressed in black. "Come in, Nancy, my dear child." Mrs Bowell's voice was falsely amiable and she waved me nearer, beginning to talk about me as if I wasn't there. "This is the young person I was telling you of, Dr Ridding. She has been with us all her life and has been most carefully trained by myself – a most obedient and helpful member of our 'family', as I like to call our little lambs." She simpered and preened herself, pausing for his praise.

He merely nodded, raised an eyebrow and then twinkled up at me. I was struck by the air of benevolence in his elderly face and a certain honesty which had a direct appeal. This surprised me. I had thought he would be a copy of the vicar who usually called to see Mrs Bowell, with his affected voice, his cold stare, his parrot-like echoing of her every pronouncement.

"I'm pleased to meet you, my dear." He spoke in a rich, rather jaunty voice, more like a squire than a churchman. "Nancy Gray, is it not? I'm Dr Ridding – rector of St James's Church in the village of Sutton

Compton. Would you like to come there and work for me? My housekeeper, Miss Jenny, is finding the rectory too much for her now, though she won't admit it, mind you, assuring me that she can manage quite well, as she has done for the past twenty years, but I know better. A strong girl about the place will be of great assistance. We live in the country, some fifteen miles from Bristol. I promise that we won't tax you too much."

"I don't want to skivvy for anybody," I muttered ungraciously.

He expressed disappointment. "I'm sorry that you look upon it thus. I'm not seeking a slave. You'll be treated as one of the family. Won't you reconsider?"

Mrs Bowell butted in. "I'm sure Nancy is conscious of the honour you do her, Your Reverence. A post in the household of a gentleman as eminent as yourself! Good gracious, it is a chance not to be missed." She stared hard at me, daring me to refuse, as anxious to see the back of me as I was to leave.

"What do you say, Nancy?" Dr Ridding ignored her, smiling encouragingly. His wide forehead was smooth, in spite of his years, and the only lines on his ruddy-cheeked face were laughter wrinkles at the sides of his mouth and eyes.

"Nancy will do as I advise – " began Mrs Bowell, but he held up a hand, gravely, courteously, and she fell silent.

"Let the child speak for herself, madam," he said with a firmness which amazed me.

"Please, sir – " I stammered, my eyes meeting his which were of a wise and kindly blue. "I think I might like it, sir." I was confused, clinging obstinately to my sulky stand, but feeling myself being wooed away from it.

"Like it! Like it! It is not for you to question whether or not you will 'like it'!" Mrs Bowell could not control herself, eyes bulging with outrage.

His face lost its good humour. "Will you kindly leave

this to me? Nancy has a tongue in her head, has she not?"

Such sternness was astonishing, putting Mrs Bowell firmly in her place. Emboldened, I asked: "Please, sir, when would you want me to start?"

He rose to his feet, small and stately, commanding attention. I found myself looking down on him which was rather diconcerting, but his brisk manner made me forget this at once. "There's no time like the present, Nancy, and I doubt it will take long to get your things." He flung Mrs Bowell a caustic glance as if knowing perfectly well how very little we orphans owned. "We will go home without delay."

Home. I could not know then that he spoke truly. The rectory at Sutton Compton became my home in every sense and I shall be forever grateful to that wonderful old man and his kindly, patient housekeeper for taking me to their hearts. It took me a long time to believe my incredible luck. At first I was guarded, suspicious of their motives; I was completely unaccustomed to people performing acts of goodness for the simple reason that they loved their fellow creatures.

One of the first things Dr Ridding did after installing me in his carriage was to take me to a tea-shop and initiate me into the delights of cream cakes. As if this was not treat enough, he then visited his bookseller and was instantly incarcerated in the back with him, poring over ancient tomes. "Is there anything you fancy to read?" he enquired, business over. "What do you like?"

I hardly knew, Nell had been the studious one, her nose perpetually buried in a book, and she had had permission to use the public library. Had Mrs Bowell been aware of the nature of some of this reading matter she would, no doubt, have banned her. But, no scholar herself, she had not bothered to enquire, so we had become familiar with the rather scandalous works of Zola, Dumas and Balzac, and the highly colourful and romantic novels of George Eliot and Ouida. Much of these we did not fully understand, but they had given us a glimpse of a world beyond the narrow confines of the orphanage.

"I'm interested in foreign parts," I ventured, and he recommended a novel by Rudyard Kipling and swept me off to the waiting vehicle. The day was grey, the air cutting the lungs like a knife, but I was aware of nothing save the glow engendered by hot coffee and cakes. I clutched the brown paper parcel containing my gift.

Leaving the town behind us, we took the road which wound into the countryside. The fields were blanketed with snow and it had been driven hard against the fir screens and those long dividing walls of local stone. My mentor talked gently to me, to put me at ease, so that my eyelids began to droop and the journey passed in a flash till I woke with a jerk as he said loudly: "Wake up, Nancy! We're home!"

I gazed sleepily out at the darkening landscape, the sun setting like a fireball behind black trees. I clambered out, my parcel in one hand, my hold-all in the other and stood there on the crisp snow, staring about me. The peace of it struck me like a revelation. There was harmony in the ancient, snow-crusted church with its gravestones nestling in its shadow, and the rectory beyond melding into its background of yews. A stream ran before it like a lively spirit. A few rooks cawed, wheeling against the sky before settling to rest. They did not destroy the calm; they enhanced it. Sky is what I noticed most clearly, grey and snow-heavy. So much sky, a vast expanse to impress a city-born child. That sense of width, of timelessness, of space. It spoiled me for town-living forever.

Miss Jenny was at the front door, silhouetted by the golden lamplight. At first she scolded him for bothering to find a helper for her in a half humorous, half annoyed manner which was not in the least intimidating. While they talked, I stole a glance at her, very conscious of my shabby second-hand clothes, my grubby hands and face.

She was about sixty, tiny as a bird, with pink cheeks and bright dark eyes. She wore a long, deep purple dress, trimmed with white, and a paisley shawl around her shoulders. A small velvet cap topped her grey hair, and it had mauve streamers of ribbon.

"Come along into the drawing room," she said after a moment, accepting the fact that he was adamant about employing me. "Don't keep the poor child standing there, catching her death. And you, sir – did you remember to take your linctus before you went off this morning?"

He confessed that he had not, giving me a wink as we went inside. I found myself in a large room, filled with panelling and dancing firelight, bright ornaments, deep chairs and carpets. The furniture was shiny with beeswax. There were red lacquered cabinets containing exotic curios, and a longcase clock with a brass face like a moon. The walls were hung with portraits and landscapes in heavily carved gilt frames, and there were books everywhere.

"Please be seated," said Miss Jenny as I hesitated awkwardly. "Tell me about yourself, and then you'll have ample time to go to your room and wash before dinner."

"But I've already washed today," I protested. I had – at six that morning, breaking the ice in the basin.

"We change for dinner," she explained patiently. "You will be able to do so too, just as soon as I've helped you select some new dresses." Then she addressed the rector who stood in the centre of the hearthrug, his coat tails whipped up to the warmth as he watched us with a smile. "Thank you for bringing Nancy to be my companion. Her speech needs to be improved, though. She has that dreadful Bristol accent."

"All in good time, dear lady," he nodded. "Elocution lessons are in order."

I was blushing hotly, wanting to turn tail and run.

"What's wrong with the way I speak?" I blurted out rudely.

"Do not argue, child," she replied imperturbably. "We know what is best for you. There is no need to glare at me like that. We want you to feel at home. Please take your hat off."

I did so, tempted to refuse but recognising the quiet authority of this tiny person. "This isn't my home," I grumbled. "I don't have a home."

Her eyes went to my head and she smiled warmly, ignoring my uncouth manners. "Why, my dear, what beautiful hair you have."

I could feel myself going even redder. I was sure that she was mocking me. My hair was a sore point and always had been. People had made so many disparaging remarks about it, behaving as if I were in some way to blame for it. Only Miss West has been kind, expressing the view that I might not be too ugly when I grew up as I had a clear skin and dark eyelashes. I found it hard to believe that this old lady really liked it. "Thank you, ma'am," I managed to mumble. "I've always been told it was hideous."

"What nonsense," put in Dr Ridding. "It reminds me of the glorious manes of those models so beloved by painters."

"They called me 'copper-knob' at the orphanage," I volunteered.

His face took on a stern expression similar to that which he had levelled at Mrs Bowell. "Ah, the cruelty of the ignorant! Forget that crude name, Nancy. Your hair is what artists describe as 'titian', and it is to be envied. Remember that."

"Yes, sir," I answered obediently, my mind spinning with the impressions crowding in on it. To my horror, a crack was slowly opening in the hard-won bastion of my distrust. I wanted to please him.

"If only the other girls could see me now," I said to my reflection later that night when seated before the mirror in the small, cosy bedroom which they had said was now my own. The windows were curtained in flowered chintz, there was a large wardrobe in which my few garments were hopelessly out of place, an impressive dressing table, and a four-poster bed. Logs spluttered and popped merrily in the stone fireplace. I had undressed and put on my patched nightgown. The novelty of using warm water and scented soap had kept me occupied for a while and then, like a lady in her boudoir, I took my place at the mirror. Awaiting me there was a silver-backed hairbrush, shining in the lamp-light. I lifted the stopper of a cut-glass bottle of toilet water and sniffed. The pungent perfume of roses filled my nostrils – a summer garden captured and pickled and poured into a jar.

All thoughts of rebellion or flight had gone, and I wished that Mrs Bowell could have been there to witness me burnishing my hair with that fine bursh. "Dr Ridding says it's a colour admired by many – not carroty," I said to her imagined face. I thumbed my nose at her and she vanished. I snuggled down in the luxury of the feather mattress, pulled the eiderdown up to my chin and lay there for a while, drinking in that room in the tender glow of the candle, almost pinching myself to ensure that I was not dreaming.

I wondered what Nell and Rebecca would have made of it and my heart ached to think of them. I had not heard from Rebecca since she left and Nell was still imprisoned in the Home. I slept soundly at last until the numerous cocks of the village woke me shortly after daybreak with their raucous crowing, another alien sound in my ears. Thus began my existence in the rectory into which I had entered with misgivings, but ended up loving, enthusiastically joining in its every aspect.

I learned so much there, things which had not been taught me in my mean, smothered life in Bristol. It was the first time that I had known air and space and freedom and, above all, consideration. My dear, good old friends treated me like a beloved daughter, though they were clever enough not to spoil me. Miss Jenny took it upon herself to help me select a whole new wardrobe of clothes, to correct my manners (or lack of them) and my deportment, so that I no longer swore or slouched or used incorrect grammar. Meanwhile that adorable, vague yet astute rector filled the appalling gaps in my education, making lessons fun. History became a thrilling cavalcade; geography a gateway to adventure; he taught me how to enjoy reading, and to express myself on paper so that I dared begin the task of keeping a journal, and he opened my eyes and ears to the joy of poetry, music and art.

Of course, it was not all plain sailing. At first I was stubborn and sulky and must have given them many moments of doubt, but their patience and love won me over. I started to listen to their advice and trust their judgement. I began to enjoy my lessons, sitting in the peaceful study with the drowsy scents of summer drifting in at the open casement or toasting my toes in winter, snug by a roaring fire while white blobs of snow pasted themselves against the panes. So, very gradually, I bloomed under their guidance, turning from a hard, loud-mouthed waif, wary of everyone, into a light-hearted girl filled with happiness and optimism. The village folk warmed to me, and I heard it said that I was a credit to the rector. This touched and pleased me and I redoubled my efforts to make the most of myself, striving to become a genteel, educated young lady.

Let it not be thought that I was allowed to shirk my duties. This was very far from the case. I had been brought there principally to work and this I did, lifting many burdens from Miss Jenny's ageing shoulders. But after the loveless, orphanage toil, any tasks were more in the nature of play in such congenial surroundings. I remember clearly my first spring and summer there.

They were magical, and I was almost tipsy with joy, revelling in the music of summer – the bees, the song-birds, the new exciting harmonies of the country – and Dr Ridding at my side on long walks, eagerly teaching me the wonder and mystery of nature.

Thus the months stretched into years, our lives following the pattern of the seasons. It was the lull before the storm – I see that now, though then, in happy ignorance, I had thought it would last forever. In September 1904 the blow fell, ripping my world apart, abruptly shattering the whole fabric of my life. I came in from a walk to find the house in turmoil. Dr Ridding had had a stroke. Miss Jenny was pale and serious. I steeled myself to mount the stairs to his room. He was still alive, but only just and, as I entered that familiar chamber, I was suddenly aware of autumn. The mullioned windows were open, the breeze stirring the curtains, bringing with it from the garden, a hint of fruit ripening against warm walls.

The sun was lying low, touching the treetops with gold and darkening with crimson the rolling slopes of the Mendip Hills beyond. Nothing broke the silence as I tiptoed towards the massive, curtained bed, but his deep breathing and the chiming of the ormolu clock on the mantelshelf. I spoke but he seemed scarcely aware, wandering ever further away from the world, entering that vast silence which finally swallows everyone forever. I tried to tell myself that he was only resting and regaining his strength.

His hands lay upon the white marcella quilt, strangely inactive. They were thin, with every vein distinct and dark, covered in blotches which I had never noticed before. His white hair was carefully combed, and he had about him an unnatural tidiness which would have amused him had he been able to see it. At long last Miss Jenny was having her way. Gone were his pipe, his books, his papers, all the personal clutter which had formed his existence. He looked shrunken and far too neat, Miss-Jenny-controlled because he was helpless, tucked in like a baby, his head resting on an unwrinkled pillow of virgin whiteness.

She hovered at my elbow like a distraught sparrow. "Your Reverence," she breathed, her face puckered, trying not to weep. "Nancy has come to see you."

My nose felt swollen with unshed tears as his blank, indifferent eyes turned towards my face. I touched one of his hands, willing myself not to shrink from the cold, clammy feel of his skin. It was already like that of a corpse. Where had he gone, my teacher, my friend? By then I knew that he was dying and wondered of what use his religion would be to him now.

His slack lower lip drooped and from his throat came a rasping sound. "He wants a drink," said Miss Jenny, eager to anticipate his every need.

For her sake I prayed that he would not linger. She was too frail to nurse him. I offered my help. His heavy head lolled when I raised him a little as she held the cup. To cheer him, and in an attempt to make contact, I began to tell him about my walk. "Farmer Wyatt has got his corn in. It will be the Harvest Festival soon, and supper in the squire's barn. I enjoyed it so much last year. We'll go, shan't we? Can't possibly miss it – "

He gave no sign of hearing me and my eyes met Miss Jenny's, reading there my own dread. I shook the pillow gently till it was smooth again and lowered him on to it. His tongue crept slowly over his lips and then withdrew into the cave of his mouth. "Nancy . . ." he croaked slowly and the effort was great. He paused, his breathing laboured, and after a moment he spoke again. "Marry Wyatt's son . . . you're a good girl . . . a brave girl . . . must be taken care of, when I'm gone."

I could never do this. I did not even like Ralph Wyatt, but I did not say so. Instead, I put my cheek against his forehead and he could not summon the strength to speak again. It was growing darker as the evening clouds drifted in, and the sun died, a ball of flame, on the rim of the horizon. Something was knotting tightly inside me, a small, dark, woeful kernel of sadness. The curtain was coming down on an episode in my life. I did not know what would happen to me now.

"What do you think, Miss Jenny? Shall I apply for the post?" I looked up from the packing case in which I was laying her treasures, carefully cocooned in newspaper. We were in her sitting room, and pursuing the conversation which had been taking place intermittently ever since I had come across the advertisement in the personal columns of *The Times*.

Miss Jenny was flustered and anxious about the safe transportation of her possessions, I noticed how much she had aged during the past month. I could see the bones around her sunken eyes and there were new lines, neat as incisions, at the corners of her lips. Strangely, I thought for the first time, and in astonishment, that she must have been beautiful in her youth. I wondered how she had come to be there and why she had spent her best years in the rector's service. Perhaps she had been in love with him. There was no knowing. I wanted her to notice my hand resting on the top of the crate, to stop ferreting through her bric-a-brac, to take and hold it in her own, but she did not.

"Well, I don't know, my dear," she answered vaguely, picking up a Dresden shepherdess and then putting her down again. "I'd never have the courage . . . but then, young people these days, they think nothing of travelling miles. You'd be most welcome if you wanted to come with me, but it is up to you, child."

Dr Ridding had died at the end of September though, to all intents and purposes, his life had ended with the stroke. It had taken us most of the following month to settle attendant legal matters and the disposing of his effects. It was good for both of us to be occupied with details, even trivial ones, otherwise we might have spent the time in futile repining. The major repercussion of his demise was that neither she nor I now had a home. She had resolved this by deciding to live with her widowed sister in Clevedon, and had wanted me to join them, but the idea of spending my days looking after two elderly ladies in a quiet seaside resort did not appeal to me, fond of her though I was.

I really had no idea what to do, faced with the prospect of carving a new niche for myself somewhere. I wished now that I had made an effort to contact Nell and Rebecca and am ashamed to admit that, after writing one letter to the orphanage and receiving no reply. I had given up. I had been so busy, so happy, that I had given little thought to the past. This was over and I was like a rudderless ship floundering on a sea of uncertainty. Financially, I could afford to take my time seeking a post. Dr Ridding had left me two hundred pounds in his will. He had also made sure that Miss Jenny would be comfortably off and had made provision for his other servants. A distant relative had come down to claim the rest of his possessions, and most of the furniture, the books and the curios had been duly packed and carted away. Miss Jenny and I were left feeling rather like discarded lumber of no real value, which no one wanted.

I now sat myself down and drew the newspaper cutting from my pocket, rereading it for the umpteenth time. It said simply: "Wanted. A capable lady to accompany a young boy abroad. Apply to Mr P. Quiller, Hennington House, Kensington, London."

I turned it over in my hands, musing on the prospect. All of my old ambitions to travel came rushing back, my imagination running away with me. Then doubts returned. Could I do it? Was it possible to pass myself off as an impoverished gentlewoman, someone suitable for such a task? Certainly I was much changed from the charity girl who had come to the rectory years before. I was rather young for such a responsibility, but I looked older than I was. It was something to do with being tall, I think.

"Could I carry it off?" I spoke aloud, capturing Miss Jenny's wandering attention.

Her mild eyes focused on me, and she knew what I meant. "Of course you could, Nancy. You are strong and fearless. You can do anything you set your heart on."

I sighed, wishing that I had as much confidence in myself as she thought I had. But, encouraged by such touching faith, I went to the writing table and applied myself to answering the advertisement. This took some time and I laboured over it, consulting Miss Jenny frequently and thumbing through the dictionary. I wanted to give the impression that I was an educated person seeking a respectable post. At last it was done and I walked down to the post office, wondering if I was doing the right thing. Once I had committed it to the scarlet letterbox there was no turning back and I was restless, eager for a reply, and the idea of returning to the rectory was almost boring.

Three days later I had that eagerly awaited summons to London. My presence was requested at an interview on the following Wednesday. In a ferment of excitement, I prepared myself. The letter had said that I would be met at Paddington station and I was a little disappointed. I should have enjoyed finding my own way about the capital, but this, it seemed, was not to be. Miss Jenny and I spent much time speculating as to who would have advertised in such a way. The address was impressive.

At last the great day came and I set out, my ears still ringing with her admonishments to be careful, to be prudent, not to choose an empty compartment, and to speak to no one but my prospective employer when I reached my destination. Paddington was like a vast cave, filled with the noise of engines, the hustle and bustle of the metropolis. There were people everywhere and I stood on the platform lost and forlorn, wistfully watching other passengers being greeted by welcoming friends. I had the sinking sensation that I had somehow become invisible. No one seemed aware that I was there. Then, out of nowhere, a smartly liveried chauffeur appeared at my side.

"Miss Gray?" he asked politely.

"Yes. Are you from Mr Quiller?" I tried to be cool, detached, as if such a trip were an everyday occurrence.

He nodded, very formal and correct, but his voice was kind. "I'm Jameson, Miss Gray. Please to follow me. The car is outside. Have you any luggage? No? Then we'll leave at once, miss."

There were so many questions I wanted to ask him but he gave me no chance, well aware of his position and I, so clumsy with members of the opposite sex, found it impossible to make witty comments or employ opening gambits. I trailed behind him and when he reached the newest of the highly polished vehicles waiting outside the station, he opened the rear door for me. I had never seen such busy streets. There were hackney cabs, omnibuses and trams, private carriages and cars, tradesmen's vans and errand boys on bicycles. The shop fronts were gay with jewel-bright enamelled signs. People thronged the pavements, some idling along, others hurrying purposefully. I drank it all in, recognising famous buildings from pictures shown me by Dr Ridding. Eventually we turned into a residential area and I was surprised to see so much greenery – parks and gardens surrounding elegant houses. The car drew up at a pair of magnificent wrought-iron gates and soon we were circling a driveway.

"Here we are, Miss Gray," Jameson announced as he held the door open for me. "You are to go to the front door."

I hesitated with my hand poised at the big brass bell. Panic shook me. What was I doing here? A charity girl! Then, marshalling the remnants of my courage, I tugged it hard. I heard it clanging somewhere in the depths of the interior. It had begun to rain, a light, persistent drizzle which looked as if it might go on forever and I hoped that I would not be kept there long, fearing for my new hat. In a few moments, I saw a shadowy shape against the stained-glass door panels and the door swung back noiselessly. A butler stood there in stately black and I stammered out my name.

"You are expected, miss. If you will wait in the hall, I shall inform Mr Quiller that you have arrived," he said stiffly.

He walked away, treading as silently and smoothly as a cat, and I sat on the edge of a gilt chair, one of several in the wide, lofty, black-and-white-tiled hall. There was much to occupy my attention. Ferns in pot-bellied jardinières; a pair of enormous Chinese vases; several large doors, carefully closed, which must lead to sumptuous rooms, I decided. There was a great mirror framed in gold roses. It reflected my healthy complexion and I put up a hand and tucked a stray lock into place. It had escaped from my carefully dressed hair on which my hat was perched at a pert angle. I was still in mourning, and this was perfectly suitable, making me look quite severe and responsible with its long skirt and wasp-waisted jacket of sensible barathea, trimmed with bands of black velvet.

A white blouse softened the starkness of my costume, and my hat had ribbons and ruching. From beneath its small brim my flaming hair stood out vividly. All in all, I was not dissatisfied with my appearance – the fur tippet, the matching muff – yet how vulgar it was to be so big and strong, I thought. No matter what I did, I feared I could never be taken for a person of quality. Acutely nervous, my spirits wilted, and I could almost hear Mrs Bowell jeering: "You're a great gawk of a girl! You've feet like a carthorse!"

I stared at my wide mouth, and the hands emerging from the lace at my cuffs, suntanned even now from too much exposure in the summer and, alas, strong as a boy's. I drew on my gloves again, ashamed of them. No wonder Ralph Wyatt had viewed me with favour. I looked well-fitted for making butter or pressing cheese. Oh, why could I not have encouraged him? By now, I would have had an engagement ring on my finger and been looking forward to becoming mistress of my own farmhouse, instead of being on this wild-goose chase. But, though wanting to carry out Dr Ridding's last wish for me, I had been unable to bring myself to do so. It was against my nature to simper and throw arch looks, as I had seen the village girls do. I despised them for their obsession with marriage, following in their mothers' footsteps. Surely there must be more to life than a round of drudgery and yearly childbearing? My experience of sexual love was nil. I only vaguely understood the romantic passages in books, not too fond of them, preferring those of adventure. Yet I was confused and curious, and found myself watching married women, looking at their eyes as they conversed with men. What was this sensation called love? This thing for which one might fade away and die, if it was not returned? I doubted that I would ever find it, and did not want to try.

I was so wrapped up in my own thoughts that I jumped when the butler returned. "Mr Quiller will see you in the library, Miss Gray," he pronounced in a stentorian tone.

My knees were unsteady as I walked in the wake of that dignified figure. He paused deferentially before a door on the right and, at his discreet tap, a voice called to enter. I stepped into a room which took my breath away. I hardly had time to take in the luxurious couch, the leather armchairs, the gilt and the glass, the glory of the floor-to-ceiling bookcases, when my attention was drawn to the man who stood before the pink-veined marble fireplace, his hands clasped lightly behind him.

"Miss Gray?" he said, coming towards me and holding out his hand. His voice was gay, musical. "I'm

Paul Quiller. I hope your journey was not too terribly tedious."

I mumbled some reply, quite losing control of speech, and was soon ensconced in a chair by the fire. Mr Quiller took a seat on the other side of the hearth, stretching out his long legs in their exquisitely cut drainpipe trousers, linking his slim hands together and staring at me with a quizzical smile. He was immaculately dressed, a handsome man in his middle thirties, with very fair hair sweeping back from a high brow, his pencil-thin moustache just a few shades darker. His was a most pleasant face, to all appearances frank and open, and his eyes were hazel, fringed by curling lashes. They were strange eyes, narrow-lidded and tilting up slightly at the outer corners, matching his peaked brows, giving him a puckish look. He was talking fluently now, treating me with great courtesy, a touch familiar, as if he addressed an equal, not someone applying for the position of governess.

"Would you like some tea?" he enquired, and rose to tug at the bellrope. "I understand that you have come all the way from Somerset. I'm Lord Renshaw's agent . . . he would have seen you himself had he been here, but he left England at the end of August. Of course, at that time there was no question of the child going with him, but subsequent sad events have now made this necessary. His mother by adoption caught a chill which developed into pneumonia and within a week the poor lady was dead, leaving Jeffrey an orphan once more."

A parlourmaid came in with a tray of silver and china. When she had poured out two cups of tea and had been dismissed, I ventured to ask a question, gaining confidence in his relaxing presence. "And Jeffrey is related to Lord Renshaw?"

He settled back in his chair, adroitly balancing a cup in one hand and passing the plate of cucumber sandwiches with the other. "Well, not exactly – he is and he isn't – an adopted child, don't you know. He was raised from babyhood by Lady Dorothea, once the wife of Sir Nicholas Renshaw's brother, Henry. I suppose you might say that the tie is strengthened owing to the fact that Nicholas is married to Lady Dorothea's sister, Lady Emily. It is natural that as there is no one else, she would want to look after him now. Lady Dorothea was quite devoted to the boy – could hardly have been more so had he been her own, for she was childless. He bears the name of Standish, her family name."

"How old is he?" I asked, struggling to take this in.

"Five years, and a capital little chap. Everyone dotes on him and he gives hardly any trouble. Till he came to London, he had been looked after by Lady Dorothea's housekeeper, but she is too old to undertake the journey to Alexandria," he answered with his charming smile.

Alexandria! My brain whirled. I had had no idea of our destination. Somehow or other, I had assumed that we might go to France, Austria or even Switzerland, but certainly no thought of the East had entered my head. The prospect thrilled me. I wanted that post more than I had ever wanted anything in my whole life. But I was a charity child and if he ever discovered my humble origin I felt sure that I would not stand a chance.

"Oh, sir," I breathed, leaning forward a little. "How exciting! Do they live there?"

"Only during the winter months," he said, steepling his fingers together and regarding me across them. "Lady Emily has asthma and suffers from poor health. The English climate disagrees with her. The family seat is in Cornwall. They have one daughter called Fleur, and Jeffrey will be a companion for her. Whoever is selected to fill the post will become the governess of both children. Tell me, have you travelled abroad before?"

This was the kind of question I had been dreading. I shook my head. "No, but I've always longed to." Now came the lies, and I was amazed by my own inventiveness. "My mother died when I was a baby, and I was brought up by my father – a schoolmaster. He and

Dr Ridding were at university together and were close friends. When my father died, he very kindly took me into his household. He promised to continue my education but now he too has passed away. He fostered my interest in foreign countries. Oh, Mr Quiller, you can have no idea how much I want to see the world!"

"A wild yearning to spread your wings, eh?" He was looking at me with those penetrating eyes under their deceptively lazy lids. "Forgive me for asking, but have you any money of your own?"

I was blushing but I faced him squarely. "A little, sir."

"And relatives?"

"I have none. That is why Dr Ridding gave me a home."

"I see," he said musingly. "So you could join us at once?"

"I should have to return to Sutton Compton and collect my things."

"Quite so, quite so . . . there would be time for that," he replied in a slow, considering manner. He did seem to be a very understanding man and I was impressed by his attitude and appearance. He was so good looking and pleasantly informal, gay and kind. If his master proved to be anything like him, then my future work could not fail to be rewarding. I opened my handbag and gave him the letter of recommendation which Miss Jenny had written. He perused it for a moment, then folded it and handed it back. "Well, Miss Gray, you appear to have all the qualities which I have been instructed to seek when choosing someone to take this responsibility. I will be frank and tell you that I have already interviewed several other applicants."

My heart sank. "I understand," I said, beginning to gather up my belongings. "So you will be considering us all before you make your choice."

He appeared to make up his mind suddenly, rising to his feet as I did so. "No, Miss Gray, I think I need look no further. As far as I can tell, you are a sensible young lady of honesty and integrity. Being an orphan yourself, you will have a common bond with little Master Jeffrey. This business of his adopted kinsman has been a great burden to Sir Nicholas. He has written giving me explicit orders to make my own decision in this matter and not to trouble him about it. Lady Emily is frequently ill and is also not to be worried; therefore, my dear Miss Gray, you will be doing me a favour if you will accept the post."

I was flabbergasted. A favour? He would consider it a favour? I couldn't believe my ears! This elegant man was actually putting the whole thing to me as a favour, an obligation which he would gratefully incur if I would save him the effort of seeking more. My heart went out to him, to the motherless child, and to the rich, illness-dogged Renshaws. I could not keep the eagerness from my voice as I replied, smiling widely: "Mr Quiller! I should be delighted to accept. But are you quite sure?"

"Quite, quite sure, dear lady." He took my hand and I was completely captivated, having no desire to withdraw mine from his firm grasp, seeing him in the glow of those opulent surroundings in his high-fashion attire, with his charm, his delightful manners. "I was almost certain the moment you stepped over the threshold. You're the very person I've been seeking. I know you are going to get on well with Jeffrey and this, surely, is of paramount importance, is it not? Do you have to hurry away? Could you not come to the nursery and meet him?"

How could I refuse when it was put to me so flatteringly? And I was burning with curiosity to see Jeffrey, so I consented, assuring him that I had ample time before my train left. We made our way upstairs. Everywhere there was evidence of luxury and wealth, the big house furnished sumptuously. Dark reds predominated – the wallpapers, like the thick carpets, were heavily patterned in floral designs. Long damask curtains hung at each window. We mounted the wide central staircase with its ironwork balustrade like delicate lace and, on reaching the top, turned off along a corridor, then went up a smaller, twisting set of steps to the next storey which was devoted to a suite forming the nursery.

How to describe my little boy? I call him mine because, from the very first, there existed a rapport between us which was extraordinary. When Quiller and I entered the day nursery, he was seated astride a rocking-horse, swaying gently back and forth. He looked towards us, his beautiful face eager, expectant, and I wondered if he had been told that a new governess might be coming. My spirits rose by leaps and bounds as he slipped gracefully from the saddle and came over to us, restraining any childish impulsiveness, remembering his manners.

"Master Jeffrey, this is Miss Gray who has undertaken to look after you on the voyage to Egypt," said Quiller, and the child made a small, old-fashioned bow which went well with his claret velvet tunic and knickerbockers and white lace collar falling over his shoulders, faintly reminiscent of the Cavaliers. Tawny curls clustered about his forehead and neck, adding to this impression. A gallant little figure indeed.

"I am so pleased to meet you, Miss Gray," he replied, and regarded me with the most wonderful eyes of deep pansy brown, shaded by thick lashes. Yet, despite the comfortable splendour, the abundance of toys and the watchful attendance of his temporary nursemaid, there was something touchingly lost about him, an ambience to which I instantly responded, that strange, solitary state of the parentless child. The fact that he had been privileged whereas I had known nothing but harshness and humiliation in early life was neither here nor there. We were comrades in adversity, rootless, abandoned by our natural kin, and it was as if something deep within him recognised it too.

"And I'm delighted to meet you, Master Jeffrey," I answered, resisting the impulse to put my arms around him, romantically dazzled by that glow of freshness which emanated from him, the peachlike bloom of his rounded cheeks, that funny, old-world air of manliness, the slightly haughty tilt of his chin which made him look for all the world like a little prince. This hauteur was emphasised when he addressed Quiller and, in an instant of surprise and puzzlement, I realised that he did not much like his uncle's agent.

"I hope you have given Miss Gray tea, Quiller," he said, his clear treble ringing firmly out, and by thus dropping the prefix of "Mr" he skilfully pinpointed the social gulf between them. With a jolt I realised that Quiller was as much a servant as any other member of staff, although he bore himself as a gentleman. I needed this sharp reminder for I must admit that I had been bedazzled by his graceful nonchalance.

Quiller inclined his head, a smile quirking his lips though there was rather a flinty gleam in his eyes. "This has been done, Master Jeffrey," he replied affably enough. "She can't stay long for she has to catch a train."

"May I hope that you'll come back soon?" the child asked, his enormous eyes searching my face, a worried little frown creasing his broad brow. Poor boy, he was no doubt confused by the people slipping in and out of his life since Lady Dorothea died.

"What d'you say, Miss Gray?" Quiller looked at me with lifted eyebrows. He was standing before the fire, his legs slightly spread in those perfect, unwrinkled trousers. His presence dominated the light, airy room whose wide windows held a view of the park. "Will it take you long to settle your affairs?"

I promised to return on Sunday, wishing that I did not have to go. I was eager to begin my pleasant work of teaching Jeffrey, of exchanging thoughts and ideas with his bright mind. On the way down to the hall later, Quiller and I discussed the business side of the appointment. My wage, set at sixty pounds a year with my keep and clothing, was more than generous and, as we parted, he added: "I can't begin to tell you how pleased I am that you are to join us." The look in his eyes brought the colour to my cheeks. "I'll have Jameson meet your train on Sunday. We shall be leaving in two weeks, which will give you ample opportunity to shop for all you need. I suggest Harrods or Whiteleys, whichever you prefer. Naturally, Jameson will be available to take you to the stores and carry your parcels."

"Oh, but I couldn't, Mr Quiller," I started to protest. "I have adequate clothing."

He raised a hand gently, silencing me. "Not, if you will forgive my saying so, suitable for a hot climate, I'll warrant. No, you must very definitely visit the shops and explain your destination. I can assure you that they are most familiar with the problems of equipping a young lady about to travel East for the first time. And please don't think that everything must be dull and sober, as befits a governess," he grinned at me impishly, but in a way which did not give offence. "I shall be going with you and you'll find shipboard life can be a lively affair, so do buy an evening gown or two. By the way, everyone here calls me Quiller – I would be honoured if you would do the same."

Was he waiting for me to give permission for him to call me by my christian name? I wondered. I was too shy to do so, but I thanked him, climbed into the car and was driven to the station. I couldn't wait for Sunday, impatient now with village life, yet parting from Miss Jenny was painful. When the time came, she gave me a bracelet to remember her by and we embraced clumsily as people will who are not used to such a show of emotion. I blinked to keep back the tears. It was not like me to cry and I was certainly not going to arrive in London with red eyes. Another period of my life was over, the door closing upon it. Closed or left ajar? Then I knew with a queer finality that I should never return again.

Chapter 3

It was dawn when we first sighted Alexandria, the *Esmeralda* rounding the point and steaming into the West Harbour. The air of anticipation was electrifying, far more so than when we had called in at other ports along the way. I joined the throng of passengers on the deck, eager for a glimpse of the ancient city. Above my head the sky was turning red, then came long bars of pink cloud, followed by an expanse of gold light, pure clarity, with here and there a small white cloud floating like an island in a fairy sea. From across the water, thin and eerie, came a strange, high singing sound – the Islamic call to prayer, ringing out from the calling-towers. My skin prickled and I held my breath, drinking in the scene – the distant minarets, the mosques and palaces forming a cascade of domes, glittering in white and gold.

Jeffrey, still rosy from sleep, came running up the companionway to stand beside me at the rail. He had with him his dreadfully shabby, lop-eared rabbit called Tippy, without whom he would not move an inch. "Look, Miss Gray," he shouted excitedly. "See the gulls on the masts of those boats over there, and that man lifting those boxes. Isn't he strong? D'you think he's stronger than the Strong Man in Barnum and Bailey's Circus? Mamma took me to see it, you know."

Before I could stop him he had clambered onto the lower rail, hanging over at a dangerous angle, fascinated by the hubbub of the quayside. I clung to the seat of his white shorts and then Quiller appeared, as cool and efficient as always. "Come down at once, Master Jeffrey," he admonished, gripping him firmly and hauling him from his precarious perch. "You are alarming Miss Gray."

Jeffrey wriggled and escaped as soon as he could, burying his face in my skirt. "I'm sorry – I didn't mean to frighten you, but isn't it all spiffing?" he breathed, throwing back his curly head, his brown eyes shining, a wide, happy smile lighting up his face.

I hugged him to me. "Yes, Jeffrey, it's all splendid. What an adventure we are having."

"I was a bit disappointed that we weren't attacked by pirates," Jeffrey said earnestly, then he brightened. "D'you think we might be kidnapped by a band of brigands from the desert? Ali Baba and the Forty Thieves, perhaps?"

"I sincerely hope not," laughed Quiller, his eye meeting mine with that warm friendliness that I had grown to expect and enjoy. "I don't think it would please your uncle if he had to pay a ransom for us."

"I'd join them," answered Jeffrey stoutly. "Miss Gray could be their queen."

Quiller and I laughed, a close, companionable bond between us. It had developed during the voyage, and I was once again gratified to be standing there with the best-looking man on board at my side. No one could have been more helpful and attentive. He had gone out of his way to make the trip a delightful experience for me. I had come out of my shell, wearing my new clothes, joining in each entertainment, Quiller giving me confidence. I lived for the moment, not thinking of anything but the present. The past was behind me, the future did not yet exist. There was only the present, that happy present when it was a joy to awake every morning in the company of Jeffrey, who filled my whole heart with love.

Now Quiller left us for a while to organise the baggage, and Jeffrey and I absorbed the colourful scene ashore.

The wharves and warehouses were buzzing with activity. Fleets of small boats plied their trades – Arab dhows, Nile river craft – and the bobbing ships of fishermen busily engaged in offering their catch to hungry customers. The heat was increasing by the minute as the sun came up in blazing glory. What struck me most was the rich smell, composed of spices and oils, borne on the breeze from the gardens and parks – cypress, camphor and olive trees, all combining into a potently heady brew.

Everyone was eager to go ashore; farewells were being said, along with those promises made and so rarely kept by shipboard friends, to keep in touch. Very soon Jeffrey and I were seated in a carriage, trunks and boxes loaded up behind. It was a Renshaw vehicle, as I was informed by the swarthy, widely smiling Egyptian in a white turban who greeted us. The wharf was crowded with porters hefting baggage, men from the poorest quarters with ragged headcloths pulled low over piercing dark eyes. It was as if we were under siege from dust and flies and beggars.

"Ignore them," advised Quiller, taking his place beside me under the fringed canopy. "Start handing out money and they'll descend on you like a swarm of locusts."

"But those poor children," I cried, horrified, as a squint-eyed old man held up a baby covered in running sores. "Can't something be done?"

"Something *is* done, my dear girl," he commented drily. "The mother has, no doubt, been deliberately making it worse to incite pity. You'll have to control your squeamishness here. Pull away, Abdul!"

I was silent for a while, a little shocked by such callousness. Quiller seemed different somehow now we had landed. The sunlight dazzled my eyes, the heat already weighing on the land though this was the winter season. The high whitewashed walls cast back the rays in a blinding glare. The shadows sliced like uneven scars down the dusty alleys through which we drove. The houses on either side presented blank, tightly shuttered windows to keep out prying eyes, their upper storeys overhanging the narrow streets which were filled with people. The colour of the men's skins varied from ebony to pale coffee, and they wore a turban or a red fez. Female figures shuffled along, thickly veiled, covered from crown to toe in enveloping black robes; children skittered about amidst the legs of laden mules and bell-bedecked camels. It was very noisy, and the smells were no longer aromatic.

"Alexandria is vastly different to Cairo. I always think of it as Mediterranean rather than Oriental. So many races mix here, each with their own language and religion, though that of Islam is the most popular. It's not really a safe place for Christians, though outwardly peaceful enough. It's a city of contrasts – mysterious, compelling." Something in his voice arrested me so that I looked at him sharply. His eyes were glittering in the shade of his Panama hat. "Once you've lived here, there's no place on earth will do as well. You may hate it, but you can't stay away for long. Every vice is pandered to here, but I don't suppose you know anything about these."

"No," I replied truthfully. "I don't."

He was laughing at me, and I glanced at Jeffrey who seemed absorbed in gazing at the picturesque crowd, but one could never be certain how much children overheard. Quiller's expression had been oddly intimate as he talked, suggesting that he knew about such things and wanted to tell me more. In my ignorance, I could not begin to imagine what he meant. All I knew of the East was fairy-tale stuff, fantasies of sultans, beautiful enchantresses and wicked viziers. I mentioned that I had read *The Arabian Nights*, and his smile deepened, giving him the look of a satyr as he replied mockingly: "An expurgated edition, I expect, suitable for the eyes of rectory-reared Miss Gray. Remind me to loan you my copy, translated from the original – quite a different version, I can assure you."

Uneasy feelings clouded my mind. I respected and admired Quiller, but he did have this ability to make me feel like a fool sometimes. I ignored him, pretending to join Jeffrey in his interest in the passing scene. This is what you wanted, I told myself firmly, this is adventure. Squeeze every drop of experience from it.

We drove along a sweeping crescent with sandy beaches on one side and houses, hotels and cafés on the other. The slums were behind us. Graceful palm trees bent before the light, hot breezes, and Europeans were beginning to venture out, to take the air, to stroll or visit the ruins. There were ladies with enormous hats, their faces veiled, parasols raised to preserve their complexions from the sun. Children walked sedately, marshalled by governesses; gentlemen positioned themselves on the stone benches of the esplanade, opening copies of newspapers. We were in the select residential area, where great houses were set back in spacious grounds glimpsed through arched gateways. On pausing at the entrance to one of these, we were ushered in by a native who leapt to attention, touching the tips of his fingers to his brow and his heart, bowing low. The driveway curved around a lawn. An old man was watering the roses and a fountain threw a sparkling cascade into the quivering air. The perfume of flowers was almost overpowering.

Then I saw the house. What an understatement! El Tarifa was a palace, domed and turreted and awe-inspiring. "I hadn't expected anything like this," I gasped in amazement.

"Bluebeard's Castle?" Quiller mocked gently. "I'll admit that it's a curious blend of Eastern and Renaissance architecture. Alexandria has yet to develop its own style of buildings. They copy everyone else. All manner of fashions and fancies intermingle in the homes of the rich." I noticed it again, that slightly acid ring in his voice when he spoke of those among whom Sir Nicholas was numbered. On the ship he had acted the part of a gentleman, whereas I had been treated by all as if I were Jeffrey's elder sister, not a governess. We had travelled first class and been accepted without question. Now, it seemed, he would have to resume a lowlier station and there was an irritability about him which had nothing to do with the humidity, though this was oppressive. My apprehension about meeting the family increased.

The front door was opened by a be-fezzed porter, wearing loose pantaloons and a short embroidered jacket, his corpulence accentuated by the wide sash wound many times round his middle. Quiller spoke to him curtly in Arabic and he salaamed and disappeared through a door at the far end of the hall. In the distance I could hear music being played on the piano – haltingly, as if a child was practising unwillingly. I can't explain why this seemed oddly disturbing. There was something lonely and plaintive about it, reminding me of the gulls which used to wail over the gorge near the orphanage, like the souls of lost children. I gave myself a shake. This was morbid and stupid. What had I expected to hear? Native drums, cymbals and flutes? Jeffrey was fidgeting impatiently, hot and tired. I wanted nothing more than to settle him in his own apartment where we could enjoy a cool drink and relax, but this was not to be – not yet. The pompous factotum returned and we followed him into a big drawing room. I could not fail to notice the fine quality of the cedarwood doors which swung back. Their handles were shaped like lion heads, beautifully made by skilled craftsmen, but I wished their mouths had not been agape in a silent, frozen snarl.

"Ah, Quiller, there you are at last. We were expecting you earlier. Nicholas told me that the *Esmeralda* had berthed," a soft, tired, petulant voice said. My eyes adjusted to the shuttered gloom. A striped awning fixed outside the French windows threw a greenish light. It was like walking through water as I crossed the carpet towards the couch, positioned so that its back was to the light. A woman reclined on it. A pair of pale blue eyes stared up at me from a pallid, heart-shaped face. Fine brown hair was puffed fashionably over each ear and drawn into curls at the back. One white, languid hand lifted a trifle as I was introduced.

"Lady Emily, this is Miss Nancy Gray," said Quiller, bowing.

She gave me a considering look. "So, you are the governess. I hope the voyage was pleasant. I never enjoy it, of course, and have to spend the entire time in my cabin – so very trying." Her eyes went to Jeffrey. There had been no warmth or interest in her tone when she addressed me, but a sudden hunger lit her face as she spoke to him. "Jeffrey – darling! My word, how you've grown! You may come and kiss me." She held his hand and studied him intently. There was a feverish look in her eyes. "I'm so glad that you are here. Fleur is looking forward to seeing you again. You must think of her as your sister now."

Jealousy was like a hot lump in my breast. Oh, I knew very well that she was his aunt and that he already knew her, but it was no consolation. Was he thinking that she looked like his beloved Lady Dorothea? Possibly comparing me unfavourably? I had been spoiled since taking over in London, beginning to look upon him as my own. She was so absorbed in him that I could stare at her without being thought rude. She had that frail boned, aristocratic delicacy which I admired. I could see the slender curve of her limbs beneath her beige silk skirt, small feet encased in high-heeled satin shoes, and crossed at the ankles. Though the morning was so hot, a tartan rug lay across her lap. Her face was oddly touching, filled with nervous intensity with extreme sensitivity in the eyes, and weakness about the drooping mouth. Petulant? Yes. Used to being pampered? Undoubtedly. Lady Emily Renshaw, invalid wife of my employer. She reached towards the carved side table and rang a small bell.

The music which had been coming from an adjoining room ceased abruptly and a small girl in a pink frock came in, hand in hand with a woman. Jeffrey and she eyed each other openly, and an emnity – which I suspected was of long standing – became apparent at once. "Hello, Jeffrey," she said, a hardfaced little moppet. "You aren't still carrying that stupid rabbit about with you, surely? I should have thought it was far too babyish for a great big boy like you."

Jeffrey coloured to the roots of his hair and clutched Tippy tightly. "What about your silly dolls?" he shrilled and I had never seen him so aggressive.

"Dolls are different," she replied primly, going to stand beside her mother.

So this is Fleur, I thought, recognising trouble, not looking forward to the job of settling their differences. I met a guarded glance from the well-dressed lady who had brought her in, and quickly learned that she was Lady Emily's companion, Veronica Leigh. We exchanged correct comments about the boat trip and the Egyptian weather, progressing to the ancient monuments which I simply *must* see, safe topics of conversation. At first I was pleased to find this young lady there. I had so much to learn and hoped that she would be friendly. A forlorn hope, as it turned out. The small talk became exhausted, and only Quiller kept going. He listened attentively and sympathised with Lady Emily's graphic description of her latest asthma attack, while Veronica and I took stock of each other. She offered politely to accompany me during our free time if I wished to explore the town. This sounded promising but at the same time I was puzzled by the congealing silence which was like a towering wall between us, the faintly suspicious expression of her features and that unmistakable air of hostility with which she was regarding me.

"Where is my husband?" Lady Emily asked on a complaining note.

"Abdul said he had been informed of Jeffrey's arrival," said Quiller placatingly.

"He should have been at the quayside to meet him." She struggled into a sitting position, the effort making her cough, a bright spot of scarlet appearing on either cheek. Veronica fussed with the cushions at her back. "Did you know that he has discovered some catacombs on that stretch of land behind the gardens, Quiller? He has become almost obsessed and spends every moment there, supervising the excavations. He's never here when I need him."

Quiller and Veronica exchanged a glance and it struck me how similar they were; he, so elegant in his pale grey sharkskin suit, white shirt and smoke-blue tie and she, the perfect model of a companion – with a fine figure, classical features of wide brow, beautiful eyes, a shapely nose and dimpled chin. She was a brunette, and her hair was thick, swept high at the sides and back. She wore a plain skirt of cream linen and a neat blouse with a flowing lacy jabot at her throat; her mien was one of gentility and refinement. The way she handled both Lady Emily and Fleur, who had decided that she did not want to show her picture book to Jeffrey, was nothing short of masterly. Unruffled, quietly controlled was Veronica Leigh, but as Miss Jenny had been wont to say darkly: "Still waters run deep." It was comforting to think of Miss Jenny at that moment – that sensible, motherly body who had done her level best to prepare me for just such a situation.

But there was one thing she could not have foreseen. Who indeed could have done so? This was the entrance of Sir Nicholas Renshaw. I heard him first, that deep, cultured, assured voice giving an order outside, then he strode through the French windows from the terrace, the shaded light dappling his face. He nodded to Quiller who seemed to visibly shrink in stature, clapped Jeffrey on the shoulder, ignored Veronica and his wife and stared sternly at me.

If Quiller had managed to make me forget my station, this was certainly not the case with his master. He, apparently, was a stickler for protocol – more than that, he did not even think about it. Everyone had their particular niche in his establishment. Born in a position of power, he did not question the rights or wrongs – it was as natural to him as breathing. I was simply Jeffrey's governess, no more, no less.

I immediately felt gauche, vividly aware of my lack of breeding. What would this arrogant-looking man say if he knew that the children were to be entrusted to the care of a charity girl? But he'd never know, I swore, thankful for the veneer I had acquired on the voyage. I stared him straight in the eye. This was a formidable experience but I managed it, though feeling, for once, quite small. He was the largest man I had ever seen – very tall and strongly built – a powerful man whose every impatient gesture hinted at a barely leashed temper. Dark eyes met mine from under heavy brows, his face thin and haughty with pronounced cheekbones, and a full-lipped mouth beneath a black moustache. His profile was that of a kestrel. His long-limbed body was clad in riding breeches and a shirt flung open at the neck, showing tanned skin and a mat of curling hair. As he came into his wife's presence, he was in the act of pulling on his jacket, though he seemed the kind of person to snub convention, perfectly happy in his shirt-sleeves. His hair was black, one untidy lock falling forward over his brow which was as dark as the devil's. This then was my new employer – Sir Nicholas Renshaw. I waited for him to make the first move.

"So – you are to look after these young rapscallions, eh?" He continued to rivet me with his compelling, unwinking gaze. "I trust you have chosen wisely, Quiller." He did not bother to look at him.

"I think so, sir," Quiller replied and, to my astonishment, his manner was almost servile. "She has proved herself to be invaluable already."

"Humm – has she indeed?" Sir Nicholas snorted, whacking the side of his breeches with his crop as if impatient to be off about more interesting pursuits. "Time will tell. Let us hope she proves more competent than that other female you engaged, my dear Emily. She was little short of an idiot!"

"She did her best, Nicholas . . ." she fluttered nervously.

"Her best! It was a damned poor best!" he thundered, a scowl drawing those alarming brows together. "She was a fool! Upsetting the servants with her silly airs and graces!" Once more he stared at me. "You're not a fool, are you, Miss Whatever-your-name-is?"

"I am Miss Gray, sir," I answered, my voice firm, indignation growing at his high-handed attitude. "If to be a fool means that one tolerates rudeness, no matter from whom – then I'm certainly not a fool!"

I was pleased to see that this barb went home. Any pleasantness left his face – and there had been precious little of that anyway – now mockery took its place. "Bravo! You're not afraid to speak your mind – Miss Gray. I hope I'm not addressing one of those educated, liberated females who put themselves on a par with men. Dowdy bluestockings most of 'em – forever making speeches about women's rights."

"I've never met any such ladies," I retorted, finding it hard to control my rising temper. "But I do believe in justice. You'll not find me lacking in respect. I shall do my work to the best of my ability but I don't intend to be browbeaten."

He was looking at me with an unreadable expression on those handsome features. A brief smile touched his lips. "No doubt Quiller has more experience than my wife in engaging staff. The last governess we had for Fleur was a disaster."

Lady Emily was watching him with the terrified fascination of a rabbit before a dangerous predator. "You wouldn't help me, Nicholas," she faltered, "leaving the choice to me when you know very well that I'm not to be upset or bothered – it always brings on an attack. How was I to know? She seemed perfectly respectable."

He flung himself into a chair, clapped his hands three times and a servant appeared bearing a decanter and glass on a tray. Sir Nicholas tapped imperiously on the goblet with his thumbnail and it was promptly filled. A curt nod and the lackey disappeared, swiftly and silently on bare feet. "You talk a lot of nonsense, Emily." His voice sliced firmly through the tense air. "Had you been less preoccupied with your so-called illness you would never have engaged the wretched creature. By George, it was a wonder that we didn't lose every single manservant! You know what these Muslims are like. They expect women to know their place – and that's not such a bad idea!"

"Well, she has gone now – and no real harm done," quavered the unfortunate Lady Emily, giving him a beseeching glance. I felt terribly sorry for her. She must have been so embarrassed, spoken to in this humiliating way before a stranger.

The sardonic lines each side of his mouth deepened and he drained his glass. There was a glitter in his eyes as he looked over at me which gave me a most peculiar feeling of animosity coupled with something else which I could not name. "Dismissed by me, my dear. You couldn't even do that yourself. I sent her off with a flea in her ear and no references."

Was this a hint that I should behave myself? I wondered, doubting my ability to hold my tongue if our paths crossed too often. Quiller was distinctly uneasy. I had never seen him like this. He was always so poised and unruffled. "I'm sure Miss Gray knows her duty, sir. A most able young lady. Master Jeffrey took to her at once."

Sir Nicholas ignored him. His eyes were still on me

and I bristled under that taunting regard. "Can you read music?"

"No, sir." Useless to lie. Dr Ridding had struggled to teach me but I had no more knowledge of it than I had of Greek!

"A pity," he snapped, a bad-tempered frown spoiling his face. "What the deuce were you doing with that piano just now, Fleur? It sounded like an elephant pounding the keys."

"I was practising, Papa," she answered sulkily. She stood in front of him, pink and frilled, her golden hair pinned away from her forehead with a bow of ribbon, then falling straight and fine as fairy-floss halfway down her back. "Miss Leigh was helping me."

"Helping or hindering?" he commented caustically and Veronica flushed, pain creeping across her face. "It was diabolical! You don't practise enough. When I was your age I spent five hours a day at my studies. You'll never make a pianist."

"She tries – truly she does," stammered his wife, thus incurring a further outburst.

"Tries! Tries! Good damnit, it's hopeless! I have almost accepted the fact that she's tone deaf and shows about as much talent as you do with those abysmal watercolours on which you waste so much time!" he snarled.

What an unpleasant man! What a bully! I thought, wanting to slap his face. There seemed to be not a drop of the milk of human kindness anywhere in his strong, domineering body or in the dark, sour recesses of his soul. Fleur had been reduced to tears. Both Veronica and Lady Emily looked as if they were about to join her. God, I hoped he was satisfied! He uncoiled his long legs and stood up. "Stop snivelling, child! I must say it will be a pleasant relief to have a boy about the house." He was already halfway to the terrace, eager to escape. "I must go back to the dig."

"Oh, Nicholas – do you have to go?" wailed Lady

Emily, following him with those sad, frightened eyes. "I have asked the Wentmores to luncheon. Can't you be present, for once?"

He paused and gave an ironic bow. "My apologies. You will have to excuse me. Today we have broken through to the second level of the tombs and I must be there. We've already found some most interesting pottery."

She sighed deeply. "You think of nothing else these days."

He frowned. "Emily, you can manage very well without me. Probably enjoy yourself more. You'll be able to indulge in sickbed talk with Sybil Wentmore. I can't waste valuable time exchanging banalities. Why don't you come and take a look at my finds? You could bring your sketching pad."

She passed a hand over her brow. "You know that I cannot tolerate the sunshine. It would prostrate me."

"Nonsense! It would do you good! You spend far too much time lying around in a darkened room." He was obviously one of those unfeeling people who was never ill and intolerant of anyone who was. "Would you like to come, Jeffrey?"

Jeffrey was watching him raptly, admiration in his eyes. I felt a pang. Oh, he would still need me, but now he had found someone to hero-worship. I hoped that Sir Nicholas would not be too hard on him.

"Oh, yes please, sir." Jeffrey was poised on tiptoe as if ready to follow his uncle to the ends of the earth.

"Tomorrow, then," Sir Nicholas promised. "You'll be busy finding your way around today." Then he stalked out on to the terrace and the room fell into an emptiness and silence when he had gone.

My room was situated on the second floor, next to those of the children. Veronica conducted me there, wearing that air of the privileged confidante which I found maddening. I pasted an insincere smile on my face and bit my tongue as she extolled the wonders of El Tarifa and left me in no doubt as to the pecking order. The only time her voice warmed and her perfect, cameo face lit up was when she mentioned Sir Nicholas. I pondered on this as we walked along corridors decorated with ornamental tilework. There were windows on all sides, the shutters thrown back, each giving a ravishing view – here the gardens glowing with verdant greens and multi-coloured flowers, there the distant city with minarets reaching towards heaven and mushroom domes shining brilliantly, the land white and hot, the sea of a sparkling, motionless blue, shimmering in the heat haze.

My apartment was a delight, furnished in splendid Eastern style, but with comfortable European additions. I had my own sitting room and a bathroom with an oval tub which stood high off the tiled floor on gold claw feet. I exclaimed with pleasure as Veronica showed me round. "Oh, this is nothing," she replied patronisingly. "Wait till you see the Renshaws' suite."

"The house in London is magnificent." I was not to be outdone. Let this haughty creature know that I had stayed there.

"I know. I've been with the family for over two years. No doubt it was a surprise to you," she said loftily, her skirt swishing as she moved gracefully before me. "I gather that you came from the country."

So, they knew my history, did they? No, not quite all, I hurriedly added to myself, only what Quiller had told them. Loyalty to Dr Ridding's memory made me exaggerate a little. "Somerset, to be precise. My guardian lived in a Tudor manor house which had been converted into a rectory. Where were you before you came to work for the Renshaws?"

A faint flush shaded her cheekbones. "My father's house was in Kent," she answered stiffly. "He was a master builder."

"Oh, a tradesman," I murmured with just the right insulting inflection. On the *Esmeralda* I had learned that anyone in business was hardly worth knowing and would certainly never have been invited to dinner! "Dr Ridding was a scholar. He had had several books published, terribly learned – educated at Oxford – a real gentleman."

Dear me, I mourned inside, though not displeased with my performance, no chance of us becoming friends now. "Really?" she sniffed, ushering Jeffrey and Fleur into the day nursery. "Of course, though you will dine with the family tonight – it being the special occasion of your arrival – normally you'll eat here, with the children."

"I see, and where do you eat, Miss Leigh?" I asked. She had put me in my place and I didn't like it.

"Sometimes with Lady Emily, if she feels unable to leave her room. At others in the dining room – with them. I'm her companion, you understand, not a servant. There's a world of difference, as you'll quickly discover." Her eyes flickered over me so that I began to wonder if I had a smut on my nose. "I'll leave you to your work, Miss Gray. Please ring that bell if there is anything you require. The native servants are a little slow, but they come eventually."

"How do I address them? I don't speak the language."

She raised one arched eyebrow, cool as ice. "French will do nicely, or if you don't speak it, English is understood."

She was about to leave when, glancing from the window, I saw a strange tableau. An elderly woman was berating one of the gardeners. She was a rather lumpy lady, grey hair wisping from under a crumpled straw hat, a shapeless garment of indeterminate colour flapping about her ankles. Mannish shoes covered her large feet, and a variety of parcels and bags were clutched to her person. Her voice was deep, booming across the lawn as she scolded the man, pointing to one of the flower beds.

"Who is that?" I asked Veronica.

"Only Miss Tranter. She's a little mad. I can't think why the Renshaws keep her on – Sir Nicholas has a fine sense of loyalty and she was once the nanny of Lady Emily and her sister. She has been helping with Fleur, but is really awfully forgetful and unreliable."

I spent the rest of the day unpacking, dealing with the quarrelsome children and accustoming myself to giving orders to the dark-skinned manservants. In the afternoon Dr Terence Armstrong came in to check Jeffrey and make sure that he had suffered no ill effects from the journey. Quiller had told me that he was Lady Emily's physican, living in the house on constant call. He was of slight build with small hands and feet, a well-shaped head crowned with unruly mid-brown hair. His eyes were at the same shade and his smile was hesitant, but when it succeeded in breaking through it lit up his face pleasantly. He was rather careless in his dress as if there were too many interesting things in the world to waste time on frivolities. I took to him at once, and the withdrawn Fleur changed dramatically when he entered, leaping from the cane chair where she had been listlessly staring out of the window, and throwing herself into the young doctor's arms while he laughed and swung her high.

I introduced myself and he told me his name, saying kindly: Look here, if you want any help or desire to go sightseeing, let me know and I'll show you round. Alexandria takes a bit of getting used to."

"Thank you, I'd like that," I replied, adding: "Miss Leigh has already offered."

"Veronica? Oh, she won't get any further than the rue Cherif Pacha where the best shops are, or will want to hang about outside one of the posh hotels in the hope that people will think she's staying there," he said with a boyish grin. "I'll take you to far more interesting places. D'you like wandering round ruins? You'd better like them if you want to please Sir Nicholas."

Later, finding that I had a few moments to myself, I

sat at the writing table near the window in my sitting room and opened my journal, eager to make a note of my impressions before they slipped away. By now, my random jottings had been transferred into a handsome, leather-bound book which fastened with an ornamental clasp to which I had a tiny key. I was not the most fervent of diarists – weeks went by when, busy about other things, I made no entries, but now I was determined to do better. One day I might be able to show it to Nell, if I could find out where she lived, certain that she would keep her part of our bargain, and that with her literary bent she would make a splendid job of it. I wasn't too sure about Rebecca, doubting that she would ever sit still long enough to perform such a task. My mind drifted as I thought about them, wondering how they were and what they were doing, and wishing that I could see them again. I was so deep in my musings that I started violently when a voice spoke behind me.

"Ah, Miss Gray – are you settling in?"

Quiller stood there and I automatically shut my book. He had changed into dazzling white and was looking very spruce. He swung a cane in his hand, and around his neck was loosely knotted a silk handkerchief of dark green. A broad-brimmed straw hat was tucked under his arm. He had that air of quiet deference, that look of pleased interest and that intimate gentleness in his voice which I found irresistible.

I smiled up at him. "Very well, thank you. Of course, it is rather strange, but very exciting. I understand that the Renshaws are entertaining us to dinner tonight."

"Well, not exactly," he corrected me mildly. "I hardly think we shall be invited to sit at table with them. They have a nice way of handling members of staff, however, and there will be a buffet laid out for us."

Of course, this would be so. Veronica's statement had been misleading. Quiller asked if he could take the chair close to mine and I readily agreed, though not forgetting Jeffrey, my ears attuned to the sound of his voice in the playroom. I liked talking to Quiller, he was so well informed, impressing me with his knowledge of the world, his experiences abroad among European society. On the journey, I had been filled with admiration by his easy way of dealing with stewards and officials, envying his tact and cleverness.

"Are you glad you came?" He was lounging back in his chair, watching me. Something flickered in his eyes, an expression which I had seen before. Was it cynical amusement at my simplicity? Possible desire? It was too fleeting to identify.

"Oh, yes, indeed!" I cried, wanting to thank him for selecting me for the post, but unsure of how to word it. Though we had spent much time together on the *Esmeralda*, there was always a certain reserve. He was the sort of man impossible to really know.

"There are even greater treats in store," he promised. "Just wait till you visit the bazaars, but don't let the merchants cheat you. Bargain with them."

"I wouldn't dare," I laughed gaily.

"Oh, you would, Miss Gray – you would dare anything," he challenged.

"I'll be able to buy some postcards to send to Miss Jenny," I fenced, wondering what he was driving at.

"Is that what you were doing when I interrupted you – writing to her?" he asked, glancing at the journal on the table.

My hand instinctively closed over it. I had written intimate secrets there and the idea of anyone, save my two friends, reading it made me acutely uncomfortable. "Oh, no." I had difficulty in meeting his eyes, though he was wearing his engaging smile. "I was merely keeping an account of my impressions."

"Of course!" He smote himself on the brow in mock annoyance with his own stupidity. "You're writing a diary, as all young ladies do. Isn't it strange how women commit their thoughts to paper? I rarely write – far too incriminating. Oh, yes – this will give you something to look back on when you are a married woman, no longer obliged to work for a living, supported by some lucky man. Then you will relive these halcyon days and read extracts to your children. I'm sure it will make fascinating reading and, my dear, sensible Miss Gray, I'll warrant it won't be an account of a misspent youth."

Something in his tone annoyed me. There was mockery there, a hint of barbed teasing which his expression, bland as milk, belied. "It's for my own satisfaction – nothing more," I protested, wishing that he would leave. His presence had suddenly become disturbing. "And as for my ever being married – I can't see that happening. It is certainly not my ambition."

At once his manner changed. He leaned across and patted my hand. "Forgive me. I didn't mean to offend you. Of course you will marry. A lovely woman like yourself will not want for suitors, but a word of advice – don't bristle so. It doesn't become you. You receive any compliment with suspicion, and you've no need of this. You are very beautiful – no, please listen." He held up an admonishing finger as I opened my mouth to protest. "There you go again – about to deny it. Where on earth did you get the impression that you are plain? My dear girl, few men could resist you – that glorious hair, and those lovely green eyes. I can see that I shall have to take special care of you here or you'll be whisked away by some sheik to his harem."

I was blushing furiously by now, embarrassed yet pleased at the same time. Quiller had such a way with words. I tried to laugh. "Oh, come – you go too far. I can't imagine that this is at all likely."

"Prickly as a hedgehog," he chided softly. "And, you know, this has the opposite effect of what you hope. It only makes you more alluring, challenging a man to try to break through such reserve. I suspect that beneath the surface you have a deeply passionate nature."

My heart was racing. Quiller was altogether too perceptive, his eyes boring into mine as if he would unravel the secrets of my soul. I started to put away my writing materials. "It's time for Jeffrey to have his tea," I said, dropping my pencil in my confusion.

He gave me his enigmatic smile and leaned over the side of his chair to retrieve it. "Quite so, Miss Gray. Your responsible attitude towards your charge is most praiseworthy."

"He's a delightful little boy, and I already love him dearly," I responded as I rose to my feet. Quiller stood up too, looking at me with those Pan-like, smiling eyes. Our faces were level for I was as tall as he in my heeled shoes.

"I'm so glad to hear it," he answered, glancing over to the open doorway where we could see Jeffrey kneeling on the floor, engrossed in a game with his lead soldiers. "I've noticed your interest and patience. He likes you too – I'm sure of that – an unusually attractive child who seems to inspire adoration in everyone who meets him."

"That's true," I put in quickly, eager for him to leave so that I might be alone to think about the things he had just said, to look in a mirror and reassess the value of my appearance. "I'd do anything for him."

"You see yourself as his champion, his shield against the ugly side of life," he remarked thoughtfully, his eyes still fixed on the boy.

"It's unlikely. He has his uncle to protect him." My words seemed to recall Quiller's thoughts from some byway down which they had gone roving, and his attention returned to me.

"Why, yes – you are right. A fortunate child, don't you think? Adopted, born Lord knows where, yet arriving in life with a silver spoon in his angelic mouth."

I called Jeffrey and he smoothed his linen suit and came running towards us, shouting: "Is it time for tea, Miss Gray? I'm hungry!"

"I'll see you this evening," said Quiller to me. "Wear

one of your prettiest dresses and leave your prickles behind."

"I'll try," I promised, wishing, not for the first time, that coquetry came easily to me. Quiller would be a good match, deep in Sir Nicholas's trust. As his wife, I should want for nothing. His attitude towards me that afternoon had been almost that of a suitor.

His smile deepened as, with raised brows, he glanced down at the book in my hand. "May I dare hope that any remarks written about me in there are pleasant ones?"

"What else should they be?" I answered guardedly. "You've proved yourself to be my friend."

All though tea, I hardly listened to Jeffrey's chatter or Fleur's complaints, my thoughts fully occupied. I wasn't sure what I really felt towards Quiller. When I was with him I was off guard, for he appealed to my imagination and my vanity in a way which was exciting. I had never met anyone like him. Till that afternoon he had always talked to me seriously and sensibly as if I were a man, but today his remarks had confused me and now I did not know what to think. Without appearing to do so, I realised that he managed me in just the same way he did the servants. He never raised his voice or lost his temper, yet lorded it over all who came within his ken. And, following the direction of the monologue going on in my head as I passed Jeffrey cake and told him to drink up his milk, it struck me that there was only one person who shattered Quiller's control and that was Sir Nicholas Renshaw.

When Jeffrey was tucked in his small white bed beneath the mosquito netting, I lowered the shaded oil lamp and left him, going into my own bedroom.

"Leave the door open," his clear voice demanded. "Please, Miss Gray – and do let me see you in your evening gown."

I promised, for he always insisted that I did so. Quiller

had once told me that Lady Dorothea had always gone into the nursery to kiss him goodnight before she went off to a party, wrapped in furs, sparkling with jewels. Jeffrey did not mention her often but I knew that he missed her very much. I pinned my hair securely on top of my head and relaxed in the warm, scented water in the bathtub, then, wrapped in an enveloping towel, I went to the wardrobe and drew out one of the dresses I had bought in London. They had seemed a wicked waste of money then, but now I was quite used to wearing them. There had been dances and parties on the *Esmeralda* and I had discovered that I never wanted for partners. I selected one of leaf-green satin and spread it out on the bed. I rummaged in a drawer and found an evening bag, gold slippers, a fan and a shawl.

I had still not become accustomed to viewing myself naked in a mirror. I hurriedly dragged my dressing gown over my body when I finally discarded the towel. It was impossible to shake off the teachings of the orphanage, they were too deeply ingrained, and we had learned to think of the flesh as sinful. My hair was still damp and I rubbed it dry. It smelled fragrant as it hung about my face. I brushed it with long, languid strokes, my mood pensive. It shone like burnished copper, and I took pleasure in seeing it, so thick and heavy. I parted it in the centre and swept it up, using combs to keep it in place, then I dressed myself in a chemise and petticoats of fine lawn, trimmed with Valenciennes lace and baby-ribbon. As this was a formal occasion, another went on top, rustling with silk, cut very plain and tight-fitting round the hips, flaring out fluffy and frilly from the knees to the floor.

With every passing moment I was beginning to look less like myself and this was a relief, like donning a masquerade costume in which one can act totally out of character. I slipped into my gown, my bare arms and shoulders rising above the low-cut bodice, the rich folds of the skirt frothing about my feet. I wore long white gloves and added Miss Jenny's parting gift of a bracelet, and a black velvet choker. I tucked a clean handkerchief into my beaded bag and went in to see Jeffrey.

His eyes widened as if I were a heavenly apparition. He beamed and flung aside his book, holding out his arms to me. "Oh, Miss Gray – you are like a queen!"

I sat on the side of the bed and took his hand while he smiled up at me from the pillow. "How nice of you to say that, Jeffrey, but I'm not a real lady, you know – only your governess."

He frowned a little at this, as imperious as a tiny grandee. "Don't say that. Perhaps I shall marry you when I grow up. I'll never have a title, of course, unless I do something very heroic and the King gives me a knighthood, but I'll look after you, just as you take care of me now."

He never ceased to delight me, this child of quaint precosity which stemmed from being constantly in the company of adults. He had been brought up deep in the country at Lady Dorothea's Devonshire manor and had had little contact with other children. He was a boy of unusual sensitivity, a very thoughtful, happy child. When we had begun lessons on board ship, I discovered that he could read and write fluently, taught by his foster mother. I was forever grateful to Dr Ridding, who had had the foresight to educate me so well. He had prepared me for this important post. Because of him, I could now taste the wine of life, my horizons widening in a way once thought impossible. Thanks to him, I could share my knowledge with this lovely boy.

With a catch in my throat, I said: "This is the first time a gentleman has proposed to me. Thank you, Jeffrey, I'm most honoured, but you may change your mind by then, you know. I shall be an old lady of at least thirty-five."

His eyes glimmered in the rosy light and his open countenance, framed by his cloud of curls, was very appealing. I reached out and ran my hand over his head. He smiled again, laughing up at me mischievously. "Then I'll wheel you out in your bath chair." His face grew serious again. "I'll always love you, Miss Gray – never doubt that."

I was lost for words, touched by his confidence in me. Such affection was exactly what I needed before facing the formidable Sir Nicholas again. I bent to kiss him, inhaling the odour of soap and cleanliness and that sweet smell of babyhood which still clung to him. He received my kiss openly, young enough to accept it without feeling unmanly. I began to tuck the sheet around him but he bounced up energetically. "Lie down, Jeffrey," I said. "It's time you were asleep."

"Oh, Miss Gray, I'm not in the least bit tired. You know what it's like in a strange bed. Can't you read to me?"

He was irresistible and I relented. "All right – what would you like?"

He held up his book with a grin, well aware of my love for the author. It was Kipling's *Just So Stories*, and we chuckled over the tale of the naughty Elephant's Child and how he got his long nose. Then I tore myself away, though I would have much preferred to remain. As it was, my fears were groundless for Sir Nicholas was not there. As Quiller had anticipated, the servants had prepared a cold supper for us and Lady Emily declined to eat, declaring herself to be without any appetite. Terence Armstrong was pleasant company, Quiller was his amiable self, in fact everyone seemed relieved that the master was away. Later, Quiller and I took a turn on the terrace. I was glad of my shawl for it was cool now that the sun had set. The beauty of the night stole into my senses. It was as if the spirit of Egypt was weaving a spell around me. There was something magical about the night. Everything was lovely and clear and dramatic in the brilliant light of the moon which sailed austerely across the purple sky attended by its retinue of myriad stars. The air was scented with spices, and as I leaned on the stone balustrade, I felt the soft breeze lift a strand of my hair and brush it across my cheek but I made no attempt to push it back. I did not move or speak for a while, lost in a reverie. I longed to stay like that forever, with tomorrow a dream, always ahead, never reached. This was so perfect that I wanted nothing to mar it, willing life to stand still.

Quiller rested his elbow next to mine and I was very conscious of his close proximity. "Enjoying yourself, Miss Gray?" he murmured.

I gave a deep sigh. "It's all too wonderful. I never expected – never dreamed . . ."

"That you would be here, just like a member of the upper classes?" he finished the sentence for me. There were large Chinese lanterns lighting the terrace, fragile painted paper spheres, and in their glow I saw that he was regarding me with a masked expression, coiled alertness in his rather indolent stance. He was wearing a dinner jacket, and succeeding in looking debonair, his white-blond hair smoothed back, a fine escort indeed. "And why should you not be? I'm sure you're every whit as good as they – if not a great deal better. I know that I am."

"I've never thought about it," I confessed, feeling rather dizzy, for the wine had been poured generously. "They have their place in the scheme of things, and I have mine . . ."

"And never the twain shall meet, eh?" He smiled without humour, and I sensed that he was in the grip of some emotion which had nothing to do with me. Then he leaned closer. I did not draw back, afraid of offending him. "Don't believe it! That's claptrap spread abroad to keep the masses quiet. I'm as good as any damned member of the aristocracy."

I was amazed at such disloyalty. "How can you say that? You accept their employment and do very well. Don't you like Sir Nicholas?"

He shrugged and drew a cigar from his breast pocket. "He's all right, as far as it goes. D'you mind if I smoke?"

I shook my head and soon the pungent fumes of Havana's finest tobacco mingled with the heavy scents of the night flowers. "If you feel so strongly about the caste system, why did you take up your present position? You could have become a tradesman or a clerk."

"My dear, sweet girl, how can you suggest such tedious occupations?" He sounded pained at the very idea. "I was born into service, if you like. My mother was a parlourmaid."

"And your father?"

Again, that careless lift of the shoulders, the red tip of the cigar glowing as he raised it to his lips. His eyes shone, points of fire. "The man she married was a butler, but whether or no he was my father is questionable. She was an ambitious girl and it was rumoured that she had had an affair with the master of the house. The butler was ordered to make a respectable woman of her.

"Oh," was all I said. My mind was racing. If this was true, then I need no longer retain the smallest feeling of inferiority where he was concerned. We were equals – bastards under the skin.

"You don't appear to be shocked." He sounded amused, still as a statue at my side.

"Why should I be? Such things happen." I was feeling bold, carried away by my dress, the splendour of the palace, and the wine. I could say anything I chose. It was an exhilarating sensation.

"Not quite the reaction I expected from a young lady who has spent her formative years in a rectory," he remarked casually, and I froze as I caught a sceptical inflection in his tone. Had I betrayed myself in some way? I wondered. I felt like Cinderella who, at the stroke of midnight, would lose her finery and revert to the scullery.

"Dr Ridding was a man of liberal views," I said

crisply. "Miss Jenny and I worked among the poor, so perhaps I've led a less sheltered life than you suppose."

"I'm quite sure of that," he drawled. "On our first meeting I recognised your earthy qualities. I like you, Nancy – I may call you that, mayn't I? I think we could go far together – as partners."

"Partners?" I had not expected this. "What do you mean?" I had been girding myself to rebuff an amorous advance but this, it seemed, was not forthcoming.

"You and I – working as a team." He crushed his cigar under his foot. "You're a bright girl, and a handsome one. I can offer invaluable service to any family, if the price is right. You can act the part of governess – companion – even that of nurse in some cases. We could travel together and get rich pickings from the élite."

I frowned at him. "But why? We have jobs already – with the Renshaws."

Although he had not moved, it was as if he was withdrawing into himself again. "I didn't mean right now – but maybe later, when we are no longer required by them. I could help you, Nancy."

"And what would you ask in return?" My delight in the evening had gone. The wind seemed suddenly cold.

"As I said – you're an attractive woman, and gentlemen are much more likely to employ a pretty face," he said as, by mutual consent, we began to move back to the house. He grinned at me as we paused by the french windows. "Don't look so alarmed. I'm not proposing that you become a lady of easy virtue, merely suggesting that masters are susceptible to charm, that's all."

"And mistresses are jealous!" I snapped. "I want none of this. I've been hired to do a job and I'm determined to carry it out to the best of my ability. I'll stay with Jeffrey for as long as I'm needed, and when the time comes to leave, I'll ask Sir Nicholas for a reference."

"You are perfectly right, my dear – always so right and full of admirable intentions," he replied gaily, but it was as if a barrier had come between us. "Speaking of jealousy – Lady Emily is fiendishly so, though you may not believe it. I've seen it in action once or twice – not very pleasant – a kind of suppressed, tigerish animosity – so be discreet."

"I'll not upset her," I answered tartly.

"Don't be too confident," he warned silkily. "Sir Nicholas is quite a one with the women."

"But he's already married."

He chuckled, but there was a hardness about his eyes. "How naïve you are, Nancy. I do hope that Alexandria doesn't corrupt you – so charmingly innocent. It would be a pity if you became a cynic."

"Like you!" I returned smartly.

"Like me," he inclined his head, smiling still, that chill smile which did not touch his tip-tilted eyes.

I went up to my room but I could not rest. The conversation with Quiller had upset me more than I liked to admit. I'd never known him so strange. I had looked up to him, proud of his friendship, but tonight's conversation had bewildered me. I paced up and down, wrestling with my thoughts, then snatched up my shawl and went out, needing fresh air. I found my way to a secluded part of the garden, a little sunken, secretive spot. The house stood above and away from it, its white walls glimmering, ghostly and cool, some areas smudged with vines and creepers. There was a pergola covered with roses, surrounded by tall cypress trees that whispered with the noise of far-off surf. I had hoped that no one would disturb me, needing my own company so that I might sift through the confusing impressions which had crowded in on me all day.

I seated myself on the rim of the basin which enclosed a three-tiered marble fountain. I trailed my fingers in the water and tried hard to be rational. Naturally, it would take time for me to adjust and get to know everyone. There was no need to panic. Quiller probably resented having to take orders again, used to being in charge, therefore his remarks might be nothing more than sour grapes. None the less they had been disturbing enough to cause a shift and drop in my spirits which was disconcerting, just when I had imagined things were going so well. This was silly, I told myself sternly, I must stop lingering about out there, courting a chill or at the very least proving an open invitation for hungry mosquitos. I got to my feet, intending to go back and attempt to sleep, when I was arrested by the sight of a darker shape against the gloom of the bushes, and there was the small, red ember of a cigarette.

The shadow moved towards me and an instantly recognisable deep male voice said: "Miss Gray? What are you doing out here alone?"

I was startled and yet, as I don't shrink from admitting, he had not been far from my thoughts. Sir Nicholas was of so forceful a personality that it was impossible to remain tepid or uninvolved with him. On the surface my attention had been fully occupied during the hours since we had met, but in the deep inner recesses of my mind, I had been engaged in an argument with his image, saying all those things which had escaped me then, clever, witty things which entirely deserted me again now.

I drew my shawl tightly around me, giving my hands something to do, and looked up at him. "I'm enjoying your garden, sir," I countered. "Is this wrong? Is a governess forbidden to stroll at will?"

I knew that my voice was sharp, but he had the power to make me angry. There was something in his arrogance, his cool assumption of superiority, which goaded me. Even the amusement in his reply added to the fire. "My dear Miss Gray, you may go where you damn well please. You're not a bond slave, you know."

"I don't want to do anything which isn't proper," I replied. "You must forgive my ignorance, but this is my first post and I've much to learn."

"And one of those lessons, Miss Gray, is that it is

unwise for a white woman to go far alone, particularly after dark." He was leaning against the hole of a tree, looking at me. It was dark save for the light of the moon, and his face was shadowed, but I could see the hard line of his jaw and the brooding curve of his lower lip.

"I'm not afraid," I said instantly, as if he was daring me.

He laughed softly. "Not afraid of the slave traffic? Of being sold into the harem of some wealthy Arab?"

"I don't think anyone would be interested in buying me."

"You underestimate yourself, Miss Gray." His teeth glimmered as he smiled; made up of black and white, he seemed – evening suit and snowy linen, black hair silvered by moonlight, the whites of his eyes. "I know of one or two sheiks who'd be entranced by your fiery hair. Don't you know that it's much prized in the East? Cleopatra was a redhead, and this was once her city."

I was becoming more uncomfortable by the minute and this made me furious. I suspected that he was making fun of me. "Please don't bother yourself on my account, sir. I can look after myself," I answered spiritedly, but was rewarded by another dry laugh.

"So? Miss Independence, eh? Is that what you were taught at the rectory?"

"I've had to stand on my own two feet from childhood," I said with all the dignity I could muster. It was on the tip of my tongue to tell him straight where I had really come from, this smug nobleman who had obviously had such a smooth passage through life. I struggled to restrain myself.

"Please don't misunderstand me, Miss Gray. But I'm responsible for you whilst you are in my employment, so don't wander too far. If you want to go into the town, I'll make sure that you are accompanied."

"Dr Armstrong has already offered," I put in quickly, "and Miss Leigh has done the same. Mr Quiller too – "

For some inexplicable reason, I did not want him to think of me as a friendless spinster.

He appeared to lose interest, already turning away. "That's all right, but don't forget, if you have any problems, come to me. Shall we walk back to the house together?"

This was put in such a way that I couldn't refuse. It was growing late and the garden, though breathtakingly beautiful, was, as he had pointed out, very lonely. It was so quiet with only the hum of insects a deep monotonous background to which the ear became dulled. Occasionally I had heard a native voice or a dog barking somewhere in the jet blackness beyond the trees and then grow still, leaving the distinct impression that some hand had deliberately stifled it.

I followed his tall silhouette and he led me to another entrance, through an arched doorway reached by a winding path fringed with prickly pear and pepper trees. We were in a passage near the music room and, as we approached, the door opened abruptly and Veronica was illumined by the light within. Her eyes went beyond Sir Nicholas, widening in surprise to see us together. "I was fetching Fleur's music, sir – she will need it for her lesson tomorrow." She had an album of piano pieces in her hand.

He nodded without comment, a smile quirking his lips, and she fled away along the corridor, though not before giving me a look which should have killed me stone dead. I bade him goodnight and made to follow her but his voice stopped me. "Miss Gray?"

"Sir?"

"I hope you will be happy here."

"Thank you, sir," I replied, and returned to my room.

I woke suddenly from a deep, dreamless sleep. For a moment I couldn't remember where I was, then I knew. The bed was strange, my room was strange – I was in the palace of El Tarifa. It was dark and very still with that unnatural hush which precedes dawn, as if the world is suspended in the void, waiting for the sun to chase away the creatures of the night. It came again, the sound which had awakened me. Somewhere a child was crying – a sad, disconsolate, disembodied sobbing.

I leapt up, recognising Jeffrey's voice. The netting round my bed trapped me like a spider's web. I fought my way free and rushed to the door of Jeffrey's room. My heart almost stopped as I crossed the threshold and saw the figure in white standing quite still in a patch of moonlight. I knew it was Jeffrey in his nightshirt, yet at the same instant a bolt of superstitious dread almost paralysed me. He looked so eerie, as transparent as a wreath of vapour on frosty air. He was staring intently towards the far end of the room, as if watching someone or something.

He's sleepwalking! I thought, and approached him quietly, careful not to wake and startle him but, to my astonishment, he turned his head and watched me cross the shiny tiles. He was not asleep and yet there was something curiously unreal about his dreamy, semi-conscious gaze which struck me with dread.

"Darling," I stammered, sinking to my knees and putting my arms about the small form. "Why aren't you in bed? It isn't morning yet."

"Oh, Miss Gray . . ." the child was bemused, his face rapt. "She was here, I saw her."

"Who, Jeffrey? Who was here?" I clutched him to me, feeling his warm, yielding body beneath the little shirt. I was trying to capture his attention for he kept peering into the gloom beyond my shoulder, looking for someone. I gave him a gentle shake. "Was it Fleur?"

"No – no – it wasn't Fleur." There was a faint note of scorn in his voice. "It was Mamma, I woke up and she was by my bed . . ."

"You were dreaming, Jeffrey," I said, as calmly and steadily as I could, considerably unnerved. "Your mamma has gone to heaven."

"No, that's not true," he cried and I was appalled by the sudden change in him as he struggled from my grasp, hitting me with his fists as if he hated me. The tears welled from his eyes and he was sobbing wildly. "She was here, I tell you . . . Oh, I want her – Mamma – Mamma – come back!"

Chapter 4

When morning came, I was able to smile at my fright. Jeffrey had fallen asleep as soon as I had put him back to bed and when he woke he was as normal as could be, appearing to remember nothing of the incident. I had a word with Terence about it and he, very sensibly, put it down to over-excitement, suggesting that I kept him quiet for a day or two.

Fortunately, I had little time to brood, there was much to occupy my mind, not the least of which was caring for my little charges. This was a challenge for there was no love lost between them, and Jeffrey was such a lively, adventurous soul that it was one person's work to keep an eye on him. In the end, I screwed up my courage and took this problem to Sir Nicholas who promptly engaged an Alexandrian to act as a kind of bodyguard. Hassan was his name, a fine, tall stout man with a rather fair complexion and a dark brown, spade-shaped beard. He dressed rather shabbily and wore a large green turban which indicated that he was a *shereef*, a descendant of the Prophet himself. Jeffrey loved being with him, and this was not surprising for he charmed us all with his fund of old ballads and tales of genies and ghouls. He spoke very good English and became devoted to his little master. His knowledge of the city, its manners and customs, was invaluable, and I grew to rely on him, enjoying his quaint, half-spiritual, whimsical conversation.

Fleur was an obstinate, selfish girl, but I was determined to win her confidence. Sometimes I daydreamed of having her play the piano perfectly to her father. That would have been a feather in my cap. By now I had realised that, among many other talents, he was a most accomplished musician and, many a night, as I lay on the very borders of slumber, I would wake fully to hear the distant sounds of the piano drifting through the scented air. Sometimes, he sang. He had a mellow baritone voice which had the disturbing power of sending stinging tears to my eyes, while my heart ached with vague longings. But he was impatient with Fleur, and she would run to her mother, burying her face in her lap whilst Lady Emily soothed her. I had heard them arguing about her, voices raised, and these disagreements resulted in her being a cold, secretive child. I had been a plain, stubborn one myself and understood that ridicule and reproaches did nothing but make her more sullen. I noticed that she behaved particularly badly when Sir Nicholas was in the vicinity, as if she almost welcomed his anger and did it deliberately to attract his attention. He, so wrapped up in his own pursuits, seemed blind to the fact that his daughter was starving for his affection.

He came and went and his presence was strongly felt; quick of speech, gesture and temper, he could not be regarded with indifference. I felt an odd, half-willing, part-reluctant, liking for him as my life began to unfold into a pattern of days. We rose early and commenced school work immediately after breakfast; then, before noon, we might take a trip to a sandy beach, choosing one which was visited only by the well-to-do Europeans. In the afternoons the children rested or played in the shade and, when they had gone to bed at night, I spent much of my time alone in my room, reading, writing my diary or simply standing on the balcony, gazing across the lawns to the dark, whispering bank of sentinel trees. Before me, a huge, ancient fig tree rustled and creaked, spreading wide its gnarled branches, the topmost of which almost reached me.

One morning, shortly after my arrival, the children and I were engrossed in our studies in the day nursery when we were interrupted. The strange, untidy figure of Miss Tranter stood in the doorway, that eccentric old lady I had seen in the garden on the first day. "Time for your treat, Miss Fleur," she announced, ignoring me. She drew a crumpled paper bag from her pocket and held it out to her. The smell of peppermint filled the air.

Fleur's blue eyes went to me and, annoyed by this disruption, I said: "We're in the middle of a geography lesson. Can't this wait till later?"

Miss Tranter girded herself for battle, pitting her will and influence against mine. "Miss Fleur likes her sweeties."

I closed my textbook with a snap. This was an important test. If law and order were to be kept in the nursery, then I must win, hands down. The children were agog. I wished that Quiller had told me about Miss Tranter. It was natural that she should resent me if she'd been used to being in charge. "I've made a few changes," I began, my voice hard and high in the still, warm room. Sounds drifted in at the open windows, the soft babble of the gardeners, the metallic click of shears, everyday noises of a busy household occupied in mundane chores. "We follow a flexible but nevertheless strict curriculum. If you wish to see Miss Fleur, then it must be done between lessons or in the afternoon."

"Ha!" she snorted, looking down her nose at me as if I were an under-housemaid. "A new broom sweeping clean?"

"I think," I said levelly, "that her education has been neglected."

"She's only a baby," Miss Tranter said indignantly.

"She is not. She's seven years old and it's high time she applied herself."

"Are you suggesting that I didn't look after her properly?" She drew herself up. "I'll have you know, young woman, that I reared both Lady Emily and Lady Dorothea, and no one ever complained. Oh, they had a governess too, but it was to me they came, my beautiful little lambs, when they wanted anything. I was left in charge. That's how much faith the Earl and his Lady had in me. 'You make the decisions, nanny,' they would say. 'You look to their welfare, we've every confidence in you.' We went everywhere together, those small ladies and I, and there was never a cross word – never!"

"I'm not doubting you, Miss Tranter." I got to my feet and the children watched with wide eyes. "But it isn't fair to indulge Fleur and Jeffrey. If they are to attend schools in England, then they must be prepared to fit in with others."

"Fit in? Fit in! What nonsense!" She glared at me, her absurd hat askew, the bunch of wax cherries adorning it quivering as she spoke. "They are not obliged to 'fit in' anywhere. They are of the nobility. It is up to the rest of the world to 'fit in' with them!" She rested a hand on Fleur's head and thrust the paper bag under her nose. "Here, child – take no notice."

Damn the woman! She was living in the past. This was my kingdom now. How dare she interfere! "Miss Tranter, I don't want her to eat sweets between meals. If you leave them with me, I'll see that she has one later."

Her face went red and she trembled. I thought she was about to fly at me. "Well!" she spluttered, fidgeting with her belongings as if searching for something to hold on to, then: "Well – I really don't know what the world is coming to. Can't give my baby sweets – putting a jumped-up chit like you in charge! We'll see about that!"

She was threatening me and I could feel anger flooding up, all part of that uneasy feeling which had been stirring in me like a caged beast ever since I set foot in El Tarifa. It was not something I could put my finger on, just an instinct, a prickling sensation of apprehension. I squared my shoulders. This must be settled, once and for all time. I was determined to be at the helm, and no barmy old hag was going to put me off.

"Very well, Miss Tranter," I said firmly. "We'll go and see Lady Emily." I turned to the children. "Jeffrey – Fleur, I want you to continue reading whilst I'm gone."

Neither child said a word and Miss Tranter, still huffing and puffing, followed me from the room. I had a shrewd idea that Lady Emily would try to avoid such a confrontation, and would have preferred to have gone to Sir Nicholas, but I had seen him ride off early. Veronica came to the door of the sitting room. Though so agitated, I noticed that she was wearing pink – a crushed strawberry moiré skirt and lace blouse. I felt dishevelled and at a disadvantage for she had that enviable china shepherdess delicacy which made me conscious of my height and my boyish figure. Men would never feel the chivalrous urge to spread their cloaks across the mud at my feet, rather they would expect me to spash through the puddles! Once this had not bothered me much, but recently, seeing her peaches and cream perfection, I had found myself wishing it were otherwise.

"I want to see Lady Emily," I said, rather too loudly.

She arched her slim brows at me. "Must you?" she enquired sweetly. "We were just about to go for a drive." This much was obvious by her big pink hat with a chin veil, pink gloves, pink handbag. She looked like a fashion plate from a ladies' magazine.

"Yes, I must. It is important," I answered doggedly, planting myself firmly on the threshold with Miss Tranter breathing heavily at my shoulder.

Veronica retreated and I heard the murmur of voices. Lady Emily's had a distinctly plaintive note. We were ushered into her presence. The ensuing conversation was far from pleasant and not very reassuring. I'm afraid I raised my voice too much and argued more than was prudent but I felt strongly on the issue. Not only was my pride involved; more than this, I had discipline to maintain. Fleur was awkward enough as it was. Lady Emily dithered, complaining of a headache. I could see that she was almost afraid to gainsay Miss Tranter, reverting to childhood, wanting to obey nanny from force of habit.

"Your attitude does seem rather unreasonable, Miss Gray," she demurred. "Surely, a few sweets, a little break from lessons can do no harm?"

I was exasperated by this time, furious because Veronica was listening, seated demurely on the couch, hands folded gracefully on the amber handle of her pink parasol. "Lady Emily, do I or don't I have the final word on what happens in the nursery?" I demanded, goaded almost beyond endurance by the prevarications she threw up like a smoke screen.

She sighed, hands a flutter. "Oh, dear, such a storm in a teacup. Really, Miss Gray, I would have thought you capable of dealing with this without bothering me. Nanny Tranter means no harm. She has been with us a long, long time, you know. Can't you come to some agreement and care for the children between you?"

God, she's so weak! I stormed within myself. No wonder Sir Nicholas loses patience with her. "Please give me your instructions, Lady Emily. An I in sole charge?"

Cornered, she was forced to admit that I was and this made Miss Tranter flare off in a tantrum, highly offended. Work had been interrupted by the incident and, on my return, I found the children seated crosslegged on the floor, listening to Hassan. Jeffrey's eyes were round as saucers. "Miss Gray," he urged, "do come and listen. Hassan is telling us about the genies."

Hassan scrambled to his feet, making obeisance.

"Dear lady – May Allah bring you great joy! I but entertain the little ones in your absence."

"That's all right," I answered, my irritation directed towards Miss Tranter. I should be unable to make them concentrate on anything I might try to teach them that day. Perhaps they would learn more from him. I collapsed into an easy chair, tired and cross.

"Tell Miss Gray about them," pleaded Jeffrey. There was nothing he liked better than stories.

"Ah, my dear young sir, the genies are a mighty race, born before Adam so it is written – huge, powerful beings, somewhere between angels and men, created of fire, and capable of assuming the forms of humans, brutes or monsters, and of becoming invisible at will," Hassan's voice rolled on. My mind drifted, half listening, half mulling over the scene in the sitting room. I was curiously deflated, wondering if I'd taken on too much, wryly remembering my joy when I'd first taken the job.

"Are they alive, like us?" Jeffrey's eyes were shining, his imagination fired. He had a retentive memory, soaking up information like a sponge. He might have another restless night later, and perhaps it was not wise to expose him to these Muslim legends, but I felt too drained of energy to stop Hassan who was in full spate.

"But of course," he nodded sagely, his dark eyes sparkling, a born storyteller. "All things are the work of Allah, the Merciful, the Compassionate."

"Even the wicked *'efreets*?" Fleur was sceptical.

"Oh, yes, for these are not all evil, being the ghosts of the departed. There are good and ill among the genies, as there are among men. The bad ones are called devils and their chief is Iblees."

"Where do they come from?" Jeffrey wanted to know.

"They live in the mountains called Kaf, which circle the whole earth."

"How can this be?" I bestirred myself to ask, watching the play of light over Hassan's proud, fierce features beneath the green swathing of his turban. "The world is round."

He frowned at such a preposterous statement. "Oh, no, *sitt*, we Muslims believe that it is a flat expanse, surrounded by the ocean which is itself contained by the mountains of Kaf."

"I want to hear more about the genies. They're much more fun," said Jeffrey.

"Indeed a marvellous race, to be sure, but one must be careful not to anger them." Hassan was only too willing to repeat colourful tales of these fabled creatures who, so it seemed, ate and drank and propagated their species (usually with the help of beautiful earth maidens) and who lived for centuries.

It was fascinating, but I thought that Jeffrey had heard enough for he was growing too excited and I feared that he might have another nightmare and sleep-walk again, so: "It's time to go to the beach," I said. "Hassan, will you fetch the gig, and children – come and collect your bathing costumes."

I clapped my hands for the Ethiopian girl, Esmahan, who helped me on the practical side, and soon lost my gloom when we drove along the coast road to where the Renshaws owned a small beach house. There was a cane basket containing a picnic in the back of the gig, and the children carried tin buckets and spades, as excited at the prospect of making sand pies as they would have been at any seaside resort in England, the main difference being that I did not have to trouble myself with umbrellas and oilskins. But no – there was a world of difference, surrounded as we were by the graceful minarets and fine old houses skirting the way, the shady parks overlooking the sea, the flowering gardens of this Queen of Cities. Of course, I was happy, who would not be in the presence of Jeffrey? We laughed and talked and his companionship was a wonderful thing, for he loved games and jokes and all the beauty of the visible world, crazy with the joy of life, as a happy child should be. It was as if he never thought about the dead Lady Dorothea, or if he did, he cleverly concealed it from me.

"Wear something sensible," Terence advised, honouring his pledge to take me out. "Can't trail frilly petticoats round old ruins."

I grinned and nodded, eager for this jaunt. As yet, my only trip into the town had been with Veronica and, as he had predicted, it had been to the shopping area only. I had bought a divided skirt in Harrods and I put it on, feeling immensely dashing, enjoying its freedom. It was of khaki cotton drill, and reached mid calf, meeting the tops of my leather boots. A matching blouse completed this ensemble and I wore a hat of the same material with a shady brim. We took the gig and he handled the reins himself.

He was a nice young man, and we had dispensed with formality by now, using our Christian names freely. He had gossiped about the Renshaws, telling me about the country seat, Revelstoke Court in Cornwall, and how Sir Nicholas had never expected to inherit it, thinking that his elder brother Henry would marry again and have children after his divorce from Lady Dorothea. He had died unexpectedly, thrown from his hunter. Now it seemed that Fleur would be the only heir. Terence was most emphatic when he said that there would be no further offspring. Lady Emily had nearly died when her daughter was born. I had been startled by the intensity in his eyes and the unusual hardness about his mouth.

He was an excellent guide and, after a couple of hours, I was stunned by the sights of this amazing city, founded by Alexander the Great, once the seat of civilisation with its Greek, Roman and Egyptian influences. We had a picnic in the square near St Mark's Church which slumbered unobtrusively behind a veil of trees, and the sparrows gathered noisily for crumbs, heartwarmingly familiar. Then we drove to see the Prehistoric Harbour and Pompey's Pillar, and finally finished up at the Catacombs of Kom es Chogafa. I had had enough by this time but did not want to hurt his feelings or give the impression that I was bored. This was simply not true; it was just that I was bedazzled and needed a respite to think about what I had already seen.

"These tombs were only discovered recently," Terence explained knowledgeably. "They are larger than Sir Nicholas's – but his are almost as interesting. Come on, Nancy, don't hang about."

I can't explain the reluctance I felt as he paid the small fee and went through the turnstile. A chill shivered through me and my feet dragged. The sun was going down, hanging like a bloody ball on the horizon, the sky livid with orange and mauve. Those fiery rays struck the hill, bathing the mosaic tiles in crimson, whilst purple shadows enveloped the broken edges and gullies. I had to go in. Perhaps Sir Nicholas would offer to take me to his own find and it would satisfy me enormously to let him know that I was not a complete ignoramus. However, I wished that there were other sightseers there, jolly parties with guidebooks and comforting chatter, all the warmth of living, breathing beings, but it was really rather late for tourists. Terence and I were alone with the past, and the dead. Cold fingers of ice seemed to be running down my spine as we descended into the gloom. This was silly, and I scolded myself without mercy. I was not going to admit that I was frightened. He would be bound to think it a joke and recount it in the music salon later that night. I could just hear Veronica cooing, eyes fetchingly alarmed, and Sir Nicholas's biting, sarcastic comments.

The place was like some marble rabbit-warren and I was glad to leave the gloomy chambers. We bade good-night to the curator who was waiting to lock up. The whites of his eyes rolled in the gathering gloom. "He's scared of '*efreets*," said Terence, tucking his hand under my elbow as we went back to the gig. "Mind you, I can't say I'd relish spending a night down there alone."

It was completely dark now, and cold. The chill of the catacombs had penetrated my very bones. I threw my cardigan about my shoulders. "I haven't been to the bazaar yet," I complained as we jogged along. The lamps which lined the main streets had been lit and the glowing orange light fell in bright pools interspersed by inky blackness. The moon was rising slowly, touching the tips of the minarets.

"It's not in a very salubrious area," he replied.

"Oh, do let's go," I insisted. "We needn't stay long. I promised Jeffrey I'd buy him some Turkish delight."

He reluctantly gave in, and soon we were leaving the squares and parks behind us, winding into the Arab quarter where the lanes were narrow and tortuous, sometimes climbing steeply and then diving down with little warning. There were few lights there, the walls of the houses sheer on either side, with closely barred windows from which no friendly beam escaped. I peered into the rubbish-strewn alleys, catching glimpses of mangy rats nosing about, skittering into the shadows. There was a white-clad figure or two, hurrying furtively along. Music wailed fitfully from behind the shutters, flute and bagpipe, then came long areas of silence. Even the sound of our horse's hoofs was muffled by the dust. Terence knew his way about, taking a route through the maze of little alleys which led to the bazaars and eating houses.

Now the streets became busy, with rows of shops lit by flares. Terence was kept fully occupied negotiating a way through and translating some of the vendors' cries for me at the same time. Each merchant sat before his tiny booth, shutters folded back to display the wares. At this stage, Terence decided to leave the gig, driving into the courtyard of a caravanserai and tethering the horse. We wove our way through the throng on foot.

"Don't pay them the asking price," he warned as I dallied, gazing at the rich variety of goods for sale. "They expect to haggle. Bargaining is the accepted thing in Egypt. They're very wily – if you finish up paying half the original sum, then you deserve a medal. A third off is the usual settlement and don't forget, they're never in a hurry. You can browse for hours in a shop and go away without buying and the owner won't object. He'll shrug and say that if he doesn't make a sale today, then he'll do so tomorrow – if Allah is willing. I think you understand the natives a little by now, don't you? *Bukra*, remember? I expect you've heard Hassan say it. *Bukra*, the tomorrow of the future, with no time limit. *Bukra fil mishmish* – tomorrow when the apricots bloom – that special Egyptian tomorrow which stretches into infinity. It drives Europeans to distraction!"

It was a scene as old as time. We could have been living when Cleopatra seduced Antony – all modernity had vanished. Those turbanned men and draped women, the street vendors, the beggars, the eerie music, possessed a timelessness which was compelling. I was dazed by the glitter of jewels on the stalls and the hues of silks, my nostrils breathing in the scent of spices and exotic foodstuffs, the rich aroma of drugs, perfumes and wax candles from the shop of an *attar*. Fruit was piled up in abundance, golden orbs of oranges, the sharp yellow of citrus, the glowing purple of grapes, and dark, shrivelled figs.

On one stall I saw ready-made garments and, in the heat of the moment, decided that I wanted that of a bedouin, with flowing burnous, an embroidered robe and baggy white trousers. Terence was amused by this but, nothing daunted, he bargained with the olive-skinned, well-dressed *tagir*, with a great deal of vehemence of voice and gesture. At last the business was concluded to the satisfaction of both parties and I was the proud owner of an Arab outfit. I bought some dangling earrings, and a bag of sweetmeats for Jeffrey, then: "Oh, Terence, my feet ache. Can't we sit down somewhere?" I said. I was hot, sticky and exhausted, but enjoying every moment. I had not realised until I left it just how claustrophobic I found the atmosphere of El Tarifa. I did not want to go back yet.

He took me to a nearby *kahweh*. It was crowded with men, full of noisy talk and the heavy odour of roasting coffee beans, musk oil and sweating bodies. A fat, jolly Greek in a crumpled suit eased his bulk along a bench to make room for me, grinning in an oily way. "He probably thinks that you are a *dame de nuit*," remarked Terence from the side of his mouth.

"A what?" I asked, staring at him, seeing the quirk of his lopsided grin.

"A prostitute. I suppose you've heard of them?"

"Of course," I answered crossly. I was getting rather tired of the charade in which I was supposed to be an innocent blossom.

"How daring," he mocked gently. "Don't let Sir Nicholas know or he'll sack you forthwith. Tell me more. What else do you know about low life?"

I wished that I had held my tongue. "Very little, Terence. How could I, in the cloistered seclusion of a country rectory? I've read novels in which they feature and, putting two and two together, can guess the rest. I must say, I'm rather impatient with the way gentlemen treat us – the non-scarlet women, I mean. We're not supposed to know anything! Our delicate little ears and feeble brains must be protected from sordid subjects. I've come to the conclusion that we're really the stronger sex. How else could we endure the earthy experience of childbirth?"

He laughed delightedly, throwing back his head, then signalled to the proprietor for service. "You're quite right, Nancy – it's all hogwash – but we men need to keep our illusions. Don't deprive us of feeling superior. We like looking after you – makes us feel important, don't you know."

He ordered a glass of *zibib*. When he added water to it, it turned a milky colour. Our host could speak English, a sad-faced man with thick black moustaches which drooped despondently. He and Terence exchanged pleasantries as he placed a dish of *kebabs* on the table. I watched the crowd as I drank my cup of thick, strong, syrupy coffee. They were a garrulous lot, good-natured on the surface, though they looked villainous. I could not understand a word they said. They used exaggerated gestures, pushing and shoving, touching each other. Musicians and storytellers hung around, performing for a few coins, but mostly ignored by the merchants and traders who were taking their ease, smoking their long-stemmed pipes or puffing at glass-bowled *nargilehs* with pliable, snakelike tubes.

"They remind me of the Caterpillar in *Alice in Wonderland*," I remarked.

He nodded towards a shelf where further *hookahs* stood in rows. The fat host took one down and put a lump of gummy substance in the burner before lighting it and handing it to a group of old men who were playing cards. "The customers bring their own tobacco, but *hashish* can be bought here and those persons over there are smoking it. They're eunuchs from one of the harems, probably from the household of some rich Osmanlee – hardly any but Turks of high rank keep eunuchs now. D'you know what a eunuch is?"

"A male slave," I answered promptly.

"A male slave who has been emasculated so that he is unable to seduce his master's wives," he corrected with a smile. "I thought you knew all there was to know? Ah, Nancy, you've so much to learn about the East, particularly Alexandria." His face sobered. "You think you understand about prostitution, but here it is a scandal. There is one particular street where children can be procured, little girls of nine and ten, not much older than Fleur – and boys too. I'm not sure that I should have brought you here. It can be dangerous, especially at night. Few English people come to this part – particularly ladies. Aren't you aware of the effect you're having!"

I was coming under a rather embarrassing and alarming scrutiny from many eyes. "They *are* staring at me," I said, feeling the blood burning in my cheeks.

"Take it as a compliment," he said easily, though I noticed that he was alert. He drank up his *zibib* and consulted his watch. "Time we were going."

I was about to gather up my parcels when, with a clash of head curtains covering an archway at the back of the room, a party of men came through. I stopped in amazement. Quiller was with them – he was wearing a fez and dark glasses, transformed, despite his fair skin, into an inhabitant of the East. I was mentally spell-bound, tongue tied, with no words or thoughts shaping themselves in my mind. He looked as startled as I but immediately recovered his aplomb, advanced upon us with a bright smile and introduced his companions.

There were two of them, a hard-faced Arab in traditional costume, black-bearded and wild-eyed in spite of his wide smile, and a slim young man who bowed politely over my hand. He was exceptionally beautiful. He was perfumed, he was rouged, and his eyes were accentuated by kohl. His coat was nipped in at the waist and he wore a silk shirt, a dark cravat, a jewelled tiepin, a bracelet and many rings. Tight black trousers and snakeskin shoes completed his very European costume. His glittering almond-shaped eyes and hair were jet black, his complexion gypsy-tinted. His name was Osman, whilst the Arab was called Sheik El-Darim.

Quiller seemed relaxed and unconcerned about meeting us. And why not? I asked myself. His friends might not be the kind of persons who would be welcome at El Tarifa, but what he did in his free time was his own business. But a change had come over Terence. He was uneasy and finished the conversation curtly, hurrying me away. We drove home in silence and he was withdrawn, quite unlike himself. Anxiously, I went back over every incident of our outing, wondering if I had said or done anything stupidly wrong. At last, as we turned into the drive, he said gruffly: "Look here, Nancy, it might be as well if you don't mention seeing Quiller with that young man."

There was something in his tone which struck me as odd. "Why?" I asked.

"I can't explain now," he replied, taking the gig to the stables where a couple of grooms uncoiled themselves from their crosslegged position on the cobbles. "He's not too particular about the company he keeps. Best not to probe, and wisest to keep a still tongue in your head."

"But what's wrong?" I persisted as we walked towards the house. The moon was high. Discs and petals of light spattered the ground at our feet. The cool, dank smell of the garden seemed to coil around us like a grey tendril thrust out from the darkness of the trees.

"Nothing is wrong." He sounded impatient and unconvincing. "Forget the incident, and don't pry."

I was aware of a drop in my spirits, the enjoyable day tarnished somehow. We said goodnight rather stiffly and I went up to my room. There Esmahan brought me supper and after I had eaten it and drunk deeply from a glass of lemonade, I undressed and stood on the balcony for a while, looking out at the night. It was in a disturbed frame of mind that I sought my bed, and there I had a most unpleasant dream.

I dreamed that I woke and found myself exactly where I had gone to sleep, and in the same attitude. Moonlight blasted through the windows and made patterns on the floor and walls. In my dream I knew what I had done that day, and for what reason I was lying there under the netting. I caught sight of my own arms stretched out on each side of me, but could not see where my hands ended and where the sheet beneath began. It was as if my fingers had melted away. My wrists showed quite clearly but I could not get the message from my brain to my hands. They would not move – I could not move. Then I slept again or thought that I slept, finding myself drifting, faces appearing momentarily, strange situations and scraps of conversation which fled at once when I jerked awake. I dozed again, yielding to the heavy, drugged feeling which stopped me from keeping my lids apart.

I dreamed that I was in a building, going down and down. There were shadows everywhere and the ground beneath my feet was soft and quivering. An awful, strident howling, which seemed to have existed since eternity began, shook me to the marrow. I felt myself being sucked into an inferno, spinning like a top. There were great rushing clouds which formed into gigantic faces brooding down on me – faces with great pits of darkness for eyes, and savage, sharp-toothed mouths, and masses of hair which streamed into and merged with the storm.

I struggled madly. The bedroom became mixed with this awful vision and I fought my way into wakefulness. I sat up, bathed in sweat, my heart thudding wildly. All was quiet, or so I thought. I tried to be logical, telling myself that I had had a nightmare caused by too late a meal and an over-indulgence in tombs and temples. I lay down again and tried to compose my thoughts, but I was mournfully aware of the traces the dream had left on my mind. It was then that I heard it. Not the ear-splitting cacophony of my dream-demons, but something else which struck as much terror into my soul. This time I was awake, and it was real. Somewhere, a piano was playing and I recognised the tune. It was that plaintive waltz which Fleur struggled unsuccessfully to master. I can't explain why it frightened me so much – haunting – melancholy. Who could be playing it at this hour of the night? It wasn't Sir Nicholas – I would have recognised his expert brilliance – besides, the sound wasn't coming from the direction of the music salon. I couldn't place its direction – it seemed to be all around me, yet faint and far away. I strained my ears to listen above the pounding of my pulse. It faded and ceased.

I was trembling as I got out of bed. My head was spinning and my temples throbbed. Somehow I reached

Jeffrey's room, breathing a sigh of relief. He was fast asleep, wearing that deceptive air of innocence which transforms the face of the sleeping child. My heart contracted with love and tenderness. He had a deep, sweet serenity, like a holy babe from some early Italian masterpiece. There was a sheen of moisture on his eyelids, the lashes lying like dark fans on his flushed cheeks, his breathing quiet and regular. In the crook of his arm Tippy was snuggled, that well-worn toy whose blue plush covering had faded to a nondescript grey. He stared up at me with his one remaining black button eye, his expression baleful. Was he protecting his master? I mused. Did such a beloved object develop a soul – a curious life of its own? I tried to shake off this morbid fancy. What was the matter with me? I had always thought of myself as down to earth. I touched Jeffrey to convince myself that he was really safe, kissing his damp brow and pulling the sheet up over his chest. He did not stir and I was disappointed, lingering in the hope that he might do so. I didn't want to be alone and it seemed an awful long time till morning. I yearned to hear his sleepy voice which would gradually strengthen into wakefulness. But he did not wake. There was no one to dispel this gloom which had descended on me, unbidden and unexpected.

"Where did you go? What did you do? And why did you buy that Arab costume?" demanded Jeffrey at breakfast next morning.

"Don't be so rude, Jeffrey," barked Fleur, digging her spoon into her boiled egg as if she were gouging out his eyes.

"Fleur, I'll correct Jeffrey when necessary. Get on with your breakfast and don't talk." I reprimanded, sighing inwardly, recognising the storm signals. It was going to be one of *those* days. My head throbbed persistently and I felt as if I had not slept at all.

"I'm only interested," said Jeffrey, staring at me with

those large, innocent eyes. "I just wondered why you bought it, that's all."

I had been asking myself the same question, shaking my head over the crazy impulse when I examined that outrageous costume on rising. Heaven only knew when I proposed to wear such a thing. A masquerade ball, perhaps? But when was I likely to be invited to such a function?" Jeffrey, you're full of 'satiable curiosity'," I replied.

He grinned hugely. "Like the naughty Elephant's Child!"

"Exactly," I said with mock severity, "and you know what happened to him."

"He very nearly ended up as the Crocodile's dinner," he shouted gleefully.

"And what did you do yesterday? It's my turn to ask questions now."

"I spent the afternoon with Aunt Emily. We sat in the shade of the tree beneath your window, and she told me stories about when she and Mamma were young. You've never told me what it was like when you were a little girl, Miss Gray. She did. She spoke about Devon – where we lived, you know – and her pony, and the larks she used to have. Miss Tranter was there too, and we had capital fun."

I experienced a niggling feeling of annoyance which bordered on jealousy. He hadn't missed me at all. It was wrong of me to be so mean and grudge his enjoyment of his aunt's company. She took a keen interest in him – too much, perhaps, her affection veering unhealthily towards that of doting indulgence. I understood why Fleur was so sulky – her mother's fickle love had been diverted from her. She was no longer the star in her firmament – Jeffrey was.

"That was nice for you," I replied stiffly, adding: "I had a lovely time with Dr Armstrong."

"Oh, I expect you did," he answered with an earnest little nod." Aunt Emily remarked that you would. I think she rather missed him. He helps her with her sketching, says it's good for her to have a hobby."

"Indeed? Then it was most kind of your aunt to lend him to me for a while." I found it hard to keep a touch of irony from my voice. Emily was such a lucky woman, and she didn't realise it, always complaining. Not only did she have a handsome husband, albeit ill-tempered, but she had this charming young doctor dancing attendance.

"She'll be happy now that he's back – she won't miss me," Jeffrey prattled on guilessly. "She'll be all smiley and pink." He glanced towards the window. "In fact, I can hear them in the garden now. Shall we take a peep?"

"Certainly not, Jeffrey," I said quickly. Really, at times he was just too precocious. "Sit still and finish your 'soldiers'."

But his words had awakened in me a suspicion of which I was not proud. I remembered the warmth in Terence's voice when he spoke of Lady Emily so, as soon as I could, I went into my room, slipped quietly on to the balcony and looked down. That small stretch of paved terrace and lawn was the place where she liked to sit. I often saw her there, setting up her easel, working on pictures of the lovely garden with its sparkling central fountain, its border of plane trees and palms.

Yes, Jeffrey had been right. There she sat, with a truly magnificent hat shading her pale face. Veronica was in a bentwood rocking chair, busy with her embroidery, her needle flashing like a miniature dagger, catching the hazy sunlight which dappled them through the branches of the fig tree. A servant girl stood behind them, swishing a horse-tail whisk at impertinent flies. Terence occupied a canvas stool at Emily's feet, transferring the view on to the sheet of paper pinned on his board. Their voices – their laughter – drifted up to me and I had never heard her so light-hearted.

My will was weak that day and the thought of lessons was wearying. I yielded to Jeffrey's persuasion and told them about the bazaar instead. Oh, Jeffrey – when he was fully grown he would have a quite fatal attraction for women, I decided. Not long before, Hassan had said to me seriously: "May Allah preserve the little master. He is too beautiful. You should dress him in rags when he walks abroad, and smear his face with dirt. Thus, by appearing to neglect him, you may ward off the evil eye which envy and covetousness may bring upon him."

I had laughed at such a ridiculous notion but he had been adamant. "By the beard of the Prophet, I speak the truth, *sitt*! Even the wealthiest women, walking out in public veiled but lovely with their lustrous eyes showing through the slits in their yashmaks, even they, devoted mothers, will not hear compliments about their children. They are deprecating and humble, lest some jealous genie be listening and may smite the little ones with blindness or a wasting disease."

So I now relented, sitting with the children and talking to them of the market, the museums, even the coffee shop, but I did not mention meeting Quiller. An hour passed pleasantly enough and then, out of the blue, Sir Nicholas appeared. "Good morning, Miss Gray," he said crisply, standing with his legs spread to balance his weight, his riding whip like a bow between his hands. "I understand from Armstrong that you were impressed by the ruins yesterday."

I was taken aback by his abruptness, rising to my feet as I must in his presence for he was my master. "I found it fascinating, thank you, sir," I replied.

It was an unusual experience for me to have to look up at a man, but this one towered above me, a good six inches taller than my five foot nine. Staring at that swarthy face, I decided that there was nothing English in his appearance for he was as dark-browed as night. Although he wore well-tailored breeches and a white shirt, his head was covered by an Arab *kaffiyeh*, a traditional headcloth of red and white striped linen, held in place by a decorated band. His skin was deeply tanned through exposure to the sun and winds and his wild hawk eyes gazed down at me from under his heavy lids, his lips compressed slightly as if musing on the subject which had brought him there.

"I would like to show you my own finds," he said quietly. "Will you ride there with me?"

I was astonished. This was the last thing I had expected. Somehow, my mind had been running on Quiller and I had thought him about to question me on his agent's nocturnal activities. "But the children, sir. I can't leave them," I blurted. I was having difficulty with my speech and my face was burning.

"Miss Tranter will look after them." He sounded amused at my confusion, strolling to the window where, in the distance, the forest of domes and spires sparkled. "Would you like to come?"

My wits seemed to have deserted me. This always happened when he was near, yet I felt strangely gay for the first time in hours. He had a disconcerting habit of staring straight back at the person he was addressing, his gaze unblinking, hypnotic. I had to look away, pretending that I was shuffling schoolbooks into a tidy pile, "Yes, sir – I would like to visit your catacombs," I managed to say, fighting to control my wayward feelings, aware of the children's eyes.

"Right. That's settled," he said briskly and, striding to the door, he barked an order to Hassan in fluent Arabic.

What was behind this sudden request? Why did he want me to go with him? Till now he'd taken very little notice of me. These questions buzzed in my brain as I changed into the clothes I had worn yesterday, and the very uncertainty of it was exciting to the point of intoxication so that my fingers shook. An imp of perversity was urging me to put on the Bedouin costume but I didn't quite dare. The proprieties had to be observed. As it was, the fact that I was shirking my duties and riding off with Sir Nicholas would cause enough talk and speculation without my donning native dress. Did he have an ulterior motive? Why had he selected me, of all people in the household, to inspect his excavations? He supplied the answer as we mounted horses in the stableyard.

"You seem a capable woman," he remarked casually, adjusting his stirrup and agilely swinging his tall frame into the ornate saddle of his shining ebony stallion. "I need someone to make notes of what we find, as we find it. I've paper and pencils with me, so we'll begin at once."

I stiffened, bridling a little at his cool assumption. It did not occur to him that I might not want to fall in with his wishes. His arrogance nearly took my breath away. The job would be exacting and time-consuming. My evenings might well be devoted to cataloguing, correlating and indexing masses of complicated material. I did not want to be involved, knowing that he would be a hard taskmaster.

He glanced at my footwear as I sat side-saddle, my knee hitched over the pommel, and he said conversationally: "I'm glad to see that you've worn boots. Snakes and scorpions hide in the ruins – nasty creatures. The bite from a black scorpion is fatal – death is almost instantaneous."

Well, isn't that just fine! I commented to myself angrily. Thank you very much, Sir High-and-Mighty Nicholas Renshaw! He bobbed his heels into the sides of his horse and we rode out, taking a path between olive trees. It was a misty morning, the sun swathed in cloud, a hint of dampness in the air. The grounds of El Tarifa were extensive and we soon lost sight of the house, passing the adobe huts of the servants, each bearing the basic talisman of the country – that symbol against the evil eye, the blue imprint of a palm with outspread fingers. The essence of lemons mingled with that of warm sand and hot walls. In my ears were mixed the sounds created by the squeaking of harness leather, the jingling of bridles, the dull thud of our horses' hoofs pounding the sandy soil and the carolling of the birds.

I remarked on this. "There are so many from England."

He nodded without looking at me, his profile carved in the strong light, deep eye-sockets, curved nose, hard line of jaw. "Like us, the birds prefer to winter here, although those over there are local inhabitants. I don't think you'd find them roosting in a Cornish oak."

He pointed with his whip. We were near a high wall with an open gate in the centre beyond which I could see plane trees, heavy with a weird conclave, gargoyled with vultures. Great, scraggy, ugly creatures, their bald heads and tattered black wings making them look like a witches' sabat.

We were in a cemetery, a hushed place, drowsing under that opalescent sky, cypress and yew nodding over the headstones. It could almost have been an English churchyard with its neat inscriptions, its railed plots, but this quiet resting place of the dead was dominated by a small white marble mosque. In the middle of the sparse coarse grass stood an imposing tomb, fenced in by spearlike iron posts, linked by heavy chains. "The Renshaw vault," he said, reining in near it. "Several members of our family lie within."

"They have been visiting Egypt for some time?" I had not realised this.

"This land and the house came into our possession a century ago," he answered as I drew up alongside, our horses lowering their heads and nuzzling the grass which grew thicker there. "The last interment was that of Lady Dorothea's infant, born when she was staying in Alexandria shortly after she had run away from my brother."

This was news indeed. I mulled it over, having had no idea that she had ever been to Egypt. I had often wondered about her but my curiosity had remained unsatisfied. A strange silence seemed to surround her. Even Quiller refused to be drawn on the subject. I wanted to question Sir Nicholas further, but he did not look as if he would welcome it, his face closed and dark, brooding on some old sore, perhaps a skeleton in the family cupboard. I knew that his brother had divorced her and this in itself had been a scandal.

He clicked his tongue and his beast moved forward again as he changed the topic to that of his excavations. "The catacombs came to light last year. Emily wanted a summerhouse built there for the view is rather fine. It was while the foundations were being dug that we stumbled upon the old site. I knew that the palace had been put above a Graeco-Roman villa. The catacombs must have been their burial place. I'm in contact with the curator of the Cairo Museum about it. Have you been to Cairo? No? Nor seen the pyramids or the sphinx? I'll take you there one day."

My mind was whirling. "I couldn't go with you," I protested. "What about the children?"

"Devil take the children?" he growled, turning the full force of his dark eyes upon me, impatience etched on every line of his face. "If I decide that we are going to Cairo – then we'll go!"

The fact that I might not want to did not seem to enter his mind. Damn the man! He had no consideration for others at all. I angrily prodded my lively mare and urged her into a canter, following his upright, indifferent back. He rode as if born in the saddle and I felt my own inexperience keenly. Jogging down leafy lanes on one of Farmer Wyatt's sturdy cobs had done little to prepare me for this. My calf muscles were cramped and my thighs sore from chafing against saddle leather. I arched my back to ease the stiffness in my spine and glared at his uncaring shoulders. The man was a selfish pig! Why on earth did Lady Emily adore him and Veronica moon after him? I was hot, tired and thoroughly disgruntled when we came to rough ground further on where the earth had been disturbed. A black hole yawned wide amidst a jumble of rocks and rubble. A couple of broken pillars lay on their sides forlornly, like the drawn teeth of giants.

There were workmen, clad in soiled turbans and loincloths, but they were knotted into a little group, their expressions mournful, their voices a low dirge. The foreman disengaged himself from the tree stump against which he had been lounging, smoking a pipe. The sight of Sir Nicholas galvanised him into action and he gabbled a stream of orders before running towards us.

"*Effendi* mine!" he cried, stopping and bowing almost to the ground. "Praise be to Allah that you have passed the hours of darkness safely. Now the day has dawned in all its beauty and we may gaze once more on your illustrious face!"

Sir Nicholas ignored this effusive greeting, and his mouth hardened at the idleness of the men. His eyes went down scornfully over the unprepossessing figure of his foreman who was as shifty as a ferret. "Out of the way, Ali, you misbegotten spawn of a crippled camel! I don't pay you to sit on your lazy backside all day!"

Ali looked hurt, whining: "In the name of Allah! *Effendi*, I pray that you let me know the crime by which I have lost the favour of your countenance!"

"Idleness!" barked Sir Nicholas, his face like a thundercloud. He dismounted and strode towards the tomb with the man hopping along like some raggle-tailed starling at the side of an eagle. I trailed behind, forgotten. "You and your compatriots are bone idle! A bunch of worthless good-for-nothings! Why aren't the men working?"

"Oh, great one, they are afraid," explained Ali, rolling his eyes.

"What has happened now?" Sir Nicholas sounded bored and very annoyed.

"After you had gone yesterday, honoured sir, a humble porter slipped and fell down one of the shafts and is like to die. And only last week, a rock crushed the foot of Acmid! Tools are lost, and strange sounds heard. There is evil here, *effendi*. It is the work of demons!"

"Rubbish!" Sir Nicholas shouted. "I expect you to see that my orders are carried out!"

"They believe the place to be haunted," Ali protested, adding in a doom-ridden voice: "Nay, more than that – to be accursed!"

"Tell them there will be a bonus at the end of it if they get the work done swiftly. I'll wager that money talks louder than demons," said Sir Nicholas sardonically.

Ali went into a muttered confab with his men, and it appeared that Sir Nicholas was correct in his cynical judgement. They began to plod down the ramp leading into that gaping aperture like rabbits into a burrow, reappearing later carrying soil in baskets, tipping the contents on to an ever-increasing mound. But their chatter was subdued, their songs sad, every eye returning now and again to the commanding figure who stood, hands on hips, watching them through narrowed lids, impatient with incompetence and sparing none the lash of his trenchant tongue. They feared Sir Nicholas more than ghosts, it seemed.

Then, remembering me, he said: "Ali, this lady has come to assist me in numbering the objects found. You'll give her every aid."

Ali raised both hands and eyes admiringly. "Oh, day of happiness! Oh, day of agreeable surprises and joy! Your beauty will banish the *'efreets, O sitt*. It will be Allah's highest bounty if I can serve you!"

There was more of this, but Sir Nicholas silenced him, taking me to the flight of earth steps which led steeply down. "I've had a door fitted so that I can lock it," he said, brushing past workers who were coming out with their baskets, their broad bare feet thudding up the steps behind us. "I've discovered many relics and have stored them in tea chests. Come and take a look."

It was dark down there, the sky a pale grey slit

between the stone walls which boxed us in. I was aware of a musty, sweetish smell that was at first refreshing after the humidity above, but soon awakened distrust with its undertones of earthy dankness as of centuries of rotting leaves and the bones of long-buried corpses.

I followed him under a carved lintel and into an antechamber. It was similar to the one I had seen with Terence, but on a smaller scale and the decorations were strictly Egyptian in style. Perhaps the builder had been a Greek official or a Roman soldier who had taken an Egyptian wife and been converted to her religion. The lighting was poor, consisting of naphtha flares stuck into rings hammered against the limestone walls, but the dancing smoky glare showed sentinel statues and bold frescos of slant-eyed priests and animal-headed gods and hieroglyphs.

"That's Anubis, the jackal-god of embalming." Sir Nicholas's face was absorbed as he gloated on his treasures. "It is he whom my Islamic workers dread. They hate dogs. Mohammed is reported to have said: "No angel enters where a dog is." Cats, on the other hand, are great favourites, even taken into the mosques. Try telling that to the canine-doting British!" He grinned at me, and the years rolled away from him, making him seem almost boyish. "You're not afraid, are you, Miss Gray? What a find, eh? Isn't it amazing? I have the feeling that it has lain waiting for me all these years. My colleagues in Cairo are green with envy."

"Don't you fear the evil eye? May they not curse you if you make them envious?" I said a trifle tartly, annoyed because he was so handsome and so buoyant whilst I was experiencing a chilly presentiment of danger.

His laughter awoke the echoes, irreverent, uncaring, challenging the gods. "You've been listening to Hassan." Then he sobered and drew something from his pocket, holding it out on the flat of his hand. "Don't misunderstand me – I'm not mocking their superstitions. Strange things happen here in the East for which there's no logical explanation, so I guard myself. This is a *mus-haf*, a miniature copy of the Koran." It was a lovely little object of perfect workmanship, housed in a silken pouch. "The magician who gave it to me said that it is a powerful charm against evil, so, you see, I can work down here without a qualm."

I was not sure if he was teasing me, but I smiled in response, thinking how charming he could be when he liked and wishing that it happened more often. His whole face altered when he smiled, winning, relaxed, filled with an intensity, which was unforgettable. "I have no such talisman," I said rather breathlessly.

"I'll soon remedy that," he announced and took from another pocket what appeared to be a cross on a chain. "This is an *ankh*, the Egyptian symbol of life. As a matter of fact, it was the first thing that came to light here. I dug it up myself and offered it to my wife but she nearly swooned at the thought of wearing anything so pagan."

He placed it in my hand and our fingers touched. It was as if an electric shock passed right through me, so aware was I of those long strong brown fingers brushing mine. Gooseflesh rose on my limbs. I felt as if somewhere deep inside me a barrier was on the point of giving way. I fumbled for words, standing quite still as he fastened the chain, every nerve in my body alive to his light touch at the nape of my neck. The *ankh* burned like a branding iron as it lay between my breasts. He turned me round to face him, his hand on my upper arm, staring down with an unfathomable look. For one brief, stabbing moment I thought he was going to kiss me. I waited, unable to tear my eyes from those lips which hovered close to mine – that beautiful mouth, the upper lip curved with a hint of contempt, the lower one full and sensual and sensitive.

I came to my senses and stepped back. "Thank you, sir. It is lovely, and I'll wear it always and feel safe." I gasped, fighting to regain my composure. "It must be very valuable. Are you quite certain that you want me to keep it!"

"I am, my dear Miss Gray," he smiled. "I wouldn't have offered it otherwise. It suits you. Gold is your colour, and you should bedeck yourself with it."

"I'm only a governess, sir, and can't afford such luxuries," I shot back at him, finding a safe refuge in anger.

"Your face is your fortune, Miss Gray," he answered gallantly, with a strange expression in his eyes. "But not only your face – for you're intelligent, my dear. And now, do you feel protected enough to work down here alone for a while? There's something I must attend to above." The glint in his eyes challenged me to refuse. "You won't be entirely deserted. The workmen are clearing the next level. We've no idea of the extent of the catacombs. It may consist of three levels, though the lower one may prove to be flooded, like that of Kom es Chogafa."

"Tell me what you want me to do." I was glad that he would be absent for I was afraid I might do something foolish if he stayed too close. When he had opened the cases, shown me the items and explained how he wanted them listed, I bent over my work and he disappeared aloft.

I used the top of an empty crate as a table, drew it closer to one of the several stone benches, adjusted the lamp and began. Each shard of pottery, every necklace, earring or grave ornament was of intense interest. I handled them carefully and made notes, reading the little labels which Nicholas had attached to them on discovery. Yes, I had begun to call him "Nicholas" in my head, and it stemmed from the moment he had given me the *ankh*. As I worked, I chafed and fretted under the irritation of my unreasonable state of mind, for I longed to be his equal now, in the position of being able to breathe his name aloud – to call him by it. Yet, all the while, I was vexed by such folly, knowing that it could never be. I wished that I had never set eyes on him. I was gnawed by a confusion of feelings and a sensation of frustration which I had never known before. It made me furious with him, and even more so with myself.

I laboured steadily for some time, forcing myself to concentrate. A curtain of silence had fallen. I was made gradually conscious of it, feeling absolutely isolated sitting there in the gloom, surrounded by relics of the past. Earlier, a stream of porters had shuffled past me, winding their way up into the light and fresh air. They had not returned and I guessed that it was probably their rest period when they would pray, facing Mecca, and then eat their meal.

I was hungry too. I stood up and stretched. The flares spluttered, the smoke stirring in the draught which seemed to come from several directions, funnelling up from the deep pit of a further staircase which plunged down into the darkness below. I was curious, wondering what lay there. I took up the oil lamp and held it over the steps. They coiled into blackness so thick that it looked solid. Beware of scorpions and snakes, I told myself and, taking a deep breath, I began to descend. I suppose I wanted to impress Nicholas with my courage and interest. How grand it would be to discover some rare, priceless treasure which would please him. And if I did, what then? He would get the credit. It would be his name which would appear in some learned paper read by archaeologists, not mine. I would merely bask in the reflected glory, warmed by his smile.

Darkness, dampness, my feet slipping on the trampled muck of the steps, down and down, like Alice in the rabbit hole. Would it lead to Australia? Should I come out in a world where everyone walked upside down, as Lewis Carroll's heroine had predicted? But no, I reached the floor of the tomb. I held my light high. There were more blind-eyed statues, more sarcophagi, more frescos. I suddenly remembered my dream, and wished that I had not, regretting my impulse to go down there. Arches yawned off into deeper darkness like the entrance to

Hades. The brave and foolhardy might have breached them, rushing on, lamp in hand, making the shadows flee before them, but not I. I had gone far enough.

There were corpses in those stone coffins and I longed for the blessed daylight. Sorrow seemed to drip from the ceiling and swell from those imprisoning walls. Who in their right mind could ever believe the dead to be content and happy? How terrible to be buried here for centuries. I didn't want to die ever – what soul in this wonderful world would ever want to leave it? I had never known how much I loved it until shut up in that dismal gloom. I yearned to see the sun, understanding why the ancients worshipped it. Ra – the sun god, bringer of life, symbol of day and everlasting hope, of everything of which mortals are made – of passion and strife, work and play, happiness and love. But Ra was not present in this chamber, only Anubis.

It was as if I could hear him howling in the wind which sighed around me. Was he coming to bear my soul away? I froze, rooted to the spot, listening for the dreadful paddings and rustlings which would herald his dire approach. Would his hand reach out and touch my shoulder? In a moment of blind panic I sensed that there really was someone behind me. A voice spoke my name, softly, silkily.

"Nancy – Sir Nicholas wishes you to join him in his picnic lunch." I spun round and looked into the face of Quiller.

Chapter 5

"I think it was most awfully brave of you to go into the catacombs, Nancy," drawled Veronica as we went into the music salon that night. "And so noble to offer to help Sir Nicholas with his work."

Ah, if one could only hear the truth behind trite, polite phrases. I guessed that what she really wanted to say was: "You low, cunning bitch! How dare you help him! I'd like to scratch your eyes out!"

I was still recovering from the pleasant shock of being invited to join in the nightly ritual of a soirée held in this lovely room. Apparently, I had pleased Nicholas and this was my reward. I had dressed with great care. They were all there: Terence paying court to Emily; Miss Tranter knitting some queer-shaped garment for Fleur as if her very life depended on finishing it; Quiller engaged in conversation with Nicholas – and Nicholas himself, wearing his dinner jacket with as much ease as his riding clothes.

The furnishings were stunning, full of the richness and sensuality of design associated with the Orient. El Tarifa had once been the palace of a Turkish diplomat. The window shutters were encrusted with ivory and mother of pearl and the ceiling was painted with floral arabesques in gorgeous colours. There were frescos on the walls, charming pastoral scenes surrounded by tulip and rose motifs in subtle greens and blues. The mosaic floor was composed of beautiful tiles. But the *pièce de résistance* was the grand piano, black and shiny and splendid, placed near the big bay windows.

Below this casement and along the walls were wide divans, covered in damask and piled with tapestry cushions. It was a place for relaxing, for talking with one's friends far into the night. But now Nicholas took his seat at the piano, running his hands over the keys. I was more than ever certain that it was not he who had played that dreary little waltz in the small hours of the morning.

"Will you sing for us, Veronica?" asked Terence, and the others joined in, murmuring encouragement whilst she feigned shyness. Her eyes met mine. If her nose had been put out of joint because Nicholas had taken me to the tombs, then she must be doubly infuriated to find that I had been granted this privilege. A wave of dislike swept over me. It was not fair that she had so many attributes. Even my green silk dress which, in the privacy of my own room, had pleased me, now seemed cheap and tawdry compared with her elegance. I regretted my panic over spending too much on evening gowns.

"Well . . . if you're quite sure you want to hear my poor efforts," she said with pretty hesitation, although she was already handing a songbook to Nicholas. She took her place by the piano stool whilst he limbered up with a few sparkling arpeggios. Everyone hushed and Veronica posed, her hands clasped lightly at her waist as he played the opening bars.

The music was very dramatic and I watched her closely as she sang. She had a clear soft voice. As I listened, I understood why she had chosen this particular ballad. Her eyes burned as they rested on Nicholas' dark head, though he was totally engrossed in accompanying her. It was the despairing song of a slave girl to her beloved master.

There was a spattering of applause when she had finished. She bowed and sat down, her face flushed, and the look of a damned soul in her eyes. I wondered if I was the only one sensitive to the intensity of her singing, the passion there which seemed to tear against the nerves. Surely, if Emily was as possessive as Quiller had suggested, she must have noticed the way in which her companion devoured Nicholas with her eyes? He was unmoved by her performance, lightening the mood by dashing off a few lilting dance tunes, and then Terence sang. It was another sad tale of unrequited love and I observed that Quiller was smiling his odd, secretive, Pan-like smile.

It was Nicholas who dominated the evening. He played as if possessed of a devil, leaving the gay tunes behind and thundering out dark, stormy cadences as if to relieve some torment deep in his soul. His face was moody as he played, set in hard lines of concentration, and I was drawn to him as by a magnet, finding that I had left my seat and inched closer, till my arm rested on the raised lid of the piano. It is a fable that the hands of a pianist should be delicate and slender. His were strong and positive, each sequence of notes attacked unmercifully yet with rapier-like precision. It was as if he sought to wrest from the instrument the depth and meaning intended by the composer. The candles in holders on each side of the music-rest illumined those hands. I could see the sinews, the faint blur of hair on their backs, the way they were bunched to attack a chord or spread wide to coax out the melody. What would it be like, I wondered, to feel them caressing me? Smoothing my hair, touching my face, cupping my breasts? I was horrified. Dear God, what was happening to me? I must not, *dare* not, fall in love with another woman's husband. The idea of becoming a second Veronica terrified me. I was sickened with disgust.

Nicholas finished his performance with a most difficult piece, played with a technical brilliance and an understanding of the lights and shades of the music which was heart-stopping. As the final, fiery notes resounded round the room, he sat back, his hands on his knees, lifting his gaze from the keyboard. Something seemed to come from his eyes, passing into mine just as the light fills a cloud at sunset and, afterwards, it was no longer from his eyes only. The same feeling was to sweep over me whenever I saw him, even at a distance, when I heard his voice and, most of all, when he touched me.

"Congratulations, sir. It's such a loss to the concert platform that you aren't in the position to play publicly, and such a pity that Miss Fleur has not inherited your gift," purred Quiller.

The spell was broken. Nicholas scowled at him, rising restlessly and seeking his glass of wine. "She'll never make a pianist. I realise this and think I'll cancel her lessons."

"Oh, Nicholas, surely not?" murmured Emily, her

worried eyes following him as he paced to the window, staring into the darkness. "It is nice for a young lady to play a little – Dorothea and I learned to tinkle – such a pleasant social grace."

He did not reply and I saw that Veronica was edging towards him, like a moth fascinated by the scorching flame which will singe its wings. "Perhaps Master Jeffrey will prove a better pupil, especially as he already admires you so much, sir."

"Can't say I've noticed it," growled Nicholas ungraciously. "He's been pampered too much – surrounded by women. Time someone took him in hand and made a man of him."

"He's so sweet – such a dear child," Emily added. "I'm amazed at such sensitivity in one so young. Why, do you know, being with him yesterday cured my headache."

"Quite the little miracle-worker!" her husband snapped.

"One must beware of growing too fond, Lady Emily, you will miss him so much when he goes away to school," put in Quiller mildly. "I think Sir Nicholas is right. He needs the harder company of men."

She was showing signs of becoming flustered, coughing and holding her lace handkerchief to her lips. "But he's little more than an infant."

"We'll begin with horseriding. By Jove, I was in the saddle as soon as I could walk. Then, I'll take him sailing and swimming and he can come to the dig." Nicholas was prowling the room, every line in his lithe body expressing that he longed to be out of doors. "Really, Emily – there is the distinct danger of him turning into a milksop if he spends too much time with you."

Veronica found the bottle of *sal volatile* and passed it beneath Emily's nose, for she was in a high state of nervous agitation, brought about by Nicholas's words and something else too which I could not understand.

To my embarrassment, she now dragged me into the argument. "This is for Miss Gray to decide. She is his governess. What do you think, Miss Gray?"

"Healthy exercise will not harm him," I replied, on my guard, "providing that his education is not neglected." I shot a glance at Nicholas, trying to read his thoughts, watching the body signals, the facial expressions, but his eyes were shuttered. "As you suggest, sir, outdoor activities will be beneficial – if you really wish to be bothered with him."

He shrugged and his smile was cold. "I'm prepared to devote some time to the lad, though I'm extremely busy. After all, I've taken on a measure of responsibility for him, though God knows why."

"Nicholas – how can you be so unkind?" Emily cried. "I know he was adopted, but we must carry out our promise to Dorothea. Oh, my dear sister! How much I miss her! You have no sympathy – no more feeling than a stone! You know how upset I was when she died."

"I could hardly fail to notice it," he said ironically. He stood before her and she shrank back against the cushions as if she expected him to strike her. "You had your way. The child was brought here and now, when I offer my help, you strive to keep us apart. Why is this, Emily? Do you look on him as the son you never had? Will he be another crawling sycophant to run your errands and obey your foolish whims? Another sympathiser for your preposterous and boring illnesses?"

"I would do anything to shield him from your vile temper!" she shouted, showing a rare flash of spirit.

"My love, you forget yourself." His voice was as cutting as a sword. "Veronica, conduct Lady Emily to her room. I think she's about to indulge in an asthma attack."

He turned his back on his wife, going to the table and pouring himself another drink, brandy this time. It was a most disturbing scene. Was this the customary example of domestic bliss exhibited nightly in the music salon? I wondered bleakly. If so, I never wanted to witness it again. I was considerably shaken and after I had helped Veronica and Terence escort Emily to her own apartment, I said goodnight and went away.

Try as I would, I could not settle. There were far too many unpleasant ripples in the ether. I listened for sounds from that magnificent bedroom which I had never entered before that night: Emily's sleeping place with furnishings fit for royalty, yet what happiness did such opulence bring to that poor lady? Foolish she might be, selfish and petty, her mind turned in upon her illness which was real enough, despite what Nicholas said. She was, after all, a human being and deserving of kindness. Doors banged below, and servants bustled, perhaps bringing the steam kettle to ease her laboured breathing. There was nothing I could do; she would have Miss Tranter there, and Veronica, besides her devoted doctor, but deep in my heart I knew that she wanted none of these. It was Nicholas she needed, and he had no time for her. I wondered why they had married, and walked about my room, watching the moon cloud over, pressed upon by a feeling of foreboding, an inexpressible anxiety and a strong premonition of disaster, aware of the dark undercurrents swirling between the various members of this ill-assorted household.

Inactivity was dreadfully frustrating and I racked my brains to think of some way in which I might assist that unfortunate woman. Then I recalled an old country remedy which Miss Jenny had made for Dr Ridding to ease his bouts of bronchitis. I rummaged among my papers and found the tattered recipe book she had given me. I left my room. My watch gave the time as midnight and the corridors were deserted. My feet made no sound on the thick carpet as I hurried along on my mission of mercy. I was unfamiliar with that part of the palace. Veronica had not redeemed her promise to take me there. Perhaps the opportunity had never presented itself for it was rarely empty. Although Nicholas was out a lot, Emily clung to her room like a hermit crab, only venturing forth when she felt well enough. I paused outside the bronzework doors, listening. Perhaps she was alone and already asleep. I had better wait till morning, I decided, but as I half turned to retrace my steps, I was arrested by the sound of raised voices and recognised Nicholas's immediately. Frozen, I could not but overhear. It was a fearsome, squalid shouting match about money and I wanted to creep away. It was difficult to believe that the studious man with whom I had spent the day, the musician who had entranced me, was this same domineering bully who was quarrelling so violently with his sick wife.

Suddenly the door was wrenched open and he rushed out, almost knocking me over. His angry eyes widened as he saw me, but he didn't stop, snarling as he made off down the passage: "Not you too! God, she expects everyone in the house to run after her!"

I did not know what to do, but the door was wide open and I could hear her desperate sobbing from within. I entered and closed it quietly behind me. She lay on the bed, crying as if her heart would break, terrible, racking sobs shuddering through her, and she was coughing too. I forgot everything else in overwhelmingly pity.

"Lady Emily –hush, you mustn't get so upset." I bent over her, stroking her rumpled brown hair. Her face was turned away from me, her hands clenched against the silk sheets.

"He hates me! Oh, God, what am I going to do?" Her voice was choked, but that wild weeping was lessening. I could feel some of the tension slipping away from her under my soothing touch.

"Of course he doesn't hate you." There was something childlike in the way she clung to me now. The barriers were down. Neither of us remembered that she was the mistress and I only a hired help. "Lord, no man could be such a monster as to hate his own wife because she's delicate."

"I can't give him an heir." Her eyes were haunted in that white face, unattractively blotchy with tears.

"But you've already done so," I assured her. "There is Fleur."

She pulled away from me, cringing to the far corner of the big bed, hunted, desperate again. She would not meet my eyes. "Yes – yes – Fleur. Of course I have my daughter – but he wanted a boy – all men want sons to come after them." She spoke in short snatches, her voice breathless. Then she bowed her head and flung her hands up over her face. "Oh, Nancy – you don't know – I can't tell you – I mustn't speak of it to anyone – I made a dreadful mistake when I was young. God, how I've been punished for it!"

"You are imagining things, Lady Emily." She was beyond my reach again, retreating into her own real or fancied guilt. "It's because you are ill – fevered – I came to offer you a medicine which I can make for you. Please let me try it."

Up came her head, naked suspicion on her face. "Why should you want to help me? What is it you want? I can't trust anyone. They all play games with me. And Nicholas – he seeks every opportunity to humiliate me – flaunting his mistress in my face!"

It was like a blow in the gut. I knew who she meant but had to ask her. "Of whom do you speak?"

"Veronica! He says that it is over – but he doesn't deny that she has been his mistress, admits that she flung herself at him and he responded, and I don't suppose she's the only one." She was panting with the exertion of her angry pain – that pain which I too was sharing. Damn Nicholas. I had a swift mental picture of his cynical smile and those eyes, so world-weary and smouldering.

"You must be mistaken." My lips felt stiff as I spoke for I knew that she was not.

"D'you think that I wouldn't be aware when he was being unfaithful to me?" She was sobbing again, cries coming from her in great, strangled gasps. "I love him so much and he doesn't want me! He never comes here – never shares my bed. What d'you think it is like, lying here night after night, knowing that he is with Veronica? He doesn't love me himself and he resents anyone else who may do so. I'm not entirely bad, Nanny Tranter loves me – Dorothea loved me – and Jeffrey, he cares. He holds my hand and says: 'Poor Aunt Emily, you'll feel better soon.' It is Nicholas's pride, his damned ungovernable pride which ruins him. His pride was hurt by something I did just before we were married. It is his pride which drives him now. He wants his discoveries to have world-wide acclaim – better than anyone else's. Oh, yes – I haven't lived with him all these years without getting to know his weaknesses. He won't let me forget mine – never lets me forget . . ."

This was terrible. I was listening to things which were no business of mine, glimpsing dark family secrets, confusing, bewildering, half hinted at. I managed to calm her down, promising to have Hassan collect the necessary herbal ingredients and make up the cordial for her in the morning. She was pathetically grateful and I left her at last when she was nearly asleep, propped high on her pillows. Back in my room I tried to make sense of what she had been saying. Jealousy twisted like a hot knife within me when I thought of him and Veronica as lovers. It was an awful feeling for which I loathed myself.

I slept after tossing unhappily for a while, but my night of trial was not over. It was the music which awakened me. I sat up with a tingling down my spine and lit the candle, but this only seemed to deepen the darkness in the outer reaches of the room where its light could not penetrate. Sleepiness had slid away like a silk coverlet and my mind was cold and keen and fully awake. The sound continued, sad waves of sound, rising and falling, calling me.

With relief I remembered that Hassan slept on a mat

outside the door. I called him softly: "Hassan! Can you hear anything?"

There was no response. He lay there, swaddled in a blanket. His arm twitched and, groaning a little, he rolled over. I shook him but he would not be roused. Was he drunk? I fumed. Or drugged? I pummelled him and shouted, eventually tugging his bulk aside by sheer force for he was blocking my way. Still he did not wake. Had he not been warm, I would have thought him a dead man. I straightened and stood hesitant, listening, my body convulsing with long shivers, from head to foot. The night was stifling, as thick as a blanket. I could hear nothing, and was filled with the dreadful conviction that I was the only person awake in the house.

In the silence my sanity wavered. I wondered whether I had, after all, only imagined that ghostly music. It might have been the edges of a nightmare. Perhaps I was still dreaming at that very moment. If so, I decided, I would dream myself back into bed and pray the rest of the night away till darkness lightened to an opal sheen. Tears slid down my cheeks with my desperate longing to hear the first twitter of a bird which would herald the dawn, enemy of those loathsome things which walked in the darkness.

But I was not asleep, much as I might wish to pretend it, and I could not rest until I had investigated the mystery. So I left the slumbering Hassan and went alone towards my discovery, whatever it might be. When I was halfway down the passage, my candle went out, plunging me into inky gloom. The music beckoned insidiously, familiar as impressions are in a recurring dream. I fled to my room, stumbling over Hassan, grazing my knee, losing one of my slippers, finding it again and thrusting it on, running forward with a cooling trickle of blood crawling down my leg, sticking to a fold of my nightdress. I fumbled for and found a box of matches on the dressing table. The wick caught, though I was shivering so much that the operation took longer than necessary, and I hurried on again, following that thin, compelling trail of sound – down the corridor and round the bend which led to another staircase, going upwards.

Then my heart bounded against my rib cage with fright as I saw two figures seated on the bottom of the narrow stairs. An uprush of relief followed. There were living, breathing beings awake after all. A shock of healthy anger doused my terror. Little devils! Such disobedience must have been instigated by Fleur who sat there with Jeffrey, gazing up into the darkness above. They were so absorbed that they did not hear me till I called their names in sharp annoyance. Slowly, two pairs of eyes swivelled to glitter at me in the wavering candle-glow. On Fleur's face there was a knowing little smirk. I felt myself scrutinised coldly, impersonally, as if I were the subject of some diabolical experiment.

"Why aren't you in bed?" I asked, feeling somehow as if I had been outwitted.

"It's such a beautiful night," Fleur answered calmly, her face as serene as a saint's. "We came to listen to the music."

It was clearer now, coming from the attics which ran above the upper rooms. "Who is it that plays in the night?" I demanded. I had the distinct impression that they had been talking of some forbidden topic which had been abruptly dropped when I appeared. It was as if there was a deluge of unspoken questions in the air which had grown almost unbearably thick.

"It is Mamma," said Jeffrey, his voice dreamy, intense longing on his face. "She always plays that sad waltz."

This was too much. My taut nerves snapped and I shook him fiercely, shook that dear child whom I loved so much, seeing his amazed expressions change to one of fear, of trembling tears, his tawny curls flopping from side to side. "Don't lie to me!" I said in a low voice. "It can't be your mamma. You know that, you naughty boy!"

"I only know that she comes to me – I see her in the night – I hear her playing," he said bravely, lower lip quivering.

I let him go then. I was ashamed of this panic which was making me cruel. "Go back to bed, Jeffrey. Stay there until I come. We'll talk about this again in the morning."

He said nothing, his thumb in his mouth, and I fell on my knees in a sudden rush of tenderness, gathering him into my arms. The little body did not give way to its customary yielding affection. He very nearly melted, then I felt his resistance, and my arms dropped slowly to my sides while he wriggled free, but delicately so as not to hurt my feelings too much. I watched them go off in the direction of the nursery and continued on my way upstairs. My hand looked red, almost transparent as I cupped the candleflame to shield it. If it went out now, I did not know what I would do.

Touching a hand on the wall occasionally to stop from stumbling, I went on. This part of the house was disused. Some said it had once been connected with the harem. Now it was a household store. Moonlight stabbed through the narrow slits of windows set high in the walls, showing me the tortuous stairs. The music faltered, almost stopped, then rang out again. Though so fearful, I wanted it to continue – wanted to confront whatever it was that awaited me – even were it the spirit of Lady Dorothea. The dead cannot harm you, I lectured myself, while my cowardly body shook like an aspen and my feet were most disobedient, wanting to run back down the steps.

When I reached the top, that thread of sound had gone, leaving only a final chord echoing repeatedly, ringing into the lonely darkness. I paused with my free hand on the doorknob, then flung it full open and stepped inside. I was met by darkness and total silence. Yet there was something lingering on the air, a sweet, stagnant odour which crawled out to meet me, as of stale perfume once sprinkled on a ballgown.

I was awakened by Jeffrey bouncing on my bed, the sunlight shafting through the shutters. "Wake up, Miss Gray – we must dash through lessons this morning. Uncle Nicholas is going to take me riding. He's going to buy me my own pony. Won't that be ripping?"

He was still in his nightshirt and, dazed with sleep, I hugged him, filled with a fierce protectiveness. "Yes, it will, Jeffrey," I said, searching his face anxiously. He stared back frankly. Either he did not remember last night's incident or he had chosen to ignore it. I could not bring myself to raise the subject. I did not know the extent of his distress at Lady Dorothea's sudden death and feared to damage him further by any mention of her name.

He ran off, singing loudly, then stopped in the doorway between our rooms, saying: "Uncle Nicholas says he'll order a tailor to make me riding breeches, just like his. He's going to take me to the catacombs and to the bazaar. Isn't it fun? I like Uncle Nicholas – he's so big and strong and everyone does just exactly what he tells them to do. Hassan says he's like a king, very much respected although he's an infidel. Miss Gray, what's an infidel? Am I one? I want to be, if that's what Uncle Nicholas is."

Nicholas was slipping very neatly into the position of being the father Jeffrey had never known. I was dubious. There were parts of Nicholas's character which were most undesirable, and I did not want Jeffrey aping them. But his influence was impossible to resist. There was a charismatic quality about him, a magnetism, combined with his high-powered personality. One might love him or hate him, but never be indifferent. What could I do to prevent Jeffrey falling under such a spell? I – who had already succumbed to it.

*

With the approach of spring, the climate changed, the winds bringing sudden storms when the skies turned from blue to brown, rushing from the desert, and Alexandria retreated into itself like a city under siege. Day became as dark as night and the sand crept everywhere no matter how closely the windows were shuttered. They were disturbing, oppressive winds and Hassan informed me that we were entering the period known as *al-khamaseen*. He added that when the plague visited Egypt it was generally in the spring and most severe during the *khamaseen*. I could have done without this news, having quite enough on my mind as it was without thinking about virulent diseases.

My work for Nicholas took up every moment of my spare time. I did not complain, happy because he needed me. I saw much of him by day and in the evenings we pored over my notes in the privacy of his study. But during all the hours we spent together, I could not tell what he felt towards me. I was conscious of a closeness which was bitter-sweet, and suffered an inner agony for which I could find no outward expression. My emotions were on a see-saw – great sweeps of elation were followed by fits of depression so deep that it seemed I could never recover from them. I had succeeded in convincing myself that Veronica meant nothing to him, reading in her furiously jealous glares and cutting remarks that he had spoken the truth when he told his wife that she was no longer his mistress. I was glad, not, I am afraid to say, because of Emily's feelings, but for the sake of my own.

I struggled to control my love for him, telling myself repeatedly that I was a fool. It was an utter waste of time and energy. He was married, albeit unhappily, and even had he been free, I was sure that he thought of me in no other way than that of a loyal servant. But I could not help it. When he was away I was only half alive, restless until I saw him again and yet, though my heart felt about to burst with gladness when he appeared, I was so fearful, so troubled that I wanted to hide. The visitations of the dark hours had stopped as suddenly as they had begun. I pushed them into the back of my mind, dismissing them as some prank organised by sly little Fleur in an attempt to scare me.

I had taken my recipe to Emily, and Terence, though sceptical, had given it his blessing. Hassan had found the required herbs and I had distilled the medicine. She declared that it helped her, smiling upon me and, from that night when I had soothed her distress, she had begun to rely on me. We often spent time sitting in the garden together, dust storms permitting, and Emily scolded Miss Tranter if she glowered at me and made spiteful comments.

"Now, Nanny – there is no need for that. Nancy has aided me – such a clever girl. Who would have dreamed that an old country remedy would have given me such relief? Your Miss Jenny must be very wise, Nancy. When you speak of her and your life at Sutton Compton, it takes me back to my own childhood." She sighed, waving a peacock fan in an attempt to stir the heavy air. She was wearing white, as we all did.

"Aye, they were good days," agreed Miss Tranter. "You were so healthy then, so full of high spirits."

"D'you remember the balls we gave at home?" Emily closed her eyes, a dreamy smile lifting her lips. "Dorothea and I met the Renshaw brothers at one of them. Those house parties were such fun. We rode and danced and all the men were madly in love with us."

"You were the fairest young ladies in the county – no, in the whole of England," Miss Tranter declared. "You could have married princes, the pair of you, instead of getting mixed up with those wild Renshaw lads. I warned you at the time, but neither of you would listen – wilful and headstrong. So, Dorothea married Henry and, a year later, you were wed to Sir Nicholas – sorry matches! Henry now, he was a bad one, treated my poor Dorothea shamefully, and your own husband is not much better."

She rambled on, nodding over her knitting, and Emily smiled across at me. "You must not take too much notice of what she says," she murmured. "It's not the whole story by any means though Dorothea was desperately unhappy with Henry. She eventually fled the country and they were divorced. I'll never forget the awful scandal."

"But she must have loved him once?" I wanted to know more of this woman who had adopted Jeffrey and whose presence he was convinced haunted the night.

"Oh, that overworked word – love." Her sad eyes filled with tears. "It is the root cause of humanity's ceaseless pain. Don't you ever think about the strife it causes, the untold misery? The poets would have us believe that love is self-sacrificing, but this is a lie. It is the most selfish emotion in the world."

It depressed me to hear her speak with such unhappiness, to see that wan, once-lovely face which now lacked lustre, like an opaque glass when the light has been extinguished. It was a hot, brooding afternoon. Even the birds and insects were silent or uttering only soft, listless sounds. A great purple-hued butterfly flitted between the camphor trees on loitering wings.

I did not know what to say to her, bewildered by the strange empathy which now linked us. Then: "How sad that you should feel like this," I ventured. "I thought that love was an uplifting experience."

Her blue eyes focused on me, the lashes spiky with tears. "Have you found it so? Can you honestly say that you're not suffering the torments of the damned because of it at this very moment?"

I was dumbfounded. I had not realised that a woman in love gives herself away in a hundred subtle ways. So much for my blind conviction that I had been successful in concealing my infatuation, forgetting that the wronged wife becomes ultra sensitive to every nuance – each glance, each vocal inflection expressed by a rival. But I was not her rival. How could I be? And I had not wronged her. "I don't know what you mean, your Ladyship," I stammered, my colour rising.

"Don't you?" she answered wearily. "Ah, well – it doesn't matter. You are a good girl, Nancy – more loyal than some."

"I try to serve you to the best of my ability," I stumbled on. "And I'd never do anything to harm you, I promise." This was true, I did not wish her harm, but if Nicholas ever said that he wanted me – ah, what then?

She smiled at me sadly. "It is not wise to bind oneself to promises."

My conscience was pricking me, and I was deeply troubled, as another vow sprang to mind – made years ago under the clock tower of the orphanage. How far I had come since then, and what a thorny path it was proving to be. I had not reckoned on falling in love.

At that moment there came a commotion from the direction of the stable block and from then on everything became a blur, merging into a continuous stream of anguish. Nicholas stood there and my heart plummeted for he carried Jeffrey in his arms, limp and unconscious. Quiller was with them, and Terence too. Emily and I were on our feet together, running towards them.

"My God! What has happened?" she screamed.

Nicholas explained as we rushed Jeffrey to his room. There had been an accident. The pony's girth had slipped and the child had been thrown. I shall never forget the sight of his little white face with the bruise purpling his temple, his head lolling against Nicholas's shoulder as he bore him upstairs. We got him onto the bed and Terence examined him, straightening at last and reporting that no bones had been broken. Shortly after, the heavy lids fluttered while I watched with bated breath. Jeffrey lifted his lashes and stared up at me. Then a smile of comprehension dawned. He knew me. He spoke, though groggily. No real harm had been done.

It was not easy to confine him to bed after the first day when he was too sleepy to protest, but Hassan came to the rescue, amusing him with stories, but to me the old Arab was intensely gloomy, saying, out of Jeffrey's earshot: "Ah, *sitt*, this is a most unfortunate occurrence. Someone is trying to harm him."

"Nonsense, Hassan," I said briskly. "It was an accident. Sir Nicholas has explained what happened."

Hassan was unconvinced. "I went to the stable and looked at the saddle girth. It is new and should not have slipped if it was properly fastened. I smell sorcery. By Allah, did I not warn you of the evil eye?"

I could not repress a shudder, my nightmares rearing their ugly heads. I was about to question him further when someone else spoke at our backs.

"Hassan, have you no work to do? Idling here, frightening Miss Gray with your foolish fancies!" Quiller had entered the room in his silent way and was frowning at the man.

Hassan retreated, touching his lips and then his turban and hurrying away. "He meant no harm," I said defensively.

"I hope he hasn't upset you. The Egyptians love drama and make a mystery of every incident." He smiled at me in a friendly way, immaculate in his dove-grey suit with a dandyish touch to the dark red of his tie, waistcoat and handkerchief.

"You examined the saddle?"

"I did."

"And you found nothing wrong?"

"Nothing at all. The buckle had come undone. A moment's carelessness on the part of the groom. Sir Nicholas has dismissed him."

"Then it was just an accident," I said, trying to accept this against the clamouring of my intuition. "After all, who could possibly want to harm Jeffrey?"

"Who indeed?" he repeated with a lift of his eyebrow. What was he hinting? I felt a panicky restlessness coming alive within me. I stared at him hard and he lifted his shoulders with a wry smile. "Lady Emily sets great store by him. I hear that she is thinking of altering her will in his favour. Oh, yes – she has a large private legacy which Sir Nicholas can't touch, though he has the rest. Somewhere in the region of thirty thousand pounds. He's a lucky boy, for he already has Lady Dorothea's house and estate – when he comes of age."

"How do you know this?"

"I make it my business to know." He leaned lightly on his cane, watching me from his slanting eyes, as if we played a chess game. I did not want to dwell on the implication of his words.

"You've been eavesdropping," I accused, his jaundiced remarks about the gentry flooding back to me.

He laughed, still gay and bland. "That's a hit harsh, Nancy. One doesn't have to eavesdrop to hear Sir Nicholas and Lady Emily quarrelling. They shout loud enough for the whole world to know. He calls her extravagant and she retorts that he has no business prying into her private fortune. He's very angry because she won't finance his excavations. I've heard her saying that the whole project can go to hell for all the interest she has in it."

It was degrading to talk of them behind their backs. I had never believed that I would indulge in backstairs gossip and yet I could not help myself as I asked him: "And what of Veronica? Do they fight about her too?"

I could have bitten off my tongue. His eyes were amused, his smile knowing. "Veronica? You want to know about his affair with her? Why, Nancy – I thought you were above such things."

"It doesn't matter a jot to me – it is Jeffrey who is my concern." I tried to shrug it off, but my brain was buzzing. I wondered if he guessed that I was in love with Nicholas. My heart sank like a stone. Very little escaped his notice, and now he had suggested that Nicholas resented Jeffrey. I fought to forget it, but the seed had been sown.

Nursing Jeffrey meant more work and though Nicholas said that he would not expect me to be in his study later, I could not deny myself the sad-happy joy of going there. I was tinglingly aware of him so close to me, his dark head bent over the papers. My nostrils inhaled the musky scent of perfumed oil which mingled with the masculine odour of his body. I wanted to touch him. We talked of the accident but more of the catacombs. This was nearer to his heart than anything else. Quiller had said that he was desperate to find the means to continue his work. He was wealthy but available funds were not endless. I dreamed of discovering that I was of noble parentage – a rich heiress! Perhaps he might care for me then. At the same time I felt guilty. I had given my word to Emily. Yet, in the intimacy of his study it was easy to forget.

I trembled when he came near me, my breath catching in my throat, my heart skipping beats all over the place. I was so very aware of his manly presence which stirred a strange, pleasurable spark that flickered along to the ends of my nerves. I ached with a desperate yearning to have him take me in his arms. My ambition had fled – or rather it had narrowed down to one thing only – of living near him forever. My loyalty to his wife was as nothing compared to this yearning to be the wellspring of comfort and love for the rest of his life. And it was so hopeless that I wanted to die.

Nothing would have induced me to confess my love to him. Wild horses would not have dragged the truth from me. I could not steel myself to face the contempt and mockery in his eyes as he rejected me – and he *would* reject me. I did not doubt that. I had nothing to offer such a man. I was not especially beautiful, talented or cultured. I was a charity child and he would find this out sooner or later. I did not want this passion which was tearing me apart, and could not understand this terrible need. He was taciturn and impatient, given to black, devilish moods, feared by the servants and cruel to his wife. Why did I go weak at the knees whenever I clapped eyes on him? It was ridiculous! But no matter how I argued with myself, the bald fact remained – I was sick with desire for him. I could not bear it, wanting to throw my arms around his neck, press my hungry body against his, and beg him to take me, then and there, on the floor, like an animal, any way he wanted.

I did not sleep well that night. This seemed to have become a habit. I, who had once dropped into a dreamless sleep as soon as my head touched the pillow, now spent hot, restless hours staring up at the netting, bedevilled by a physical craving the like of which I had never known. My thighs throbbed; the light pressure of my nightgown across my breasts made them tingle; lust coiled tightly in my loins, burning for relief. I tossed and turned, thumping the pillow, then lying on my back, hearing his voice, imagining his kisses, so tormented that I groaned aloud. Ah, his mouth – his beautiful mouth – how I craved to have his mouth exploring mine, lipping over my skin. I now knew the full meaning of those desolate night hours, called by some "the hour of the wolf", when one's heated longings, self-accusations and disillusions stalk abroad.

I was contemplating getting up and finding a book to drag my thoughts away from him, when I heard something. A sound? A sigh? I could not be certain, but I sensed that I was not alone. Cautiously, I pushed aside the netting and peered into the room. The sound, if that is what it was, had died away. Silence fanned down on me once more, heavy and charged with a waiting quality. There was no wind. The air seemed to hang like dissolved curtains in space. I stood up, my toes curling at the chill of the tiles. The slanting moonlight, falling through the windows like a shower of ice, took on a sinister aspect. It was so cold, inimical – in league with whatever it was that had disturbed me.

Don't be such a fool! I told myself sternly. There's no despairing little waltz tonight. You've already been into the attics and found nothing. It is only Hassan's stories about ghouls which have stirred your imagination.

I lit a candle and walked towards Jeffrey's room. This is where the sound had originated. If those little demons are out of bed again and up to tricks, I'll smack their backsides, I threatened mentally. But it was hard to be brave. The very candle itself had an expectant air and, as I held it in my hand, it lit up the room with a yellowish uncertainty. My shadow loomed large and grotesque on the wall, part of my tousled head merging into a fantastic pattern with the moulding at the edge of the ceiling.

The door was ajar, and as I pushed it open my candle guttered and went out. I stared inside, looking towards the white hump of the bed, and there I saw a figure, hooded, shapeless, bending over the child. I was so shocked, so much caught up as if in a nightmare, that I could not move. In that split-second pause, the apparition disappeared to the far side of the bed, hidden by the curtains. I cannot recall motivating my feet, but found myself running in pursuit. There was no one there. I thought I heard the door into the corridor close softly.

A quick glance at Jeffrey showed me that he was asleep and breathing normally. I opened the door and leaned out into the passage. It was deserted – nothing was visible in that eerie light from the great windows overlooking the garden, nothing but the faint trace of perfume – sickly – stale – that which I had inhaled once before. I locked the door, checked Jeffrey again, and went back to bed, sick with fear. Had Lady Dorothea really succeeded in returning from the grave? Jeffrey was convinced that he had seen her. But why here? Why now?

I had always scoffed when asked if I believed in ghosts. Of course not! They did not exist. But now terror made me duck down under the bedclothes, every grisly tale, each superstitious story of haunted houses and graveyards inhabited by denizens from the netherworld, returning in all their horror. Then a sudden thought banished phantoms. I sat up sharply. Ghosts don't close doors behind them, they go through solid matter as if it was water. And if it was not a ghost, what was a living human doing in Jeffrey's room? It could have been a woman though that odour of musk meant nothing; every male Arab I had met loved to smother himself in perfume. Perhaps it was a prowler who had strayed into the room with robbery in mind. If so, I should raise the alarm, but it would be too late to catch him now. I did not sleep, watchful, alert, until I heard the dawn prayer chanted by the *mueddin* from the nearest call-tower.

I could visualise him, his rapt, sightless face raised to the sky. Shivering, I crept onto the balcony to welcome the day – that blessed light which he would never see, chosen for his office because he was blind and unable to look down into the harems of the surrounding houses. The sky was turning to a pinkish sheen, great splashes of colour spreading out as the mighty sun rose, dismissing the pale moon, dissolving the fragile wisps of cloud, sending the things who walked in the darkness back to their lairs. It came in a burst of splendour, gaudy greens, orange and mauve, flaming through the haze of pink and gold and delicate greys. Its great bulk, like a melting mirror, dribbled and spread over the vast sky, chasing off the night, banishing the tendrils of mist that hung over the garden.

The harmonious, sonorous voice of the *mueddin* rang out clearly, a simple, solemn melody which was answered from minarets all over Alexandria. It was an awesome moment. It made me feel tiny, insignificant, dwarfed by such fervour. I yearned to be enveloped in such a creed, to give myself up to faith. Allah was Good! Allah was Bountiful! Sadly, I knew that I had no such prop, no omnipotent bosom on which to lay my burdens. I was alone and desolation settled over me.

I questioned Hassan later. "Did you go into Master Jeffrey's room last night?"

His eyes were round, his brows drawn down in perplexity. "No, *sitt.* Why should I do such a thing? Why do you ask me this?"

I hesitated, reluctant to stir up a hornet's nest, then: "I heard a sound and went in. There was someone standing by the bed. Whoever it was disappeared when I entered."

His face paled and his hands worked in a wringing motion of agitation. "Oh, dearest miss, it was an *'efreet*! Sir Nicholas should not have disturbed that ancient tomb. The dead are angry. They will seek revenge. Already one of the workmen has died, and now they will strike nearer home. They mean to harm Master Jeffrey."

I felt a prickling in my scalp, denying it and shouting. "Stuff and nonsense! There are no such things as ghosts!"

"Ah, that is foolish talk," he reproved earnestly. "I know many who have seen them, although 'tis said that those with a clear conscience are never tormented by spectres. Is your conscience troubled, *sitt*, that the veil is lifted from your eyes and you see these restless, wandering shades?"

This observation alarmed me. How much did he or the other servants know of my guilty love for Nicholas? I retreated into dignity, saying tersely: "I've nothing to be ashamed of, Hassan, and I definitely do not think that ghosts exist. Do they leave the smell of perfume behind them? Can they close doors?"

He nodded sagely, tapping the side of his long nose. "They can do, *sitt* – oh yes, a ghost can adopt any form. You may imagine that you know the face which rises unexpectedly before you. You see familiar eyes, hear a well-known voice, but it will be a crafty *'efreet*, wishing to deceive you. Master Jeffrey is in great peril. Oh, I beg you, seek the advice of a saintly *murábit*."

The mystery remained unsolved. No one had entered the night nursery and my enquiries subjected me to queer looks. I did not tell Nicholas about it, fearing his mockery and, from then on, I was careful to lock every door leading to our rooms after dark. There were no further disturbances. Jeffrey recovered completely and, by way of celebration, it was decided that we should hire a boat and sail along the coast towards Fort Agame where there were beaches and excellent, safe bathing. This was Nicholas's idea and it was quite an undertaking. Everyone went. The morning was warm, the winds had died and a light fall of rain had revived the beleaguered city. The changes in the weather at that time of the year were most erratic. Hassan blamed the genies.

We went aboard a Nile vessel, a simple, elegant craft about forty feet long, with two triangular sails. There was much to watch as the crew prepared to leave, and I could not fail to note how much at home Nicholas was. Terence and Quiller were sporting white flannels and navy-blue blazers, just as if fresh from a yachting club, but Nicholas wore brown breeches and boots, white shirt and headcloth with its glittering *agal*. The sailors looked like pirates, much to Jeffrey's delight, turbanned, half naked, and the captain who strode the deck was enough to strike terror into the very heart – short and thickset, with hair and beard of hennaed red. The fabled corsair, Barbarossa, sprang to mind. Once the Mediterranean had been his stamping ground. Seeing Nicholas in close confab with this man, I thought how much like some barbaric sea wolf he was himself; those hard dark eyes, that eagle nose, the way he swaggered, a commander of men. Ah, to be transported back in time – I might have been his comrade at arms, fighting at his side, dying for him, going out in a blaze of glory, making the supreme sacrifice to save his life.

Dreams, dreams – those hopeless dreams which now beset me. They were my comfort and my bane, and the very humiliatins and self-reproach I felt when I saw Emily watching us only served to make me more ashamed. God knows I did not want to wound her, but knew that I inadvertently did so every time he talked to me of his work. She had not really wanted to go on this trip, but was doing so to please him. Veronica, on the other hand, had eagerly agreed, taking great pains with her appearance. Both of them were dressed as if going to a garden party rather than a day on the beach.

As the anchor came up, I stood on the deck which lifted and fell beneath my feet, feeling the slow vibration, hearing the rush of water against the rudder. It was far more exhilarating than when we left England on the steamer, a lifetime ago, but then I was not in love, I reflected. This half-crazy state heightened even the simplest actions. I saw how the horizon cut into the waves, while the white spume raced by; I smelt the sea's heady odour. The gulls screamed and wheeled and I felt an answering call deep within me, a force, a power, a savage wanderlust.

I leaned on the rail beside Nicholas, my pulse racing like the ship. The imprint of his muscular shoulder felt as though it was burning into mine – elbows touching, shoulders touching, arms resting on the carved support. He smelled clean and fresh, with that male scent which was so disturbing. I sneaked a glance at his craggy profile as he stared ahead, lips narrowed, eyes half-closed against the glare. He looked harder, bigger and more dangerous than at any time I could remember, blending into this environment where savagery lurked beneath the surface. The weather could be so unpredictable, whirlwinds and squalls could strike without warning – like his uncertain temper.

Hassan believed that such disturbances were the work of genies, and that the *zoba'ah*, a mighty pillar of dust which sometimes swept across the fields and deserts with alarming ferocity, was caused by the flight of supernatural beings. "The genie rides the whirlwinds," he would say. It was if that demon possessed me too. I leaned against Nicholas and fancied that he was almost superhuman himself. The white *kaffiyeh* and his black hair streamed behind him. My throat ached with love and longing. Thoughts of Emily became clouded. If he wanted me, no matter for how brief a time, then I would gladly surrender, and to hell with the rest!

Quiller and Terence were not far away. I could hear them talking but their words did not penetrate my mind. I was much too conscious of the even rise and fall of Nicholas's chest and the warmth of his body which was drugging me. Even my responsibility towards Jeffrey was of little account, but he was happy enough, seated with Hassan, listening open-mouthed to the marvellous adventures of Sinbad the Sailor. Too soon for me we reached our destination, a tiny fishing village surrounded by reefs and small islands. We found a spot to set up camp and I was delirious with sheer happiness. I had a whole long, lovely day to spend with Nicholas.

The children could not wait to explore and when I had prepared them, I hid behind the awning and changed, putting on my bathing dress with its short-sleeved tunic belted at the waist over knee-length baggy breeches. The men too had changed into swimming costumes. Whilst keeping an eye on my little charges as they splashed in rock pools, I watched Nicholas, admiring his superb physique, my desire mounting.

He raced up and down, did strenuous exercises, sent pebbles skimming across the surface of the water, and generally behaved as if he was enjoying a holiday. This mood prevailed over all. The other men joined him in this athletic competition whilst Emily and Veronica encouraged them admiringly from their nest of rugs and pillows beneath the shade of an olive tree. Jeffrey left his play, trotting behind his uncle like a small, faithful dog, eyes wide with wonder at these splendid antics. To show that he could be every bit as manly, he began to climb a steep, rocky outcrop. I leapt to my feet, shouting: "Jeffrey! Be careful!"

Hassan was already winging towards him. "Don't worry, *sitt* – I'll fetch him."

We had lunch and rested for a while but, after a short pause, Nicholas was on his feet again. There was always a huge concentration of energy in him. He could never remain still for long. "Who's coming for a swim?" he demanded, staring down at Terence who sprawled on the rug, leaning on one elbow and finishing a dish of fresh fruit.

"Not yet, sir," he grimaced, pained at the idea. "Must give the old grub a chance to go down, what?"

Nicholas looked at me, a challenging gleam in his eyes. "What about you, Nancy? Will you put this lazy beggar to shame? Can you swim?"

I had learned during those idyllic summers at home, taking to the water like a fish, spending hours in the lively little river, under the watchful eye of Dr Ridding, busy on the bank with rod and line. "Yes, I can swim," I answered eagerly.

"How very unladylike," drawled Veronica.

This drove me to my feet at once. "It's a useful thing to know," I retorted, stuffing my hair into my bathing cap.

"For tomboys perhaps," she replied, languidly waving her fan.

"It might save you from drowning one day," I almost shouted, vowing never to rescue her if the occasion arose.

"Oh, I'm sure some gallant gentleman would be only too eager to leap into the briny if she was very threatened by Neptune," said Quiller, running the warm, soft sand through his fingers and watching us with his knowing eyes.

I walked to the sea with Nicholas, matching my steps to his long, swinging strides, and I spent some fruitless energy on grimly planning several ugly methods for Veronica's disposal. Once in the water, however, I lost my anger in enjoyment. The rocks were sharp, bruising my feet, through my pumps and there were drifts of seaweed, but I did not care. I struck out and swam strongly, following his brown arms cleaving through the waves ahead of me. Then I lay on my back, cradled by the clear water, so happy to be near him, so proud to be his chosen companion, that my heart sang. How I savoured my triumph. What price pale, silky skin and fragile looks now? I was his equal. I stood shoulder to shoulder with him in his endeavours. His helpmate. His aide. I rolled over and swam as if possessed, challenging him to race me, seeing how he reared up through the foam, shaking back the dripping hair from his eyes. He caught and held me, laughing like a boy. I would have been happy to have died then, in all the glorious joy of feeling his arms about me, his wet, smooth skin, his muscular body keeping me captive.

He swam to shore before I did. Just one more moment, I thought, kicking lazily through the tepid water, so clear and steeped in sunshine that the white stones on the bottom gleamed like pearls seen through blue-tinged gauze. I could feel the sun beating down on my arms. They were already tanned through working in the open. Veronica would sneer when I wore evening dress. To hell with Veronica! I thought. She had had her day with Nicholas. Now it was my turn.

"Where's Master Jeffrey?" I asked as I waded through the shallows, pulling off my cap and shaking out my hair. I squinted up the beach to the group under the striped awning which, tasselled and Arabic, gave them the appearance of nomads. I could see Emily and Fleur but where were the others?

"He's gone exploring. Don't worry, *sitt*, the gentlemen are with him." Hassan held out a towel for me. "If one stands on those rocks over there, it is said that one can look down into the water and see a submerged city." He clicked his tongue reprovingly at me, adding: "Oh, lady mine, it is not seemly for you to swim like a man. Look at you – dripping on the sand without even saying '*Destoor*', asking permission or craving the pardon of any genie who may chance to be there."

I had more on my mind than angry genies. Where

the devil was Veronica? I stared towards the rocks which jutted out from the cove. The sea thundered and boiled there and the rocks were high. I picked out the small figure of Jeffrey, climbing steadly, helped by Nicholas. Veronica struggled along in the rear. In furious haste, I tore off my wet things and dressed. I was all fingers and thumbs. Veronica had no more interest in sunken cities than she had in flying to the moon. She was only doing it to capture Nicholas's attention. How silly she looked, mincing along, having trouble with her high-heeled shoes, her skirt and her parasol. Vain bitch!

I clapped on my sensible canvas hat and went in hot pursuit, sinking almost ankle deep in the slippery sand. They had disappeared from view. I wondered what she would be saying to Nicholas. Pouring poison into his ear about me, no doubt. As I drew closer, I could see that the rocks were far higher than they appeared at a distance. The waves were deafening as they thundered away on the other side. I spotted Veronica. She was halfway up and I only wished my curses could be transformed into a stupendous boulder which would go hurtling down and crush her. She had seen me. I could tell by the set of her shoulders. She was on a flat shelf of rock, taking a path which led her out of sight around a sharp bend. I made better progress than she had, shinning up quickly, soon taking that pebbly route myself.

Rounding a corner, I saw her leaning over a natural barrier of stone, gazing down at something. The salt spray hit my face as the waves boomed, battering that sheer drop. About ten feet below us, Nicholas, Quiller and Terence stood on a wide ledge. There were a couple of native guides with them. Boiling water rushed up, foaming and frothing at their feet, before being sucked back down a gully. In panic, I saw Jeffrey who had ventured even further, onto a promontory which jutted dangerously. He was jumping up and down, waving his arms. I could see his mouth opening and closing as he hurled defiance at that dizzying, raging torrent, but I could not hear him above the uproar.

I cupped my hands and yelled: "Sir Nicholas! Make him come back!"

He saw me and jumped the narrow chasm which divided us, still below me. "He's all right!" he shouted up. "Do him good! You women want to wrap him in cotton wool!"

"He'll fall in and be battered to death!" I was sobbing with anxiety.

"It's not as bad as it looks when you're down here!" He scowled, annoyed because I was interfering. "Go away if it upsets you."

He leaped back across that yawning void, as sure-footed as a mountain goat. I could see him talking to the others and they began to move towards Jeffrey. It is strange how, when disaster strikes, one is aware of it almost before it happens. I knew it, yet couldn't believe it as I saw Jeffrey slip, falling against Nicholas. Everything happened very fast, yet seemed draggingly slow at the same time. There was a confused jumble of figures on the edge of the gully, but Jeffrey had gone. I think I screamed, then I saw Nicholas dive into the threshing waves, sucked from view.

Quiller clambered up to where I stood. "Quick!" he yelled. "Run to the beach. Get help!"

I do not remember leaving the rocks, only aware that I was running along the sand, my heart giving a great leap when I saw Nicholas's dark, wet head come sweeping into view. But he was alone. It was Hassan who dragged Jeffrey out of the water further along where the undertow had taken him and, miraculously, he was none the worse for his ducking. Rather pleased with himself, in fact, as he was borne to the camp where he was petted, scolded, dried out and given brandy to drink.

"Did you see me swimming, Miss Gray?" he kept asking through chattering teeth. "I dived in! Did you see?"

I could not speak, hanging on to him. Nicholas treated the incident lightly, which was wise I suppose, clapping Jeffrey on the shoulder and promising to make a champion swimmer of him. Emily was so upset that we decided to leave. The sun had gone and the wind had sprung up boisterously. "Come along, young sir, we don't want to be caught in a storm," said Hassan as we walked to the harbour. "*Allah kereem*! He has saved you this day, but do not tempt fate further."

Jeffrey grinned up at him. "It might be Sinbad's storm. That would be exciting. We could be shipwrecked and washed up on a desert island – perhaps the one where the mighty Roc lives. I can swim now – almost. I should be all right if the ship went down."

"What a nasty, selfish little cockroach you are," butted in Fleur, walking primly along with not a ribbon out of place.

They wrangled all the way to the boat, but I was not listening. I could not forget that awful moment when Jeffrey disappeared. Why had Nicholas taken him there?

"You're very quiet, Nancy," said Quiller as I sat in the bows on the return journey. All joy had gone and my thoughts were as bleak and heavy as the clouds lowering over us. He sat beside me on a hatch cover, smoking a cigarette. Alexandria was coming into view, like a mirage in that weird light. The evening sun lurked somewhere behind those muddy clouds, giving them a golden aura. The minarets seemed to be on fire.

"I don't feel awfully jolly after what happened today," I replied. "I'm worried about Jeffrey. This is the second time something unpleasant has occurred."

He drew on his cigarette, then glanced at me. "Two accidents, Nancy. He's bound to get into scrapes."

His calmness restored some measure of balance to the imprisoned thoughts which were like bees swarming in my head. He was probably right. I would just have to accept boyish pranks and minor injuries which were part and parcel of bringing up a healthy lad. Then I remembered that shrouded figure hovering over him in the dead of night. I told Quiller, laughing rather mirthlessly as I concluded: "Hassan is convinced that it was a ghost."

"More likely some servant that Sir Nicholas dismissed and who is holding a grudge – a flesh and blood ghost, no doubt. Perhaps he sacked an idle workman and, in revenge, he seeks to frighten you." I heeded his words, for Quiller knew the country well, I felt better after talking to him, his urbane smile and quiet manner bringing me to my senses.

"I hope you're right. But we'd better keep watch. Shall we tell Sir Nicholas?"

He lit another cigarette, smoking calmly, staring at the view. The lights of the port gleamed against the dark shore, like a string of amber beads around the neck of some black giantess. "I'll deal with it. Leave it to me."

"I feel so responsible for him, you see, more than that – I love him, and would do anything to keep him from harm." Even then I could not bring myself to tell him about the ghostly music, or Jeffrey's conviction that he saw Lady Dorothea. It sounded so far-fetched, so I pretended to be only concerned about realities. "I do hope you find out what is going on."

Quiller tossed his butt over the ship's rail and I could not read his expression in the gathering gloom. "If there *is* anything 'going on', as you put it. It sounds terribly melodramatic, my dear. Are you sure you haven't been reading too many penny dreadfuls or scribbling overmuch in your journal? You do still keep it, I suppose? Imagination can be a dangerous thing."

"Did I imagine Jeffrey's mishaps? And what about the unknown person in his room?"

"Nancy, if you let yourself believe that those accidents were something else, then you're allowing fancy to run away with you. As for the apparition? I think that you had a nightmare – that's all. Don't worry so much. Trust me. I'll soon find out if anyone really is trying to alarm you or get back at Sir Nicholas. Try to relax. You are strained – overwrought. You are working too hard, becoming a little too involved with Sir Nicholas's ambitions for his catacombs. He uses people, you know, quite ruthlessly. You've never been East before, and don't understand that the hot spring winds can play odd tricks with a Westerner's mind. Be careful, Nancy, that you don't destroy yourself in an excess of zeal and wrong-headed courage."

Chapter 6

The shocks I had suffered because of Jeffrey had sharpened all my senses. I felt as if I were a shield. I was to stand before him and protect him, from what I was not sure, and this made it worse. I began to watch everyone in a kind of stifled suspense, nerves quivering like bowstrings with that hidden tension which, I feared, might well drive me insane.

I had never thought of myself as nervous, nor was I normally troubled by malaise of the spirit. Physically, I had the constitution of an ox, but now I was jumpy and on edge. How strange, how unpredictable life is. I had longed to find work which involved travel. My prayer had been granted but I had lost my peace of mind. I was totally committed to one small boy, and in love with his uncle. I wavered between doubts and uncertainties. Quiller had said Nicholas was hard, ruthless, and in need of money to complete his work. He used people. He was like a man possessed when it came to his precious excavations. Hassan had remarked that he feared his master was bewitched – such an obsession with disturbing the dead could not have come from the angels!

I was fast losing my sense of proportion. Jeffrey had

been lectured soundly for his carelessness, and everyone else seemed prepared to make light of the incident on the beach. Life continued as before, as normal as could be, though I was aware of being caught up in strange events whose meaning eluded me. Amidst the commonplace routine I felt that something beyond my control was hiding.

Then, to add to my problems or possibly because of them, I developed a fever. At first Terence thought it was malaria, but it proved to be nothing more serious than a cold. He ordered me to bed for a few days. This inactivity was galling, but I was feeling too ill to protest, sneezing and coughing miserably. So, waited on hand, foot and finger, with plenty of books and my journal to keep me busy should I feel inclined, I tried to make the best of it.

"Not a bad place to be in this weather," joked Terence, putting away his medical paraphernalia after examining me. "The season of the *samoon* is upon us, those hot winds from Africa which spoil the summer. They're even more oppressive than the *khamaseen*. Dust and sand everywhere. Most unpleasant. Never mind, they only come in short bursts, but I should have thought Sir Nicholas would have wanted to return to England by now."

"He doesn't want to leave till the catacombs are fully dug out," I croaked. "We may have to stay the entire summer."

"That won't be good for Lady Emily," he frowned, "far too hot – but I doubt he'll consider her. He's a selfish devil."

My head ached and once I had swallowed my medicine, I lay down, hot and feverish, listening to the wind thrashing the palms and whistling round the walls. The fig tree groaned in protest at this brutal force. Through my window I could see tattered clouds fleeing before the onslaught, and all the while my mind was wandering off down side tracks too dreamlike to be called thoughts. I suspected that Terence's draught had contained laudanum. Visions of death kept rising in my mind, replacing one another – the churchyard at Sutton Compton where Dr Ridding rested – the Kom es Chogafa catacombs – Nicholas's excavations. I struggled into a sitting position and tried to read but my eyes ached too much and I tossed the book aside.

Although the wind shrieked like a thousand demons outside, within the room was quiet and dim. The dust penetrated everywhere, lying on shelves, creeping among clothing, drifting across the floor. I dabbed at my forehead and cheeks which were running with sweat. The bed creaked as I shifted my position and, somehow, it was as though the rasping sound became transposed into a wisp of uncanny mist that curled through my awareness so that I fidgeted and glanced around me. The opiate was producing a drowsiness which I fought hard to resist. Jeffrey! What about Jeffrey? Then I remembered that Hassan would look after him. Nevertheless, I had an urge to remain awake and alert, feeling terribly vulnerable. There was a menace in this oasis of stillness. I dared not shut my eyes in case I was overwhelmed by some stealthy horror only waiting for the opportunity to pounce. I buried my face in the pillow to avoid this intangible thing. I suppose I must have slept at last, yet it was a strange sleep for I thought that I could see every detail of the room, the wall decorations, the rich furnishings and, at one point, could have sworn that someone was standing at the foot of the bed, masked by the cloudy netting.

I woke later. Though weak and light-headed I felt better. The wind had died and I could see sunshine outside. It was late afternoon and I had been asleep all day. Esmahan brought me water and I washed and tidied myself. Terence came in to see me, satisfied with my progress.

"Then I'll be able to get up tomorrow," I said, fretting because Nicholas would have to manage his work alone.

He shook his head. "Oh no you don't, my girl. You've been overdoing it – the rest will do you good."

"But it's only a cold," I grumbled through my stuffed-up nose.

"We'll see what you're like by the end of the week. Now, no more arguing. Take your medicine and shut up!"

"But Jeffrey – " I started to say.

He silenced me with a gesture. "He's perfectly all right. Stop worrying. Lady Emily had him in her room this afternoon. He spent a most happy time winding the gramophone for her."

"What about Sir Nicholas's relics? I'm supposed to finish the cataloguing. He wants to ship them off to Cairo."

"Veronica is helping him," he replied and a dark rush of jealousy flooded through me.

Forced to stay in bed, I had too much time to brood. I could not get Nicholas out of my thoughts. I half believed Hassan's tales of witchcraft. It was as if some malicious person had slipped me a love potion. Nicholas, oh, Nicholas, where were you now? In your study, perhaps, with Veronica's head close to your own. Were you taking her in your arms at that very instant, whispering against her cheek? You were lovers of long standing, knowing each other's moods, having memories to share. How could I possibly compete? Veronica, he may despise you, may no longer care for you, hating himself for that jaded stirring of the flesh which your beauty can still arouse, yet you are closer to him, perhaps, than I can ever be. Even his dislike of you betrays some kind of emotion. For me, he feels nothing – an indifference which is more damning than downright loathing.

I could not control these morbid thoughts. The heat had increased in intensity. The shutters made it worse. I got up and opened one of them, making my way unsteadily on to the balcony. The garden, glittering in the sunset, reared up in dense walls, shutting us in. It had a rigid, listening look as though we were held in an enchantment. I found myself listening too, for there was a couple walking below me, coming to rest under the fig tree. For one panicky, sick moment, I thought it was Nicholas and Veronica, conjured from my delirium. Then I recognised Emily and Terence. He began to speak and I was riveted there.

"Oh, Emily, I can't stand it!" he said in low, anguished tones. "The way he speaks to you! My God, I want to hit him!"

"You mustn't, my dear – don't provoke him – he'll send you away from me," she pleaded, her hand resting on his sleeve, her face turned up to his.

"What d'you expect me to do? I can't watch the woman I love being abused by that brute! Why don't you leave him? Come away with me." There was an intensity in his voice which bordred on madness, a madness which I knew only too well. "I'll look after you. I swear it."

"I can't," she sobbed. "You don't understand. I'm fond of you, very fond – but I'm in love with Nicholas."

"How can you be?" he groaned.

"I owe him so much," she began, but he stopped her, seizing her hands and holding them tightly against his chest.

"You owe him nothing! He has the bulk of your fortune, and wants to get his greedy hands on the rest. He parades his women in front of you – Veronica, and now Nancy. How can you say that you still love him?"

"He has that power," she said softly, sadly. "No matter what has taken place between us, I would follow him to hell if need be. There is nothing so low that I would not do for him. If he asked me to whore for him, I would agree."

"Where is your pride, Emily?" He was holding her gently, and her head lay against his chest.

"I have no pride where he is concerned. There must

be something wrong with me, Terence, for the worse he treats me, the more I want him."

"Will you let me be your lover?" he asked, his lips against her head where the white parting showed.

"No. I am his wife. I gave him my vow. While he lives, I can't break that promise. Besides, there are Jeffrey and Fleur to consider."

"You could obtain a divorce."

"He would take the children." There was desperation in her voice. "Dorothea would have lost her baby to Henry, had it lived. She was forced to stay very quietly in the country after her divorce. No one would invite her to their houses. People cut her dead if she passed them on the street – even old friends. Ah, no, my dear – a divorced woman is shunned like a leper, even if she is innocent. I couldn't stand the disgrace nor could I bear to be parted from the children."

"He wouldn't want them," he exclaimed. "He doesn't like his daughter and has little time for Jeffrey either."

"He would do anything to prevent Jeffrey having any of my money. If I left him, I should will it all to the boy. Nicholas knows this." She gave a deep tired sigh. "Besides which, have you thought of your career? If you were cited in a divorce case, you would no longer be able to practise medicine. I'm your patient. It would cause a terrible scandal."

"So, while he lives, I must be denied you," he said and there was an ominous note in his voice. "And if he were dead?"

"Then I should be freed from this torturing bondage," she replied, her voice thick with tears.

I saw him kiss her passionately, reverently, with all the lovely concern of a man who is deeply committed, then they disappeared from view. Suddenly the sunshine took on a sickly quality – harsh and garish. I went back to bed, the unwilling party to their guilty secret. It had come as no surprise and I was neither shocked nor dismayed. I wanted to help them, laughing weakly and rather hysterically as I lay among the frilled pillows, mocking myself for being such a hypocrite. It was not them I wanted to help – it was myself.

By the weekend I was up and thankful to be with Jeffrey again. He flung both arms around my waist. "I've missed you. They wouldn't let me visit you in case I caught the cold too."

Hassan bowed, his face wreathed in smiles. "*Bismallah*! Praise be to God that you have recovered. I consulted a wise man who prepared an incantation for your speedy return to health. Now I can have a little peace from this rascal who forever plagues me. He has me running everywhere. I'm built for comfort, *sitt*, not for the speed of a young gazelle!" But as he scolded, he beamed at Jeffrey, patting him on the head.

"Thank you for your prayers, Hassan," I replied, and then voiced a niggling worry which had been gnawing at me since I got up. "Have you seen my *ankh* anywhere about?"

I usually wore it, but it had vanished whilst I was ill. Hassan shook his head and I went on searching fruitlessly. This was not the only item which mysteriously disappeared during the following days. I kept losing things, and they sometimes turned up in the most unexpected places. Not only my own possessions, but those belonging to others as well, and they were invariably discovered later – in my room. I could not understand it, racking my brains to try to remember if I had, in fact, moved them and then forgotten. It was peculiar and most unnerving. I was more than just distressed at the loss of my *ankh*. Nicholas had given in to me, making it doubly precious.

Then something else happened which shook me to the core. I entered my room one morning and found that my journal had been opened. I stood wth it in my hands, staring disbelievingly at the broken clasp. What use now the little silver key which I always wore around my throat? Clasping this very private book as close as a threatened baby, I rushed through the house, upbraiding Esmahan and the other servants, trembling with fury. I was frantic. I had poured every emotion I felt for Nicholas into that diary, never dreaming that anyone would read it. My rage was useless. Everyone protested their innocence, looking at me askance. Hassan calmed me eventually, mending the clasp so that I could lock it again. I was beginning to feel hunted, hiding my journal furtively, finding a new place of concealment daily.

I seemed appallingly slow in recovering fully from my indisposition, subject to headaches and a feeling of lassitude and deep depression. I lay on my bed for hours at a stretch, listlessly staring at the ceiling, feeling drugged although I had stopped taking my medicine. Fantasies smothered my mind, as they had done when I was feverish. Perhaps it was the weather, for it alternated between sunny days and the terrible *samoom*, howling and beating and seeming to fill the very mind with sand. I never got used to the feeling of grit – beneath the feet, under the fingernails, in the food – hot sand and hot winds – winds that drove men mad, so Hassan said.

Nicholas and I worked when we could and a further tomb had been discovered. Perhaps it was due to spending so much time among the dead which was giving me this sensation of unreality. What was substance and what was shadow? Was I really there at all? I dithered between hope and despair when with Nicholas. Sometimes he ignored me – but sometimes, on a few magical occasions, he would put his arm affectionately through mine and we would talk on all manner of subjects. It was conversations like these which made me forget any doubts about his integrity. So he was hard and had lost his faith in women. Perhaps I, and only I, could restore it.

Emily, poor creature, courted me as a friend now, but the trouble is that if you feel guilty about someone, then something sad and knowing within them recognises it. Thus our friendship was strained. I was ashamed because I wanted her husband and dreamed of making him mine. Nothing had been said, but there were tensions in the air impossible to dispel, unspoken words which quivered and hung there – gestures which could mean something significant or nothing at all.

Then dawned that terrible day which I shall never forget as long as I live. I woke late. Though sleeping long and heavily, I was still stupefied with weariness and leapt from my bed guiltily, wondering why I had not been called. "Jeffrey!" I shouted, pulling on my dressing gown. "Jeffrey, come along, we shall be late for breakfast!"

Yawning widely, I went to the door of his room. He was not there. I frowned, puzzled, wondering if Hassan had taken him out – though this was unusual, we always did lessons in the morning. I looked at his bed. It was smooth, unwrinkled. Had Esmahan already made it? Then a terrible thought struck me. Had it been slept in at all?

With a supreme effort I controlled my sudden panic, calling the servants, asking again and again, as I did throughout that dreadful day: "Have you seen Master Jeffrey?"

The house and grounds were thoroughly searched. Nothing was found. Hassan too was missing. At first no one but myself was seriously concerned. Hassan and Jeffrey often went off on their own, but not so early, I kept insisting, not when the child was due in the schoolroom. Hassan would not have taken him away from his lessons – unless, unless – the idea was too awful to contemplate – unless he had been lying ever since he came to El Tarifa. I refused to believe that he could have been so cunning, pretending love and concern if he really intended to harm Jeffrey.

By the afternoon I was nearly out of my mind. Nicholas came in, hot and dusty. He had been riding around the grounds and the fringes of the desert leading a search party. The servants were subdued, whispering about evil spirits. Terence returned from scouring the town, equally unsuccessfully. The police arrived with their official questions, their chief a very smart Egyptian in a white uniform and a red tarboush. They promised to do everything in their power to find Jeffrey. But it was Quiller who eventually came in as dusk settled over the house and his face was long and serious. He went into Nicholas's study whilst I waited in an agony of suspense.

I remember reflecting on the strangeness of civilised behaviour as I sat with Emily, Veronica and Terence in the drawing room. Each of us knew very well the dark direction of the others' thoughts – the horror – the fear. Yet as if by some silent, mutual pact, no one voiced it. Even Emily was controlled, though deathly pale.

Nicholas returned with Quiller, his face drawn, the deep lines each side of his mouth carved as if in granite. Terence's head went up and we all, save Emily, rose to our feet. "Well?" he asked. "Is there any news?"

Nicholas poured out a drink for himself and his agent. "Yes, there is some news. Not about Jeffrey – well, indirectly, I suppose. Hassan was found late this afternoon, floating in the Mahmoudieh Canal with his throat cut from ear to ear." He turned and placed a damp, limp object in my shrinking hand. "This was in the pocket of his robe."

For an instant, I did not recognise it, then my fingers closed over the soggy, bloodstained plush of Tippy. No one moved, struck dumb with horror. My mind went blank, a merciful anodyne before a thousand fears rushed in. I was given no time to think. Emily suddenly jumped up, her face a white, grotesque mask, mouth opening on a glare of teeth as she started to scream. It was a sound to strike terror into the bravest heart – a terrible, grating noise which went on and on. In the midst of those screams, there were words – pouring out of her in a torrent. She was like a snared animal, every trace of control banished.

"No! No!" she yelled, her hands clenched against her

head, shaking her whole body to and fro. "No! No! Tell me it isn't true! Where's Jeffrey? What has become of him? Oh, God forgive me – I didn't mean – no harm – no harm – "

She started to run across the room, blindly seeking escape. Nicholas caught up with her as she headed towards the door. She was not going to turn or stop and he threw his arms about her. And then, at last, she reacted, struggling like a wild thing, but with her face twisted to one side and her arms flat against her sides, trapped by his. "Emily! Emily! Stop it!" he shouted, in a mixture of fury and anxiety. "We'll find Jeffrey. It is Hassan who is dead."

Through taut slit-mouth, she spat out: "Don't touch me, you bastard!"

He braced his feet and shook this creature who no longer resembled his wife. There was something mad and horrifying in the way she threshed from side to side, trying to escape him. She kept repeating: "Leave me alone," almost imploringly. Then she suddenly stopped struggling, standing still and tense, her tearstained face averted, eyes tightly shut, lips clamped together. A kindred tightness gripped me, like a giant fist squeezing my heart. I kept seeing Hassan's face, his wise eyes, his affection for Jeffrey. He was dead – but rather that than finding he had betrayed us. The picture faded, and I saw him being dragged out of the canal, his robe muddied, bereft of his proud green turban, the blood oozing from the wide grin of his slashed throat.

Emily's hysteria had lasted no more than a minute, just time enough for Terence to gather his wits and rush to her aid. His control had snapped and he shouted: "Emily! Darling – it's all right – I'm here!"

Nicholas's eyebrows shot up and, with a taunting, tigerish smile, he released her, almost flinging her into Terence's arms. "My God, so that's it! You want her? Well, you can have her! But I'll break you, doctor!"

Emily's hands went out, blindly groping for her

husband. "Nicholas." She spoke his name on a choking whisper for forgiveness.

He hesitated, something flickering in his eyes, then he turned on his heel, snarling: "Get her out of my sight! Give her a sedative, Armstrong – do as you damned please with her – just keep her away from me!"

Terence led Emily out like a little girl, speaking to her gently, and Veronica, after one searching glance at Nicholas, went after them. Nicholas stood with his back to me, his hands pressed flat on the table, then he straightened up and his face was haggard. "I must go into the town," he said sombrely. "Hassan was my servant and the police will want information about him. I doubt if his murderer will ever be caught."

"Shall I come with you?" asked Quiller, but Nicholas shook his head.

"No, stay and keep an eye on things here," he answered in a preoccupied manner. He had not looked in my direction since that scene with Emily. I doubted that he was aware of my existence. I was left alone with Quiller.

I found my voice at last, a queer, shaking voice which did not seem to belong to me. "How did Hassan come to have this?" I held out the bedraggled toy. "They must have been together – Jeffrey wouldn't go anywhere without Tippy."

Quiller pulled a wry face. "I can't say, Nancy. There are several possibilities. He could have been kidnapped, maybe Hassan died trying to prevent this. We'll know if they send a ransom demand. On the other hand, he may have been abducted by slave traders. Perhaps Hassan was in their pay, but proved awkward so they did away with him. An attractive boy like Jeffrey would fetch a high price." Seeing me shudder, he added: "It's a common enough practice. Alexandria is a corrupt place. Pretty children are much in demand. It's like some enormous vat, fermenting every known perversion. The poor are so very poor, you see – they'll do anything for money."

"But it's too horrible." I could hardly speak from the sheer enormity of his suggestion. "He's only a little boy! Will they hurt him?"

"How can I say?" He was smoking quietly, leaning against the table. "They won't spoil his looks, that's for certain. But it may not have happened, I am only surmising. The police are quite likely to find him. Possibly he took it into his head to pay a visit to the bazaar. You know how adventurous he is."

"And Hassan?"

He shrugged his lean shoulders under the well-tailored coat. Somehow, no matter how serious the crisis, Quiller always managed to look immaculate. "Who knows? A personal quarrel? A jealous husband? An impatient moneylender? I've no idea."

"There must be some connection." My mind was working fast, examining every possibility. I would not allow myself to face the fact that Jeffrey might be dead.

"Why should there be? Ah, Nancy, you don't know these people like I do. Though deeply religious, they can't agree on their creeds – Jews, Muslims, Copts – they are always at each other's throats. Murder is commonplace, particularly in the lower quarters."

"And this is where Hassan was found?"

"Yes, the canal is not far from some of the most notorious streets."

"D'you think Hassan took Jeffrey there?" My whole body was taut, my mind at fever pitch.

He frowned a little, as if irritated by my persistence. "I've already told you – I don't know."

"Will you go there? Make enquiries? You've friends among the Arabs, haven't you?" My control was slipping away. I began to pace up and down, anything was better than just standing there – waiting – waiting.

He promised to do all he could, then suggested that I should get a sleeping draught from Terence. "You look awful, my dear. You'll make yourself ill again, if you aren't careful, and then what use will you be to Jeffrey when we find him – or to anyone else for that matter?"

I was grateful for his kind concern and did as he advised.

Sleep. How cheap it seems when we can get it easily, how precious when we cannot. I did not sleep that night nor on the following ones. Jeffrey, oh, Jeffrey! Over and over I turned in my mind every little thing that had happened lately, searching for the smallest clue. I suspected everyone of conspiring against him – and against me. My thoughts were wild and irrational and, the more exhausted I became, so these fantasies grew beyond all bounds. Nicholas was the prime suspect of my fevered brain. Nicholas, the only one who would gain from Jeffrey's removal. But I loved him still – ah, how I loved him. Burning, grieving, even now waiting to catch a glimpse of him. He was hardly ever in the house, still searching for his nephew or giving that impression. His work at the catacombs had stopped. The whole tenor of our lives had been disrupted. The only one who seemed unaffected was Fleur, saying to me coldbloodedly, "Is it true, Miss Gray, that Jeffrey may never come back? Is he dead?"

A demure little doll in her sprigged dress and frilled pinafore. Lucky child who was always well dressed, clean and amply fed. How unlike my own girlhood. I stared down at her, unable to curb my resentment because she was there and my boy was not. Narrow, mean little face, a faint glimpse of triumph in the china-blue eyes. The usurper had been deposed and she once more reigned unchallenged in the nursery.

Emily's condition was deteriorating. She had not recovered from the shock, and never stirred from her room. I went to see her and she stared at me blankly, like a somnambulist. She had not bothered to dress, wearing her nightgown and a lace-trimmed negligee, her unbound hair falling over her shoulders. Terence was keeping her sedated and she sagged in her chair. Her face was as white as chalk, her eyes staring out from brown, crepey circles. She looked old. I wondered if I too had aged, so unaware of my appearance that I could not remember looking in a mirror during those dreadful days.

"How are you today, your Ladyship?" I asked, not knowing what else to say. What could one do but voice banalities to stop oneself from screaming?

"Nancy, have they found Jeffrey's body?" She came straight out with it, nearer to reality than any of us, having drawn so far away from everything normal.

"His body? Why, no. What makes you so sure that he is dead?" Somehow, I managed to speak, though I had to sit down.

Her eyes glistened, as glazed as one in a hypnotic trance. "Did I say that?" She faltered and fear peeped out from those ghastly eyes. She drew in a deep, rasping breath, began to speak and then stopped, making a despairing movement with her hands. I waited for her to go on and, with a pathetic attempt to be conversational, she said with a kind of awful brightness: "How nice of you to call, Nancy. Isn't it a lovely day?"

It was indeed. The garden smiled under the sun; the birds sang joyous hymns in its praise; yet I trembled with fear, feeling that at any moment I might gouge a hole in that gorgeous façade and glimpse the unknown evil it hid. Life was full of ugliness, hate, ignorance and cruelty. I had been a fool to learn to trust, to love, forgetting the stringent lessons of the foundling home. Dr Ridding and Miss Jenny had worked a miracle, turning me into a warm, caring being, but now all my old concepts had come back. What use was it to open one's heart, and let love pour in? I had loved Jeffrey and he had been taken from me. I loved Nicholas, but it was destroying me.

I did not answer Emily. There was no need; she had gone meandering off into a world of her own. I looked out of the window for a moment, as if the sunlight could cheer up the dreary atmosphere which filled her magnificent room. What good did it do her to be surrounded by such luxury if she slept in that ostentatious bed alone? I knew the agony of longing for one person only to lie by my side at night, and I had never experienced the actuality of it. She had done so, had known a physical union with Nicholas the joy of which I could only guess. Her pain must be a million times greater than mine. No wonder she was tottering on the brink of insanity.

I had made up my mind to look for Jeffrey myself, saying nothing, slipping away into Alexandria. I had mastered a little of the Arabic tongue, and the thought of taking some positive action made me feel much better. I could not shake off that instinctive feeling that Emily knew far more than she was willing to tell. She was desperately sick, of course, but I dared not let pity weaken me, so I leaned across and shook her by the arm.

"Lady Emily, you must help me. Do you think Jeffrey is in the Arab quarter?"

"He may be," she said, vaguely, uncertainly, in barely a whisper. Her eyes were like those of a hurt child. "Why don't you ask Nanny?"

Conversation with the mad Miss Tranter was the last thing I wanted. I tried again. "He wanted to visit the bazaar, didn't he? Is there anything you can tell me?"

She pressed her hand to her forehead, her features crumpling like melting wax before my eyes. "Why do you keep pestering me? Where's Terence? What right have you to speak to me in that rude way? You're only a governess! Leave me be!"

She was on her feet and I thought she was about to spring at me, but instead she burst into hoarse sobs which seemed to tear into my very soul, and flung herself across the bed, beating at the quilt with impotent fists, then lying lax and boneless as a rag doll, allowing the waves of hysteria to buffet her uncontrollably.

Terence burst in. He rushed to her side, glaring at me as he passed. "Go away, Nancy! Can't you see that you've done enough damage?"

He had changed so much from the kind young doctor I had once known – or thought I had known. Had I been deceiving myself? Had it been a game he was playing – that they were all playing? I fled away, though hardly knowing which direction to take, beyond tears, beyond anything except that one thought of seeking Jeffrey.

I sped in the direction of my room but did not reach it. Someone barred my path. His sudden appearance deepened my confusion, though why I was surprised to see him I cannot say; this was, after all, his private part of the palace. Nicholas stood before me, his face cold and hard, whilst I stared back at him as if he too was my enemy.

"I've been looking for you, Nancy," he said, his tone like ice. "I want a word with you in private."

I followed him without speaking as he led me down into the drawing room, too numbed to protest. It was dim and cool there, and such secluded closeness should have made me happy, but dark anger radiated from him. "What is it, sir?" I asked, while dread clutched at me. "Have you some news of Jeffrey?"

"It doesn't have anything to do with my nephew." His eyes held mine, keen, unblinking. "It concerns yourself."

"I?" This surprised me further.

His black brows were frowning and he loomed over me, hands thrust deep into his trouser pockets. "Quiller has come to me with a most disturbing story. He thought that I should know of it, risking my anger by so doing. He has been most anxious about you apparently – says that you've been working too hard and that your health has suffered in consequence."

"Have I proved unsatisfactory? Has anyone complained?" I asked sharply, on the defensive.

He was very controlled, still as a crouching panther, never taking his eyes from my face. "No, not at all. If anything, Quiller hints that you've been over-conscientious, driving yourself to the edge of a breakdown."

"I only had a cold," I protested, preparing to do battle over my fading reputation for efficiency.

"I'm not talking about that. There's something else much more serious. I understand that you've been acting oddly since Jeffrey's accidents – suspicious of us all, as if someone in the household was responsible and trying to hurt him. I can't have you going about repeating such things. Quiller tells me that you seem to be losing your memory – misplacing objects – and that you are subject to hallucinations – thinking that you've seen an apparition in Jeffrey's room."

My knees were trembling, my fists clenched into tight balls, and his beloved, handsome face wavered in the shuttered gloom. I did not know what to say, unable to believe that he could be talking to me in that cold, stern manner. Then some of my old, fighting spirit struggled into revival, coupled with a heartening flash of anger. "But Jeffrey has disappeared. Is that imagination? Hassan is dead. Is this the product of delirium?"

"Absolutely not. Everyone is most distressed, but we don't look at each other with suspicion, asking all kinds of awkward questions. You've been well treated here. Jeffrey was happy. Lady Emily and I have done everything we can for him, though he was only an adopted relative. Can't you see how wicked you've been to distrust us? Who could want to harm him? If there has been foul play it is the work of kidnappers." He sounded so positive, so convincing that I began to look back over the past weeks. Was there truth in what he said? I did not know what was right and what wrong any more. I had become so strained, so restless, my brain whirling with half-formed plans, hopes and ambitions which were in themselves a kind of madness. They had centred on him, but I could not tell him this. Perhaps I *was* on the verge of mental collapse, unable to cope with the torment and frustration of wanting something that belonged, by right, to someone else.

"You think that I'm losing my reason," I said flatly. A stillness held me as if I were encased in ice.

He shrugged. "Who am I to judge the disorders of the mind? I blame myself in a way for giving you extra work. This was hardly fair, but now, Nancy, that is over. You must leave here."

My heart nearly stopped. To go away – never to see him again. It was unthinkable. But coupled with this overwhelming misery was something else. "Are you trying to get rid of me?" Again, that sane or insane suspicion. My head was spinning. "I can't go. I must be here when Jeffrey returns."

His mouth was set in a grim line, eyes like shards of steel. "No, Nancy, I cannot allow this. You are most unsuitable to be his governess. Quiller has told me something else, you see – something much more damning. I understand now why you made such a hysterical fuss when your journal was tampered with – I thought at the time that it was odd, but now I see that you had much to hide. With your background, I wouldn't dream of allowing you further access to the children."

He knew! My heart was pounding like a drum. All my worst fears had come true. "What do you mean?" I whispered.

His smile was wry, mocking. "Oh, come now, don't play the innocent. You were brought up in an orphanage. Why did you lie about it?"

"I wanted the job," I burst out. "I wanted to travel. I had spent the last four years with Dr Ridding and saw no reason why I couldn't be a governess. I've been a good one, haven't I? What right have you to condemn me for something which is no fault of mine? Quiller engaged me. If anyone is to blame it is him. He should have looked further into my history."

"Oh, but he did," he answered, his voice cool now,

very factual. "He's most apologetic, in the light of recent events. Apparently, he considered you most admirably suited for the post when he interviewed you in London. Time was short and he had to find someone quickly. But, whilst you were in the country, collecting your belongings, he made a few enquiries. It was his duty to do so. He wrote to Miss Jenny."

"She didn't tell me." I felt betrayed on every side. Why hadn't she mentioned it? Was it to save me from worry? She knew how much the appointment had meant to me.

"You thought you were going to get away with the lie, did you?" His voice cut me to the quick. "A pity, Nancy. I don't like liars. Quiller says she was most cooperative, writing to tell him that you had come from an orphanage in Bristol."

"Very well, sir, I admit that it is true." I was facing him with my head high, glad that my secret was out. At least I no longer had to fear exposure. "I'm not ashamed of it. I concealed the fact, suspecting that this would be the general attitude. It's so unfair – can't you see that? Why didn't Quiller tell me that he knew?"

His face was black as thunder. "He says there wasn't time to alter the arrangements. I'm extremely displeased with his handling of the matter. He had no business employing you, but he thought you such a level-headed young woman. It is only lately that he's begun to have serious doubts – that is why he came to me to confess his error."

"Because I was a charity child? What has that to do with Jeffrey's disappearance? Or my 'odd' behaviour? Charity children are human beings too, you know – not some entirely different species!" I was raging with indignation. It was as if I spoke on behalf of every foundling brat who had ever been born, pleading their case.

"Don't take that tone with me, Nancy!" He was as furious as I, but I didn't care. My boats were burned anyway, so it no longer mattered what I said or did. He despised me. He was going to banish me from his sight for ever. "I would have overlooked this, prepared to give everyone a fair chance, but I can't keep you on after hearing how your mother died!"

"My mother? They never told me anything about her."

He raised a sceptical eyebrow. "Really, Nancy? You expect me to believe that you never knew how you were taken away from her as soon as you were born? She died in a lunatic asylum. She took her own life."

It is strange how deep shocks hold one in a kind of suspension of belief, a natural shield so that the brain does not snap under the pressure. This is how I received this damning information. I refused to believe him, wondering sickly if I were the victim of some ghastly practical joke. "I didn't know this," I whispered. "How did Quiller find out?"

"He wrote to the authorities. Oh, yes, it has been verified. So you see, you are not fit to look after children." He was so cold, so serious. The horror began then, growing in me until it swamped all else. I hardly heard that stern voice rolling on. "Quiller says that he had a letter from a certain Mrs Bowell, who wrote that you had shown no signs of instability, but that you had been rebellious and troublesome."

"I swear to you that I knew nothing of this." In my mind a thousand torturing doubts held sway. My mother had died in a madhouse. She lay in a suicide's grave.

Something in my face must have convinced him for he paused, then collected himself and went on. "You must see how much this alters the situation. You suspect everyone around you – but just supposing that I begin to suspect you? The unbalanced mind develops strange fancies. Could it not be that you have hidden Jeffrey yourself in a mad moment which you cannot now recall? Perhaps prompted by your desire to protect him."

I could bear no more. I had to get away. I turned

and fled from the room. Somehow I reached my own chamber, locking the door behind me and leaning against it. I was shaking and my heart seemed to have lodged in my throat. I sat on the edge of my bed and forced myself to be calm. Was it true that the seed of insanity had been passed on to me? Now it was of even greater importance that I find Jeffrey, to prove to Nicholas that I was as sane as he. Nothing must hinder this. I dared not even peer into that yawning pit of terror which his words had opened at my feet. I was *not* mad. I had *not* done away with the child. I could not even consider this dire possibility. How could I be sure that Nicholas was telling the truth? It might be a ploy to successfully silence a damaging witness.

I made myself concentrate on my plans, but pain kept surging up. Nicholas wanted to send me away. He cared nothing for me. Stop it, my mind screamed, don't think about it. Now, how was I to get into town? Walk, of course. It was some distance away. My next problem was how to achieve this, so recognisable as a European. Also, Nicholas might have me followed. In a flash of inspiration I remembered my bedouin costume. The flowing white wool burnous would hide me. With hands that shook, I put it on, pulling the hood up over my head. I filled a drawstring pouch with coins and armed myself with the long, curving dagger which had come with the costume.

I let myself out through Jeffrey's room, seeing that neat white bed, forlornly empty except for Tippy whom I had dried out in the sun. He lay there on the pillow, looking dejected and abandoned – lop-eared, scruffy old rabbit, stained with those ominous, rusty-brown patches which had refused to yield to my vigorous scrubbing. Hassan's blood? Or Jeffrey's?

In a terrified, bewildered turmoil I reached the heart of Alexandria. Disjointed thoughts churned in my head. If I wasn't already mad, they were enough to drive me to the brink. Was Nicholas telling the truth? Why had Quiller confessed to his mismanagement at this precise moment? Were they plotting against me? My love for Nicholas refused to accept that he could be so vile as to have become involved in a plan to hurt his nephew. Yet there had been no evidence of the work of kidnappers, no demand for money. The police said he had vanished into thin air. It was true that I had been feeling ill, unable to think clearly. Could I be following in my mother's footsteps? It was horrible, unbearable.

When I saw Nell in the bazaar, it was like a miracle. My rationality returned and with it my determination to vindicate myself. It was as if I had been crawling through a swamp, feeling myself being sucked into the depths, then suddenly finding a strong branch to cling to. Nell would help me, always so clever, and I arranged to meet her later at her hotel. I still felt that the *kahweh* might hold a clue, but the meeting with the beggar and the acceptance of the accursed metal disc were enough to convince me that it was useless. Through a blinding dust storm, I had made my way back to El Tarifa, forcing myself to enter its portals once again – that place of cold magnificence – hostile – evil – which had never welcomed me. A place of secrets, haunted perhaps by the spirits of the ladies of the harem who had once been imprisoned within its marble walls.

I remembered that sad, wistful waltz which had haunted me there. It haunted me still – half heard – distant as the wind – calling, crying. Somehow, I stumbled to my room. I met no one on the way. Every corridor, each sumptuous room seemed deserted and the silence was like lead. Like a terrified child, I crept on to my bed, clutching my journal, reading it until far into the night.

Now I am forced to add a very sad and terrible footnote to my narrative, one so entirely dreadful that I tremble as I write. I would avoid setting pen to paper, but Nell must be in possession of every fact, no matter how painful. I shall have to leave for her hotel as soon as I have finished this, and have already told the grooms to prepare the gig.

The house is in an uproar after this latest tragedy, and they will not notice me slip away. I am shaking as if the fever is upon me again. My room, once a haven, has become a dreadful place. Fascinated, I am drawn to the balcony again and again, looking down, still witnessesing in my mind that which I saw as dawn stole over the city, the *mueddins* waking the echoes with their calls, the sea touched with bloody fire. It was the most awful moment of my life, and now I must describe it in detail. Perhaps, by so doing, I can exorcise the horror.

Having read for hours, I fell at last into sleep, my journal still open in my hands. I was awakened by a sound, opening my eyes to see the room becoming lighter by the second, the birds trilling in the treetops – but it was not their innocent carolling which had roused me. No, it was a squeaking, repetitive noise, like a rusty piece of machinery which needed oiling. It had the quality of a persistent pain that would not go away, monotonous, compelling, insistent. It came from outside, drifting in at the open window. I rose, still drugged with sleep, stiff and uncomfortable. My shoulder and arm were numb down one side from being too long in an awkward position.

Following the sound, I went out on to the balcony where the top branches of the fig tree brushed the iron-work. I looked down and – dear God, how can I bear it? There – below me, in a leafy gap, I saw a face suffused with dark colour, upturned towards me pathetically, horribly, as if imploring my aid. The eyes were shut, the head screwed unnaturally to one side. Disappearing into the foliage was the white linen of a nightgown. Emily swung there, floating, suspended, a terrible laxness to her limbs as if she were a puppet hooked up by the neck in a showman's box. The sound which had summoned me had been her strangling gasps for breath.

I don't remember how I reached the garden. I must have rushed to the table and picked up my dagger, thinking of nothing but cutting her down. My next impression was of seeing Esmahan, screaming to her to follow me, and rounding the corner of the wall where I had to face that ghastly sight again, head on this time. Emily was hanging in the tree, a length of sheeting twisted tightly around her throat, the other end knotted to the branch above her head. It was as if she stood in mid-air. An overturned chair lay on its side beneath her dangling feet. She must have climbed up on to the wall to secure that improvised rope, the noose already circling her neck.

Esmahan let out a piercing yell and stopped dead at the sight of her. "Don't just stand there!" I screamed. "Help me! We must cut her down!"

She clapped her hands to her mouth. "No! Don't go near her! She's blue! She's dead!"

Still unbelieving, I reached up my hand and touched Emily's leg, and she swung away, almost coyly.

BOOK TWO

Eleanor

The Devil, I safely can aver,
Has neither hoof, nor tail, nor sting;
Nor is he, as some sages swear,
A spirit, neither here nor there,
In nothing – yet in every thing.
He is – what we are; for sometimes
The Devil is a gentleman;

Peter Bell the Third, SHELLEY

Let thy love in kisses rain
On my lips and eyelids pale.
My cheek is cold and white, alas!
My heart beats loud and fast.
Oh press it close to thine again
Where it will break at last.

The Indian Girl's Song, SHELLEY

Chapter 1

Meeting Nancy in the bazaar had excited and upset me. Filled with the resolve to honour that childish vow made at the orphanage and help her if I could, I waited for her next day on the wide, pleasant verandah of the Stanley Hotel. I fretted impatiently, longing for her to come, terrified that something might have happened to stop her. It was so odd that we should have met in Alexandria of all places, after four years. Stranger still that brave Nancy should be so frightened. With relief, I saw her, neatly dressed in a dark skirt and frilly blouse, a shady hat on her red hair, but this turned to dire alarm when I took in her white face and listened to her horrifying story. I yearned to keep her with me, but this was impossible. I had to let her go, promising to assist her, convinced that she was telling the truth. I had no premonition then that my attempts at help would bring bizarre and tragic results in their wake. To explain how this happened. I must go back many years, to the beginning of my tale.

I can remember my father clearly. A tall, lean man who would swing me high, looking at me with loving eyes and laughing as I grabbed at his beard. We lived alone at the top of a narrow dark house. He was scholarly, forever writing, and he taught me to read at an early age. I was content, thinking that we would be together always but, one wintry day, he woke me early. "We're going on a train, Eleanor," he had said and there was a gravity in his manner which had disturbed me.

I'd never been on a train and I skipped about excitedly as he dressed me in my best frock and buttoned my gaiters, wrapping me in a white fur coat and pulling my hat snugly about my ears. The station was alarming, the great roaring monsters of steam engines, the bustle on the platform, but I didn't show it. I sat by his side in the dingy compartment, swinging my legs and watching the houses, fields and trees flash past. I imagined that there were huge knives attached to each side of the coach, sweeping flat every obstacle as we rushed onwards. When we arrived in Bristol, he said: "I'm going to take you to live with a lot of other little girls. There will be so many to play with."

"Will you be there too, Papa?" A finger of doubt chilled me.

"No, petal. I must go away for a while, so you'll have to be brave and manage without me. But I'll come for you soon."

Shortly after this we came to some iron gates behind which I could see a large house and a grim tower with a clock at the top. It looked very dreary through the drizzle and I didn't want to go in there. When I met Mrs Bowell, I was even more reluctant. I didn't want to be left with this fat, stern woman; I didn't like the stuffy room into which we had been shown. My father and she talked for a while, then he drew me against him, his arm hurting me with the intensity of that clasp, saying in a queer, choked sort of voice: "Now you won't cry, will you, pet? Mrs Bowell will look after you and I'll be back. I promise."

He handed her a paper parcel which contained my clothes and gave her some money. I was bewildered, standing very still, dry-eyed but with a pounding heart. He left quickly, the door closing behind him. Mrs Bowell tried to take me by the hand but I wouldn't let her, backing away. "Now, come along!" she snapped. "Let's get you out of those fancy clothes and into your uniform."

"No!" I shouted. "Go away!"

She grabbed me then, but I kicked and screamed like

a miniature fury till she slapped me hard about the head. The surprise and outrage of that hard blow stopped me dead. I'd never been smacked before, never been spoken to in that angry way. Every sensitive feeling within me froze. She dragged me off to her storeroom and stripped off my clothes, then pulled an ugly frock over my head, her fingers harsh and uncaring. A label was attached to it with a number printed on it.

"I'm not a number. I'm Eleanor Sheldon," I protested.

Another clout around the head shut me up. "Here you're a number and your name is Nell," she said grimly. "We don't put up with no airs and graces." She pushed me on to a stool and took up a pair of shears. Snip, snip, snip. My fair ringlets lay at my feet. "We don't hold with long hair neither. Harbours nits."

I didn't know what nits were, putting up my hand to feel that strange, bristly shortness. She had taken everything – my papa, my clothes, my curls. I hated her. She was like some horrid black crow with a nasty, sweaty smell. The horror of that day remains with me still – the bleak dormitory, the crowd of hostile girls, that first meal in the bare, cheerless dining hall. Mrs Bowell yelled at me for being finicky and faddy when I refused to eat the mess of overcooked cabbage and potatoes swimming in greasy gravy. "If you don't eat it now, Nell, it'll be served up cold at every meal until you do!"

The other children tittered but were silenced by her glare. My stomach rose as she forced a spoonful into my mouth. I was sick over her apron. She beat me with her wooden ladle. By the time evening came I felt that there could be no deeper misery in the world. Wearing the coarse cotton nightgown provided, I crept beneath the scratchy blanket. Hard bed, lumpy mattress, unfamiliar odours. I stared at the distant gaslamp and anguished for my father. I hadn't even the comfort of my rag doll, Mopsy, to cuddle. She had been packed with my clothing and locked in Mrs Bowell's cupboard. Thus, at five years old, I entered the Cardwell Asylum for Exposed and Deserted Young Children. I never saw my father again.

•

The days ran into one another – long, terrible days. There were lessons, the teachers armed with switches which they whacked down on bare knuckles without mercy. At first, clouded by despair, my wits deserted me. I was called stupid and idle, and caned and caned again. Pain sharpened my mind and I remembered all that my father had taught me. I displayed my ability to read and write, but learned that it didn't pay to be too clever or one was caned for that too. There were chores to do, plenty of them, and sewing and knitting. I was always cold, my toes and fingers swollen with chilblains. Mrs Bowell walked amongst us with her thin, whippy switch ever ready. I began to bite my nails down to the quick.

I expected my father to arrive at any moment and take me away from this hell. He did not come. The other girls were right, it seemed – they had said he wouldn't. I grew very thin and survived in that infantile jungle by lashing out with my tongue. My peers were even more cruel than Mrs Bowell, picking on me because I was small.

The leader of this gang of tormentors was a large, red-headed, green-eyed girl who had been in the orphanage all her life. She was loud and coarse. Her method of expressing herself when we were unsupervised would have made Mrs Bowell's hair stand on end. I envied her physical strength and the way in which she always came out on top in a fight. She was a bully and had singled me out for her attentions. They called her Nancy.

On one particularly gloomy afternoon, the girls had decided to relieve their frustration by playing the cellar game. It was my misfortune to be the victim. The cellar was a fearsome place, the home of large, hairy spiders.

Nancy was in the lead, pinching my arm as she dragged me towards that black, bottomless pit of terror. "Want to go in the bogey-hole, Nell?" She mocked my fruitless, struggles, while I spat and swore. "There's a ghosty-wobbles down there waiting to pounce on you!"

"Let me push her in, Nancy." A lumpy, spotty girl barred the way, challenging her. "You always do it."

"Get out of the way, Connie, you fat cow!" shouted Nancy, her eyes beginning to blaze. "She's my slave, aren't you, Nelly? She has to do what I tell her!"

They were like two dogs snarling over a bone. In the end, Nancy punched Connie in the eye and she retreated bawling and threatening to tell on us. Nancy turned on me triumphantly. Her hard fingers bit into my arm. The cellar door was wide open, that damp, mouldy smell of darkness and cobwebs rushed up to envelop me. I tried to tear myself free, shouting into her face: "Why d'you treat me like this? I haven't done anything to you! When Papa comes, he'll box your ears!"

Nancy stared me in the eye and I steeled myself for her expected blow but she grinned instead. "Bloody sauce!" she said. "And who the hell do you think you're talking to, slave?"

"Leave the brat alone, Nancy," came a voice from the rear of the kitchen and another girl pushed her way to the front of the interested crowd watching me defy Nancy. "Much better to wallop that bloody tell-tale Connie. Shove out of the way, you lot. Come on, let's have a look at you, Nell. Lor', but you're a funny little object."

This was Rebecca Smale, and I had only seen her from a distance till now. I was impressed. Rebecca carried herself like a queen, her close-cropped dusky head was held proudly, poised on her slender neck as lightly and delicately as a flower. Her eyes were big, golden-brown and imperious – there was something in their expression which was untamed. She was a girl you couldn't help looking at, making you think of an eagle or a panther, something wild and solitary. She seemed to put space around her as she moved, and had such an air that the others stood back and Nancy let me go.

Then a most strange thing happened; simultaneously, Rebecca and Nancy reached out and took my hands in theirs. I stood between them, unable to believe it. I think I can still capture that sudden flash which passed through the three of us. It was almost a recognition, as if we had known each other before, in another life perhaps, and now met again as old friends. All I know for certain is that from this moment onwards, I was no longer alone and abandoned. I had them and they had me. An alliance was born in that drab kitchen which was to illumine our lives. I felt as if some great book where the pattern of my destiny was written had turned a leaf and showed me a new page. Now I no longer grieved for my father. I even forgot him for days at a time. The bond between Rebecca, Nancy and me grew even stronger. An incongruous friendship perhaps; the strapping, fearless fighter, the foreign-looking beauty, and myself – fair of hair and skin, small of stature, my sensitivity masked by sarcasm.

The years rolled by. We survived, united in our hatred of the home, Mrs Bowell and her lecherous, hypocritical husband. We became adept at flouting authority in a hundred ways. Miss Winifred West came to teach music and English. I admired her tremendously for she was kind and earnest, her sallow face flushing with pleasure when I showed a genuine love of literature. I tried to interest my friends in the fabulous world of books, but they were far too restless. Often we talked of what we would do when we left the orphanage, meeting in the sheltered doorway of the clock tower, our favourite hideaway. Nancy was usually in the lead, her hooded cloak flying out behind her, hair straggling untidily about her square face. She always moved with a fast, swinging gait, constantly reprimanded for this hoydenish stride, but she didn't give a damn. She'd always wanted to be a boy, a strong, vital girl, vigorous and adventurous, possessed of a fierce spirit of courage and indomitability. This was betrayed in every movement of her body and each expression of her alert face. Both she and Rebecca would be fifteen soon. The prospect of being left behind was bleak indeed. I was more than a year younger.

I remember meeting them there one summer day not long before Rebecca was due to go. Rebecca was beautiful. She had all the looks of a pagan princess, so dark-skinned and golden-eyed. Her black hair sparkled with highlights, and her eyes danced as she performed a little pirouette on the warm stone steps, filled with an irrepressible zest for life. At that age, many girls are conscious of their limbs and carry themselves awkwardly, but not so Rebecca. Her breasts slightly swelled her dingy cotton frock, her waist was tiny, her legs long and slender, and her face was ravishing. I loved her so much that it brought a lump to my throat. I hid my emotion, of course, saying coolly: "Stop showing off! You won't be dancing so much when you've got to earn a living."

"Don't you believe it, Nell," she tossed her head, speaking in that joyously reckless voice of hers. "I'll dance and sing my way to fame. Just you wait. When I'm rich, I'll send for you both and we'll have a wonderful time."

"Ha! That'll be the day! Bet you'll forget about us!" I commented, but I felt as if a gulf a mile wide was already yawning at our feet, dividing us.

"Is that what you want, Rebecca? To be rich and famous?" asked Nancy, suddenly serious. She was frowning as she stared at our lovely companion.

"Yes – oh, yes!" Rebecca's eyes were dreamy and she moved restlessly, as if her feet were itching to carry her on her way to glory. "I want to wear gorgeous clothes, and have all the mashers running after me. I'll spurn 'em, of course! Tell you what – never, never, as long as

I live, will I be called Becky again. I'm Rebecca. My mother gave me that name, even if that's all she did give me. I'm going on the stage and to hell with the orphanage! I can't stand being Becky Smale! That can be left here to rot when I go. I need a new one, though. What shall it be, Nell? Help me to choose. You've read hundreds of books – you must be able to think of something. Give me a grand name – something that rolls off the tongue."

Nancy came up with one or two absurd suggestions, and I tried to conjure a noteworthy title. Rebecca was certainly fiery and Spanish-looking. The name Costello floated into my brain, culled from some half-forgotten romance, no doubt. I mentioned it and she clapped her hands delightedly. "That's marvellous! Just the ticket! Clever old Nell! It'll look bloody great on a programme, that will. Rebecca Costello!"

"But you've never been to the theatre. How d'you know you want to act?" Nancy asked, her dark brows frowning. I knew what she was thinking. Often, Rebecca's wild ambitions alarmed us. There was a ruthless determination in her. Nothing or nobody would stand in her way.

"Peggy told me about it. I've seen pictures of the actresses, and she says that some of their lovers are titled gentlemen. They drip with diamonds! The stage-door Johnnys send 'em whacking big bouquets and take 'em out to supper in posh restaurants. They even drink champagne out of their slippers! Think of that! Who wants to be a skivvy when you can live like a queen? Not me! Not Rebecca Costello!" She was smiling with sheer happiness at the idea, linking her arm with mine. "And you, Nell – always so calm, cool and collected, what d'you want to do? You're so damned clever, you ought to go to university."

"I'd like that but I'm not sure the men would. I'd knock 'em into a cocked hat!" I replied lightly. "I don't know how best to employ my amazing talents."

This was not quite true. I had an ambition which I divulged to none. I wanted to write, a part of my mind continually inventing plots, seeing vivid scenes peopled with my own creations. I changed the subject, suggesting to Rebecca that she cross-question Nancy.

"I'm going to travel," she answered at once. "I want to see the world. D'you think I could dress as a boy and enlist, going to fight the Boers in Africa?" She started to march up and down, swinging her arms in a military manner.

"You'd never get away with it – not with that chest," I laughed.

Nancy slapped her bosom. "What's wrong with my chest? It would support a fine row of medals."

"There's not a thing wrong with it – there's just a bit too much to hide under a uniform, that's all."

Nancy pulled an exasperated face. "Then, I suppose, I'll just have to get a job as a nursery maid or something equally boring, looking after a swarm of horrible brats."

"How dreary," agreed Rebecca, throwing her arms above her head and opening them wide as if offering up a prayer to the sun. She was on tiptoe, stretching like a cat, her face lifted to the sky, eyes closed, a smile curving her lips. "Oh, isn't it a lovely day? Lor', don't it make you want to tear off your clothes and run about on a sandy beach and dive into a blue, blue sea – as naked as the day you were born?"

"Don't talk so daft," said practical Nancy. "Girls don't do that! Boys can, mind – they can do as they damned well like, but girls have to be careful – Peggy said – or they might find themselves lumbered with a little come-by-chance. D'you think that's what happened to our mothers? You can't run around with no clothes on. Whatever next! You're crackers, you are, Rebecca. Where could you do it, anyhow? Weston-Super-Mud?"

Weston was the only seaside town we had ever visited, taken there in an open, horse-drawn bus, on rare outings sponsored by the orphanage committee. "Christ no!

Who's being daft now?" Rebecca said with a scornful toss of her head, hands on her hips, feet tapping as if to music running through her head. "The sea never comes in there. It's a dull, dirty hole. I hate it! Common place – full of common, boring people! No, Peggy was telling me about the South of France and Monte Carlo. The swells go there. She got it from one of those novelettes she reads. Then there's Italy – and what about Spain? All that glorious hot, hot sun!"

I took fire at her words, watching her, so full of lovely life. I loved to see her dancing, and sometimes she sang in a rich, mature voice. Was it true that she might come from gypsy stock? A child of the south, she seemed, and I longed to be there if she ever did find the shore of her dreams, to watch her dancing naked, her limbs sun-kissed. It was indeed the time of year to lift even the hearts of such as we. The deep blue sky arched above us unmarred by the smallest cloud. Larks vibrated far, far up, while blackbirds whistled in the trees and the air was sweet with the smell of freshly garnered corn and ripening brambles. This is how I always think of Rebecca, against such a summer backdrop, a sun-worshipper rejoicing because she had been born in this season and was so much at one with it.

"It's August now," she announced, flinging herself down on the steps. "I'll be fifteen in a week, then I'm off!"

"I've got to wait till January." Nancy sat beside her, elbows on her knees, staring across the quadrangle where the children were having a break from lessons. Miss West, supposedly in charge, was sitting on a low wall reading a book. She would be the only friend I had when January came.

It was shortly after this that we were involved in an incident in the dormitory. Though Connie was mostly to blame, it was Nancy, Rebecca and I who were savagely punished; Nancy most of all. Mrs Bowell took the whip to her whilst I watched in helpless agony, feeling the smart of each lash as if it was cutting into my own skin. I hated injustice but, worse than my own thrashing, the heavy chores and lack of food, was the soul-destroying separation. Rebecca arranged that we should meet the night before she left. It was not easy for me to escape but I planned it well. I had been having lessons in strategy from Peggy who had secretly given me her gay, feckless support. She was a bold girl, cheeky to everyone, including Mrs Bowell, yet she possessed a virtue to which that lady could never aspire – a shrewd understanding of human nature. She used this to further her own ends and bore no grudge for her humble status as a kitchen drudge. Indeed, she changed it into an advantage, turning the misery of poverty and illiteracy into the plus of "knowing her way around".

She taught me to accept every small benefit that came my way as the proper weapon of the sharp-witted battling against fools. It didn't pay to be honest and outspoken. Much better to be cunning and devious, exploiting the weaknesses of others. I put this into practice with regard to the drinking habits of Mr Bowell, and was soon able to twist him round my little finger with the promise of an extra bottle or two.

Thus I was able to ensure that he would cause no trouble on that night of storm when I met my friends under the clock tower to say goodbye to Rebecca. It was a dramatic moment which made a deep impression on me. I joked about the vow Nancy insisted that we make, that promise to fly to one another's aid, if need be, but this was only to lighten the intensity, to help me seem cool and unemotional so that my heart did not break with sorrow.

It was Rebecca who had suggested that we keep journals. We had sworn to record our adventures faithfully, keeping nothing back, so that we might one day share these experiences. I did not attempt to carry this out whilst still at the orphanage and it was not until that wonderful day when I looked my last on that hated place, that I obtained a suitable book and began my task.

I suppose I can truthfully say that my existence really began on a certain sunny day early in June 1901. When I awoke, I had no inkling that this was a momentous dawning. The morning started normally. I rose at five-thirty, washed in cold water and hurried to the hall for prayers. There were chores to do till nine, followed by three hours in the classroom. Later, I was sitting in the playground, dreamily watching the movement of the fluffy clouds, when Miss West came out of the door. She saw me and beckoned urgently. I wondered what I had done wrong now, looking back over my most recent essays, filled with guilty thoughts of untidy handwriting. I ran towards her, then pulled myself up for we were not supposed to rush about in an unseemly manner.

She was smiling, having about her an air of importance which I guessed concerned me. "Nell, my dear – Mrs Bowell says you are to go and put on your Sunday-best clothes at once. Wash your face and tidy your hair. I'll come and help you."

"Yes, miss – all right, miss. But why?" I ventured as we walked swiftly in the direction of the storeroom.

"You have visitors," she said mysteriously, and her face was almost merry.

My heart leaped and I nearly stopped, but she would not have me dally, taking my hand and pulling me along. "Who is it?" I gasped, and all the time hope was ringing a joy-bell within me.

My father has come, I thought, the pent-up disappointment of years rushing through me like an avalanche, bursting down the barrier of cold, uncaring reserve which I had painfully erected. It must be him. Who else would visit me? It could not be Nancy or Rebecca. They wouldn't have had time to establish themselves in positions where they could return in triumph and, knowing their stubborn pride, this was the only way they would ever come back.

"It is not for me to say," Miss West replied, but her voice was light, as if she was bubbling with a secret she was dying to divulge. "You'll just have to wait till you get to Mrs Bowell's room."

I took off my soiled dress and donned a clean one. Miss West brushed my hair, then helped me to set my cap straight, even allowing me to look in the mirror. I stared at myself critically. There I stood, neat and well-scrubbed, a presentable daughter for any man. Oh, what would he think of me? Would I recognise him? Miss West had said "visitors" so he had not come alone. The idea that he might have married again was like a knife thrust into my heart. My mother had died when I was a baby, so he had told me, and when he had spoken of her it had been with love. I prayed that he had not been disloyal to her memory.

I felt sick as I waited at Mrs Bowell's door. I was shaking and my palms were wet. I wanted to run. Supposing he was disappointed in me? What if, having checked to see that I was all right, he went away again? I knew that I shouldn't be able to bear that and, with a feeling akin to hysterical panic, I turned the doorknob when Mrs Bowell called me.

I stepped inside and closed the door behind me. I was blind for amoment, my mind registering nothing. Then the blur formed into vision and I saw her rise, coming towards me, putting her arm around my shoulders and leading me forward. "There you are, Nell, my dear child. See who has come looking for you." Her fingers dug into my flesh and the message was as clear as if she had hissed the words into my ear: "Behave yourself! Disgrace me in front of them and it will be the worse for you!"

There were three people in the room and none of them was my father. I refused to believe it, my eyes still seeking him. Two middle-aged ladies were seated on either side of the fireplace, staring at me as if they had seen a ghost. A thickset man with iron-grey hair and fiercely twirled military moustaches was fixing me with his eyes, an expression of astonishment on his tanned face. He found his voice at last, and: "Jove!" he gasped. "She's Marianne to the life! Extraordinary! I've never seen anything like it!"

"The child is overcome," gushed Mrs Bowell. "Such a sweet temper and very clever too. Of course, I have personally supervised her. Always top of her class and a shining example with her modest, obedient behaviour. We're like one big, happy family here, Colonel Curzon, and it will grieve me to part with her. She'll miss me as well, I expect. Won't you, my love?"

Again, the pinching finger on my shoulder. Her arm was heavy and I wished she would lift it. I was so bewildered that I forgot myself, shrugging her off, rounding on the man and demanding: "Where's my father? I thought he had come for me. Who are you?"

I met his keen scrutiny and he did not seem in the least shocked by my outburst. Indeed, he was overcome with emotion and quite as disconcerted as I. His voice was commanding and cultured, but there was a break in it as he said: "Steady there, m'dear. I realise that this must be a tremendous surprise for you, and I'll explain if you'll give me half a chance. I'm your grandfather on your mother's side, and these ladies are your great-aunts – Miss Maude and Miss Louisa Curzon. We have come to take you home to Cheshire. I can't begin to tell you how delighted I am to have found you." He drew out a large white handkerchief and blew his nose resoundingly.

My grandfather? My aunts? Suddenly, I had a family – and I was leaving with them. It was really happening, this thing I had dreamed about but, as I've since found is often the case, life had given me what I wanted, yet not quite in the way I had wanted it. "My father . . ." I said, my voice expressionless. "Where is he? He promised to fetch me."

The ladies were glancing at one another uneasily, then

at me and lastly, at their brother. He cleared his throat and fidgeted with his watch-chain, pressing his lips together thoughtfully as if not knowing how to frame his reply. Then he brought it out abruptly, and how else could such news be broken? "Your father has been dead for nine years, Eleanor."

Dead? My father was dead. I felt cheated, outraged. How many silent tears had I wasted? How many hours had I spent, planning what we would do when he came for me? All the time, he had been rotting in his grave. I should have known. If there was any truth in God and his holy angels, then they should have appeared in a vision, and told me. Nothing – no hint, no feeling, no supernatural knowledge that it was hopeless. In vain I had pleaded for someone, somewhere, to let him return to me.

I stood mute and, no doubt moved by my unhappy face, the Colonel reached out one of his gnarled hands and patted me on the head. "There, there, child – don't grieve. He was very ill, you see. That's why he brought you here. He knew that he didn't have long to live and wanted to be sure that you were sheltered and cared for. There was no one else to help. Your aunts and I were abroad. It's a long, sad story and I'll tell you about it later. Come, cheer up – get your kit together, say goodbye to Mrs Bowell and we'll be on our way. We've a train to catch and a lengthy journey ahead."

The younger of the two ladies smiled across at me and said: "I do so hope you will be happy with us, Eleanor. We were absolutely delighted when we arrived in London and found a letter with our solicitor telling us about you. My dear, it will be splendid to have a pretty young person to look after, instead of a crusty old soldier like your grandfather." Here she twinkled at her brother. "And think what fun we'll have taking you shopping!"

Aunt Maude was more plainly attired than Aunt Louisa, and she looked as if she could be something of a martinet, yet there was kindness warming her voice as she added her word. "You'll have to help us, Eleanor. We haven't lived in England for years and I dare say things have changed somewhat."

It did not take long for me to pack my meagre possessions. All the while, I neither spoke to nor looked at Mrs Bowell who hovered, unusually nervous, at my side. Then my newfound relatives conducted me to a hansom cab which was waiting at the gates. I felt it move, rolling smoothly, bearing me away from the orphanage. It had happened too swiftly for me to begin to sort out my thoughts and I sat there silently while my aunts chattered.

"Lord, what a grim place!" said the Colonel, his hands clasped round the silver-mounted top of his cane. "Disgraceful to think that Marianne was brought to such strains that her child became a foundling. How could Stephen Sheldon have allowed it to happen?"

"I suppose he had little choice," murmured Louisa, smoothing the wrinkles out of her lavender kid gloves thoughtfully. "What else could he have done? We were in India, and he had no family."

"He was a fool!" came the growled reply. "He should never have married her, snatching her from me. Runaway matches rarely prosper, and my poor daughter died as a result."

"Hush, Frank – the child," murmured Louisa, casting a warning glance at me. There was no further talk for we arrived then at Temple Meads station. By this time, the pain of my father's death had diminished to a dull ache, and my ears had pricked when they mentioned my mother. The actuality of the situation began to take hold of me. This was no dream.

My control had returned, so that I was able to enter the first-class compartment as if born to travel in such luxury. The train steamed out of the station and before very long a white-coated steward announced that luncheon was being served. Soon I sat on a padded red plush chair with a small table dividing me from my grandfather. Across the gangway were my aunts, stiff-backed and elegant, the ostrich feathers in their huge hats nodding gently over the menu. I kept finding my grandfather looking at me with that air of disbelief, but he controlled his emotion, unaccustomed to letting his feelings get the better of him. I stared back at him. He was well over sixty, but his upright bearing was that of a much younger man. There were laughter lines around his mouth and creases about his eyes as if he had spent much time peering into the distance in search of the enemy.

Lunch was certainly far removed from orphanage fare. The Colonel ate sparingly himself while I tucked in, then he poured two glasses of red wine and sat back, dabbing his lips with a napkin. "You look as if you were starving m'dear," he remarked quietly. "Didn't they feed you properly?"

"We never had enough, sir, and if we were naughty they put us on bread and water." I answered promptly, encouraged by the compassion in his eyes.

His face became stern. "Then Mrs Bowell was lying. I'll report her to the authorities and see that she's kicked out!"

I loved him from that moment onwards. He was my champion – an elderly King Arthur. During the afternoon, as the train roared onwards, he talked to me. From him I learned my history and the tale of my mother, Marianne, and Stephen Sheldon. There was much in it to appeal to my romantic nature. Marianne had been born in India and spent her childhood there until her mother died of malaria. She had been sent home to England to be reared by Maude and Louisa. All went well for a while, but she grew to be headstrong and, at sixteen, fell in love with her tutor, the man who was my father.

I was fascinated, as one always is when it is something to do with one's own entry into the world. I leaned my head back against the white antimacassar protecting the carriage seat, and his voice rolled on, mingling and merging with the churning of the wheels. Occasionally I asked a question and the Colonel was quite frank in his answers, keeping nothing from me. I was grateful to him for that, it made me feel mature, as if he trusted me to be sensible. He said that, as time passed, letters from his sisters had become increasingly anxious.

Maude and Louisa joined in then, filling in details. Marianne had been so lovely, but so wilful – she simply would not listen when they told her that Stephen was not of her class – it was unthinkable! Why, a tutor was not even invited to eat with the family who employed him, let alone court one of the daughters! The Colonel had come home on leave. He and Marianne had quarrelled violently. He had forbidden her to see my father again and had packed her off to a finishing school, returning to his regiment in Bombay. Two weeks after his departure, she had eloped. She and my father were married at Gretna Green and every trace of them was lost. In a black rage, the Colonel had shut his manor in Cheshire and shipped his sisters out to join him.

"But they loved one another," I said at last, when he had grown silent, lost in thought. "He was a fine man – kind and good."

He sighed as if suddenly terribly tired, and the lines on his face were deeply carved, lines of grief, sorrow and regret. "I know that now, Eleanor."

"We tried to find her – we really did," put in Louisa. "We thought that perhaps they had emigrated to Australia. It was not easy to make enquiries as we were in India."

"We were very busy there. Your grandfather was an important man and we put his interests above all else," added Maude, her eyes resting on her brother lovingly, protectively. I later realised that she was almost maternal in her devotion, whereas Louisa was of a flighty disposition, much more fun to be with than her serious sister.

"Shouldn't have know of your existence, child, had it not been for my poor health," the Colonel continued. "Damn fool of a medic said I must retire on account of a dicky heart. So I handed in my resignation and we took the boat home. I visited my solicitor and he gave me a letter, left with him by your father, years ago."

"What did it say?" I was on the edge of my seat by now.

"In it he begged my forgiveness and expressed his abiding love for Marianne." His voice was gruff and he stared unseeingly at the landscape flashing past the train window. "He said that they had been so happy during the brief time they had had together. Unfortunately, his fortunes had declined. Work was hard to come by. They were poor, though he did a little tutoring whilst working on his manuscripts. He aspired to be a writer, you see – an uncertain occupation. Marianne was ill. The doctors said it was consumption. He couldn't afford medical treatment and she, so proud and stubborn, would not allow him to ask me for help. After she died, he struggled on, bringing you up, but he had caught the illness from her and knew that there was no hope. That's why he took you to the orphanage, but, even at the last, he thought of you, entrusting the letter to my lawyer. We don't know what happened to him, but presume that he died in a workhouse hospital."

A stange peace stole over me now that I knew the truth. I had roots, forebears and relatives. My parents had been married and I was not a bastard. I was important. I was Somebody! I was on my way to Henford Grange, the family seat in Cheshire.

It was to be my home for the next three years. It was a quaint old house with a steeply gabled roof and mullioned windows. It had irregular rooms with pointed casements dating back to the fourteenth century, and thick oaken doors. There were cellars and attics, outbuildings and stables, a Great Hall, a Long Gallery, in fact everything to delight me. I fell in love with it at first sight on that evening when we left grimy Macclesfield behind, proceeding by carriage along a road which wound upwards between richly wooded hills.

I remember that it was sunset, and the herons were coming to roost in the fir trees, long shadows lying across the moors and deep dales. The coach stopped when we reached the moated grange. From the crooked chimney-pots smoke curled lazily, and each diamond-paned window was aflame with the light of the dying sun. I knew the place, how I cannot tell. Perhaps it was something in my blood which recognised it for it had been in the possession of the Curzons for centuries. Bristol seemed a million miles away. It was as if I had never left Henford Grange. No aspect of it surprised me and, when I explored further, I had that same feeling of belonging.

The Colonel was overjoyed at my interest and I adjusted to my new life with hardly any effort. Of course, like any Cinderella, I had much to learn, but I took it in my stride. Louisa expressed amazement at my cool acceptance and I think it rather baffled her. I recall that she remarked when I had been there some time. "You are always so unreachable, Eleanor. You don't appear to want anyone to be close to you."

I was unstinting in my admiration of the house, though. I like to think that the old place which had dozed unoccupied for over fifteen years now stretched and awoke, restored to its former glory. Every room was spring-cleaned, money and time spent on repairs and restoration. While this was happening, with an army of workmen moving in with paint pots and hammers, the aunts and I shopped.

Money was no object, and I was soon equipped like a princess with outfits for every occasion and each hour of the day. My grandfather bought me a horse and taught me to ride. I spent hours with the dressmaker and when she had done with me, there were lessons with drawing, dancing and deportment masters. I was being groomed to take my place as the Curzon heiress. It seemed that the Colonel was determined to put the clock back and treat me as he might have done my mother, had circumstances allowed. In his mind, I think, he confused us. Sometimes, he even called me by her name. He could be forgiven for this, for my likeness to her was uncanny, as photographs showed.

Gradually, he resumed his old position in the country, a much respected member of the community. Despite his doctor's warning about avoiding too much excitement and exertion, he became Master of the Hunt. These were halcyon days. I rode with my grandfather or, wearing rubber boots and oilskins, tramped the wild moors with Aunt Maude, a stickler for outdoor exercise. Louisa, however, encouraged my interest in the extensive library and portrait gallery and told me the life story of every member of the family who stared out from the gilded frames. She was an incurable romantic and often spoke of one Douglas Parco-Stanley. He was the lost love of her youth and she adored being reminded of him. I played on this, keeping his memory in reserve for really important occasions requiring her collaboration. The portrait of a dashing cavalier ancestor in the Long Gallery reminded her of Douglas. So did every other handsome man she ever saw, never mind his size, shape or colouring. Darling Douglas, who had been slain by Kurdish tribesmen whilst serving with his regiment, had, as the years passed, gathered a halo of sainthood.

I was still very young. My hair had not been pinned up and my skirts were mid-calf and, despite my impatience, would remain so until my seventeenth birthday. However, I was sometimes allowed to stay up and attend the soirées which my fun-loving Aunt Louisa persuaded her brother were a necessary part of establishing our return to Cheshire. He was proud of me and enjoyed introducing me to his friends, the local squires and landowners and their ladies, who began to leave their calling cards. Louisa hinted that he was seeking a good marriage for me among the sons of his acquaintances, when I came of age. But this seemed a long way off and I did not bother my head about it.

It was as well that I enjoyed those years. Looking back, I see them as an innocent oasis of peace and contentment, vouchsafed me as if in compensation for my misery in Bristol, a serene interlude where, unbeknown, my spirit rested and gathered strength for the trials which lay ahead. It was not until I was nearly seventeen that I met Charles de Grendon, the man who was to turn my world upside down, and tilt the carefully balanced, harmonious scales so essential to my wellbeing.

Chapter 2

I woke on a lovely morning in early October and remembered at once that there was to be a hunt meeting in which the Colonel and Maude were to take part. I had been forbidden to join in as I had had a slight cold, but there was a party planned for that evening and this was some compensation.

My maidservant, Bertha Blakeley, bustled in with a jug of hot water, setting it down on the washstand and going across to draw back the sprigged dimity curtains with a jangle of brass rings. "Looks like the Colonel's going to have a fine day for his hunting," she announced and helped me into my dressing gown. "My word, but there's a fuss going on downstairs, miss. Anyone would think he's preparing to defend the place against a siege."

"On the warpath, is he?" I yawned, knowing how agitated he became, organising everything as if it were a military campaign.

"That he is, miss – no disrespect, of course, but he does like everything done just so. No half measures with Colonel Curzon. And Miss Maude is like his second in command. She never can forget that she was a *memsahib*, used to ordering darkies about."

"They're thoroughly enjoying themselves, Bertha," I said as I washed. "Loving every fraught minute. Where's Miss Louisa?"

"In the kitchen, miss – driving Cook crackers! It's going to be a splendid party, isn't is, miss?"

I nodded and we exchanged a smile. Bertha was three years my senior. It had only recently been decided that I needed the services of a personal maid and my aunts had been fussy in their choice. Bertha was a local girl, a niece of the housekeeper, and she knew her job, but this didn't mean that she was starchy and strait-laced. On the contrary, her beaming good nature and sense of fun were what I needed in this household of elderly persons. She was pert and energetic, rosy-cheeked and plump, filled with lively interest and curiosity, mingled with a fund of backstairs gossip and common-sense wisdom. I had not realised, till Bertha came, how much I had missed young company. Tactfully, I withheld the knowledge of our friendship from my aunts. They were fantatical about people keeping to their proper stations.

"You're going to wear that new dress, aren't you, miss!" Bertha's face appeared momentarily in the dressing-table mirror as she stood behind me, brushing my hair till it shone like gold satin. "Think of all the fine young gentlemen who've been invited. Why, you might be engaged to be married by this time next year."

I shrugged this off. I had not met anyone who remotely resembled the gallant heroes of my daydreams, although Louisa, her motive as transparent as glass, was constantly introducing me to this young man or that, praising their good looks, their breeding, their financial prospects. I was not sure that I wanted to marry. The physical aspect of it terrified me for I had had a most unpleasant experience with Mr Bowell once, when he had cornered me in the apple shed. He had been far gone in drink and had exposed himself.

Bertha was disappointed at my tepidity. She loved parties, eager to attire me and catch a glimpse of the other guests. "What are you going to do with yourself today, miss?" She changed the subject adroitly. "Will you help Miss Louisa?"

"There are one or two little tasks she has allotted to me. I have to assist with the floral arrangements," I replied, wondering why I suddenly felt so gloomy and unsettled. The memory of the disgusting Mr Bowell kept flashing into my mind. I remembered how he had pulled me close to him, breathing hard, mutering hoarsely. I shook myself and added: "I may go for a walk later. I thought I'd stand near the copse when Grandfather rides that way."

Yes, that's what I would do, I decided, a brisk walk would clear the cobwebs from my brain, so after performing my duties for Louisa, I pulled on my jacket and cut through the kitchen garden and across the fields to the spinney, there to await the passing of the huntsmen. The autumn sun was low over the meadows; wind buffeted the coarse, tussocky grass and lifted my hair. Shafts of sunlight glanced and flickered about me, lengthening and shortening as the breeze shifted the close-growing branches. The withering leaves shivered above and around me with a persistent dry whispering, a continual moving canopy of sound. In the distance, I could hear the calling of the horns through the clear air, and the sharp, excited barking of the hounds.

Then I saw the fox, a red-brown streak circling the hedge. He darted along in a zigzag manner while I stood still as a stone and he was unaware of me. For the first time ever, I was sharply aware of how horrible it must be to be hunted. I'd never thought about it when caught up in the fever of the chase, borne along on a hot wave of excitement as my horse pounded along beneath me. "Go it, fox," I whispered. "Give them the slip!" He found a break in the undergrowth and disappeared into the woods.

I heard the approach of hoofs and wanted to divert the rider, to give the fox a chance. The lane curved and I could not see who was galloping so fast. I scrambled down the slope, then my foot caught in a rut and I tumbled the rest of the way, sprawling in the mud. At the same moment, the horseman came charging round the bend. His mount reared and plunged as he reined in sharply to avoid trampling me. I saw the great beast's eyes rolling and his iron-clad hooves flying above me. I heard a deep, masculine voice swearing violently.

I got to my feet, muddy and dishevelled and furiously angry. The horse yielded to the pull on the bit and the terse commands of its owner. It quietened, blowing down its nostrils and tossing its mane.

"What the hell d'you think you're doing, jumping out like that, frightening my horse? You could have bloody well unseated me!" shouted the rider, his face black as thunder.

"You should look where you're going! Charging round that corner like an express train!" I yelled back, staring up at him. I had a quick impression of height and darkness and great breadth of shoulder beneath the hunting pink. He had lost his hat in the struggle for mastery. I was pleased to see that it had fallen into a puddle. A bright beam of light gleamed on his tousled, curling chestnut hair.

"You saucy bitch!" he snarled. "Get out of the way!" God, but he was arrogant. His very mien, his haughty face and cultured voice shouted it aloud.

"You owe me an apology," I glared at him stubbornly. "My skirt is covered in mud!"

"I've no objection if you take it off," he said with a wicked grin. "I'll dismount and help you, if you like."

He was insufferable. I felt at an immediate disadvantage, standing there at his stirrup, forced to look up at him. I could not but be aware of how the red wool jacket fitted his arms and shoulders to perfection, nor of how the white breeches revealed the hard strength of his legs, ending in shiny black boots. A high stock collar emphasised the sun-brown skin of his throat and hard, square-jawed face.

He was staring at me, his anger replaced by something else, equally alarming. As my eyes met his openly assessing gaze, my heart increased its tempo and I felt a crazy stab of excitement. They were the most unfathomable grey eyes I had ever seen, having a cold, clear, irresistible glitter in them which gave me a strange, melting sensation deep in my body – a sensation which I would much rather not have felt. His features had a magnificent regularity, with slightly flared nostrils and high, flat cheekbones, but it was his eyes, deep set under dark brows, which distinguished him – the extraordinary power and persuasiveness of his eyes.

With a great effort, I tore my gaze away. Who did he think he was gawking at? "This is my grandfather's land," I said stiffly. "I can have you thrown off it, if I wish."

A puzzled frown drew those formidable brows together. He turned his head to face me fully and, with a shock of surprise, I saw that the right side was marked by the thin line of a scar. Strangely, this in no way spoiled his looks, in fact it gave him a swashbuckling appearance which had instant appeal, suggesting that he had acquired it during a duel. I saw it and then promptly forgot it, mesmerised by his mouth which was curved into another impudent grin.

"Your grandfather?" he replied with a touch of disbelief. "You mean to tell me that you're Colonel Curzon's long-lost granddaugther?"

"Yes," I answered with tight satisfaction. "I'm Eleanor Sheldon. I think you will agree that I've more right to be here than you. And I didn't jump out, as you so crudely put it – I slipped."

I could have bitten off my tongue for this seemed to amuse him even more. He threw back his head and laughed mockingly. "Oh, dear me. Well, Miss Sheldon, it seems that I shall have to apologise after all." His eyes met mine again, bright and cold, the dark lashes making a fringed shadow round them. "Will you accept it? It would be pleasant if we could get on, for we're close neighbours, you know."

"Yes, I'll accept it," I said, stiff with dignity, stifling my rage at his derision. "I didn't realise that you lived near here. I've not seen you in the village."

"I've only recently returned from abroad," he replied, and I wished that he would stop staring at me like that – it was extremely rude of him. I had the distinct feeling that he was trying to imagine what I would look like without my clothes. "I'm Charles de Grendon of Combermere," he added, with an ironic bow over his horse's ebony mane.

The horn rang out again, followed by a renewal of the furious barking. His head shot up and his strong hands tightened on the reins. "You'd better go," I said coolly. "I'm sure you don't want to miss the kill."

Again, that maddening smile, that slow, embracing glance. "I need my hat," he said. "I'm certain that you wouldn't want me to risk cracking my skull without it."

"Mr de Grendon," I answered levelly, "I shouldn't give a damn if you broke your neck!"

He clicked his tongue reprovingly. "Tut, tut! Such language. Well-bred young ladies aren't supposed to swear. Wherever did you learn it? Come along, be a good girl and pick up my hat."

Our eyes locked in a fierce battle of wills. I was tempted to grind my heel into his topper, but I couldn't. To my vexation, he beat me down, winning in the end.

With a snort of annoyance, I swooped on the thing, snatching it up and holding it out to him. "Blast you to hell!" I muttered. "Take your bloody hat!"

He seemed about to say something cutting, then changed his mind and smiled warmly instead. The total transformation of his features when he wished to be pleasant was quite remarkable. He captivated me with that smile. I remember thinking how unfair it was that he could turn on so much charm and yet act like a brute. My heart flipped right over. Without understanding anything at all about the complicated chemistry of desire, I instinctively recognised that here was a man whom most women would go mad about, and none could forget.

He took the hat as if it was his right to be waited on by me, then suddenly seized my hand and kissed the back of it. I felt the brush of those firm, warm lips, too astonished to move. Raising his head, he murmured: "Thank you for retrieving my rather soggy topper. I hope we'll meet again, Miss Sheldon."

"Not if I see you coming!" I retorted.

He grinned, clapped it on his head at a jaunty angle and took the lane at a brisk trot without glancing back. I was so confused that I stood there like an idiot, my hand burning with the imprint of his mouth, gazing after him even when he was lost to sight among the trees. I could see nothing but his hard stare, enigmatic smile and those terribly compulsive eyes. I shook myself, as if waking from a trance, and began walking up the winding path which led to the moors. As I went, I called Charles de Grendon every unpleasant name I could think of. He was an arrogant, overbearing bully and I'd like to teach him a sharp lesson. It occurred to me to complain to the Colonel about his behaviour, then I realised that he was of the hunting fraternity and, as one horseman to another, Grandfather would no doubt agree with him that I had been silly to startle his already high-strung mount.

This angry and, I'll admit, alarmed monologue went on in my head as I climbed. The damned man had succeeded in smashing my calm reserve. I never let anything touch me, if I could help it, my emotions firmly controlled, but he had raised such a storm of anger within me that I wanted to scream and stamp. It was degrading. I never wanted to clap eyes on him again.

Presently I reached the windy top of the crag where the moorland rolled away from me, bright with wide sheets of purple heather and ruddy clumps of cloudberries. Here and there lay darker patches of green where the peaty water had formed into treacherous bogs. Curiosity took me to a spot where I could overlook the next dale. He had said that he owned Combermere and there it lay, like a toy at the base of the hill, a sprawling homestead. A thick group of trees and a rough stone wall guarded a ragged, grass-grown courtyard. In the grey light, it looked cold and desolate, with a steep roof and latticed windows. At the rear were a cluster of outhouses and sheds, dropping away to barns and shabby farm byres. There were ornamental chimneys and dormer windows like scowling eyebrows, and the front door was imposing, but the rest of it was low and tumbledown and forsaken. So this is the castle of that unfuriating individual! I thought, pleased to see that it was nothing like so fine and well maintained as Henford Grange. Devil take him! He certainly had little to be proud of.

The moors were dark and sombre now. I snuffed the quiver of rain in the wind before even the first faint webs floated down from those weird, orange-tipped clouds – huge grey clouds, rent and ragged, loaded with moisture, moving ponderously yet swiftly above the tossing gorse. Yellow and russet leaves went whirling over my head, the increasing wind roaring through the valley. It was raining hard as I retraced my steps, the storm in keeping with my mood. Lord, how it could rain on those hills. The steely clouds massed over the crags, the heavens opened and the rain descended, drifting in sheets, blotting out the landscape, soaking me within a few minutes. Good, I thought bitterly as I squelched through the slough of water-filled ruts, he'll be as wet as I. That should cramp his style, the bastard!

I liked the rain about as much as a cat does and was in a truly foul temper, my skirt waterlogged, my jacket and blouse clinging to my skin, my hair dripping down my face, my only consolation being that he must be as cold and drenched as I. But the devil looks after his own, so they say, and ensured that his hunting was not blighted. Away over the hills there was blue sky, and before I had gone far, the storm rolled off. Everything looked brighter for its wetting. When the sun burst out, tiny diamonds sparkled on the heather and crystal drops lay on every bilberry leaf, while the wind shivered a glittering shower from the evergreens. Glumly, I supposed that he had probably been sheltering under some trees, laughing and joking with other members of the hunt – particularly the ladies.

At seven o'clock that evening we were ready to receive our guests. Bertha had helped me to dress and I wore a simple white lace dress which swirled out just above my silk slippers. Louisa had given me a necklace from her jewel case, a fragile thing of seed pearls and gold, saying that it would look well with my delicate colouring. I went in to display myself, twirling around so that she might view me from all sides, and she expressed her satisfaction. She rose, elegant and stately and – with fan, cashmere shawl and beaded bag – was ready to leave her chamber and descend the staircase.

There was a tap on the door and Maude appeared, asking if we were ready. She was resplendent in velvet of a purple shade which did not agree with her full-blooded complexion, holding herself so correctly that it looked as if she had a poker for a backbone.

"Ah, there you, Eleanor. Is your cold better?" she

said on seeing me. "My word, you do look smart. Pity you couldn't ride today – capital sport. Couldn't wait to get into the saddle when I was a girl. Blooded when I was twelve. D'you remember, Louisa? You were rather squeamish, I recall."

"Really, Maude, must you talk of it?" Louisa said, rather pained. "And I do hope that the conversation at dinner doesn't follow similar lines. There are other topics, you know."

"Nothing else worth talking about – not in the country," said Maude heartily and, bickering half-heartedly, they led me to the landing where there was an uninterrupted view of the Great Hall. Some of the guests were already there. They had been selected with care and by now I was familiar with the social distinctions. There were simply certain classes of people with whom one did not mix. Army or naval officers, diplomats and higher clergymen might be invited to lunch or dinner. The vicar could be asked to Sunday luncheon, if he was a gentleman. Doctors and solicitors sometimes attended garden parties, but anyone engaged in the arts, the stage, trade or commerce, no matter how well connected, was never invited to the house at all.

The men had left their hats and coats in the vestibule, and were waiting for their ladies to emerge from the dressing room. They disappeared within as mere chrysalids, swathed in furs and wraps, later returning as gorgeous butterflies, shimmering with greens and blues and mauves. As each came floating out, her escort offered her his arm and they made their way to the drawing room.

Grandfather was below, very handsome and distinguished in his evening suit. With shoulders squared and posture erect, he greeted his guests as they entered. I saw him step forward to shake hands with someone who had just come in. I stared hard, recognising him with something akin to panic. There was a cloaked lady with him.

"Well, bless my soul," breathed Louisa, pausing at the head of the stairs. "I know that man, though it's years since I've seen him. It's Charles de Grendon and his sister, Cordelia."

I was unable to take my eyes from that tall, powerful figure, seeing how at ease he was. The ladies dallied to talk with him and my aunts were no exception, though I hung back, listening to their voices and his drawled rejoinders, until the Colonel put out an arm and drew me into the circle. We were introduced and my embarrassment was acute, especially when Charles's grey eyes lingered on me with amusement and he held my gloved hand an instant longer than decorum permitted. He didn't mention that we had already met, and neither did I, but this shared secret infuriated me. I wanted no bond of any kind with him. The general talk was of the day's sport. The conversation dipped and swelled as we stood in the ancient hall with its decorations of crossed pikes, shields and tattered banners, with a minstrels' gallery high up on one side. And then, as the dinner gong boomed, Cordelia de Grendon stood poised in the doorway, looking across at us. It was a dramatic entry and she held it effectively.

She was extremely beautiful, the most striking woman there. The resemblance to her brother was very marked, but in her case the de Grendon features had been softened by femininity. She had the same pronounced cheekbones, the same proud, narrow nose, but nature had been more gentle in the moulding. Though her hair was of a similar rich chestnut shade, her eyes held the changing greys of a stormy sea, not the cold steel of his.

'Cordelia, how delightful to have you living here again. We are all of us like exiles returning to the homeland, it seems," said the Colonel, bowing over her hand.

"You have the edge on us, sir. We have but recently left Europe, whereas you have been back some time." Her voice was low and yet gay, and she drew every glance.

I stared at her whilst trying to appear not to. She was taller than I and her figure was lush. Her gold satin gown fitted her body closely to below the hips where the skirt belled out to the floor, swirling into a train. The bodice was a deep oval, and her superb bosom swelled alluringly above its cream lace trim. Her shoulders were bare, two tiny sequinned straps keeping the bodice in place, and her fine arms were naked above the long white kid gloves. Jewels sparkled in her ears, at her throat and wrists, and her hair was most elaborately dressed about her handsome head.

She rested her hand lightly on her brother's arm as they sauntered in the direction of the dining room. His head was bent to hear something she was saying, and her laughter rang out. Were they talking about me? I wondered angrily. Had he told her about the incident near the spinney? I was convinced that he had.

When I took my place at the long oval table, I was relieved to see that the de Grendons were far down on the opposite side. The room was magnificent, filled with Hepplewhite furniture. The fireplace had been designed in marble by Adam, the hangings at the narrow windows were of rich damask, the whole scene lit by three enormous chandeliers sparkling with hundreds of candles. It glowed on the snowy linen, the silver cutlery, the wineglasses, and the service of Copeland china. Against the wall was a great walnut sideboard on which stood the decanters. Under the stern eye of the butler, the smartly liveried flunkies played their part, bearing in the numerous platters of food.

Our guests chatted whilst they ate and their subjects were almost entirely hunting, shooting, archery and croquet, the weather and the latest mismanagements of the government, but they soon drifted back to country matters again. Though one of them was a magistrate, it seemed that poaching was regarded much as smuggling had been in the past, with a certain feeling of sympathetic toleration. Then, above the general buzz of conversation, I saw a jolly, ruddy-faced man lean across Cordelia and address her brother. "So, you lucky devil – you've just come back from Monte Carlo, have you?"

Charles gave his unrevealing smile and nodded. "That is correct, Major Arlington, my sister and I have been out of the country for over three years. It's good to be home."

"Dammit, is it as long as that? Thought I hadn't seen you about – missed you at the races." The Major was smiling at Cordelia who cast her eyes down demurely. "Hope we'll see a lot of you now, eh what? Did you visit the casinos? How was the play? Damned costly sport, what? I like a game of cards, of course. Play faro at my club, but stick to racing mostly – nags are more trustworthy than croupiers, don't-cher-know?"

Louisa was nudging me and I realised that one of the footmen wanted to remove my plate. I missed Charles's reply, but he must have made some witty comment for the Major was guffawing loudly. Round and round rippled the talk, accompanied by the clink of glasses, the arrival of further dishes.

"You are very quiet, Eleanor," said Louisa. "Aren't you feeling well?"

"I'm perfectly well, thank you, Aunt," I answered calmly. I knew that she was piqued because I wasn't talking to the youth whom she had purposely placed next to me, no doubt hoping that a romance might blossom. His father was an earl. Then Aunt Maude caught the ladies' eyes and they collected their fans and shawls, and we left the gentlemen to their port. She marched us to the drawing room.

"Isn't Eleanor a charming child, Miss Curzon?" gushed one amiable dowager. I bridled at her patronising air. It was as if she was viewing a circus freak, gazing at me through her lorgnette.

"I didn't realise that Marianne had had a daughter," commented Cordelia who had draped herself gracefully on a small couch near the fire. "This must have been a shock for the Colonel. She looks very like her mother."

"Not so much a shock as a pleasant surprise," corrected Maude, levelling her a stern look.

Cordelia shrugged her shapely shoulders and half turned to converse with one of the younger women. She had spoken as if she had known my mother and I detained her, my hand on her arm. "Please, Miss de Grendon, were you friends?"

Cool grey eyes stared into mine, shuttered, aloof. She exuded a polite, unhelpful warmth. "But of course, my dear. She was older than me, but we were companions when she came back from India." Those eyes considered me carefully. She was confident and self-possessed but I stared back at her with lifted chin, equally assured.

"I would so much like to talk to you about her," I said. "You see, I can't remember her for she died when I was a baby. I've seen photographs of her since I came here, but I would appreciate anything you can tell me." Though convinced that she and I could never be friends, there was something fascinating there. She was such a splendidly handsome creature.

"I should be delighted," she drawled, sounding very much like Charles. "You must come and take tea with me at Combermere."

I sat on the edge of my chair, my hands folded sedately in my lap, but inside I was in a ferment. These people had known my mother. Although my aunts had filled in many details of her life, I was eager to learn more. The other women were talking of their children, interminable tales of lazy nannies and governesses and I guessed that Cordelia must be as bored as I. After a while, she butted in, launching into rather scandalous anecdotes of her life in Paris, Venice and the Riviera. I suspected that she was amusing herself at their expense. They viewed her askance. She was too lovely, too worldly and, worst of all, still single, a threat to domestic peace. Though perfectly acceptable in the social sense, she had about her the unmistakable stamp of the adventuress. Their hackles were up.

This was turning out to be a most disturbing evening and, under my façade of calm, my thoughts were running wild. It was Charles who had robbed my heart of serenity. It was as if his face and form were seared into my brain. A thrill of anger, alarm – and something else as yet unnamed – raced through me. I recalled his tall, broad-shouldered body, that aura of reckless passion which had seemed to reach out and engulf me as I had picked myself up from the muck of the lane. Bedevilled and infuriated, I told myself vehemently to stop being so foolish, mooning over a conceited bully who would most likely bore me to death with his eternal talk of gambling and hunting. I was tortured by dislike and attraction, flung in at the deep end of sexual arousal without having the least comprehension of the dark, violent force which was about to swamp me.

Presently, I slipped away, unnoticed by anyone save Cordelia who watched me go with a musing smile playing about her crimson, cushiony mouth. I knew that soon the music salon would be filling up, for an entertainment was planned. I wanted to be alone to collect myself before facing Charles, so I went out on to the terrace.

It was chilly there but I did not mind that, standing by the stone balustrade, my fingers idly tracing the swags and festoons on a bronze urn. Time seemed to be in suspension. It was as if the night held its breath – waiting, waiting – as I did. It was misty, with a young moon brightening the mist to a luminous, half-transparent veil. From the flower beds came a damp, aromatic scent. I was expecting to hear footsteps and, sure enough, they came, light and swift from the direction of the house. There stood Charles, a cigar glowing between his fingers.

"Hello – tired of the chitchat?" he asked, as if it was the most natural thing in the world to find me there.

"I'm glad that I'm not a woman, condemned to such tedious nonsense. You don't object to tobacco smoke, do you? The Colonel said I wasn't to light up in the dining room for the smell would offend your aunts. So I thought I'd take a turn out here. They're not so fussy abroad – I've seen ladies smoking there."

I could find nothing to say to him, and he leaned back against the balustrade, long legs stretched out, calmly smoking and staring at me in a quizzical way. "Are you still annoyed with me?" His voice was like the purring of a jungle cat. "I'm sorry that I reacted so violently, but I was concerned for your safety. My hunter is a fiery old fellow."

I wondered why he was going out of his way to be so polite. "That's perfectly all right, Mr de Grendon," I replied frostily. "I suggest that we let the matter drop."

"Will you visit us at Combermere?" There was a challenge in his eyes.

"Your sister has already very kindly invited me." While my lips formed the correct words. I was marvelling at my ability to do so when all I really wanted was to sample the things which his mouth and eyes promised.

"Good. Make it tomorrow – after you've met me in the spinney." He spoke in a matter-of-fact way as if everything was arranged between us.

"I can't meet you. Don't be so ridiculous!" I protested, but while I spoke these conventional words of protest, my heart was saying yes! Yes!

He reached out and touched my face, tipping my chin up until my eyes met his. There was something in them now which made me feel hot and uncomfortable. "You can. You will." The intimate note in his voice made me shiver. "Don't even dare to refuse me. How old are you?"

"Seventeen in two weeks." I was glad that he had released me, stepping back a pace carefully, struggling to make it appear that I was moving naturally, because

I wanted to, not through the fear of what I might do if we stayed close.

"Seventeen, eh? The same age as your mother when she ran off with her tutor. Oh, yes. I know the story, though there are some here who don't remember. So, you were the result of this hasty union. Your grandfather found you in an orphanage, didn't he?"

This made me angry again. Why did he have to mention it? He might have had the good grace to keep his mouth shut! Did he think that because of this stigma I was easy game and he need not respect me? Grandfather had considered inventing a different tale to spread abroad but he had opted for the truth. It would have been better for me if he had lied. I tried to brazen it out. "You seem to be well acquainted with the facts. Yes, I was raised as an orphan. It was not an experience I wish to remember."

"I'm sorry." He was instantly contrite. "I didn't mean to hurt you, but it's as well that there are no secrets between us from the start."

The admiration in his eyes disturbed me; the charming smile on his lips disturbed me; everything about him disturbed me in a way which was both potent and important. I was achingly aware of him standing so near me. "It is always better if people speak the truth," I said primly, trying with a kind of frantic desperation to throw up barriers.

He laughed, and his expression was sardonic. "That depends, the truth can sometimes be painful. You, my lovely ice maiden, are very young and, I would say, totally inexperienced. You have much to learn and I shall love teaching you – when we are married."

"Married!" I gasped. "What do you mean?"

This seemed to amuse him, a slow smile began to curve his mouth and his eyes roamed lazily over my face. "I intend to ask the Colonel for your hand. Is there any reason why I shouldn't? What could be more natural than the joining of two such illustrious families? Do you find the prospect displeasing? Am I repulsive to you?"

I stared up into that intensely masculine face, a queer, choking sensation in my throat. Such cool assumption took my breath away. "I don't want to be married, and certainly not to you," I said tartly.

"Why not?" he chuckled. "A lot of women would jump at the chance."

Such conceit was not to be tolerated. "You're much older than me," I flared back at him.

If I had hoped that this would bring him down a peg, I was sadly mistaken. "And is that such a bad thing?" he replied gaily. "A young bride needs a man of the world who knows how to make love to her. Some awkward, fumbling boy would not suit you at all. I know what's good for you, and your grandfather will agree. It will be an ideal match, of benefit to both parties. He'll recognise this."

"And if he doesn't?" My head was whirling.

His eyes gleamed with wicked humour, yet there was a ruthless slant to his mouth. "Then, my dear, I shall seduce you. For the sake of your reputation, he'll have to agree. I want you, Eleanor, and am determined to have you. You'll learn that I always get what I want, by fair means or foul."

"You are frank – I'll grant you that!" I snapped, quivering with indignation. "But how dare you presume to know what's best for me? I have the right to choose my own destiny. I have no intention of marrying yet, and when I do it will be to a man I love and admire – someone who will care for me all his life long."

"Look no further. I am that man," he countered, almost indolently relaxed and unconcerned, as if he were perfectly certain of the outcome. It was most galling. He was a vain, high-handed dictator, and I wanted to tell him exactly what I thought of him. To my chagrin, he seemed to read my mind and his amusement increased. "Go on – say it," he urged, coming closer. 'Look into my eyes and tell me that you hate me. Tell me that you don't want to marry me."

"Very well!" I shouted desperately. "I do hate you and you're the last man alive I want to marry!"

"You are a poor liar, darling," he laughed. "You know as well as I do that the die was cast this morning." He sobered suddenly, his voice low and tense. "Don't ask me how or why it happened. I only know that you're the most beautiful girl I've seen in a long time. There's something about you so attractive to me that I'll move heaven and earth to possess you. Let's give the locals a fresh item of gossip, shall we? We'll announce our engagement on your birthday."

"You're very confident, aren't you?" I said shakily, feeling that I was being carried along by a tidal wave.

"But of course. Why not?"

Why not indeed! He had the assurance of the ruling classes. He was handsome and he was wealthy. At least, I supposed him to be, though the appearance of Combermere hinted otherwise. I knew nothing about him, and I was annoyed to find that I wanted to know.

I could hear people entering the music salon. Now I could get away from him. He stabbed a quick glance at the curtained windows. "I must go in," I whispered.

His hands came out to grip me round the waist. I arched my back but he gave me a little shake. "No, don't struggle. Hush, we don't want them to hear us, do we?"

His breath was warm with brandy and Romanoff cigars and the combination had a powerful effect on me. Of their own accord my hands came to rest one on each of his upper arms. Beneath the cloth of his coat, I felt the muscles ripple as if they were separate entities running to do his bidding. It was an alarming, wonderful sensation, the like of which I had never experienced or imagined. Something leapt and sang in my blood.

He drew me against him, and I knew a moment of sheer terror before his mouth fastened on mine in a long, deep, possessive kiss. Any romantic, childish notions about love between men and women flew straight out of the window, never to return. The feel of his lips, warm and devouring, infused through my whole body a delicious, aching desire which made me moan and cling to him, my arms creeping up about his neck, my fingers burying themselves in the thick, curling hair at his nape. It was a strange, throbbing, treacherous feeling which robbed me of thought. I wanted nothing but that it should go on and on.

Somewhere from the deepest recesses of my mind, danger signals were gradually interfering with the paralysing quality of his kisses. I began to push away from him, hearing him chuckle deep in his throat. He lifted his head and looked into my face, his eyes hard and metallic in the dim light. "A passionate little witch, eh?" he murmured as I buried my face against his chest, trembling as if feverish. "I knew it at first glance, when you looked at me with those great eyes, so angry, so indignant, but I knew better. You were trying to deny your own nature."

"Let me go," I pleaded, afraid and angry. My own body had betrayed me.

He did as I asked, withdrawing from me, and at once I wanted to be back in his arms. I forced my wayward hands to stay at my sides. "You'll meet me in the spinney tomorrow afternoon," he said. It was not a request – it was an order.

I wanted to defy him, to break this spell which was binding me, but I was literally speechless with emotion and desire. I saw his teeth gleam in a brief smile and then, completely composed, he strode to the door and disappeared within. I stayed there for a few moments, fighting to regain a semblance of calm. My pulse raced. My thoughts were jumbled. I needed to talk to someone about this. Oh, how I wished that Nancy would suddenly appear with her logical brain, or Rebecca – she'd know how to deal with such a persistent man. But my friends were long gone, and I had no idea how to reach them. Then I remembered Bertha. I would question her about Charles.

Filled with this resolution, I felt steadied enough to face the crowd inside. But: "Where have you been?" hissed Aunt Maude as I sidled round the window curtain in an attempt to slip into a chair unobserved.

Fortunately, there was a diversion as the Colonel managed to prevail upon Louisa to play the piano. She was escorted there by him while someone else was granted the privilege of turning the music sheets for her. She explained that she was terribly rusty, although I knew that she had been secretly practising for the past fortnight. She drew off her gloves and put them down on the piano lid with her fan, her rings and bracelets, then she ran her fingers up and down the keys as a signal for the chatter to cease.

Thank God for Aunt Louisa, I thought, now I could bury myself in my thoughs, quite undisturbed. My mouth burned from Charles's kisses and I felt almost delirious. Cordelia looked at me and one of her brows arched slightly, her eyes shining with amusement. She knows, I thought bleakly. I didn't dare glance at Charles, though every nerve in my body was aware of him seated beside her on the other side of the room. He seemed so cool, so politely interested in Louisa's performance that it was impossible to believe that only a few moments ago he had been making love to me and proposing marriage. I still heard his words ringing in my brain – "Tomorrow, at the spinney."

Useless to pretend that I wouldn't go. My fate was moving onward with remorseless inevitability. The rest of the concert passed in a dream and at last the carriages were announced and the guests said goodnight, with smiles and compliments. Charles and Cordelia were about to leave and he bowed over my hand, the message in his eyes clear and direct. He did not expect to be disappointed when he rode out next day.

Part of the entry in my diary for that day reads: "October 4th. I think the party was a great success and dear Aunt Louisa was the star of the evening. As for Charles de Grendon – well, what can I say? He's certainly very rude and domineering. He kissed me tonight and it was an astounding experience. Now I know why I have admired strong men for so long without really understanding the reason. Now I can appreciate why women fall in love with the most unsuitable rogues, throwing away their honour, their reputations, their very lives! I am determined not to tumble into this trap. He has offered me marriage. The impudence of the fellow! I refused him, of course, I have no intention of meeting him tomorrow!'

Chapter 3

My state of mind when I awoke the morning after the party can easily be imagined. I talked to Bertha about Charles de Grendon. To my dismay, her face clouded over when I mentioned his name. Born and bred in those parts, she knew each member of the families in the big houses. Gossip was the stuff of life to her.

"The de Grendons? Oh, yes, miss – live over at Combermere, they do. Leastways, they did live there till a while back when it was shut up and they went abroad. There's just the two of them. Their parents died years ago." She hesitated, and I sensed that there was more.

It was almost time for lunch and I had been fretting throughout the morning, unable to settle to anything, wracked by uncertainty. I ordered her to fetch my latest autumn outfit. "Are you going out, miss?" she asked, round-eyed with curiosity.

"Possibly, I haven't made up my mind," I answered

casually. I changed and then lingered in the doorway before I went to seek my aunts. "Bertha, what else do you know about the de Grendons?"

She gave me a penetrating look. I could feel my colour rising, realising that whatever I had discussed with her that morning – be it clothes, the party, even the weather – it had somehow or other turned back to them. "Well, miss – it's a noble family to be sure. It was a tragedy when their father and mother died, in an accident, I believe. Old Mr de Grendon was a fine man, a friend of the Colonel in his youth."

"And Miss Cordelia? She seems nice. I talked with her last night."

"Oh, she's a handsome woman, miss, but she's never married, though many have courted her." Bertha had grown serious, a frown puckering her brow. "They say she's devoted to her brother and has no desire to leave him and have a home of her own. They've travelled all over the place, and I'll hazard a guess that she was the belle of the ball in the smart resorts, while he would have spent his time at the gaming tables."

"He's a gambler?" This was nothing unusual. Most men of his class played cards for money or bet on horses.

"Yes, miss, he's a gambler and no mistake." I didn't much care for the way she said this, but I was intrigued. "He doesn't have the interest in the estate which his father had," she continued. "It's gone downhill since he inherited it, and I don't mind telling you, miss, around here he's considered to be a ne'er-do-well – a wild, unsettled sort of man."

"That's just idle gossip, Bertha," I exclaimed. "He's rich – he must be. You can tell that by his clothes and manners. I expect he made a pile abroad and the village hasn't got wind of it yet."

Bertha sniffed, offended by my tone. "Maybe so, miss. I know it isn't my place to speak ill of my betters, but if I was a young lady in your position, I'd steer well clear of him."

Rather disturbed by this, and also by the speed with which I had leapt to his defence, I left for the morning room. My aunts were resting there, recovering from the rigours of entertaining. Louisa said as soon as I entered: "Miss de Grendon asked me if you might go to tea at Combermere this afternoon. Isn't that nice? So kind of her to take an interest in you. I expect she will tell you about France, and do listen carefully, Eleanor. Your grandfather is thinking of sending you to a finishing school in Paris."

She lay on the chaise-longue. Her pekingese was curled up grumpily on her lap. She had named him General Goring, after her favourite royalist soldier, a roistering fellow who had served Charles I a couple of centuries before. So much attention last night had taken years off her. I loved her, my dear, frivolous Aunt Louisa. She had no objection to my meeting the rather notorious de Grendons. Bertha must be wrong in her assessment. Even Maude did not fault them, saying as she stumped across the room towards me: "She's a first-class horsewoman, bless my soul if she ain't! And as for him, well, there's no finer shot in England."

"And he's so handsome," sighed Louisa, playing with General Goring's silky ears. "He reminds me so much of poor, darling Douglas – he had that very same air of melancholy and reserve. I think he carries some sad secret in his soul, poor boy – crossed in love, perhaps."

"I don't know about his looks," said Maude rather severely. "I think he's a bit sinister with that scar."

"Not at all!" scoffed her sister, round and rosy as a cherub in her lavender dress and lacy cap. "It happened when he was at university. A fencing bout when they had forgotten to replace the buttons on their foils. He told me about it last night. Of course, they shouldn't have done it, the naughty things, but isn't it rather romantic and splendid! Just the sort of prank Douglas would have taken part in. He was born too late, I always said – should have been a courtly gallant."

I could feel myself softening, losing my grip on my resolve to spurn him. In my heart, I suppose, I wanted to think well of him. This process went on through lunch. Louisa seemed most taken with the glamorous brother and sister. I declared my intention to walk to Combermere. Louisa instructed me to allow Charles to drive me home as it grew dark early now. So, still uncertain but unable to keep away, I made my way across the fields towards the copse.

The afternoon was warmed by the pale sunshine which broke through now and again. I found the lane which followed the course of a clear stream. It was quiet in the valley and I paused on a small stone bridge which spanned the water, leaning over the gurgling water and thinking. I could deceive myself no longer. I wanted to see Charles again most desperately, but I was fearful too. Something warned me to consider it well. The bridge was a kind of no-man's land between my old life and the one now offered. I lingered there, wishing that time would stand still, thinking of carefree summer days when I had watched the wagtails make little sallies from the willows, catching the dancing gnats. Now many of the birds had gone, great sweeping arcs of them migrating in a southerly direction before the onset of winter. The robin was still about, bright-eyed and impudent, and a white-breasted dipper curtsied to me from a boulder. I had grown to love this country. The tree-crowned hills, the rugged escarpments, the open moors – they were a joy in any weather, at any season, so far removed from smoky Bristol and the orphanage.

My gold fob-watch told me it was three o'clock. I couldn't put it off any longer. I must either go on, or return to the safety of the Grange and forget Charles. I made my decision for good or ill, leaving the bridge behind me. When I came to the spinney, I felt a sharp pang of disappointment mingled with relief. He wasn't there. I paused, wondering what to do. I knew the direction of Combermere and was about to follow the path which led to the de Grendon land when I heard the jingle of harness close by. I spun round, seeing him leading his black horse from among the trees. My heart bounded up, and I was immediately annoyed because he had been clever enough to keep me in suspense. I had the feeling that he had been watching me. I was conscious of the sinister aspect of his scarred countenance, then he smiled and I forgot it, hypnotised by those unblinking grey eyes.

"Oh, I thought you had changed your mind," I said lightly, refusing to give him the satisfaction of knowing that I cared.

"And I feared that I had alarmed you last night." His voice was low, caressing, and he took my hands in his. When he touched me, every coherent thought fled, and I was reduced to a weak, bewildered state bordering, I think, on a kind of insanity. Reason left me, along with all remembrance of propriety, decency and decorum. My grandfather need not have bothered to waste his money on tutors or attempted to turn me into a lady. I became a primitive animal with no more control than the pagans who had once roamed these hills.

It was a raw, tribal feeling. Gone were my dreams of a noble knight who would woo me gently. Within the core of me now stood a wanton creature who responded to the touch of this man. I recognised the suppressed violence of him – he was strong, physically and mentally. I wanted him to hold me, to kiss me, to perform that act which Mr Bowell had attempted and from which I had shuddered away in disgust. The orphanage girls had whispered about it, making it seem so sordid. My aunts had never discussed it, but they had hinted that a refined lady did not enjoy her husband's embraces, bearing them nobly, from a sense of duty. It was only common trollops who liked it. In that case, I was exceedingly common, for I had never known such pleasure as his kiss had given me. This side of myself was a shocking revelation and it brought me to my senses.

I snatched my hands away. "I came to see your sister," I said. "Not you."

His face darkened and he scowled at me. "Really? You acted differently on the terrace, but no matter – I shall ask your grandfather if I may court you. In spite of what you say, we shall be married."

"You will be wasting your time." This was better, with distance between us I could defy him.

"I don't want an argument." I was glad to see that I had shaken him. He looked angry enough to strike me.

"You're not going to have one. I'm telling you plainly, this time you won't have your own way. I'd like to talk with Cordelia. I'd like to see Combermere – but that's all."

He did not answer for a moment and I held his gaze. The light was striking between the branches, running into his eyes, silvering them, then down across that bold nose and touching his lips. "I'm sorry that you feel like this," he said and his expression was sombre now. "You see, I've waited a long time to meet someone like you – beautiful, unspoilt. You have an austere quality which I admire, and are exceptionally mature for your age."

"Oh, come – you must have known many women," I protested while a thrill of pleasure ran through me.

"Yes, I have. I freely admit it, but I've been grievously disappointed in them and had practically made up my mind to remain single." He gave a wry smile and his eyes were sad. That look went straight to my heart. It was flattering to have such a man say that I was the woman of his dreams. Someone has hurt him badly in the past I thought. Aunt Louisa had noticed it too. It would be a challenge to prove to him that females could be loyal and loving.

But, still guarded, I replied: "I can't believe that you've been unlucky in love, though come to think of it, you were most rude to me yesterday. If you treat every woman you meet in such a boorish fashion, then it's not surprising that you've been unsuccessful."

He sighed, his long fingers stroking his horse's mane. "I expect you are right, but you see, I've grown to expect women to be foolish. You are different. I respect you – oh, yes I do – don't smile in that doubting way. If we can't be lovers, perhaps we can be friends."

I was not prepared for that. It was a moving moment. Friendship I could understand. This had been my salvation in the orphanage – the friendship of Rebecca and Nancy. "I would like that," I said, very low. "I know the value of friendship."

His eyes blazed and he smiled with delight, sadness slipping away from him. He took a step nearer to me and I did not move. "Ah, my dear – if this could only be so," he exclaimed, reaching for my hand and twining his fingers in mine. "It would give me such happiness. I've so much affection to give, and there's been no one to share it, apart from my sister. You see, we too were orphans, as parentless as yourself, though brought up at Combermere, with no lack of material comforts. We had an uncle who was our guardian, but he was unmarried and used to his freedom. He simply didn't know what to do with us. We rarely saw him, and he left us in the care of his valet, Joseph Duffield, and a governess. Cordelia and I were inseparable till I went away to school."

I was touched, picturing those two children, richly endowed with everything except loving parents. A curious, almost maternal feeling swept over me. I wanted to take him in my arms and kiss away the bitterness. "I know how you must have suffered, truly I do," I said. "It is terrible to know that there is no one in the world who really cares. You were lucky. You had your sister. I was so lonely until I met Nancy and Rebecca – they were orphanage inmates too. We formed a close bond."

"The loneliness. Yes, that is the worst part of it. How

sensitive and understanding you are, my dear." His mood had changed, the sadness gone, and I thought it was because of me. His smile was so brilliant that I could hardly bear to look at it. Very slowly, hesitantly, he reached out and lifted one of the ringlets which lay across my breast, lifting it to his lips. Then he said, soft as a conspirator: "Come, kiss me, friend."

Thus it was that passion took me, swiftly, unexpectedly. I had hoped that I might fall in love one day, but this had happened prematurely, without warning, giving me no chance to rally my forces, seek advice, pause for cogitation. As on the previous night, the touch of his lips on mine shook me as if there had been a violent explosion and, when he took his mouth away, I felt cheated, empty, incomplete.

He led me into the woods to a glade well hidden in the trees. There, he shed his jacket, spreading it out for me to sit on and then stretched out beisde me, drawing me into his embrace once more. He kissed me long and deeply, his hands wandering over my back and waist and I felt a tremor run through him. At last, as breathless as I, he withdrew that provocative mouth, holding me a little away and laughing down at me.

"Steady there, darling – we aren't married yet. Where did you learn to kiss like that?"

"I've never been kissed before," I answered shakily.

"Never?" He seemed surprised.

"Not by a man, Rebecca and Nancy kissed me sometimes. We loved each other like sisters – we needed affection, and sometimes we tried it because we wondered what it would be like with a man."

"Ah, I see." He gave me a mysterious smile, rolling over to lie on his back, his hands clasped under his head, staring up at the whispering firs. Then he regarded me through half-closed lids. "Three young virgins, eh? Burning with curiosity about love."

I knelt beside him, brushing back a lock of hair which had strayed forward over his forehead. This was all so new, so fascinating – the crisp feel of his hair, the smoothness of his skin, the male smell of him. He captured my hand and kissed the palm. "Of course we talked about men," I smiled into his eyes. "Girls always do."

"You must tell me about your childhood, dearest," he murmured, pulling me upon him with both arms. "We've so much to learn about one another, but there will be time enough for that later," and his hands moved behind my head, bringing my lips down to meet his.

I lay there savouring the warmth of his body, feeling his long legs pressed against mine, and the hardness of his muscular shoulder beneath my cheek. He had everything in his favour, he was older than me, worldly and experienced; he was handsome and had, above all, appealed to me for friendship. There was no way I could resist such a potent spell. His very restraint was in itself a challenge. He stroked my hair, leaning over me while his mouth explored my face, my chin, my throat, with light, delicate kisses. It was as if he cherished me, almost afraid to touch me lest his big hands do some damage to my tender female form. And he wooed me with words as well as caresses. Looking back now, knowing his sensual nature, I can only marvel at his self-control. But then – he had other considerations in mind. So, he refrained from carrying his practised lovemaking to its conclusion, making me burn for his kisses by the simple expedient of withdrawing them.

I was puzzled when he slowly released me, rising to his feet and holding out a hand to assist me. "We must be on our way. Cordelia will be waiting."

I brushed the leaves from my skirt. "Must we go yet?"

"Indeed we must," he said firmly. "I'm only human. Don't you understand that I'm struggling to be honourable? If we stay here much longer, I shan't be able to control myself."

I didn't know whether to be glad or sorry as, with an arm slung carelessly about my shoulders, he walked with me to where his horse waited. Then he surprised me still further by suggesting that I tidy my hair, waiting patiently while I found my comb. What a strange mixture he was – a creature of moods. He tied the strings of my cloak beneath my chin and I was intensely aware of a desire that he remain in this soothing, fatherly frame of mind. He lifted me on to the front of his saddle, swinging up behind me and clasping me close against his chest. Thus we made the short journey to Combermere.

The clouds were thickening over the uplands, blotting out the sun, and the lane wound higher towards the moors. The wind whistled through the heather and the curlew lamented. I was glad that I wasn't alone, fancying that spirits lurked in such lonely places, hiding behind mounds, ready to spring out.

Everything was so quiet and still, and Charles made no comments as we breasted a rise. There, below us, in the wooded vale, lay his house. We began to descend, branches sweeping across to block our view as we passed beneath a tunnel of interlocking trees. Ahead of us lay a straggling wall, over ten feet high in some places, and a gatehouse giving access to a cobbled courtyard. It was completely enclosed by the wall at our backs and the three sides of the house. Once, long ago, it had been a fortified manor. There were the remains of a moat, and a walk for bowmen. Every window was complete with heavy oaken shutters. Charles dismounted and helped me down, and I stared up at the covered gallery which ran round the upper storey, connecting with the bedrooms, and having two wooden staircases leading down to where we stood.

"Rather like a miniature castle, isn't it?" Charles said. "An ancestress of mine held it under siege for six months during the Civil War. The Roundheads had to give up. She was a spunky lady, by all accounts."

Though neglected, the place had a powerful beauty, but it was a severe, unyielding, almost threatening kind of beauty. An old man came from the stable to take Charles's hunter. He was as tall as a weathered tree, his face gaunt and hollow-eyed and, like the house, there was an ominous air about him.

"That's Jonas," explained Charles as we went towards the front door. "He looked after Combermere whilst we were abroad. The stables were once the quarters for a private army but that was many years before my time, I'm afraid." He sounded as if he would very much have liked to be the feudal lord with a gang of rascally, cut-throat mercenaries at his beck and call. We walked through the massive, dark door, and I found myelf in a panelled hall where logs roared in a huge stone fireplace which was carved with mythological figures and a central coat of arms.

"Cordelia!" Charles shouted, throwing his whip on to a side table. "Where the devil are you?"

She appeared from a room at the back, advancing to meet us, her hands outstretched to him, smiling widely as her eyes met mine. "Welcome to Combermere, my dear Eleanor," she said, gracious as a queen. "Do come into the solar. You must be cold, or was it quite warm and cosy in the spinney?"

There was candid amusement in her eyes, as if she knew exactly what had been taking place. This made me feel uncomfortable, but I didn't show it, listening politely as she took me into the solar, telling me that it had once been a pleasant corner where the ladies of the house could sit and work at their tapestry. Now it was furnished with comfortable, though shabby armchairs and rather threadbare rugs, but a fire burned brightly in the hearth and it was much more friendly than the hall. There was a stained-glass oriel window in one corner, and narrow casements which faced outwards over the garden beyond. Family portraits stared down from the walls, and there were several sporting prints too, along with hunting trophies. Books lay among ornaments on the shelves, and everything was dusty and untidy. As we entered, two enormous dogs rose from their places on the hearthrug, greeting Charles with furious wagging of their tails.

He gave each a caress, then ordered them to lie down. They slunk away, to flop down with their chins on their paws, rolling their large brown eyes at him adoringly. "They're longdogs – purchased from the gypsies," he said, flinging himself into the wing chair by the fire. "They call them lurchers, and there are no better hounds for chasing hare or bringing down deer."

"They look awfully fierce," I ventured, eyeing them cautiously.

He laughed. "Not at all. They're as soft as butter, when you get to know them."

"Are you interested in field sports?" asked Cordelia, smiling across at me.

"I like riding," I answered, slipping off my cloak and letting it lie on the back of my chair. "I learned rather late, I'm afraid, but then I was not brought up in the country as you were, Miss de Grendon."

"You must call me Cordelia," she insisted. "After all, you'll soon be one of the family. Charles has confided in me and I heartily agree with his choice."

Has he, by God? I thought, that niggling feeling of annoyance returning. Their cool assumption that I should comply with their wishes was rather daunting. "Aren't you rather taking things for granted? The Colonel may have something to say about it," I replied sharply.

Charles's quick flashing smile curled round me like an embrace. He added a generous measure of brandy to his tea, and I suddenly realised that I had already tasted it on his lips. He passed the decanter to Cordelia. "I don't think we need worry, my dear. He lost his only child because he objected to her choice of husband. I don't think he'll risk doing the same to you. He wants a peaceful life now. Haven't the doctors warned him against upset or strain? I think it's damned unlikely that he'll raise objections."

"If he gives you any trouble, I'll persuade him to relent." Cordelia's eyes were sparkling. I noticed that she wore paint, subtly applied but unmistakable. There was rouge accentuating her cheekbones, her eyelashes were darkened, and her lips bright scarlet. Her dress was most informal. When I remarked on her rather unusual costume, she said that she had bought it in Paris where Eastern styles were all the rage, designed by Paul Poiret who created for the famous fashion house of Worth. He had done away with the corset and those pastel, sweet-pea shades which had been in vogue. Now fierce colours took the stage and more daring, exotic gowns.

I absorbed this information, admiring her straight skirt of vivid green which she wore below an orange tunic. This was richly embroidered, and caught in by a belt of a contrasting colour. Her gleaming hair was dressed simply, coiled up at the back with a huge tortoiseshell comb. Around her neck was a long string of jade beads and wide bangles decorated her slender wrists. When she moved, a wave of musky perfume wafted from her, and it had those Oriental undertones which, so she kept assuring me, had taken fashionable Paris by storm. I drank in every word, though pretending that I knew all about it, responding, as always, to everything beautiful and luxurious. It was as if I hungered continually for lovely, harmonious sights to fill my eye, and soothing sounds to entrance my ear. At Combermere I was amply rewarded for, if the house itself chilled me with its sombre, decaying grandeur, its owners certainly did not. They did everything in their power to make certain that I enjoyed my visit.

They were so easy to talk to and Cordelia was remarkably skilled at recounting their travels, making them seem gay adventures, glossing over trifling difficulties, transporting me into the realms of high society where nothing, it seemed, was of more importance than clothes, wit delivered with rapier-like precision, and love affairs carried out with grace and aplomb. Charles mentioned the casinos in a way which suggested that gambling was the only possible pastime for a gentleman of leisure.

"Of course, the English countryside has its compensations," she said at last, refilling my teacup. I noticed that the level of brandy in the decanter had sunk rapidly. By now, I too was enjoying it. It diffused a warm glow in the pit of my stomach and I lost some of my reserve. "And London! Well, my dear – London is something else entirely. We must go there after you and Charles are married. I love the theatre. Do you?"

I was forced to admit my ignorance and she stared at me aghast, her eyes very wide. "We weren't allowed to attend theatrical performances when I was at the orphanage," I said defensively. "And since I've been here, I was only once taken to a pantomine in Macclesfield."

"What! Never seen a play or a musical comedy? We'll remedy this, won't we, Charles?"

He nodded, lounging in his chair, those long, slim legs in the well-fitting riding breeches stretched out to the fire, booted feet crossed at the ankles. His shirt was unbuttoned at the throat and his chest was tanned and covered with curling, reddish hair. There was an intimacy about this casual mode of dress which was exciting, yet there was a subtle hint of danger to him, that held-back feeling I had sensed from the start. He was holding a brandy glass between his hands, sniffing its bouquet appreciatively. "We'll take her to the newly built Gaiety Theatre," he remarked.

"If you marry soon, we could go to London for a while. What fun!" she enthused, but I experienced a drop in my spirits. I had thought that a honeymoon was a most private affair. Now it seemed that she intended to come with us.

"They're putting on *The Country Girl* at Daly's," said

Charles, stretching lazily. "So you two will be fully occupied whilst I go to my club."

"Oh, Charles, you're such a spoilsport," she pouted archly. "But if you are mean and won't accompany us, then I'm sure I know at least a dozen jolly chaps who will."

He laughed carelessly, not in the least put out because his sister was organising our honeymoon. With a shock, I realised that they spoke of it as if our marriage were a foregone conclusion. I was aware of a terrible hollowness that came with a feeling of defeat. This was odd because by now I wanted to be his wife more than anything. Cordelia was being so kind and understanding, and I should have been in the seventh heaven of delight. For some unaccountable reason, I wasn't.

"Can you dance, Eleanor?" she asked suddenly, leaping to her feet and running to the gramophone which stood on a dower chest against the wall. She wound it vigorously, selected a record, and waltz music blared from the brass horn. Without waiting for a reply, she pulled me from my chair and we whirled round madly. She was singing the refrain in my ear. "Swing high, swing low, swing to, swing for, that's how they set wedding bells ringing, you know!" And she was laughing hilariously and squeezing my waist.

It was impossible not to respond to her high spirits. She was so beautiful, her body curved against mine, her exotic perfume sultry and seductive. Life at Henford Grange had been rather sedate. Now I had fallen in with a dominating couple who were not afraid to flout convention. When the record stopped, she kissed my cheek and left me to attend to it. I found myself in Charles's arms instead of hers. His face rested against my hair and my body relaxed, moulding into his, my mind dizzy. I drifted to the music as he danced effortlessly, with surprising grace and lightness. I found that I was smiling as I dreamily anticipated a future which must surely be composed of happy times like this. There was no haven for me now, save the strong, safe haven of Charles's arms. I forgot everything when he held me, consumed by an intense physical longing which was none the less insistent because I was ignorant of its true meaning.

His arms tightened, and we stopped dancing though the music continued. I let my head fall back, feeling deliciously tiny and crushable, something of little account before the passion which was sweeping me. His mouth swooped down, capturing mine and his lips were hard and bruising, forcing mine apart, his tongue exploring deeply. I experienced a second of outrage, thinking frantically, he's drunk too much brandy – then I was caught up in a web of such exquisite sensations that I was powerless to stop him. I didn't want to stop him. I wanted more and more.

Then something, a movement, a gesture perhaps, caused me to open my eyes. Cordelia was watching us, her hands clasped against her breasts. Charles felt me start and lifted his head.

She grinned and clapped her hands. "Well done, brother. I'm glad to see that your bride isn't a shrinking violet. Don't lose that healthy animalism, will you, Eleanor?"

"Sit down, Cordelia," scowled Charles, releasing me. "Give me the key to the cellar. I need another drink before I take Eleanor home."

Her face was flushed and she moved unsteadily, coming to sit by me on the couch as Charles left the room. "If you want to know anything about sex, come and ask me," she said. Her arm was about my shoulders, and her warm body scent drifted up from the unfastened neck of her tunic. "Sometimes the hypocrisy of English society makes me want to scream. All those taboos. Religion is occasionally mentioned with bated breath, but as for sex, birth, and passion, they are never spoken of. It's not the same on the Continent – there's a wonderful freedom there. The damned Englishmen and their double standards! They lock up their wives, load them down with a parcel of brats, give them no love and fondly imagine that it's only themselves – these lords of creation – who are capable of getting any pleasure in bed. I can assure you, Eleanor, that the Almighty hasn't limited desire to men. Women enjoy themselves too, you know."

This outburst left me speechless. She giggled and hugged me, giving me time to recover from my astonishment. "I don't doubt it, Cordelia," I managed to bring out calmly.

"There are many women who think as I do," she replied airily. "I'll introduce you to some of my friends who move in artistic circles. They believe in free speech and free love. I want my brother to be happy with you, so take my advice. If you please a man in bed, that's half the battle. No, I've never been married but that doesn't mean that I don't know what I'm talking about. Oh, and another thing – you don't have to have children if you don't want them. There are ways of avoiding pregnancy. I'm speaking of anti-conception – the control of birth."

Cordelia had been right. These were subjects never, never talked of at Henford Grange. The aunts would have been most deeply shocked if they could have heard her, but I found myself responding, excitement thrilling through me at the boldness of her views, the suggested laxness of her morals. I was shamed that she should think me green and ignorant, so answered levelly: "Ah, yes – I have read of this."

She lay back against the cushions, watching my face. "It's nothing new, really, and has a very long history, though it's far from being accepted as a practice to be used by 'decent' people. Only tarts are supposed to know anything about it. The Church hates it, of course, blathering on about it being demoralising to the character and hostile to national welfare. What rot!"

"Don't listen to her, Eleanor." Charles had come in

unnoticed. He was leaning against the door frame, watching us, tipping the bottle to his lips. He frowned at his sister. "I want children – lots of 'em. There'll be no damned anti-conception for us. Will you give me babies, Eleanor?"

Babies! Good God, I was only just getting used to the idea of marriage! Then I thought of handsome little boys who looked just like him, and tiny, dainty girls in frilly frocks – my children who would have the love and advantages that I had missed. "Yes, I would like to do that," I answered quietly.

"Ugh! How can you?" Cordelia shuddered, holding out her glass for Charles to fill it. "To feel sick for months and lose one's figure! To have to deal with nurse-maids and tyrannical nannies! No thanks. That's not for me!"

There was a sardonic expression on his face as he strolled over to stand just behind me, his hand coming out to caress the back of my neck so that I shivered. "Don't you want a stake in the future, Cordelia? To know that your descendants will follow after you? Isn't that a kind of immortality?"

"Ha! I don't need it!" she said with a toss of her head. "I positively know that I'm going to live forever and never grow old. There's so much I want to do – places to see – and for a start, Charles, we must make changes here. The house is dreadfully inconvenient. You must buy a motor car, then we can go for drives and get to town quickly. Horse-drawn carriages are such a bore. Can't we have a telephone installed, and electricity?"

I glanced up into his face. It was closed, unreadable. "All in good time, sister," he said.

It was growing dark outside, with rain falling on to the cobblestones. The wind sighed through the nooks and crannies of the old house. I glanced out of the window, never happy in the dark, my quick imagination peopling it with the wailing, wandering spirits of the lost. Charles lit the lamps which stood in ornamental holders on the wall, and took a spill to those standing on the table. The house was certainly not as well lit as Henford Grange where there were candles and lamps in abundance. I shivered suddenly, envisaging long winter evenings. I told myself firmly that I would get used to it. Combermere would be my home and Charles would always be there to protect me. When I thought of the nights which would be spent in our bedchamber, my fears vanished, replaced by impatience and anticipation.

"I'll take you to the Grange now, Eleanor," he said, shrugging on his jacket, then holding my cloak, his hands resting on my shoulders as he draped it round me. He was smiling, his teeth extremely white in his sun-browned face. I noticed, abstractedly, the fine lines etched at the corners of his eyes, and the deep cleft in the centre of his chin. Cordelia took up a lamp and accompanied us to the front door. The hall was gloomy, its pictures and relics swallowed up in the shadows which reigned where the lamplight did not reach.

"We've much to discuss about the wedding," she said as Charles lifted me on to his horse.

"I'm sure Eleanor's aunts will make quite certain that she's the loveliest of brides," he answered.

"I'm not talking about *her*. What about me?" she trilled back, her voice high and brittle in the damp air. "Of course, you realise that I'll have to have a completely new outfit, with the most amazing hat I can lay my hands on?"

He said nothing, wheeling his horse out under the arch. "My sister is mad," he said indulgently. "You'll get used to her ways."

There was something bothering me. "Where will she live – when we are married?" I asked.

I felt him stiffen, then relax again, his arm holding me, the horse moving smoothly beneath us. "Oh, here and there. She's a restless soul." He didn't enlarge on this and I decided not to pursue it. He was brushing my cheek lightly with his lips and, once again, I was unable to think clearly.

When we reached Henford Grange, he swung me from the saddle, keeping his arms around me. A light wind blew over the trees; the clouds parted and the moon shone golden, illumining his face, his searching eyes, his halo of hair. Ah, yes, I thought him a man indeed – upright, gracious, intriguing and handsome. His eyes were so deep, so alive, so fearless that they were almost frightening, because it seemed as if they must read one's most intimate secrets.

"Dammit, the drive is wet," he said and looked down at my shoes. "Those thin little things – you mustn't soak them through," and with that he lifted me as easily as if I were made of thistledown and carried me across and set me down on the steps. He was on the one below me and now my eyes were nearly level with his. He kissed me solemnly, and he smelled of the night and the dampness and that touch of frost in the air. Our breath hung about us like a mist.

"Won't you come in?" I whispered, hating to lose him for a moment.

He shook his head. "Not now. Tell the Colonel that I'll call on him in the morning. Say nothing about us to anyone until I've spoken with him."

I understood. We were behaving most unconventionally, and this made it doubly exciting. It was not the way such important issues were conducted in well-to-do society. He should have courted me tepidly, then sought my grandfather's permission to ask for my hand. I was beginning to have an inkling of just how very different he and Cordelia were.

With a quick glance around to make certain that we were alone, he kissed me again, and it was a brief, affectionate touching of closed lips. Then he strode back to his horse, saluting me with his whip, and leaving me feeling extremely confused, still a little angry at his rushed courtship, yet blinded by physical passion. I already missed him, fretting to see him again. Henford Grange no longer seemed a warm, happy and satisfying place.

Chapter 4

"November 26th. This morning at twelve noon, Charles and I were married."

Such a simple sentence in my diary, but every bride will know how much this covers. I had jotted it down hastily when I had retired to my room to change after the reception in the Great Hall, before leaving on my honeymoon. There had been no time for more, no time to describe the upheaval, the excitement, the carefully compiled guest list, the gifts which arrived daily – now on display in the drawing room – to say nothing of the extra work given to the servants. The house had been cleaned from attic to cellar in readiness for the event. Aunt Louisa had been in her element, borne on a wave of exalted romanticism, perhaps pretending that she was preparing for her own union with the saintly, long-departed Douglas.

As Charles had predicted, the Colonel had given us his blessing. He was a sick man and wanted to see me happy. I was rather puzzled by his lack of concern, but then, he had been absent from the area for a long time, particularly when the de Grendons had been in residence and therefore their reputation had most probably not reached his ears. He had brushed aside any rumours as so much servants' gossip. In his eyes Charles was a stout fellow – a member of the hunt – the master of a fine old house and substantial estate.

When Charles approached him, he had summoned me to his study, that sacred place where he retired to don his smoking jacket and enjoy a pipe, and asked me, point blank, if I wanted to marry him. I suppose that my starry-eyed reaction must have convinced him. Thus I found myself betrothed to the most exciting man in Cheshire and, caught up in the whirlwind preparations, I allowed myself to be radiantly happy, my dreams of love coming magically true.

I saw Cordelia frequently, and it was she who helped me to decide on the style of my wedding gown. It was of white brocade and cut like that of a medieval princess. I wore a floor-length veil, and because the day was cold with snow clouds darkening the moors, I was wrapped in a white velvet cloak, lined with snowy fox. Grandfather gave me away, and one of Charles's friends acted as best man. Cordelia was a bridesmaid, dressed in yellow silk with an eye-catching hat, lavishly bedecked with artificial tea roses. At the reception she drank too much champagne and flirted outrageously with every man from eighteen to eighty.

Louisa adored every moment of the day. Maude bore herself magnificently, and the Colonel looked superb, every inch the military man, as he escorted me down the aisle to where Charles waited. The ceremony went without a hitch and the church was full, the villages around turning out in full force to witness the alliance between two such well-known families. We were married in the local church with its Norman tower and its oak door which still bore the scars of Cromwellian musket balls. I had turned my back on religion having had too much of it at the orphanage, though to please Grandfather I had made a habit of going with him twice on Sundays, and now I was glad of this church ceremony. My marriage was a sacred thing, this dedication of my life and myself to one man. I wanted every blessing to fall on us.

But there was one person who was not pleased to see me become Mrs de Grendon, and that was Bertha. As I turned down the aisle on my husband's arm, I caught sight of her face – white, tense and unhappy. She was only my maid, I told myself crossly, and had no business trying to warn me off, but she had done, almost continually, since the betrothal was announced. "Don't do it, miss. Please – he's bad and dangerous," she kept repeating.

For a stabbing moment, fear touched me, thrusting through the serenity and peace of the church, putting a cold finger on my happiness, and then I saw Cordelia, looking on with her wide smile, and she winked at me. By the time we had reached the porch every unpleasant thought was forgotten. The photographer organised us as the sun came out momentarily, and he disappeared beneath the black cloth shrouding his camera. A flash, a pop, and we were recorded for posterity.

We did not go to London for our honeymoon, and Cordelia was left behind. The weather was threatening frost and snow as we took the trap and clopped through the lanes. Charles refused to tell our destination and this added to the wonderful sense of adventure. I was so pleased to wave goodbye to Cordelia. She seemed very content in the company of some half a dozen lively young gentlemen who had arrived to attend the wedding. Charles said they would be staying at Combermere for a while. I can remember details clearly now, though at the time a golden haze seemed to hang over every word and action. I was aware of extreme tiredness, yet flying high with a curious kind of elation. It was cold, but I didn't feel discomfort, cuddled close to Charles's side, a fur rug wrapping me snugly. I rested my head against his shoulder and he smiled down at me.

"Where are we going?" I asked sleepily.

"Wait and see."

Up and up we went, leaving the village behind and passing a copse of firs. Steeper still and more stone-littered, the moorland-edged road mounting between grit walls, until beyond the rounded knolls I saw a building on the skyline. Great rough pastures stretched to the unfenced moors. It was wild country and, above us, a peregrine hovered seeking grouse. Charles pointed it out to me, saying: "I knew a parson once who lived near here. He flew his falcons and tiercels on these slopes, chasing the screaming ousel along the mountain streams with his little blue merlins. He did much to revive the lost art of falconry. A grand sport. I'd like to get some hawks. We must clear out the mews at the back of Combermere."

I shivered, wide awake now and aware of cold. Why did he have to talk of killing things on our wedding day? As for repairing the tumbledown mews, I thought there were more important projects on which to spend my dowry. The Colonel had been generous and whilst knowing little about the management of an estate, I could see that these were cottages, leased to the farm and forestry hands, which demanded attention. Even I was not blind to the fact that Charles was inclined to leave such matters to his bailiff, a somewhat indifferent landlord. But his pride in everything pertaining to his home was self-evident, as was his gratitude to my grandfather for endowing me so lavishly. My fortune, when he died, would be responsible for the rebirth of Combermere, my husband's kingdom. Though he might leave it for long periods, Charles was extremely territorial, proud that the de Grendons had owned this land from the time of the Norman conquest. Neglect it he might – but he would never part with it.

Yes, I mused, this was his kingdom and I was his consort. He was acting the role of the man of the country now. His tweeds were of the finest quality; his riding gear fitted him like a glove, in the evenings his formal wear would have graced a prince. Philippe, his French valet, took great pride in him, and so did I.

I sneaked a sideways glance at him. His profile was etched against the sky. He had that same air of distinction which had impressed me at our first meeting. I was his wife. I couldn't believe it. I kept repeating the word to myself, as if by so doing it would solidify into reality – a reality which I had not yet begun to feel. I am his wife. He is my husband. Over and over, matching the steady clopping of the horse's hoofs, until at last we came to the end of the journey. We arrived at a lonely inn called the Cat and Fiddle.

We were expected, and the host came out, smiling and effusive, in his waistcoat and striped apron. Ostlers ran to take the horse and trap, and his round, beamy wife ushered us into the taproom. We were the only guests. "Too late in the year for many to venture this far," the landlord said, seating us at a round table close to the fire. "This is the highest licensed house in England," he added proudly, laying out cutlery on the red checked cloth. "Stands over a thousand feet above the sea. Other public houses dispute it, but I know for a fact, that there's none to top it. Now then, sir and madam, would you like to eat before you go up to your room?"

A servant was already bringing in our bags and disappearing aloft with them. I glanced at Charles who was throwing off his greatcoat. "I only want a pint or two of your excellent ale, landlord," he said, his eyes meeting mine. "What about you, my love? Some soup, perhaps, to warm you." He lowered his voice and murmured into my ear: "I don't appreciate freezing feet in my bedmate."

I ate the soup and we lingered at the table. A couple of farmers clumped in, wearing breeches and gaiters, rubbing their cold hands together and slapping them against their sides. Charles engaged them in talk and they shouted for the potboy, while he downed his third mug of ale. From my shadowy corner, I could see his face in the firelight, my heart filled to overflowing. How awful now seemed my childhood in the orphanage. I had been blessed with the love of my grandfather, I was the wife of this fine man, and warmed by the hospitality of these simple country folk.

My drowsy soliloquy was brought to an abrupt end. "Eleanor, wake up. You're very nearly asleep there. Go on to bed. I'll be with you soon," said my husband, looking across from the table where he was playing cards with the farmers.

I woke fully at the sound of his voice. I found it difficult to believe what he was saying. This was our wedding night! Did he intend to spend it gambling? I drew my cloak around me and held my head high. I stared at him coldly, disappointment weighing my heart. "You wish me to take the place of a warming pan?" I said. "No need for that. I'm sure the inn-keeper's wife will have aired the bed."

There was a wicked glint in the grey eyes which now regarded me above the spread of cards – a glint which seemed to reflect the gold sovereigns on the table. Damn him, he found it amusing to keep me waiting. I could feel my anger rising. The farmers were grinning. "That's right, sir," remarked one of them, as red and rugged as a turnip. "Start as you mean to go on, I say."

I flung him a withering glance and stalked out in the wake of the landlady. She was smiling and flinging me knowing looks, leading me up the winding staircase whose treads were worn down in the middle by the countless feet of generations. The bedroom was under the eaves, low-ceilinged and with sloping floorboards, the tiny dormer windows facing on to the moors. She bade me goodnight and there was a certain familiarity in her glance which made me bridle. An unwelcome thought flashed into my mind. Was Charles a regular customer there? And was this really the first time he had brought a woman with him?

It was beneath my dignity to ask her if she knew him, but when she had gone, I couldn't get this question out of my head. I remembered certain disquieting conversations we had had during the past weeks. When he was in a dark, disturbed mood he could be unkind, I had discovered, baiting me about my lack of experience, saying that at seventeen he had already bedded his first woman, a lady much older than himself. I had tried not to be hurt, telling myself that I must be sophisticated about his past – as Cordelia would have been. A man as attractive as he must have had many mistresses. I was appalled at the jealousy which twisted like a burning iron in my stomach.

I unpacked slowly, missing Bertha. A shower of confetti, paper rose petals and rice cascaded to the carpet, probably put there by that prankster Bertie Hollis, the rowdy best man. He had made a speech at the reception; his humour had been broad, filled with sly innuendos. Charles had gone to London for his stag night, meeting his friends there. They had returned in high spirits the day before the wedding. Louisa had been enthralled by this sudden flux of men, laughing immoderately at their rather risqué talk, reproving and applauding, as gay and coquettish as could be. Of course, she was at pains to explain, they did come from very good families. I didn't care for them much.

"A man is known by the company he keeps," I said to myself, rather too late in the day. "But they are school friends," insisted that part of me which would think no ill of him. I scolded myself for petty jealousy and turned my attention to unpacking.

My trousseau was extravagant and sumptuous. Macclesfield, though adequately provided with shops, had not suited Cordelia's plans for me, and she had made a special trip to London, coming back laden with cardboard boxes bearing the crests of Harrods and other smart emporiums. The Colonel had given her *carte blanche* to buy whatever she considered essential for a bride. She had not needed a second bidding. I was to learn soon enough that, in common with her brother, there was nothing she liked better than spending someone else's money.

Bertha had not packed all these exquisite items for Charles did not intend to spend long away from Combermere, and the rest awaited me in the Master Bedchamber there. My case contained half a dozen pretty chemises and matching knickers made of the finest lawn, lavishly trimmed with lace and ribbon, and the same number of nightgowns and peignoirs. Cordelia had insisted that I include one of black silk, daringly transparent. My petticoats were a mass of frou-frous, made of flimsy, flounceable fabrics. Every undergarment was seductively feminine.

When I had stowed my clothing in the corner cupboard, I stared at the nightdress spread demurely on the bed. Ignoring Cordelia's advice, I had chosen one of purest white. The black could come later, when I had experienced – when I had learned – I stopped quite still, my heart racing. The mind is a funny thing, filled with bits and pieces and snippets of incidents lying dormant, waiting to spring up when least expected. In a flash of repugnance I visualised not Charles, but Mr Bowell with his slack, drooling mouth and the raw lust in his eyes.

I tried to shake off the feeling of frigidity brought on by this vision, resolutely taking off my jacket and blouse and washing at the toilet stand. Why did I tremble? Why was I so afraid? I loved Charles and hungered for his kisses. He had pushed me away sometimes, freeing himself from my demanding arms and he had groaned as if in pain, saying that we must wait until we were married. Then, fevered and impatient, I had longed to have him take me at once. But tonight he had offended me deeply, so engrossed in the cards. It seemed that he was so sure of me that he had no qualms about this neglect – tonight of all nights.

I removed the rest of my clothes and pulled the nightgown over my head. I drew out the pins and combs which held my hair in place. It whispered down across my shoulders and I took my time brushing it. I had no desire to get into bed, delaying the moment. The room was warm and pleasantly lit, cosy with its dark furniture and cotton curtains. How nice it would be to lock the door and spend the night in that comfortable brass bedstead, quite alone. An imp of mischief was urging me to do it. What would Charles say, I wondered, if he found the door bolted? I rose, halfway across the room, hand outstretched to do it, when I pulled up short, dismayed at myself. This was no way for a bride to act! You wanted to marry him, said that horrible little nagging voice inside me. Oh dear, I did – I *do*! My mind was racing like a frantic squirrel in a cage. I needed him to calm these bridal nerves and he wasn't there. It will be all right when he comes, I thought.

In this I was correct, or very nearly so. He came in much later. I heard his step on the stair, heavy and slow, and he swayed a little as he ducked his tall head under the lintel. I was standing by the window, gazing out into the darkness. I refused to give him the satisfaction of turning and welcoming him. He came behind me, his arms clasping me about the waist, chuckling when he felt my angry resistance. "My darling ice maiden," he muttered, and his speech was slurred. "That's what you pretend to be, but I know different – I've had you sighing and shuddering in my arms, and now I've come to give you what you want. My child bride – my golden-haired and golden-pocketed too. What more could a man ask?" One of his hands came up, cupping my breast and my heart leaped at the touch, fear vanishing. Gently, he pushed the nightgown from my shoulders and his fingers slid along my flesh. It was like fire engulfing me. Oh, how I had yearned for him to caress me like that, but he had not done so, till now.

His lips were brushing my neck, my throat and he pulled my unresisting body closer. I arched back against him, feeling the hardness of his desire pressing intimately against my hips. He raised his head, his eyes fixed on the black window, speaking very low as his fingers continued to tease my breasts. "See that dark hump of hill over there? There's a cairn on top where the Celts used to worship their great god Teut. Beltane fires roared there at certain seasons. Who knows, perhaps witches still revel and hold their covens in that sacred place? Perhaps, tonight, we should offer a sacrifice to those mysterious deities of Toot Hill."

I spun round, clinging to him, burying my face in his chest. He chuckled because he had frightened me. I was so tense and I wished that he would stop. Outside, the branches of the trees had looked like crooked arms and bony fingers. I heard the wind sighing, and the sound of a brook bounding down the incline. In the warm sun of day it would be a pretty, beguiling sight. Now it had the wild sound of racing water in the dark. I was angry with myself as the fear inside me churned and grew.

Charles felt me shiver. It excited him, and his voice was urgent as he said, "Get into bed. You are cold. I will soon warm you."

A strange bed is never comforting, and this one seemed vast. I lay waiting for my bridegroom, torn between desire and apprehension. He was stripping rapidly, red as a demon in the dim ember-light. I had never seen a man naked before and, fascinated, I couldn't keep my eyes off him. I remember thinking how hairy were his arms, legs and chest. Then, in the still and breathless room, he came to me and initiated me into the delights of the flesh. My body changed from that of a girl and I became a woman. The process was not without difficulty and Charles, who I realised was drunk, was not very patient. He stifled my cry of pain with his mouth, crushing my lips with his until I could taste blood. He raised his head and I saw his eyes shining above me. "God dammit," he muttered. "Virgins are hard work!"

I started to struggle, tears of pain on my face, but Charles would have none of this. Snarling a curse, he had his way, penetrating me with brutal force, surrendering to the demands of his body and increasing his rapid movements. This is what I recall of the moment when I lost my virginity – the taste of blood, searing pain and the sensation of being overwhelmed and crushed. But once he had reached fulfilment, Charles was content to be tender with me, an intent look on his face as he lay there and explored me. There was no denying the increasing heat in my loins as his fingers invaded me, touching me where I ached to feel them most. Oh, he knew what he was about, there was no doubt of that, playing with me, teasing me, bringing me to such a pitch of hunger that I leapt to meet his touch, begging him for release. Then he relented, laughing low, and giving me my first taste of sexual completion. I was gripped by an intense need to have him take me again. I arched my hips, as if seeking his possession, and he, sensing my readiness, spread wide my thighs and covered me with his body. This time it was with a sense of triumph that I felt his frame shudder with the intensity of the pleasure I was giving him.

Although his possession of me was physical, it was also a spiritual awakening, and I was bathed in a rosy afterglow as I lay beside his sprawled satiety, my heart racing, holding my breath with the wonder of it. Emotions too complicated for mere happiness rushed across my consciousness as I stared up at the ceiling. Slowly I relaxed as he slept with his legs entwined with mine and his arm across my breasts. I experienced the bruised peace of a fighter who had unexpectedly conquered. I had ceased being a child, now accepting the cares and responsibilities involved in adulthood.

I felt wise and smug, pitying ladies who did not love their husbands or wish to share this savage and strangely wonderful union . . .

In the barnyard a rooster was crowing, announcing his supremacy over his harem. It was odd to wake and find myself nestling in the curve of a naked man's arm. The events of the night came rushing back, and I seemed to see life with heightened perception, brilliant and exciting. Charles caressed me sleepily, grunting and pulling me into his arms, burying his face in my breasts. He was so beautiful to feel, every part of him alive, the flesh firm and smooth, the muscles under the flesh so perfect in movement, the whole body so strong. I ran my hands over his back. It was like silk, only more polished, more resilient. When he had made love to me again, he got up.

Watching him gave me the greatest pleasure as he moved about the room with that controlled grace of his, standing, bare to the waist, screwing up his face as he shaved with a cut-throat razor. He squinted in the mirror, propped up near the window. I sat in bed with a breakfast tray on my knees. It was a scene of domesticated intimacy which was heart-warmingly normal. Yet, when I rose and joined him, the damp mystery of the view alarmed me. Below, the treetops floated in a white mist which blew against the inn and billowed over the shoulders of the hills. The window was shut, but I could tell that all was silent. I shuddered.

Charles turned, one side of his face still covered with soapy lather. "What's the matter?" he asked. "Don't worry about the mist. It will lift presently and we'll take a walk, so put on something sensible."

So casual, I thought, and now my fear seemed foolish, yet I felt that something evil had been shown me; this rugged countryside, smiling in the day, had secrets while I slept. Beltane fires? Sacrifices? They had sacrificed virgins, hadn't they? Then he smiled at me and my knees felt weak. I didn't mention that sense of foreboding. How do you explain things when you can't understand them yourself? I forgot it as soon as we set out for our walk and, as he had predicted, the mist lifted and the sun appeared. We leaned on a gate and my eyes followed where he pointed. On one side were the hills and dales of Derbyshire while away to the west was the great plain of Cheshire. It was just possible to glimpse the Mersey estuary and the bluish mountains of Wales. Grey patches of smoke marked the various towns.

Close at hand we could see the well-wooded valley which seemed to fall from the very inn itself, and it was there that Henford Grange and Combermere lay. We had not been away from them for many hours and yet it seemed like a lifetime to me. Charles was in such a gay, pleasant mood, delightful to be with. He was considerate and loving, holding my hand, whispering sweet nothings in my ear, dazzling me with his charm. The whole rich panorama of the wintry scene ran past my eyes, a wealth of life which seemed created by my love, a newly evoked existence that I'd never really noticed till my senses were awakened. The excitement of it spurred passion in me so that my throat hurt and an ache came in my breasts. I hung on Charles's arm as we strolled back to the inn, and rubbed my cheek against his sleeve.

We had lunch and then went up to our room to love, to sleep, and wake to love again, through the dusky afternoon. Now I saw why so much attention was paid to a trousseau, happy to adorn myelf in the most provocative garments, only so that he might take them off and lay me on the bed. "You're an apt pupil," he laughed later.

"Do I please you as much as your experienced older woman?" I asked, running my hand lightly over his chest. Against the white sheet his skin was almost startlingly bronzed.

He chuckled, bending his head to kiss my waiting lips. "So you remember that, do you? Are you jealous?"

"I wish that I had been the first woman you made love to," I cried vehemently. I *was* jealous, wildly jealous of his past, no matter how much I pretended otherwise.

"Don't think about it," he whispered, and it was so easy for him to distract me. "Why torture yourself? We are together now, and nothing else matters."

He was right, of course, my lord and husband. "Make

love to me, Charles, make love to me," I urged, wanting to lay the ghosts of other arms, other lips, to make him think only of me. I closed my eyes, forgetting everything in the pleasure he gave me. He needed no prompting, rousing me till I reached that explosion of the flesh which made me cry out. When he had finished, I was ashamed of my jealousy and suspicions, for the fact that I felt so much physical delight made my silent questioning seem not only ungrateful, but downright improper. What had happened to him before we met was none of my business. If it had served to turn him into such a highly skilled lover, then this was all to the good.

Thus passed the first three days of my married life. On the morning of the fourth, Charles announced that we were returning to Combermere after breakfast.

I shall always remember the Cat and Fiddle with affection. Its hospitality had given me those precious days of love when life had promised everything and there had been no cloud to mar this bright expectation. It is as well that we cannot predict the future or its dark shadow would spoil our enjoyment of the present, our fearful eyes turned to that which was to come.

It was snowing by the time we reached the house. The clouds had been gathering ominously all morning, and now flakes drifted from an iron sky. They looked so pretty, settling on roofs and hedges, filling standing carts, collecting on the ornamental gables which crowned Combermere. It would be a lie to say that I was pleased to be there. I didn't like the place, and Charles had already changed, oddly morose yet with a kind of eagerness too, as if he couldn't wait to set foot over the threshold. I wondered if he was bored with my company; certainly, when we took a breather from games in bed, we had little in common. He had a disconcerting habit of looking at me impatiently sometimes, as if I had said or done something which he thought foolish.

Cordelia was in the hall, and she was not alone. Bertie and his cronies were still there, as much at home as if they owned it. A cheer arose as we came in, and Charles brightened. There was much back-slapping and shaking of hands and I shrank into a desperate, icy dignity as Charles laughed and answered their most personal questions about our wedding-night activities. Cordelia's musical laughter rang out among the deeper chuckles of the men.

It appeared that we had either arrived in time for lunch or else the litter on the table was the remains of breakfast, even possibly the supper of the previous night. There were dirty plates and bread curling up at the edges, the surface of the refectory table sticky beneath the muddle of mugs and wineglasses. Empty bottles lay where they had been discarded on the floor. Half-empty ones stood, uncorked, on the boards. A big, heavy man with immense whiskers was lying full-length on the couch, purple and swollen, snoring loudly. The others tried to rouse him, pulling at him and shouting in his ear, but to no avail. They were unshaven and haggard and Cordelia looked as if she had been up all night.

Charles went to one of the windows, flinging it wide amidst general protests. "Dammit all! It smells like a bar parlour in here," he said, but he was grinning. Bertie handed him a pint pot and he threw himself into a chair, his dogs fawning at his knee.

I said, rather stiffly: "If you'll excuse me, I'll go up to our room and change."

"That's right, m'dear," nodded Bertie, a large young man, rather too portly and florid, with lazy blue eyes and a sensual smile. He was wearing the loudest of check suits and the most extravagant of ties. "Get into bed and wait for that randy old dog to come up. Hope you had a nightie made with fur around the hem."

"Why?" I asked, falling into the trap.

"To keep your neck warm!" he shouted, bellowing with laughter.

"Oh, shut up, Bertie," yawned Cordelia. "That joke came out of the ark!"

"It's snowing hard," commented Charles, instead of coming to my rescue.

"Good," said another man with a worn, dissipated look on his pale face. He was leaning against the mantelpiece, cigar between his lips. "Then we'll be here till Christmas."

"What about women, eh?" chorused the others who were seated, talking excitedly, all of them intoxicated. "Should have brought some of the Gaiety Girls with us – that would've livened things up."

"I'm all right," said Bertie smugly, with a meaningful glance at Cordelia.

"Bloody selfish pig," growled the pale man. "You always were a one for seeing that you didn't go without. We'll have to seek female company in the village. Any willing girls about, Charles, old boy?"

"A few, Harry," he remarked drily, tankard raised. "If you know where to look."

"I'll bet *you* do," answered Harry sulkily. "Feudal lord, and all that. *Droit du seigneur*, eh? A fine old custom. Taking the yokel bridegroom's place on the wedding night. What a compensation for the responsibility of being a landowner. There's supposed to be many a farm brat around my old man's estate in Norfolk that bears a distinct resemblance to our family."

"It doesn't happen like that now, Harry," Charles replied, glancing at me. I fought to maintain a cool exterior as if this bawdy chat left me unmoved. He held out an arm and summoned me to his side.

Harry refused to be put off, very argumentative. "So you say, you damned old liar," he scoffed, weaving on his feet. "Bet you've your fair share of bastards, littered about Cheshire. Don't be so deuced miserly, Charles. You're the host. You should provide us with entertainment."

"Used to be different in the old days when that valet

chappie was here. What was his name? Duffield – that's it, and Cordelia's governess was in charge," recollected Bertie, stumbling as he made for the table and a further bottle.

"Miss Annette," amended Cordelia, watching him with her feline smile.

He slapped himself on the brow. "That's it. Lord, didn't we get up to some larks! Remember, Charles? That was before you were expelled from the old school, what?"

"Why were you expelled?" asked Harry, screwing up his eyes in the effort to focus. "I was in a lower house and never heard the full story."

"They said I was corrupting the other boys," Charles replied, his mouth curved in a cynical smile, his grey eyes hooded and smoky.

Harry hooted with mirth. "What the devil did you do? Initiate them into the joys of manhood? Smuggle tarts into the sacred precincts? I'll bet you taught them how to drink and gamble too, didn't you, you scoundrel?"

Charles shrugged. "Maybe it was a combination of sins. I can't remember," he said indifferently.

"Didn't we have some good times down here during the holidays?" Bertie went on. "Duffield and Miss Annette didn't give a tinker's cuss what we did – lived like savages, didn't we? What days they were! Girls, booze and money, and those two lording it as if they owned Combermere."

The lines on each side of Charles's mouth deepened, his scar showing clearly. "There's no one quite like the privileged servant for taking advantage," he said. "My uncle was at fault – if fault there be – for leaving Cordelia and me in their hands."

"He trusted them, I suppose," put in his sister, one leg crossed over the other, her foot swinging in its black patent shoe. Bertie seemed bewitched by that slender ankle, but she was looking not at him, but at her darkly brooding brother.

"What happened to them? I completely lost touch for a while – went to Rome – damned sweaty and full of dagos – was in hot pursuit of an heiress but she went off and married some other blighter!" Bertie was indignant, unable to comprehend how any girl could possibly prefer someone else to his alcoholic charms. I could understand it, bored and affronted by this silly young man, yet I lingered, listening to their conversation, eager to know Charles's background.

"They are dead." His voice was flat and unemotional, but there was a factor withheld, his reserve cloaking it. "It happened years ago, when I was twenty-one and had come into my inheritance. Duffield was found with his head bashed in, lying in a ditch. He had been to the inn, and had taken a fall from his horse on the way home."

"And Miss Annette?" It would have been better if Bertie had dropped the subject but he was continuing with drunken obstinacy.

"She went berserk when the news came, moped about for days and then disappeared. Later, her body was dragged from the mere. I had to go and identify it – not a pretty sight for she'd been there for some time, caught in the weeds at the bottom."

Charles said this as coolly as if they were discussing the weather. Bertie shook his head sadly. "Damned pity that – she was a fine, handsome woman, as I recall. Besotted by Duffield, of course, but she liked we lads, didn't she? Good to us too, in her way. Never mean with her favours."

"Neither was he," added Harry darkly. "Man, woman or dog, it was all the same to Joe Duffield."

"You're so crude, Harry," complained Cordelia, regarding him sleepily as she reclined in her chair. "Please remember that there are ladies present, and we don't want to know about the dirty little habits he taught you."

This seemed to amuse them further, and they laughed as if she had just said something stunningly witty. I knew little about intoxication then, but realised that they had been drinking steadily ever since the wedding, a feckless crew who had once been Charles's companions at public school. The friendships had remained, like calling to like. How true are some of the old saws: "Birds of a feather flock together. A fool and his money are easily parted." I collected quite a few of these during the course of the next months.

What a winter that was. Blizzards swept down from Scotland, blanketing the exposed moors, snow settling hedge high in the valleys, followed by severe frosts. The roads were impassable, and Charles's guests did not leave until the green tips of spring began to appear through the melting slush and the thaw set the streams gushing. Their long-term visit would have been an endurance test for a mature wife, let alone a girl of seventeen who wanted to be alone with her husband. Hatred is too mild a word to describe my feelings for them – I positively loathed them.

Quite apart from the nuisance of having them constantly underfoot was the crippling expense. They ate us out of house and home and emptied the cellar. I was labelled kill-joy if I lost my temper and criticised them. I could no longer reach Charles. He and Cordelia rejoiced in the bedlam which turned every day into a continual party. Bertha was my mainstay, serving me faithfully under these trying circumstances. She stoutly fended off the amorous advances made to her, and sat up with me far into the night when, sickened by the drinking, the gambling, the brutal cockfights in the hall, the drunken quarrels and the equally drunken reconciliations, I would retire to my room to wait for Charles. Often now, he did not come to bed at all, sleeping where he had fallen, across the hearth or with his head on his arms on the table. I grew up rapidly, at first refusing to believe what manner of man I had married.

I remonstrated with him, making myself unpopular. He had a wealth of excuses. Then it was Christmas and there was a certain amount of seasonal revelry, but it dragged on too long. Sometimes a local squire or two braved the snow, attracted to Combermere by the liquor and the gambling. Sometimes we made short journeys on foot on return visits. At first, I went along because I disliked being left in the gloomy old house. I had hoped there might be women there with whom I could converse, but I quickly discovered that the only place to which we were invited were the homes of bachelors or widowers, men who lived alone with only a servant or two. They were all the same – run down, unkempt, used for sleeping and boozing, stinking of ale and spirits.

I felt like the skeleton at the feast. For all the notice Charles took of me I might not have bothered to accompany him. Cordelia, on the other hand, entered into it with zest. Charles and I began to quarrel bitterly. "God, you and your friends are disgusting!" I would rave on the rare opportunities when we were alone. "Small boys playing at being men!"

"Christ! Are you saying that I'm not man enough for you? Come here, bitch, and I'll prove it to you!" he would shout, grabbing at me, his eyes bloodshot, his breath poisonous.

I knew that the slightest slur on his masculinity was a fine weapon and, reckless with anger and disappointment, I used it without mercy. "Call yourelf men!" I would sneer. "You're loud, vulgar and embarrassing! As for this so-called virility of which you're always boasting, when it comes to the test, you're too damned drunk to prove it!"

And all the time, I was weeping inside. It wounded me to see Charles degraded by drink. His whole character changed, the very worst aspects of his personality coming to the fore. It was as if some demon possessed him. He became truculent, quarrelsome, easily offended. His handsome features were wild and flushed, eyes heavy-lidded, speech slurred, fists clenched, ready to fight. My condemnation infuriated him. "Come here, woman!" he would shout aggressively, showing off to his friends. "Where are you? Dammit, I want my woman!" Then he would seize me by the arm, his fingers like talons, spinning me round to face him. "What's the matter with you? Why aren't you laughing? Don't you think me witty? Don't you love me? Bah! You're like all the rest! You cold bitch! Why the hell did I marry you? And why the hell did you marry me? You could've had any charming nitwit alive, but you chose a brute instead! What a fool!"

There are some people in the world who set out on a course of self-destruction, almost taking a dark, perverse pleasure in feeding the element which will bring about their ruin. Such was Charles. He feared death greatly, talking to me of it sometimes – those good times when we could still communicate. Oh, no – it was not all despair – not at the beginning. Then I forgave him his drinking bouts, always believing that I could change him. He had been lonely, misunderstood, I told myself – now that he had me to love him things would improve. My dowry would enable him to make improvements at Combermere, but the days slid into weeks and he showed no desire to bestir himself.

I was still in love with him, putting on a brave face when we visited Henford Grange. I was stubbornly proud to be his wife, and cheered because my grandfather was so fond of him. Perhaps this was not so strange for he could charm the birds off the trees when it suited him. He flattered the Colonel, engaging him in endless sporting talk, and as for Aunt Louisa, she blushed and fluttered when he flirted with her. He was even nice to General Goring, though in private he voiced the opinion that he was a fat, pampered little bastard unworthy of the name of dog. Yes, she adored Charles, and he brought her little gifts, earning himself a reputation for open-handed generosity. I would sit back and watch, thinking that there was no man alive who could ooze affability from every pore as could my husband, when it was profitable to do so.

He still wove his magic around me. I could not resist his overpowering physical attraction. He might infuriate and wound me, but he had only to take me in his arms, spinning his web of lies, stopping my spitfire tongue with his mouth. As I melted into sighing acquiescence, I would think, while thought was still possible – tomorrow we'll have a serious talk about his extravagance, tomorrow I'll ask him when Cordelia is leaving – but tomorrow never came.

Time and again through that harsh, bitter spring, I went to the moors, longing to look down into the valleys and see the first delicate flush of green spreading out to soften and blur the view. March went out, then April. May came in with raw winds and stinging sleet. The leaves seemed blasted, blossom was beaten off the branches before it was ever full. But at last my horrible guests were going. At last! At last!

Charles had bought a car by that time, and they piled in, effusive in their promises to return soon. I heaved a deep sigh of relief as the vehicle made its noisy way towards the gatehouse. He was to drive them to the station and see them on to the London train. Now everything would be all right. I should have my home to myself – apart from Cordelia. She wore a sulky expression, red lips drooping petulantly as we closed the front door. "Hell, but it's going to be most hideously boring now," she grumbled.

"There will be plenty to do," I said brightly, starting to clear away the bottles. "You'll be moving soon, won't you? I haven't been inside the lodge, but it looks so pretty. Is it furnished? Will you need to take things from here?"

I said this in all innocence for they had been talking vaguely of her taking up residence in the lodge-house. I assumed that she would want a home of her own. There she could hold orgies to her heart's content. To my astonishment, rage twisted her face into an ugly mask and she glared at me. "Damn it, Eleanor – nothing's been decided! I'm not to be fobbed off like some poor relation! There's masses of room here. Besides, I'm not sure that I want to live alone."

"I'm sure that you won't be alone," I said crisply. "Bertie will jump at the chance."

"Damn Bertie! And damn you!" she yelled and slammed from the room.

Not for the first time I felt like an intruder. Cordelia was difficult to fathom. Sometimes she seemed to dislike me, at others she wooed me, making me feel uncomfortable with her caresses, taking my part against the men. With all my heart I wished that she would marry Bertie, though the prospect of having him as a brother-in-law was depressing. I knew that they were lovers for she'd made no attempt to hide the fact that he had shared her bedroom during his stay. My sense of right and wrong was becoming blunted by the company I had been forced to keep. They appeared to scorn the manners, morals and mores of society which my aunts had instilled in me. Was she in love with Bertie? They way they spoke to one another did not bear this out. The tone of their relationship was flippant and cynical.

For a short while my life improved. Cordelia did not move, but she did go away for a holiday, visiting Buxton. I had Charles to myself and sampled the task of being a housewife, taking the helm of the establishment. I examined the acount books. Everything was in total disorder. There was a pile of unpaid bills and I had the strong suspicion that Jonas was cheating us. I spoke to Charles of this and he promised to look into it, telling me not to worry, taking me in his arms and carrying me off to bed. It was so easy to be lulled by him, to enjoy the hot summer days and languorous nights, to do as he said and leave well alone. Jonas had managed for years, so why make a fuss?

"Of course he cheats a little," Charles laughed, "it's one of the perks of being a butler. Don't worry your pretty head about it." He went on to say that he had plenty of money – the farms were showing a profit, the land yielding up its harvest – and he'd had a lucky run at cards. "Leave everything to me," he insisted. So I did.

I stopped arguing and swallowed my growing resentment. Also, I was learning to fear him. Yet when each day ended and we were in bed, he would make love to me with that expertise which brought me to a screaming pitch of ecstasy. But when it was over an insistent inner voice kept crying out for something more. What was it I wanted? I would ask myself as I lay beside his sleeping form. Certainly not more bodily pleasure, he gave me my fill of that – when he was sober. What was wrong with me? Why was it that when he was there, his body hard against mine. I heard that terrible voice again, ringing in my brain, asking even as I reached fulfilment: "Where are you, Charles? Where are you?"

I refused to let these awful misgivings destroy my happiness but, try as I might, they were there, deep in my heart, and though I held them in check most of the time, I could not ignore them. So I plunged myself fully into everything I could do to make him happy. I devoted myself to him, prepared to spend my every waking thought in his service. He seemed to be responding, much more the Charles I had first known. I recaptured joy, filled with a tingling sense of wellbeing. He even drank less and the future looked bright. Then Cordelia returned from Buxton. I remember how glad he was to see her. They stood in the hall and her mouth was wide open. She was laughing – he was laughing – closely embraced, they rocked with glee.

As the autumn approached, we went to London. We

stayed in the Colonel's residence in Kensington and, because he wished me to enjoy the London winter season, he did not put a limit on spending. He wanted us to make an impression as a newly married couple, and this we most certainly did. We gave parties and attended galas. I went nearly everywhere with Charles – and so did Cordelia. Bertie and company descended on us and before I knew what was happening, they had practically moved in. Encouraged by Cordelia, I was rather extravagant, buying a number of expensive garments. I wanted to be a credit to Charles, appearing at important functions so that he might show me off as his beautiful, wealthy wife. And always, deep in the night, he would bring me to that peak of satisfaction which had become a craving with me, a terrible need which was at once bliss and torture.

It was nearly Christmas time again and I had been expecting to stay in London, planning a New Year party. But one morning Charles received a letter and I recognised the Colonel's handwriting. My husband's face darkened as he read it. He did not divulge the contents, but cancelled further engagements and said that we were leaving for Cheshire at once. Cordelia stormed, bullied and sulked, but to no avail. By the end of the week we were once more entering Combermere. The mist rolled over the moors and the dark old house seemed to envelop me as I went in, and the embrace was not of warmth and security but of fear. Charles had been in a foul mood throughout the journey and Cordelia had scarcely spoken a word.

"What's the matter with them, Bertha?" I asked her as she started to unpack. "It's pleasant to come to the country for Christmas. I don't mind forgoing the delights of London one little bit. We shall be able to visit Henford Grange. Why, there will be carol singers, a decorated tree, all the traditional fun."

She saw through my attempt at joviality, her face guarded as she busied herself with putting gowns on hangers and laying undergarments away in drawers. "I can't say, I'm sure, madam. It's not my place to question Mr de Grendon's moods – not hers neither."

There was always a touch of venom in her voice when she mentioned Cordelia. "It was something to do with the Colonel's letter, wasn't it?" I persisted, taking out the pins and removing my hat. "Oh, come along, Bertha, don't pretend to know nothing about it. What's being said below-stairs? Hasn't Philippe commented on it?"

She gave a contemptuous sniff. "Him! I don't care to listen to him, madam – he's much too French, if you know what I mean. I wouldn't trust him further than I could throw him."

So much for Charles's rather smarmy valet. But I was sure that she knew something, she had that air about her, and it was a well-known fact that nothing happened in the drawing room and bedchambers of their masters which was not discussed in detail in the servants' hall. "Please help me. What is going on?"

She was taking out the dress I would wear for dinner. Her face appeared, ghostlike, in the mirror at which I sat. "I think it has to do with money, madam," she replied slowly.

"Money?" I paused, meeting the eye of that mirror image. "But Grandfather said we could go to London at his expense as a kind of second honeymoon. I'm sure he would not have objected to my having new clothes and entertaining."

"Of course not, madam, but he did object to paying Mr de Grendon's gambling debts," she said crisply.

"He hasn't been gambling," I snapped, then knew at once that I had been living in a fool's paradise. Tiny vignettes flashed through my mind, uppermost of which was that air of feverish excitement which had glittered in Charles's eyes at times during our stay. I had put it down to alcohol and I suppose I was right, but it had been combined with his obsession for gaming. He had often gone to his club and I had assumed that he sought male company. I had been cleverly sidetracked by Cordelia. She had a talent for discovering entertainment and the enjoyments she had offered had been so manifold and varied that I had been given little time to concern myself with his absences. As long as he was there in my bed at night, I had convinced myself that all was well.

I was aware of an intense chill, although the fire leapt and the curtains had been drawn snugly, shutting out the dark evening. Bertha's hands were gentle on my hair. "I'm afraid that isn't true, madam. Someone wrote to Colonel Curzon telling him the extent of the money your husband owed and that letter was the result. Now Mr de Grendon may have to mortgage Combermere to pay his usurer."

"Oh, God," I groaned. "But he's so possessive about everything which belongs to him. He'll hate doing that." My heart ached for him. Poor Charles. Anger rose up in a hot wave. "It's those damned friends of his!" I exclaimed furiously. "They lead him on, I'd like to kill them!"

"Madam, I did try to warn you," she began. "This isn't the first time by a long chalk that he's run into trouble. Everyone in the village knows him of old. I'd hoped that he might have turned over a new leaf when he married you – but leopards don't change their spots!"

"He has changed, Bertha – of course he has. There must be some mistake," I replied angrily. I refused to discuss it more, finishing my toilet quickly and going to find Charles.

I looked in vain. He did not appear at dinner. Cordelia and I ate alone in that shadowy hall. Our attempts at conversation dwindled. She sat at one end of the long table and I at the other. The candles struggled to overcome the pressing darkness. Jonas waited on us and Cordelia kept drinking and staring at me. "God, I'm so bored!" she announced suddenly.

"You'll have to get used to it," I grated, nerves jangling as I gave vent to the irritation which her continual presence caused me. "From what I hear, we'll have to live quietly for a while. No more trips to town – no parties, no visits to the theatre, and no new clothes." I brought this out with a savage satisfaction and my inner feelings about her obviously came through. She permitted herself a small smile but there was a waiting in her eyes.

"And what exactly have you heard, Eleanor? Has Charles discussed the situation with you?" She was inferring that he hadn't, wanting me to know that she was perfectly *au fait* with the matter. I was sick to death of playing second fiddle to her – they were so damnably close, those two.

"Where is he? I want to talk to him alone," I rapped out.

She yawned and stretched and took the decanter to her glass. "He's ridden over to Henford Grange."

"To see Grandfather?" Hope and fear warred in me. I wished that he had told me he was going. I could have gone too.

She nodded, maddeningly cool, holding up her glass and staring into the golden liquid. "He thinks the Colonel is being unreasonable. Naturally, we spent a lot in London, but he wanted you to have a good time, didn't he?"

I had difficulty in swallowing and my hands were clammy although the room was damply cold. Damn her. I didn't care if she sneered because I had been listening to servants' gossip. Something had to be said. "It wasn't that, and you know it. The trouble is about Charles's gambling."

Cordelia did not bat an eyelid. Her smile became fixed and those eyes, so like her brother's, were steely. "This is nothing to do with you, Eleanor. Mind your own business."

I had not quite realised just how much anger, resentment and jealousy was bottled up inside me until that moment when she spoke to me as if I was a silly child.

I threw my napkin on the table and stood up. "It *is* my business. I'm his wife, and I don't like everyone thinking that he's a spendthrift and waster."

She remained absolutely composed, apart from that tight smile. "Well, my dear, that's exactly what he is," she drawled. I was flabbergasted. "How can you sit there so calmly and say that? He's your own brother?"

"Precisely – and I know him better than anyone else. We've stuck together through thick and thin. He's often been in trouble, but usually manages to come out of it unscathed. Sometimes he wins at the tables – at others he loses heavily. This is a great deal of bother about nothing."

I was shaking with rage, appalled by her attitude. "But this time Grandfather is involved. He's an honourable man, even if Charles isn't. He'll insist that the debts are paid in full and curtail our allowance so that it doesn't happen in the future," I yelled at her.

She rose and strolled towards the fireplace, stretching out her slim hands to the flames. "Oh dear – such righteous indignation. Very tiresome, I must say, and if you think I intend to curtail my pleasures you're in for a shock."

Sudden suspicion flashed like lightning on a dark night. "Is that why you left Monte Carlo? Because he was in debt?" I demanded.

She shrugged, subsiding into a chair and crossing one leg over the other. "Maybe. I don't want to talk about it. You married Charles and must accept him for what he is – the bad along with the good."

There was a red haze covering my vision. I wanted to hit her across her beautiful, ruthless, uncaring face. Hatred poured through me in an uncontrollable torrent, too long stifled. "I love him and I do accept him, but does this mean that I have to tolerate you too? Why don't you go away? Leave us in peace? I can't stand it! All right, so you're used to living in each other's pockets, but this has changed. He's married to me. He doesn't need you. Make your own life. Find yourself a husband and go away! Go away!" I screamed, beside myself with fury.

It would have been easier if Cordelia had shouted back, possibly even attacked me, but her very calm was more menacing than a show of temper. "How stupid you are," she replied frostily. "You understand nothing – know nothing. How dare you suggest separating my brother and me?"

I opened my lips on a slashing retort but at that moment Charles came in through the door, shedding his overcoat and flinging it down. He brought with him a blast of cold night air, and I was conscious of that same intense, irrational excitement which I had felt on meeting him for the first time. I had no chance to read his expression. His opening words left me numb.

"The Colonel had a heart attack shortly before I arrived at the Grange. I'm afraid he is dead."

Chapter 5

Almost a year to the day after my wedding, I attended my grandfather's funeral. Snowflakes drifted from a pewter sky to settle in the churchyard. I could not but help remembering how I had stood there as a bride, receiving congratulations. Afterwards, we went to Henford Grange for the reading of the will. I was stunned by grief, walking like someone in a trance, sitting when told, helped in and out of carriages, answering the kind condolences automatically. I couldn't believe it. I had known he was ill, but he had taken such an active part in country life, probably doing too much – this was what everyone said. My aunts corroborated Charles's story of how he had gone there to find grandfather dead. They blamed themselves for having gone out about some charity work or other, leaving him in his study, but it could have happened at any time, and they must not feel guilty. No sisters could have been more devoted to their brother, concerned friends insisted.

So I unexpectedly found myself in the possession of a substantial fortune, and Henford Grange. My aunts, after a decent time set aside for mourning, moved into the Dower House. I didn't know what to do with such a large, rambling manor, but my husband had plenty of ideas. "We'll take over when we come back from abroad," he said as we lay in bed one night. "Cordelia can stay at Combermere. I shan't have to mortgage it now. We'll need a bigger house. I want to give weekend parties. Bertie can come down and stay. Cordelia has ambitions to inch her way into the Marlborough House set – with a bit of luck and so much money, she might even catch the eye of the King."

I shifted impatiently in the circle of his arm. He had been so nice to me since the funeral, but there was always Cordelia and her welfare. My heart had leapt when he mentioned her remaining at Combermere, but now he was talking of using Henford Grange as the stage by which she might launch herself into the court circle. It's my damned money after all, I thought resentfully, but this was not strictly true. I was married to Charles, therefore my fortune became his, apart from a small annuity which the Colonel had so arranged that it could be touched by no one save myself.

"Cordelia – Cordelia – it's always Cordelia and what she wants," I muttered, and the hand which had been caressing me grew still.

"She is my sister," he murmured, his lips against my forehead.

"You are as thick as thieves," I said, unable to keep that shrewish edge from my voice. "Why should we go on supporting her? She spends money like water.

Grandfather didn't leave me his wealth to pour into her greedy hands."

"He should have left her something." His voice sliced through the candlelight gloom and I could see a warning smile on his scarred face. "As his mistress she deserved it."

It was like a blade slipped into my heart, chilling my blood, making me sit bolt upright, staring into the dusky recesses of the room and hardly breathing. No. It wasn't possible. Charles was lying. Slowly the breath left my lungs and I lay back on the pillow. "Stop teasing, Charles. The joke's in bad taste. Don't be so ridiculous. He was an old man."

"And old men like a bit of fun, same as every other fellow," he answered lightly. I looked at him as he lounged on one elbow, and there was something in his eyes which terrified me.

"I don't believe you." My voice was low and taut, bewildered pain making my lips stiff.

"Who'd you think she went to Buxton with in the spring?" he asked slowly, and I saw the gleaming steel colour of his eyes, honed to a sharp, cutting edge.

"It's not true." I clung to my image of the Colonel stubbornly. He had been so honourable, so trustworthy. The image became distorted by suspicion.

"Ask Cordelia," he answered and swung his legs over the side of the bed, padding naked into the corridor. I heard him tapping at her door and the low murmur of their voices. She sounded amused. Soon they appeared together, she in her black silk nightgown and over-robe, and Charles as bare as the day he was born. Neither was in the least embarrassed, and they should have been for there was something in this scene which was exciting my husband.

He slipped in beside me; she sat on the coverlet, and: "Come on, Cordelia, tell Eleanor about it. She refuses to believe that you went to bed with the Colonel."

"Of course I did," she smiled, that hateful woman,

bizarre and sensual and treacherous. "He gave a good performance too, for a man of his age – he worried about his heart a bit, but I soon made him forget that."

"You deliberately set out to seduce him, when you knew perfectly well that such exertion could shorten his life?" I whispered, stunned as much by her callousness as her immorality.

"We didn't want him hanging on too long," said Charles. "Not after I'd stuck my neck out and married you."

"We planned it between us," she confided brightly. "It worked like a charm – and he gave me lots of jewellery and pretty things. He doted on me, you see, and I think I made his last months very happy. He was able to convince himself that he'd regained his youthful vigour, poor old thing."

"You're nothing but a whore!" I spat out, prickles of loathing crawling over my skin as she tried to take my hand.

"A most expensive one," she corrected with a smile. "I prefer to think of myself as a courtesan."

"You did well, Cordelia, I'll give you that," remarked Charles, stretching lazily under the sheet, one arm about me, the other hand holding a glass. They had been drinking all through dinner. "And he didn't like it a bit when I told him that if he refused to settle my debts, I'd make bloody sure that everyone knew about your little affair."

My mind was slipping notches, blanked by a kind of disbelieving shock. "When did you see him?" I gasped.

"Before he died."

"But you said that you'd not seen him that day – that he was dead when you got there."

"I thought it prudent to bend the truth a little. No one saw me enter the house, you see. I used a secret door which Cordelia told me about. It connected with his study, useful for clandestine meetings. They were most discreet. I don't think anyone suspected, not even your nosy old aunts. I told him, point-blank, that I'd come to demand a settlement with my moneylender. It was embarrassing me. I couldn't go to my club until the slate was wiped clean. He refused, so then I said that I had some rather passionate love letters which he had written to my sister, besides the receipts for their stay in a hotel in Buxton. I advised him to reconsider." Charles's voice was gay, as if recounting some amusing story. I couldn't grasp the enormity of what he was telling me. "I really didn't expect him to get so angry. He exploded with rage and attacked me. Then he suddenly stopped, clutching at his heart. His face turned a strange colour and he struggled for breath. Before I knew what had happened, he'd collapsed. I could see that it was too late to do anything, so I scarpered. I waited a while, then rode up to the front door, suitably amazed and most distressed to find that he'd just been found dead of a heart attack."

They were both smiling at me, that terrible pair, very pleased with themselves, as alike as two peas in a pod. All the drifting truths which I had been avoiding for months came to a halt then and hung in the air as grim reminders of my own foolishness. "So now you have my inheritance, and you think you've nothing more to worry about," I said quietly.

"It's worked out perfectly." He eased down under the covers and his hand came across to rest on my breast. "I don't like blackmail – an ungentlemanly occupation, and now it isn't necessary. My debts are discharged, we've plenty of cash, the future looks rosy, and I'm going to take you away on a long holiday in the sun."

"You are a murderer." I brought this out calmly, unemotionally. It was the only way I could function at that moment.

"That's a very nasty word, my dear." He was nibbling my neck and then smiled up at me, rakish, charming, his chestnut hair falling loosely over his forehead. "I'm pleased with the way you're taking this. I thought you were about to throw a fit of hysterics."

To my eternal shame, I must confess that, even now, my body responded to his touch. I was like two people then, one experiencing that fevered intensity, the other hanging back, appalled. Pictures of my grandfather kept impinging on my mind, and there I sat with the two villains who had engineered his death. It was like some terrible nightmare. A hard, rocklike core of bitterness filled me, but there were no tears – not yet. Grandfather, I cried in my soul, how could you? What made you so foolish as to become infatuated with such a woman? All the parts of the jigsaw were falling into place – his toleration of Charles, his acquiescence to my marriage – these had been paths which led him to Cordelia's arms. There are so many hidden reasons for what we do, I thought wearily. Even the reasons which seem clear are often wrapped in disguises. How painfully well did I know that. Who was I to condemn a man for seeking a little love, a little happiness? What upset me most was that he had been so gullible. I had respected him, now I could no longer do so, even in memory.

"What's to stop me going to the police?" I said suddenly.

I felt him stiffen, and Cordelia was watching me, lynx-eyed. "A wife can't give evidence against her husband," he reminded. "Besides, how could you prove it? I didn't kill him. I didn't lay a single finger on him. I should merely say that you're unbalanced by grief. Cordelia would uphold this. We might even get you committed to an asylum for the insane."

Was this really my husband speaking? I felt a sickening surge of fear. "How can you say such things, Charles? I'm your wife. You love me, don't you?"

He and his sister exchanged a smile, secretive and intimate. "Love? What is love? Have I ever said that I loved you?" he asked musingly. "I wanted you. I still do and, through you, I'll now be able to live in luxury for the rest of my days. It's not such a bad bargain."

"A bargain? I never thought of our marriage as a bargain," I whispered and all the time I was remembering – ah, so much. Those heated nights of passion, his overwhelming lovmaking – yet never, as I recalled, had he confessed to being in love.

"All marriages are bargains in some form or another. You got a personable husband who opened your eyes to more physical delight than you had ever dreamed existed, and I was given you in return – a lovely wife with even lovelier prospects. I was prepared to overlook the fact that you'd been reared in an orphanage, and that your father wasn't a gentleman."

At any other time I should have risen to the bait, but his insults could not penetrate the paralysis which gripped me. "You knew about me when we met?"

"I made it my business to find out as soon as we returned to England and I heard that the Colonel was ensconced at Henford Grange, bringing with him a long-lost granddaughter." In a few cynical words, he destroyed my illusions. I had believed it to be a romantic love match. Dreams, crazy dreams – all the time he had carried out his courtship in a coldly calculating manner.

"But why me?" I asked, thankful for this numbness which deadened feeling. "Surely there were plenty of suitable girls, daughters of the gentry?"

"Ah, but you see, they've been living here for years and years, and knew of us before we went to Europe," put in Cordelia conversationally. "Apart from the scandal which had surrounded us when Joe Duffield and Miss Annette were here, there was the affair of the landlord's wife at the Ship Inn. It was because of this that we decamped when we did."

Though dazed, my mind was working frantically. The Ship Inn. It lay in the next village. We had been there not long before we left for London. Charles had insisted on driving his shiny new car. We had stalled in the village and he had been in a hellish mood, storming off to get help. Cordelia and I had waited in the courtyard of an inn. A woman, black-eyed and comely, had come out to bring us refreshments. It was then that I had noticed the child. He was playing in the doorway of the stable, a lively toddler whose features were vaguely familiar.

Now Cordelia supplied the brutal answer. "One of Charles's bastards lives there with his mother. He got her pregnant, and her husband came round threatening blue murder. We went away till the fuss had died down. We needed a change anyway – life was terribly dull." She was sprawling on the bed, her robe falling open, her magnificent limbs glistening through the transparency of her nightgown. "It's all right now, of course. Her husband died and she runs the inn. These things happen, you know, but it was just as well that your grandfather was out of the country at the time."

Bertha had known. Bertha had tried to warn me. Yet if she had come straight out with it, I wouldn't have listened. Even now, I loved him, with a sick love which was like a throbbing wound within me. I was prepared to forgive him, telling myself bravely that we would make a fresh start now that he had been frank with me. We would go away together, quite alone and, perhaps, we might rediscover that spark which had brought us together for, despite what he had just said, I refused to believe that he was nothing but a scheming opportunist. There had been more! I couldn't accept the alternative.

Love is blind, so they say, but though I struggled not to see, I was forced to – no longer able to excuse him, or even to hope. Cordelia and he were reminiscing about the old days and, as I listened, it seemed that my love was crumbling, bit by bit, its diamond brightness chipped and tarnished by each cynical word.

"Of course, he had to go when I came of age," Charles was saying. "That damned Duffield! Christ, what a high opinion of himself the fellow had! Thought he was master here, but I soon changed his tune, the bastard!" But even as he spoke, there was gruding admiration in his tone.

"They'd been in control for so long, Charles," Cordelia added. "How many years was it? Ten at least. Uncle was only too happy to let them make every decision concerning us, far too busy with his own life to bother his head about a couple of orphans. Just as long as he had regular money from the estate, that was all he cared about. I can't say they were bad times. I enjoyed them, and they certainly taught us a lot."

He grinned, one eyebrow going up. "Didn't they just! He took your virginity and she robbed me of mine." He looked at me in such a way that I instinctively shrank back, but Cordelia was on my other side. "She was the older woman I told you about, Eleanor."

"She was a lady," said Cordelia. "Albeit down on her luck."

"So she might have been, but he was certainly no gentleman for all his pretence," said Charles grimly. "D'you remember how they taught us about sex? We used to watch while they demonstrated."

Her tongue crept out to run over her drooping lower lip. "I shall never forget. It was the one lesson I enjoyed."

"It usually ended in a free-for-all – four in a bed," he laughed, then his face sobered again. "But you had to get rid of a little bit of trouble, didn't you?"

She shuddered. "Don't remind me. Miss Annette took me to a dirty old hag in the back streets of London. It was horrible! But it had to be done for the father would have been Joe Duffield – "

"Or myself," he put in casually, "in either case, not good for the reputation of the de Grendons."

Comprehension dawned in a blinding scarlet glare. I gave Cordelia a violent shove. "Get out!" I screamed, pummelling at her with my fists. "Get out of my bed and out of this house! You filthy bitch!"

"Who the hell d'you think you're pushing?" she blazed back at me, clinging to the bed curtains. Though rage gave me strength, I couldn't shift her.

"Charles, tell her to go. Help me!" I shouted, in a paroxysm of rage, despair and disgust.

My husband was laughing. I shall never, as long as I live, forget the sound of that laughter. "Don't look so shocked, Eleanor. It happens when boys and girls are growing up together."

"Not brothers and sisters! It's unnatural! Horrible! Get her away from me!" I was trembling so much that I could no longer move, hemmed in by the de Grendons.

"Often brothers and sisters, I can assure you. And why not? We are so fond of one another." He was smiling still, his calm making him hateful. "You know so little, Eleanor, but we'll teach you. Now that the Colonel is gone, you'll have no one to turn to but us. Don't you fancy the idea of Cordelia sharing our bed? What a pity, for it rather appeals to me. You might even enjoy it. She's highly skilled, you know, and makes love to women as well as men. I'd like to lie back and watch you – then you could both turn your attention to me."

"Leave me alone!" I cried as he reached out to pull me against him. I swung up my hand and slapped him across his mocking face.

His return blow was so violent that my head jerked back and struck the wooden panelling of the four-poster. Through spinning sickness, I heard him growl: "I'm master here and don't forget it! You'll do as I say, now and always!"

"If she doesn't leave this house immediately – then I'll see a lawyer! I'll divorce you! You won't get a penny of my money!" I defied him through my pain.

His face wavered in the candlelight, devilish, evil. "Don't provoke me, bitch," he snarled. "I didn't kill the Colonel, but I did put an end to Joe Duffield. His horse didn't throw him – I clubbed him to death. I'd not think twice about ridding myself of a troublesome wife.

Accidents are easily arranged, and the inheritance would come to me. Be careful what you do."

Our bedroom was well away from the servants' quarters. Cordelia would be his willing accomplice. They were drunk and very dangerous. Amoral, unprincipled – to call them animals would have been an insult to noble beasts. All this ran through my mind, coupled with dread. My defiance had been foolhardy and I was about to be punished for it.

I screamed as I tried to leap from the bed, but it was Cordelia who grabbed at my nightgown, pinning me down, tearing it from my body. I threshed wildly, hitting out, my fist meeting flesh and hearing curses. Charles twisted my arms behind me and roped my wrists. His face was no longer handsome. It had become a horrible mask. He ground his knee into my thighs, forcing them apart.

During those hours of pain and cruelty, I learned that whips, obscene devices and every orifice of the body became vehicles for their perverted pleasure. In my memory, everything is distorted by the outrages inflicted on me. I cannot be certain who abused me most, Charles or his sister. Eventually they tired of me, turning to one another for further gratification. Bruised, bloodied, almost unconscious, I lay and watched as she took her place beneath him. I swore to be revenged on them, if it took me a lifetime.

Six weeks later, Charles and I went to Liverpool and there boarded a Bibby Line mail steamer bound for Egypt. He was bored with the Continent, he said, though I thought it more likely that he had outstayed his welcome in the casinos of the French Riviera and Italy. We were going to Alexandria where there was a colony of wealthy Europeans and fine gaming houses. Cordelia did not come with us. She had expressed a wish to open up the London house and spend the summer entertaining lavishly.

We made a most attractive couple. Everyone on board said so. He was so distinguished and charming, whilst I was deemed pretty and amiable, and they all agreed how very delightful it was to see such a happily married young pair who were obviously so much in love. Charles was at his sparkling best, a different man now we had left Combermere and Cordelia, but nothing could dispel the bitterness which ate into my heart.

We had never spoken of that weird, unnatural night spent in the Master Bedchamber. Next day, they acted as if nothing unusual had happened. I wondered if I had imagined it, although the welts on my skin had been proof enough, the memory never to leave me. I had waited in fear and dread for them to try it again, but they left me alone, wrapped up in each other. I was so glad to leave Combermere. Its very walls now seemed impregnated with sin, as if the unquiet spirits of Duffield and Miss Annette walked there still. With a sick fascination, I had found myself drawn to the mere where she had ended her wretched life. It lay in a great hollow, bordered by a thick wood, a gloomy spot where hidden moorhens uttered broken, rusty cries. This was where that miserable woman had drowned. Miss Annette, the governess who, with her depraved lover, had debauched those children left in her care, sowing seeds which had distorted their lives.

I wrote to ease my mind, but furtively now. I didn't want Charles to read my journal and, before we left, I took it to the Dower House and asked Louisa to look after it. Charles was amused by my interest in "scribbling", as he patronisingly described it, and I made copious notes on the journey which, years later when I became established as an author, were published as *By Sea, to the Land of the Pharaohs*. But I digress and must waste no more time in telling what happened next.

We chugged down the coast of England and it was not until we reached open water that I became seasick. This misery lasted for days and I missed a good deal of shipboard fun. Not so Charles, whose stomach was like cast iron. He spent his time drinking and playing faro with other male passengers. As we left Gibraltar and entered the calmer waters of the Mediterranean, I recovered a little and then realised that it was not only the motion which had been making me so sick. I consulted the ship's doctor who confirmed my suspicions. He smiled broadly and congratulated me on my pregnancy. I had to sit down, my knees suddenly weak. I forced a smile to my lips. Yes, of course I was delighted, I said, but in my heart there were reservations too dire and deep to confess. I didn't want Charles to know. It was absurd, probably inaccurate, though times and dates suggested it, but I felt instinctively that the child had been conceived on that awful night of revelations. It was as if it was Cordelia's baby as well as ours. Every time I looked into its little face, I should recall that humiliation, that depraved union which had nothing to do with love.

I asked the doctor to keep my news a secret, saying that I would tell my husband in my own time. He laughingly agreed, no doubt accustomed to the fancies of expectant mothers. I knew that Charles wanted a legitimate heir, but there was a great burden of sadness in me. My love was a sick thing now, devoid of joy. I feared him and could no longer trust him. He had shown me that it was possible to feel lust without love and I nurtured this feeling, letting him know when he took me in his arms that the magic had vanished. He seemed content with our animal mating, my hardness and resistance an amusing challenge, I think.

There was much to distract me from my melancholy brooding. I adored the Eastern ports of call, but these were as nothing compared to Alexandria. It was early summer and terribly hot, with winds and sand storms spoiling its beauty sometimes. Bertha and I were bubbling with excitement when we landed and, after the usual fuss with customs officials and baggage-handlers, we found ourselves being driven to the largest, most expensive hotel in the town. We could have been staying in Torquay or Brighton, so well-appointed were our apartments. It had a most British atmosphere, complete with splendid bathrooms and palm-decorated dining room where a string quartet played softly, but there were exotic scenes glimpsed through every window, and white-robed, tarboush-wearing servants.

The other guests were a cosmopolitan crowd united by the common bond of wealth and titles. Once we had settled in, we did all the things expected of foreign visitors, going on conducted tours of the temples, museums and tombs, shepherded by agile-tongued guides. In the beginning, Charles came along too, but soon became bored. I continued to sightsee with Bertha, whilst he disappeared in the direction of the rue Rosette, a notorious gambling area.

This made me angry. I hated to think of my money being wasted in this way. I was not so intimidated by him that I was afraid to let him know exactly how I felt about it. We quarrelled violently, the ornate bedroom resounding with our blistering words. I was confident that he wouldn't hit me whilst we were staying there. He was acting the part of the perfect English gentleman abroad. A battered wife would have spoiled this image. I couldn't stop him of course and, muttering threats, he would storm off to the fashionable gaming clubs to indulge in the high play.

After one such scene, I went out with Bertha, furious and disheartened. We were driven to a bazaar in the Arab section. Leaving our guide at the entrance, we entered alone, and I was cheered by our little adventure. There were so many fascinating things on sale. Bertha and I lost one another in the crowd, but I wasn't worried for we had anticipated this, arranging to meet under the entrance arch in an hour. For a while I forgot Charles, enthralled by the sights, sounds and smells. It was while I was haggling at a booth selling silks that I noticed one particular bedouin. A tall person with something about him which was oddly familiar. He turned and stared at me. A light-skinned hand came up and pushed back his hood. To my astonishment I saw flaming red hair framing a face that I knew. She had changed – older, more mature, the rounded profile of girlhood gone. It was Nancy.

In an instant we were in each other's arms, overcome with emotion. It had been so long – so much had happened – there was so much to say that we were speechless for a moment. But once I had recovered from the shock, I became alarmed at her manner. Oh, yes, she had changed all right, but then so had I. Taller than I remembered, well-spoken too, the rough edges had been polished and she had become quite beautiful, though gaunt and hollow-eyed as if she had not slept properly for ages. We did not talk for long. She was very agitated and desperately anxious to be on her way, her fear communicating itself to me and this too was odd, for I had known her to be utterly fearless. It was as if she was being hounded by something awful. I readily agreed when she begged that she might visit me, although I was doubtful of Charles's reaction. Like an apparition from the past, she reminded me of that vow made beneath the clock tower, holding me to it.

When she had disappeared, as mysteriously as she had come, I was left feeling distinctly jittery. When a voice spoke behind me, I started and swung round. It was the merchant, hands folded in his sleeves as he bowed low. "Lady, do not forget the purchase you were about to make. This is stuff of rare quality, too good to miss."

He was dark and hawk-featured, handsome as so many of the Arabs were, dignified and well versed in the English tongue, yet now he frightened me. I paid him the price asked, too scared to bargain, seeing menace in that alien scene which had seemed pleasant until I met Nancy. I was terribly conscious that I was the only

European present, alarming tales of the white-slave traffic flashing through my thoughts. Was this what Nancy feared?

"Thank you," I said as calmly as I could.

"May Allah protect you, lady," he replied, but as I was about to turn away, he spoke again in a low, hurried voice. "Permit me to give you a word of warning. I saw you talking with the English miss. Ah, no – her wearing of native robes deceives no one – have nothing to do with her, I beseech you."

"What d'you mean? She's a friend of mine," I snapped back.

"I do not wish to offend you, lady, and am humbly impressed by such loyalty, but there have been dire happenings at El Tarifa, the palace of the nobleman, Sir Nicholas Renshaw, for whom she works as a governess. It is a subject of much gossip and speculation in the market-place, and it is believed that the family are accursed!" He wagged his black beard earnestly. "Keep away from her, and may the blessings of Allah shower upon you and yours."

I gave him a sharp stare, considerably shaken, but could read nothing in his dark, veiled eyes. I did not reply, took up my package and searched for Bertha, relieved to see her fair, honest countenance among so many swarthy, secretive ones. I could not keep my news to myself, telling her about Nancy. She smartly dismissed the merchant's warning as so much foreign nonsense, having little time for anyone who wasn't downright British. We were close, she and I, and now, more than ever, I needed her steady common sense. We returned to the hotel at once and it was as well that we did for a sand storm whirled through Alexandria, hot and oppressive, blotting out the sun. It added to my feeling of apprehension, driving home the fact that we were in the East where strange, incomprehensible events could take place.

Charles came back from the casino in time for dinner

that night. The storm had died, calm restored to the elements and, by his almost friendly mood, I guessed with relief that he had been winning. It was a pleasant change and my spirits lifted a little. I wore my favourite evening gown, cream satin overlaid with lace, whilst he was extremely elegant in his well-tailored dinner suit. We ate by candlelight in a secluded alcove off the main dining room which was resplendent with pink marble, potted palms and gilt mirrors. In the background, the orchestra played soothingly. What a façade, I thought, and what are Nancy and I doing here, for God's sake? Both of us unhappy, both feeling threatened. I knew that I should have to tell Charles that she would be visiting me.

"The most extraordinary thing happened today," I began, as we lingered over the Turkish coffee. It was most difficult to put it into words. "I wonder if you can guess who I met in the bazaar?"

His big hands were folded round a brandy goblet. One of his dark eyebrows shot up. "Lord, how do I know? The Caliph of Baghdad? Rameses the second? A sheik propositioning you? Do tell – I can't wait!"

The sarcasm rolled from his tongue like the hiss of a serpent. Annoyance stiffened my backbone. "It was an old friend. D'you remember my mentioning Nancy and Rebecca?"

"Ah yes – your little girl lovers from the charity home," he jeered.

"It was Nancy I met. I hear that she's working as a governess – at El Tarifa, the residence of Sir Nicholas Renshaw."

"A governess, eh? Like Miss Annette? How charming. I've heard of the Renshaws – a Cornish family, I believe. My dear, you do seem to have this unfortunate predilection for underlings – Bertha, for example, and now a governess."

"You're a fine one to talk! Didn't underlings teach you the facts of life?" I snapped back. Then I controlled myself. I needed his cooperation. "I've asked her to tea here tomorrow."

His brows drew together in a scowl and he set his empty glass on the table. "Have you indeed? Remind me to be out."

"You weren't always so averse to governesses," I reminded sharply. His face hardened, the thin white line of his scar showing up starkly against his tanned cheek.

"It depends whether they're good looking and willing," he answered, eyes the colour of flint. "Is Nancy willing? Renshaw has a reputation with women, I recall, so I'll hazard a guess that she is."

"Why d'you constantly reduce everything to the lowest level?" I was angry on my friend's behalf. She'd not had time to tell me anything, but I doubted very much that she had succumbed to her employer. I remembered her to be resilient, uncompromising and brave, and there had been nothing about her that afternoon to suggest that her character had changed, though certainly she had been afraid. "She was a dear friend. Can't you receive her as such, Charles? My God, I've had to endure your friends often enough, and a damned nuisance they are too!"

"Eleanor, my dear – I think that you are forgetting yourself," he said with a tight smile which warned me that I would pay for it later. "So hot to defend this Nancy person. I always suspected that you were in love with her. You should introduce her to Cordelia."

"Damn you," I hissed between clenched teeth. "It wasn't like that."

He sighed and shook his handsome head. "Is that the way to speak to your loving husband? If this is what contact with Nancy does to you, then I'll have to put a stop to it – for your own good, my dear."

Fear lanced me. I had to see her. She was in trouble. His jibes had enraged me but I swallowed my pride. "I'm sorry, Charles," I said, my voice low, stabbing about in my mind for words to soften his temper. "Please forgive me. It's the heat – it makes me irritable. Can I see my friend tomorrow?"

He was egotistical enough to believe that he'd succeeded in browbeating me, and flung me a hard stare of impatience and animosity. Then he stood up. "Do as you damned please, but don't involve me. I'm going out now. Don't wait up for me. Oddly enough, I've recently met another of Renshaw's employees – his name is Paul Quiller. I'll ask him about this woman. What did you say she was called?"

"Nancy – Nancy Gray," I replied, my thoughts already stretching away to that desolate wasteland which would form the remainder of the evening.

There was little pleasure in his company these days, yet I could still feel sad because he preferred the roulette wheel to myself. I was nervous too, the words of the merchant haunting me. What did we English really know of the Eastern mind? Depression swamped me, that wretched lowness of spirit which dissolves into helpless tears and is a symptom of early pregnancy. There will be the baby soon, I whispered to myself in an attempt at comfort, then you'll be no longer alone. This seemed a terribly long way off, and I wondered how it would affect our lives. I found it hard to visualise Charles as a loving father. In vain I yearned for the security I had once known, weeping for my grandfather, wanting to see my aunts. It had been so peaceful at Henford Grange before I was overwhelmed by the maelstrom of passion.

Nancy arrived at about four o'clock on the following afternoon and was shown on to the wide verandah where I awaited her. I saw her first, and was shocked. Her face was white, ghastly, and there was a pinched look about her mouth. I waved to her and she ran towards me. I leapt up and our hands met. She was icy cold and trembling. I pushed her into a chair. "My dear girl, whatever is wrong? Here, drink this." I poured out a cup of hot, sweet tea, giving it to her for she was unable to speak. "Don't worry – I know a little of why you are in Alexandria and who you work for."

Her eyes lifted to mine, blank with terror. "Who told you? How do you know?" she whispered.

"It was the silk merchant. He warned me to have nothing to do with you. As if that would stop me." I tried to laugh scornfully but it stuck in my throat.

She had the look of a hunted deer. "He knew me then? They all know – I can't trust anyone. Oh, Nell – someone has put a curse on me. I'm doomed."

Superstitious dread crawled down my spine. "Nancy, my dear, how can you believe in such things? Is that what has upset you so?"

"No – no – something dreadful has happened. God, I'll never forget it – " she started to say, then paused, still seeing horrors.

"What is it? Tell me!" I urged.

"It's Sir Nicholas's wife – Lady Emily – she hanged herself this morning. I found her!"

My imagination painted the terrible picture. "How horrible! What did you do? Is this what you feared yesterday?"

"No. I didn't dream she'd do that. I wanted to see you about something else – but now – oh God – poor Lady Emily!" The cup was rattling against the saucer and I took it quickly, thinking that she was about to faint. "It was the sound which was so awful," she continued shakily. "I keep hearing it, over and over. It woke me from sleep, that weird, grating noise – she was strangling, you see, hanging from the tree beneath my balcony – her face was turned up towards me, as if she wanted me to hear – wanted me to help her – but it was too late – too late."

It would have been better if she had broken down and cried but she was beyond tears. I took her cold, clenched hand in mine. "It's the shock, dear. You'll feel calmer after a while."

She seemed hardly aware of me, staring straight

ahead. "Her doctor says it will haunt me for years. He's in a bad way too, poor Terence – he was in love with her."

There was so much that I couldn't even begin to understand. All that concerned me was Nancy. "What about her husband? He must be dreadfully distressed."

"Oh, Nell – so many unhappy things have happened recently. The boy I was engaged to look after has vanished."

"How? Why?" My bewilderment was growing.

"I don't know. He disappeared days ago, my dear little Jeffrey. His bodyguard was found murdered. They say it may be kidnappers, and the servants whisper of evil spirits, but I've a feeling that it's the work of someone much closer – even a member of the family. I'm trying to find out, but I'm blocked every inch of the way. I'm watched, Nell. I know I'm in danger."

This was hysterical talk, but Nancy had never been given to flights of fancy. "You must be mistaken," I insisted.

"I swear that I'm not." Her eyes held mind, desperate green eyes struggling to convince me of her sincerity. "I'm not mad. I'm not imagining it. You must believe me."

She recounted some of the story. It was garbled, disjointed, but shining through was her own devotion to Jeffrey. "And Sir Nicholas? What does he say about it?" I asked when she paused for a moment.

Her face flushed. "Nicholas? One never knows for certain what he thinks." Her use of his Christian name took me aback, but she was too upset to notice the slip, rushing on. "I don't want to implicate you, Nell, but please do what you can. It won't be easy, but there are places where information can be bought. Everyone has his price here. You could ask – no one knows you."

"Bertha will help," I said.

"Bertha?" Suspicion flared in her eyes.

"My maid, she's loyal and can be trusted."

"No one can be trusted," she muttered, her fingers mangling her handkerchief.

"Why don't you go to the police?"

"I can't. I daren't. They are searching for Jeffrey, falling over backwards to assist Sir Nicholas."

"Then everything is being done." I tried to give her the reassurance which I was far from feeling. So, Nicholas Renshaw was a gentleman and, at one time, I too would have deemed him above suspicion. But not any more – not after my own experiences with the de Grendons.

"I think that Jeffrey has been murdered," she said.

Around us teacups clinked. There was the subdued murmur of small talk from every table. The orchestra played a Gilbert and Sullivan selection, and we sat there speaking of murder. "This can't be true," I breathed, struggling to hang on to rationality.

Then the dam burst. She held nothing back, speaking rapidly, intently, filling in the details which she had omitted before, even confessing her love for Sir Nicholas. When she had finished, I sat there silently. Had it been anyone else but my practical old friend, I would have thought the tale to be the product of delirium. But I believed her when she said that she would have laid down her life for him and the child. My own life had taken such devious twists and turns, so what could I do but believe her?

"I'll do anything I can to help you," I said at last.

She sighed and became much calmer and I realised how lonely she had been. Partly to take her mind from her own troubles, I recounted my own adventures. Not all, of course, there are some things which are not discussed, too complex to put into words. "Are you certain that you're happy?" she asked, and I could not meet her probing gaze.

"As happy as most married women," I shrugged. She had enough problems without my adding to them.

"Charles is handsome, and we're rich. What more could I want?"

She was listening to me, glancing around her nervously, her body taut as if ready to spring up and make a bolt for it. The tense quality was infecting me too. "Will your husband help me?" she asked.

"I don't know." I thought it most unlikely, but did not wish to discourage her.

Waiters were hovering to clear the tables. It was time to leave. Nancy drew a leather-bound book from her bag and slipped it on to my lap. "This is my journal. I've written everything there. It's already been tampered with. I don't know who did it, but someone fears what it contains. Read it. Guard it well. Do what you can for me. Here's the address of the Renshaw palace. I can be reached there, but don't mention anything damning if you write to me. I know this must sound absurd, but I'm in deadly earnest."

I walked to the entrance with her. She seemed reluctant to leave, yet too agitated to remain. I noticed how she peered into the hot, dusty street, looking this way and that before finally departing. I stood there for a moment, watching her tall, erect figure hurrying away.

I didn't know what to make of it and when I reached my bedroom, I went out on to the balcony overlooking the bay where the water was a deep, rich blue. The hazy distances were pinpointed with a blaze of gold from the mosques and minarets. Poor Nancy, was she deluded? Had love turned her brain? I marvelled at the strangeness of our meeting in Egypt of all places. What weird concordance of events had brought that about? Fate, destiny, the will of Allah? I tried unsuccessfully to discuss this with Bertha when she came to help me dress, but she was an avid believer in coincidence and had a sensible explanation for everything.

When I was attired for the evening, she left and I sat down and unlocked Nancy's journal. I had thought that I would have time to glance through it before the dinner gong boomed, but Charles came into the room, pulling at his tie and tossing his coat across the bed. I jumped, and tried to hide the book. I was too late. "What have you there?" he asked, reaching my side in a couple of strides.

"Just one of my diaries," I lied, my hands pressed over it.

"Give it here. I want to see what you've written about me." He was looking down, his eyes narrowed, holding out one hand.

I was wary and confused, then: "I can't do that. To tell you the truth, it isn't mine. Nancy asked me to look after it for her."

He became very still with that quietness which I had learned to dread, more menacing than his violent outbursts. "So you saw Nancy Gray. Quiller had been telling me about her."

I remembered that name. Nancy had said he was Sir Nicholas's agent. She had seemed unsure of him. "What did he say?" I asked.

Charles poured himself a whisky and lay on the couch. His face was beaded with sweat, his hair plastered to his forehead. He wrenched at his shirt buttons, tearing the garment off. He always looked bigger without his clothes, savagely uncivilised. "He told me quite a lot," he drawled and, with a drop of my spirits, I recognised that beneath that quiet exterior, he was angry. "I've had a hell of a night, and the day hasn't been much better. The luck was against me."

I hadn't seen him since dinner the night before and this had been a relief, leaving me free to concentrate on Nancy. "Did you lose much money?"

"Yes, I bloody well did. Then I won some back and went on playing, hoping to recoup it all, but it was just not my night for winning," he growled. It was the same old tale that I had heard so often. This compulsion was beyond my comprehension. "I'll have to go to the bank tomorrow and arrange for more cash to be transferred here. Unless, of course, I do well tonight," he continued.

Oh, why won't he stop? Anger surged in me. We were rich, but our resources weren't unlimited. On shipboard he had played constantly, drinking as well, and the more befuddled and annoyed he became, the higher he pushed the stakes. And here it was not only cards – in the casinos the roulette wheel revolved ceaselessly.

He was lounging at his ease, long legs in their narrow grey trousers stretched out on the couch. "Quiller tells me that there was a tragedy at El Tarifa this morning."

"I know. Nancy spoke of it." I wondered what was going on behind those mocking eyes.

"Lady Emily was quite dotty. Hung herself from a tree in the garden. Things haven't been going well for them lately. A nephew has disappeared – a servant found with his throat cut. Did Nancy tell you about this too?"

"Yes, she did." Now was the moment to enlist his aid and, at one time, I wouldn't have hesitated, thinking him the soul of chivalry. Now I wanted to laugh at my own folly.

The room was filled with the glow of the setting sun, crimson as blood. Long bars of colour lay across the sky, and I could hear the chanting, spine-chilling call to prayer. I thought of Nancy and her awakening at dawn. She had looked at death then. Philippe was moving about in the bathroom which annexed our chamber. There was the sound of water running into the tub. Charles stirred and I thought he was about to bathe before dinner, but instead he sat up and fixed me with those cold eyes. "I don't think you should see Nancy again, Eleanor. Quiller spoke well of her, but he also hinted that she'd been acting queerly. He described her as a hysterical woman who's spreading all manner of unpleasant rumours concerning the Renshaws. I forbid you to become involved."

"Listen, Charles – I've known her practically all my life. There's no one more level-headed." I retorted, gripping her journal. "What d'you know of Quiller? Who is he anyway? If he's a friend of yours from the casino, then he can't be much good."

"Oh, listen to Miss Prim," he jeered. "Is that what you think about me, my dear? You and your charity-brat friends! At least Quiller has spent years among the best sort of people. I'd take his word against hers any day." He towered above me and his face was dark with fury. I caught the smell of whisky on his breath. "I shan't tell you again, Eleanor. You are not to meet her. Give me that journal. God knows what poisonous rubbish she's been scribbling there. You're so stupid that you'll believe anything – even the ravings of a madwoman!"

"I'm not so stupid as I was when I fell in love with you, nor so naive!" I shouted. "You and your loathsome sister have taught me a great deal!"

His hand shot out and struck me across the face. "Shut your spiteful mouth!" he grated. I tasted the salt of blood and tears, but had not realised that I was crying. "I know what's best for you," he went on and his voice was cool now. "You mustn't concern yourself in this affair. Her wild accusations are nothing more than fury because Sir Nicholas ended their liaison. She was his mistress."

"That's a damnable lie!" I tried to rise, but his hand was on my shoulder, pushing me down. His fingers caressed the bare skin but it was a touch which I knew could turn into pain if he willed.

"No doubt we'll read about it in this diary of hers. Let me have it."

"No!" I struggled to keep it but he prised my fingers apart, snatching it up and holding it high, out of my reach. "Oh, Charles – don't. She trusts me! I promised to keep it!"

"I'll take great care of it, don't worry," he replied, his mocking laughter ringing through the room. "Now, send for Bertha and repair your face. You'll look especially beautiful tonight, my dear. I'm taking you out."

"I don't want to go anywhere with you."

"Ah, but you will." There was an ominous note in his voice as he stalked towards the bathroom. "I've arranged to meet Quiller and some friends of his. One is a rich Arab who has begged me to introduce him. He saw you from afar the other day, and declares that you are the lovelist of creatures. I've told him that I'll bring you with me tonight."

"You owe Quiller money."

"Yes, a large amount of money, but I intend to win it back. You'll have a softening effect on him perhaps, so you'll be damned civil or I'll want to know why."

Chapter 6

I could eat little at dinner, assailed by that sickness which swept over me willy-nilly these days. Charles no doubt thought my lack of appetite was due to the scene we had just had. I could not bring myself to tell him that I was with child – I'd told no one, not even Bertha. So we sat there, the epitome of the happily married couple enjoying a sojourn in the East. We were extremely well behaved, in public. No one would have guessed that there was a perverted streak in my husband, a heartlessness which made him capable of cruelty, an immorality which led him to demonstrate to his wife his incestuous relationship with his sister.

I had recovered my equilibrium to some extent, and by the time Bertha had helped me tidy up, a feeling of deadly calm had descended on me. She could see that I had been crying, her eyes anxious, face indignant every time she glanced towards the bathroom where Charles was talking gaily with his valet. I said nothing and she did not probe, knowing her place, but every line of her stocky body proclaimed that she was for me, one hundred per cent.

"I'll finish my brandy and then we'll go," Charles said, smiling into my eyes. "You'll enjoy a visit to the casino, won't you, my dear? I might even permit you to indulge in a small flutter." He leaned across to kiss my cheek, and the other diners smiled indulgently, wherepon he made a great display of husbandly devotion, whispering in my ear so that everyone thought he was speaking words of love. "You'd better enjoy it and please Sheik El-Darim, or you'll regret it when we get back."

I looked into his face, challenging him, the cold expression in his eyes leaving me unmoved. "You devil! What have you done with Nancy's journal?"

He tapped his pocket significantly. "Don't worry. I have it safely here, beloved."

It was terrible to love him and yet know that he was not worth loving. And even more terrible to be so aware that, curled in the darkness deep in my body, was growing the child which should have been the perfect result of love. Had things been different, I should have been so proud and happy to give him an heir, yet this was now soured by knowledge and disillusion. I wanted to weep again, but all the tears in the world would not wash away this sense of betrayal.

We stepped out into the warm, star-spangled night and entered a waiting carriage which took us along the Corniche road, glittering with strings of coloured lights. On one side were grand houses, nestled amidst glorious gardens, and on the other, the long stretch of curving bay. All too soon we reached the mosque-like façade of the casino. Its door stood wide, ablaze with golden light, luring the foolish to cross the threshold. Nearby stood a large tree, overshadowing that grandiose frontage. It was a gnarled olive tree and it had a sad and sombre effect on me with its long, pointed leaves of dull green lined with a chilly pale tint, ancient and venerable, almost sacred, little in harmony with the flowering shrubs around it. I felt chilled to the marrow, remembering Nancy's grisly tale of Lady Emily's suicide. The atmosphere seemed thick with menace. There was something impending, something frightful, so real and tangible that it seemed to close about me, dark with threat.

There was nothing about the building itself which could have engendered this feeling. It was marvellous in every respect, lit by electricity, gorgeously decorated in exotic Eastern style. We passed through the gilded foyer to the gambling saloons beyond. I hung on Charles's arm as he stood looking around for his friends and I was struck by the quiet solemnity. Everyone spoke in whispers. There was something religious in the intensity of the proceedings. The large, spacious rooms were unfurnished, save for the long tables and chairs for those who played steadily and with enormous concentration, victims of that dreadful disease called play-fever.

Pallid-faced, sleepless, flinty-eyed croupiers spun that fatally fascinating ball in the roulette wheel, and mechanically swept in with their rakes the piles of money staked and lost by the infatuated players. Others crowded at their backs, silently waiting their turn. I saw cadaverous, yellow-skinned old women, their scrawny necks and withered arms covered with jewels, and others, beautiful and reckless, evidently in the pay of the croupiers, acting as decoys. Some of the men were hardened and ruthless, others young gentlemen having a fling, waiting eagerly to clutch their winnings or pale, unhappy looking, seeing their money dwindling away.

I glanced up at Charles and was sickened by his expression; it matched theirs. His eyes were veiled, hypnotised by that spinning ball, yielding to that mad, selfish compulsion which would not be denied whatever the cost. Further along were tables where even higher stakes were laid. *Trente et quarante* was perhaps a little more favourable to the customers than roulette, though it depended on the shuffling of the cards. Gold and notes were scattered on the baize, either for or against the numbers backed turning up. There was a barely leashed impatience in Charles's voice as he explained all this; he couldn't wait to begin playing, but he had to wait, and it was nearly an hour before his friends joined us.

"Ah, thank God! They're here at last," he exclaimed, and I turned towards the door, seeing a thin, blond man weaving his way through the crowd, accompanied by a robed sheik and a handsome youth.

"Mr de Grendon," he said, a quietly spoken Englishman who bowed when he reached us. "How nice to see you again, and this, I presume, is your charming wife."

I observed him closely, this Paul Quiller who knew Nancy. He was a smooth-tongued individual with perfect manners, almost foppish in dress, with white gloves, a white bow tie, white waistcoat. Good-looking too, in a rather effete way, but there was total lack of warmth in the hazel eyes which regarded me, although he smiled readily enough. This was the trouble, I think – he smiled too much.

"Mr Quiller, I'm pleased to meet you," I plunged in recklessly as he kissed my fingertips. "I understand that you know a friend of mine, Miss Nancy Gray."

One of his peaked eyebrows lifted and I saw him exchange a glance with Charles. "Why yes, indeed I do, Mrs de Grendon. An unfortunate young lady who is rather unwell at present, I'm afraid. We've had trouble at my employer's house."

"I know. She told me," I interrupted, rather unwisely. "May I hear your account of what's happened there?"

I had that wild sense of having nothing more to lose. I was suddenly tired of the pretence, wanting to smash through this veil of half-truths and secrecy. Nancy was depending on me. Charles refused to assist, therefore I must do it alone. Quiller seemed friendly; Nancy had told me that he was the one who had engaged her in London, but as we talked further, I found him baffling. He had a clever way of giving the impression that a question had been answered when, in reality, it had been deftly sidestepped. He also had a highly effective method of casually slipping his own questions into the conversation so that I answered without meaning to.

He presented his companions to me. Sheik El-Darim was a big man with a hooked nose, olive skin and a black beard. He grinned at me, displaying even white teeth, and his eyes undressed me in an embarrassing way. His compliments were effusive and, as he pressed closer, I was enveloped in a warm wave of heavy perfume. His English was good, and he told me that he'd been educated at a public school on British soil. He owned the casino, and a great deal of other property, an influential figure in Alexandria. Charles was not in the least offended by his blatant interest in me.

The other man was very different. There wasn't the slightest danger that he would try to seduce me – even my inexperienced eye could tell that. Talk about beauty! Heavens, he was a veritable Adonis. His features were classical, his eyes the colour of jet, and his crisply curling hair was raven black. There was a touch of petulance about his lips and his rounded chin was not quite firm enough for a man. He wore a midnight-blue jacket and a pink silk shirt, open at the neck where a paisley-patterned cravat was knotted with careless elegance. His waistcoat was of gold brocade, his trousers skin tight, and he spoke with an accent, partly Greek, partly Arab, making play with his delicately beautiful hands which sparkled with rings. His name was Osman, and it was strange to see him flirting openly with my husband.

"I pray that you will do me the great honour of entering my private apartment," purred El-Darim, and he led us to an arched doorway at the back of the saloon.

I stepped over the threshold and the full decadent opulence of the East burst open me in unrestrained bloom. The fine rooms of the casino faded into insignificance beside it. It dazzled the eye, a vision of Islamic art in vivid blues, umbers and yellow, contrasted with white. Overhead, magnificent lamps were suspended on chains, their oil giving off a sweet, powerful odour as the wicks burned. The ceiling was domed with stained glass, catching the light in a million rainbow shards. El-Darim took us to a massive divan, heaped with brocade cushions, seating himself upon it and inviting us to do likewise. Refreshments were brought – salvers of *kebabs* and dishes of Turkish Delight. There were silver jugs of sherbert and carafes of wine and *zahib*, along with a pot of coffee and tiny, handleless cups. The slender-stemmed tobacco pipes were produced, and a *hookah*. The sheik was showing the customary hospitality of his race, and everything was conducted in a leisurely fashion.

I began to hope that Charles had been mistaken in thinking that the object of our visit had been gambling. It was most civilised and I started to lose some of my tension. El-Darim was a cultured man, as much at home discussing the opera houses of Europe as the merits of his thoroughbred racehorses. His compliments were like balm to my bruised feelings. I warmed to him, catching Charles's smile, and it was not flattering to know that my husband was encouraging me to please another man.

El-Darim looked on sardonically, then took the amber mouthpiece of the *hookah* from between his thick red lips and said. "There are some dancers waiting to entertain you."

"Female?" asked Charles as he accepted the proffered *hookah* and inhaled the smoke deeply. "Ladies of your household?"

El-Darim shook his head. "Even I cannot permit my women to appear in public unveiled, liberal though I am. These are dancing girls, the *Ghawazee*, from a tribe who've been entertainers for centuries."

He clapped his hands thrice, and a small band of musicians came in. They arranged themselves at the far end of the room and then, at the first wail of flute and beat of the drum, four dancers glided in on bare feet. They were unveiled and skimpily clad, wearing tight, low-cut bodices and gauze skirts slit to the thigh. Ornaments jangled as they moved seductively. Two of them wore rows of gold coins across their foreheads and another had a nose ring. They postured and gyrated, sensual and provocative, lovely sirens with their aquiline noses, high cheek-bones and slanting eyes outlined with kohl, the tips of their fingers, their palms and feet stained red with henna patterns.

The effect on Charles was dramatic and I grew cold as I watched him. He reached out to grab at one dancer in particular each time she whirled past him. She had the face of an Egyptian queen, almond eyes filled with bold invitation, and lips pouting promises. He succeeded in catching her, pulling her down across his lap, pouring wine into her mouth. She lay there, laughing up at him, before wriggling free and running back to dance. El-Darim joined in the sport, seizing the skirt of another girl and hauling her into his arms, filling her bodice with coins while she giggled archly.

Osman yawned behind his hand and remarked: "How boring. Can't think why El-Darim engages these street sluts. In reality, they're nothing but whores, and that old crone over there is their procuress."

Quiller smiled at him. "Don't be petty, Osman," he chided. "Our visitors are enjoying the local colour."

"Well, I'm not!" replied Osman huffily consoling himself by watching his gold bracelet flash as he moved his hand. "I thought you were going to play cards with de Grendon again. You did frightfully well last night. Weren't you intending to give him the chance to recover his losses! That would be a sporting gesture."

"I'm not given to gestures, as you well know." Quiller's smile was pensive. "Not generous ones, that is."

"I would disagree with that, Mr Quiller," I countered.

"Nancy told me of your kindness when you gave her the post of governess to Master Jeffrey."

"Did she now," he said slowly, his expression bright, his eyes keen. "And what else did she have to say about me? Or the Renshaws?"

"She was very fond of the child and desperately worried because he is lost." I did not intend to reveal more at this juncture. Let him make the next move.

He sighed deeply, and his face folded itself into a suitably mournful expression. "So sad – poor little chap. We've searched high and low, and the police are doing their level best to solve the mystery, but Alexandria is a strange city. Perhaps there was a servant with a grudge – or the work of a slave trader seeing gold in the form of such a pretty child. Who knows? Maybe we shall never know. No, don't shudder from the facts, dear lady – life is harsh here – harsh and cruel."

"Still talking about Miss Gray?" Charles had turned his attention to us. He scowled at me, trying to focus. "Didn't you say she was going off her head, Quiller? Suspecting the lot of you at El Tarifa – hinting at skulduggery? Convince my wife of this. Tell her that her friend is barmy. She wrote it all down in a book and gave it to Eleanor to guard with her life! Lot of bloody nonsense!"

"I believe that she was in the habit of keeping a journal," said Quiller smoothly. "I'm sorry to distress you, Mrs de Grendon, but it is true that she seems to be rather unbalanced. I should like to see what she's written and I'm certain that Sir Nicholas would too. We don't want malicious gossip circulating – all quite false, naturally. Will you help us to aid your friend? Sir Nicholas has offered to send her to a good doctor. Where is the journal?"

"I have it." There was that drunken truculence about Charles which I dreaded. "It's here – in my pocket – thought it best if my wife kept out of the business. Don't you agree, Quiller?"

"I'm afraid I do," Quiller said regretfully, patting my hand. "You mustn't upset yourself, dear lady. We will take good care of Nancy, I promise. She must have medical treatment and forget her crazy notions about Jeffrey's disappearance."

The dancers had retired to a corner to count their money. Servants came in to set up a card table with chairs drawn around it. The gentlemen commenced play. My eyelids were heavy, the divan was too comfortable and I longed to lie down. An old man continued to play on an instrument which was a cross between a violin and a cello, drawing a bow over the strings with a weird, wailing sound. The game dragged on. Charles was sweating. I could see beads of moisture on his brow and upper lip. Quiller was cool and collected, winning consistently. El-Darim and Osman sat near them, watching keenly. I heard Charles swear foully and say: "You're having the most infernal luck, Quiller – just like last night. Damnit, if I wasn't in such distinguished company, I might accuse you of being a sharp!"

Quiller smiled his catlike smile, patted Osman's knee, and continued to win. Time crawled by and I was nodding now, then I suddenly jerked awake as Charles got to his feet, scraping back his chair violently. His face was black with fury. "But you must allow me to play on!" he shouted. "You have my word for it that I'll pay you."

"When?" asked Quiller softly, still seated, looking up at my furiously angry husband. "You lost five thousand pounds to me last night, and now you've doubled the amount."

"I'll visit the bank first thing in the morning. They'll transfer the money from London." There was desperation in Charles's voice, but I could feel no pity for him. The size of the debt was staggering, and I wondered bleakly how much of my inheritance remained. We had spent extravagantly since the funeral; this trip had been costly, and there was Cordelia at home, doubtless living as if there was no tomorrow.

"I'm afraid that won't be good enough." Quiller was spreading the cards into fans with his fingers. "How can I be certain that you've enough, even in London, to meet it?"

"D'you think I would have played if there was any doubt?" Charles's eyes were blazing. I thought he was about to punch Quiller's nose. The sheik said nothing, his shrewd gaze going from one man to another. I saw him then as a calculating leech who made huge profits from the misery of those caught up in play-fever. There was one person who never lost, and that was the casino owner.

Quiller shrugged his lean shoulders, lips pursed in thought. "What security can you give whilst we await the arrival of the money?"

Charles scowled, unsteady on his feet. Quiller edged the wine bottle towards him across the table and he seized it, tipping it to his lips, then: "I've nothing of great value here – no deeds, nothing, unless you accept my wife's jewellery."

El-Darim leaned over and murmured in Quiller's ear. He nodded, smiled like a satyr and spoke to Charles again. "There you are wrong, de Grendon. The sheik has just reminded me that you own a pearl beyond price."

"A pearl beyond price?" echoed Charles groggily.

"Yes. Your wife!"

"Eleanor? What the devil are you getting at?"

"He's very taken with her and wants to add her to the collection of beauties in the harem," Quiller continued. "He suggests that she remain here until you settle with me or, if you prefer, he'll pay the sum himself and keep her for ever."

This was like a bad dream. I didn't believe what I was hearing, yet an awful, hollow emptiness was beginning in the pit of my stomach. I had never seen Charles lost for words before. He subsided into a chair and I seemed to hear his brain whirring – weighing, assessing, prepared to do anything to save face amongst the gambling fraternity. "But how could this be?" he said at last. "There would be awkward questions if I returned to England without her."

He was seriously considering selling me to El-Darim! Quiller's nimble mind supplied the answer. "If you said that she had deserted you – falling in love with an Arab – then you could divorce her."

"Henford Grange, the London house and the remainder of the money would be mine," Charles muttered, and now he was cold sober.

"Exactly. What do you say?" Quiller's voice was as precise as a lawyer's.

Charles did not look at me. I'll grant him that. There was a scrap of shame left in his black soul. He nodded and said: "That seems a fair arrangement. Quiller."

So much for love, I thought as I rose to my feet, so much for those vows made in the dark, the passion, the bitter-sweetness. "Fair to whom?" I asked icily, drawing every eye. I rounded on Charles. "Fair to you? You despicable bastard! I refuse to have any part in it. How dare you make such a bargain? I don't care if you're declared bankrupt! I don't care if you're disgraced and barred from every smart club from here to hell! I don't give a damn if you rot in jail forever, but you're not going to use me in your filthy games!"

"Eleanor, stop it! Can't you see it's only a temporary arrangement?" he said, still with his eyes averted.

"No, I can't," I shouted. His behaviour was appalling. He was prepared to leave me with the sheik, sacrificing me on the altar of his obsession. There was something missing in his character – the normal, humane capacity for caring. Both he and Cordelia lacked it completely.

I could have told him then about the baby, but my pride would not let me. If he didn't care enough about me to find some other solution, then I wasn't prepared to offer his heir as bait. I'd rather become El-Darim's concubine, finding a savage revenge in bearing my child in the harem. Charles would never know of its existence. Damn all men! I thought despairingly. I didn't want the sheik – I didn't want Charles – they were all of them out for their own ends. "I'll kill myself before I consent!" I declared.

"Oh dear, how very dramatic," sighed Quiller. "Sit down, Mrs de Grendon. Let's talk this over calmly." He turned to Charles. "Sir, I have another suggestion to make."

Charles stared at him suspiciously and El-Darim scowled, none too pleased to see his chance of possessing me slipping away. "Well, what is it? Speak up, man."

"I'm prepared to wipe out the debt in exchange for something which is of no value to yourself." Quiller paused, loving this game of cat and mouse.

"What are you driving at? Out with it!" Charles's temper was at boiling point. Usually the one who called the tune, he hated being at a disadvantage.

"I speak of Miss Gray's journal," said Quiller blandly. "Give it to me and I'll sign anything you want exonerating you. I know a certain party who would dearly like to lay hands on it."

The relief on Charles's face was quite shocking. He even managed a grim smile. "This person must want it deuced badly."

"Oh, he does. Sir Nicholas has been most worried about what that silly woman may have written concerning him. She's already threatened blackmail."

"Nancy? I don't believe it," I gasped. I swung round to my husband. "You can't do it. No one should read it without her consent."

"It's either that or you go to El-Darim!" He was as savage as a wounded bear trapped in a thicket. "You're lucky to have a choice. Suit yourself!"

"What d'you say, Mrs de Grendon?" Quiller was

waiting with a tension about him which hinted at strictly controlled excitement.

I did not reply. I looked at them slowly, committing each hated feature to memory, and neither of them could meet my eye. Finally, I stared again at my husband. I had married him, given him my promise, and I had the baby to think of. It was the hardest thing I had ever been called upon to do, but I bowed my head in assent.

Charles took the journal from his pocket and flung it down on the table. "Take the damned thing. I'm glad to be shot of it. Now, you keep your side of the deal, Quiller. Write a letter clearing me."

Soon it was over. I had betrayed my friend and her secrets would fall into the hands of Sir Nicholas, the man she loved. Love? My God – love! My love had died that night, but one has to go on. I was left with my desire for Charles and the cynical determination to make the best of a bad job. I would accept him for what he was – cheat, liar, murderer and all – but I didn't know how I was going to face Nancy.

This proved to be unnecessary for Charles ordered me to pack as soon as we reached the hotel and, at noon next day, we went aboard a steamer returning to England. He gave no reason for this sudden decision, and I couldn't bring myself to speak to him, let alone question his actions. I stood on deck, watching the misty, fairy-tale domes of Alexandria slipping away on the horizon. Oh, Nancy, what have I done? I cried in silent anguish. What danger threatens you now? I knew that something terrible was going to happen to her, caught up in a certainty quite beyond me, an inner voice, a silent conviction which demanded recognition. Then, as I clung to the rail for support, I remembered Rebecca. I would find her, tell her what had happened and beg her aid. This idea was like a ray of hope unexpectedly flashing in the very dim world in which I now found myself.

BOOK THREE

Rebecca

For she was beautiful – her beauty made
The bright world dim, and everything beside
Seemed like the fleeting image of a shade.

The Witch of Atlas, SHELLEY

And pale Fear
Hunted by ghastlier terrors than surround
Moon-blasted Madness when he yells at midnight.

Religious Musings, COLERIDGE

I rise from dreams of thee
In the first sleep of night –
The winds are breathing low
And the stars are burning bright.

The Indian Girl's Song, SHELLEY

Chapter 1

At my birth, the good fairies must have put their heads together and decided to bestow a gift on me – the ability to act and sing. God knows I needed some advantage – illegitimate, and left on the doorstep of an orphanage when only a few days old.

I accepted my life there because I had never known anything else, but I hated being called Becky. Nancy and Nell always used my full name, and I blessed them for it. We were inseparable companions and I was devastated to leave them, lanky Nancy with her untidy, fiery mop of hair and fearless disposition, and little Nell of the keen mind and sharp tongue. She had always had an elusive, well-bred air about her, at variance with our humble status. I envied her blonde beauty, though people said that my dark looks were attractive. Yes, it was with a heavy heart that I met them under the clock tower on the night before I departed. It was an emotional scene, and we made a vow to rescue one another if any of us landed in trouble, and promised to keep journals so that we could compare notes when we met again. This vow appealed to my sense of drama, and I took it seriously. It is not in my nature to go back on a promise. I suggested the idea of the journals, I can't remember why for I was too scatterbrained then to want to put pen to paper. Why sit and scribble when I could be singing and dancing?

However, I did do it. Later when I settled into my job in London, Mrs Linton gave me a diary for Christmas. I thought it a shame to spoil those beautiful white pages with my spidery writing. There was a lock on it and a small key; I could safely put down secrets galore. "What shall I write in it?" I asked her when I saw it on the table among my other presents. She had smiled and kissed me on the forehead.

"The story of Rebecca Costello," she said, and everyone there had laughed agreeably.

I had left the orphanage shortly after my fifteenth birthday, summoned to a final interview with Mrs Bowell. A strange pair, the Bowells, she so fat, ugly and bossy, whilst he walked in her shadow, a hypocritical toad of a person. I knew that he fancied me. He was always trying to get me alone and succeeded once when we were in the storeroom where he was fitting me for a new pair of boots. His hand had slid upwards from my ankle, fondling my knee and attempting to go higher. His breath smelled abominably, and I knew exactly what he was after. Peggy, the skivvy, had told me about men and their animal appetites. In a way it was a kind of backhanded compliment that he found me desirable. I stood still, staring down into his face, quite unafraid, and he remained there on his knees at my feet. Quite right too, I thought conceitedly, that's where every damned man should be! There was a foolish grin on his lips, a bright expression in his eyes, like a hopeful dog. I said nothing, merely removed myself out of reach and, giving him a look of what I fondly hoped was withering scorn, I stalked proudly from the room. I was rather amused by the incident.

Mrs Bowell had added a few personal touches to her room which betrayed her lack of taste. It was crammed with small tables and bric-a-brac, trivial pictures and overstuffed chairs. A pair of quite hideous china dogs sat stiffly on the mantelpiece, guarding a sombre malachite clock which looked like something from a cemetery. Above this miniature mausoleum hung a portrait of Sir George Cardwell, and one was expected to genuflect before it. When much younger, I had been confused between this picture and an image of the Almighty. We were taught a lot about God and, I'm afraid, I saw him not as a loving deity, but rather as a tyrant, spying out the smallest misdeeds, with the burning lakes of hell waiting for the transgressor.

Mrs Bowell cleared her throat and shuffled papers on her desk. "You'll need work, Becky. I know of a respectable family in Redland who want a scullery maid. I hesitate to recommend you to anyone after your bad behaviour, but these are God-fearing folk who will guard your moral welfare, and report to me."

"No, thank you, ma'am," I answered firmly. "I can look out for myself."

"Can you indeed?" she said dubiously. "Let's hope that you'll not be leaving an unwanted infant here before many months have passed."

"I'll never do that," I replied, not as she might have thought because I intended to lead a blameless life. I vowed that I'd rather die than let any child of mine endure the misery of an institution.

"I'm glad to hear it," she answered, getting the wrong end of the stick, as usual. "Perhaps my teachings haven't fallen on stony ground after all." She folded her hands piously in her immense lap, and ran an eye over me. "I see that you've been fitted out with clothing supplied by the kindness and generosity of the Ladies of the Foundling Association." She was making certain that I didn't leave without being reminded of my unworthiness, a recipient of charity still.

"Yes, thank you, ma'am," I said coldly.

I had been excited when dressing that morning, laying aside for ever that hated uniform, the itchy woollen camisole and drawers, all worn and darned, every garment bearing a label declaring that it belonged to the orphanage. I supposed that now some other unfortunate would inherit them. This was my special day and I took my time. I was leaving – they had no power over me any more. My new underwear was nice, trimmed with tiny linen buttons and lace inserts. The costume was simple, a high-necked blouse with leg-o'-mutton sleeves, a dark red skirt and jacket and a petersham belt. Though it was second hand, I'd never had such a fine ensemble and I danced around the dormitory, feeling the skirt swirl about my legs, even enjoying the painful ecstasy of the tight, high-buttoned boots donated by some wealthy lady.

I strained on tiptoe to peer into the looking glass. We were only allowed to use this to brush our hair and set our caps straight, mirrors being frowned upon, vanity a cardinal sin. I thought how grown-up I looked, sweeping my hair to the top of my head, imagining how I'd wear it when I was old enough. I let the locks fall again, the thick curls springing round my fingers. Gypsy hair. They called me "gypsy" and "dago" and I wondered if they were right. My skin was certainly of an olive tint, my nose thin and straight, while my mouth was too wide, too full-lipped to conform to the fashionable cupid's bow. And my eyes gave me a decidedly foreign appearance, slanting slightly up at the outer corners, golden-brown and black-lashed.

Oh, well, I thought, I don't mind being a gypsy, and I sang as I gathered up my tatty old carpetbag. No one would ever stop me singing again. I'd give voice to whatever tune I pleased, no longer confined to dreary hymns. I kicked up my heels and sang that loud, vulgar music-hall ditty, "Ta-ra-ra-boom-de-ay!" I'd learned it from Peggy who'd actually been to the theatre and heard Lottie Collins sing it in person. I had noticed that Peggy was quiet these days, drooping around the kitchen, and I wondered if her soldier-boy sweetheart had managed to "have his wicked way" with her before he went off to Africa to fight in the Boer War.

I should be able to go to the theatre whenever I wanted now. I was free! With a whoop of joy, I snatched up my straw hat and rushed off down the corridor, still singing and giving an extra high kick at every "boom-de-ay!" But now that I was with Mrs Bowell, some of my optimism was evaporating.

"And how d'you propose to earn a living?" she was saying gloomily.

"I want to be a singer," I announced, meeting her jaundiced eye boldly.

Her scanty brows shot up and her mouth turned down. "A singer? You can't be serious, girl? Respectable women don't parade about on the stage for every Tom, Dick and Harry to gape at!" She spoke as if I proposed becoming a streetwalker "Forget such stupid notions and get yourself an honest job."

"As a servant," I said scornfully.

"Of course, it's the only thing for the likes of you. Mark my words, if you get mixed up with the theatrical people, you'll come to a bad end. Most of those actresses are no better than they should be!"

I had heard this expression before, and still didn't understand it. To me, the life of the stage seemed a most wonderful one. I couldn't think of anything I wanted more. Peggy's chatter had impressed me deeply, as had the picture postcard she had shown me of the glamorous Lottie Collins, all spangles and feathers and short skirts. What did Old Mother Bowell know of such divine creatures?

All I wanted was to be off to seek my fortune. "May I go now, ma'am?" I asked impatiently.

"There's one other thing, before you leave." She lumbered across the room to a cupboard, taking a key from her chatelaine and opening the door. She took out a parcel and placed it on the table in front of me. "As you already know, you were found in the porch, and were judged to be about three days old. You were wearing these, and this letter was pinned to your shawl."

My fingers were unsteady as I unwrapped the paper, the smell of mothballs rising from the neatly folded pile of baby clothes. I took out each one and examined it closely as if, by looking hard, I might unravel the secret of my identity. They were quality garments, different indeed from the poor little things which clad the babies of the Home. There was a long cambric gown, yellowed in the folds but beautifully made, showing that someone had worked on it lovingly. It was adorned with feather-stitching and point-lace whipped on with almost invisible silks. Next came an equally lovely petticoat, a back-flannel, a tiny vest and pilch, a crocheted bonnet with rosettes of white ribbon, a carrying cape bordered with swansdown, and a shawl knitted of wool so delicate that it resembled cobweb. These fine articles had clothed my newborn body when I was abandoned.

That stuffy room and its stout occupant were fractured across by my unshed tears. I blinked them away and opened the fragile scrap of paper which had been fastened to me. It was dated August 12th, 1885, and the faded ink showed an educated hand. It said: "Please take good care of my baby. Her name is Rebecca, and this is from her unfortunate mother who, to preserve a reputation, is obliged to part with her though she is almost dearer to me than life."

I stood for a moment, reading this sad little note. Someone had loved me once. Maybe, she still lived, and I wanted to find her and say: "I'm here, Mother. Don't give me away again!" But this was locked in a deep recess of my being. I didn't let Mrs Bowell know that I was so moved. I said nothing, placing the letter with the clothing and retying the string, then I tucked it in my bag. I left quietly, closing the door behind me, no longer Becky Smale, that hated surname given me by a whim of the Bowells. I was Rebecca Costello now.

It had stopped raining, the drizzle melting into a fine, golden day, pleasantly warm, faintly nostalgic, tinged already with the rich russets of late summer. I stared up at the clock tower, shading my eyes. This is where I had said goodbye to my friends, and it occurred to me that my mother must have passed beneath it, carrying the swaddled bundle which had been myself. Had she slipped there furtively after dark, placing her precious babe in the doorway, then ringing the bell and hiding to make certain that someone answered? It was rather dramatic and I was gratified to be the central character. I liked to think of myself as a love child, not a bastard, but dared not dwell on the anguish she must have suffered.

I shivered as if brushed by the wing of an invisible angel, then turned and hurried towards the high double iron gates, coming to the road outside. I knew that I must cross the city to reach Chipping Sodbury, so I adjusted my hat, hoisted up my bag, and began to trudge in the direction of the Hiring Fair.

I'd never been to a fair before and didn't know what to expect. First, I walked to the centre of Bristol and took a tram, spending a penny of my meagre savings. Chipping Sodbury was almost a country village, and the tram didn't go all the way, so I had to walk several miles from the depot. It was odd to be out on my own, with no teacher snapping: "Don't dwaddle! Don't slouch! Keep in line!"

The suburbs straggled untidily, an ugly confusion of red brick dwellings and allotments, with larger, detached villas in their own neat gardens. Each house had a door with a brass knob, three white steps and a tiny porch. All the windows had lace curtains. Traffic rumbled past me; horse-drawn tradesmen's vans and an omnibus or two. The houses thinned and fields banked the road, and the crowd thickened, heading in the direction of the fair. The number of carts increased, some containing pigs and cattle, while a group of horses was herded by drovers with long whips.

When I reached the village, the principal street was thronged with people giving themselves up to the fun of the occasion. There were family groups and holiday-makers, farmers, hucksters and blowsy country lasses hanging on to the arms of their young men. The fair had spread from its proper place in the meadows, out into the street. Beyond, I could see the big-top of the circus with a Union Jack fluttering lazily from the main pole, and heard the thrilling roar of the big cats, and the shrill trumpeting of an elephant. On every side of me were booths and cheapjacks and fancy quacks, and at the far end were roundabouts, glittering with bright paintwork, while the pipe-organs played.

I was unsure of which direction to take, bedazzled by the colour, noise and reek of the fair, jostled by the crowd. The whole pageant was bewildering, and the smells of roasting meat, popping corn and sweetmeats reminded me how hungry I was. Thick, swaying tendrils of smoke crawled about the food stalls, rising to the waving pennants, the flaunting flags. A band of tumblers from the circus were performing near the inn, flashing figures in sequinned costumes, leaping and balancing, forming a human triangle, while clowns passed through the crowd, encouraging them to come to the show. I was caught up in the fever, almost carried off my feet, pressed against smelly clothes and warm, sweating flesh.

I managed to struggle free, passing several stalls where the farmers were getting drunk, quaffing cider. I found the hiring section, where those in search of employment had gathered. Those who already stood in line had some mark of their calling about them. Shepherds wore a tuft of wool in their hats or carried a crook, carters flourished a whip, and dairymaids held a milking stool or a pail. I had nothing but I brazened it out, standing next to several women and trying to look pleasant, able and willing. I felt terribly out of place. This wasn't what I wanted in the very least, and I angrily vowed to get even with the world one day. I suppose this rebelliousness showed, for although several couples paused and questioned me, they passed on without striking a bargain or giving me a "fastenpenny", thus securing any services. One or two drunken louts made saucy remarks aimed in my direction. I longed to slap their silly faces, staring through them coldly.

One farmer almost engaged me, but then his wife arrived, eyeing me jelously and ronouncing me as unsuitable. They took on the plain girl who stood next to me. I was getting desperate by now; most of the others had found places and I was alone except for an ancient shepherd and a slow-witted boy. It was at that moment when my feet were aching, my bag seemed to weigh a ton and I was close to tears, that I was rescued by Mr and Mrs Linton.

I had marked their approach, watching them with interest for they were strikingly different – an outstanding couple who commanded respect, so that people stepped aside for them to pass. Henrietta Linton was about thirty years old and bore herself regally, her dark hair piled up and topped by a hat with a curly brim adorned by a stuffed bird of paradise in the centre. She had a gracious, rather theatrical air, and wore a flowing black gown, and a sweeping cloak with an enormous fox-fur collar. I thought her rather stout, though I later realised that she was pregnant. Albert Linton was equally impressive. He was tall and good looking, though his complexion was rather florid, his brown hair was winged with silver at the sides, brushed back from a fine, broad brow, and worn rather long. His clothing was flamboyant; his black overcoat was slung carelessly over his shoulders; his hat had a wide brim and was tilted at a dashing angle, and there was the little figurine of a nude woman mounted as the handle of his ebony cane.

She regarded me through smiling dark eyes. Her glance was shrewd, assessing and kind as she looked me up and down. "Dearest, what about this girl?" Her hand tightened on his arm as he was about to stroll past me. "Don't you agree that she has something about her? She's so pretty too, and you know that I can't bear ugly people about me at this time." She patted her thickened waist.

He was so dignified and distinguished, and I was rather awed as he turned his heavy-lidded brown eyes to me. "Whatever you say, my angel," he replied, and he pronounced every syllable as if it had to be heard at the back of an auditorium. "I know you've set your heart on having a country lass. Yes, she's comely," and here I was subjected to a truly professional scrutiny. "Do you like children, Miss – eh?"

"Costello," I said quickly. "Rebecca Costello."

"That's a fine name. Are you sure you didn't invent it?" he asked with a smile. "It would look splendid on billboards."

"I don't understand, sir."

"Hoardings – advertising theatrical performances, you know," he continued with a satiric lift of his bushy eyebrows.

"You are on the stage?" I stammered.

"Well, not exactly – not at the moment," put in his wife. "My husband and I are 'resting', as we say in the profession. Waiting for the chance to tour again. We're not idle whilst we wait – oh, no. I sing and play the piano, and Mr Linton recites monologues or speeches from Shakespeare when we are invited to entertain at parties. Why, some of the best houses in London hire our services. Yes, my dear, I think you will suit us, but it's essential that you get on well with children for we have five under ten years old, and this new baby will be born in the autumn." A sudden anxiety seemed to strike her and she turned her eyes to her husband. "Oh, Albert, do you suppose that our dear little ones are well?"

"Of course, my treasure, having the time of their young lives, I shouldn't wonder. We shan't be able to maintain any discipline when we return, and heaven knows, we had precious little before," he answered indulgently, and they were so absorbed in one another that I realised, with surprise, that they were in love. Two people whom I considered to be terribly old, with a large brood of children, were actually still deeply in love!

Pacified, Henrietta turned to me again. "You'll have help. It's just that we have an extremely busy household and Elsie, my general assistant, can't manage it all. I'm rather incapacitated at present, and shall be taken up with the new arrival very soon, so we're seeking someone to live in."

"You look honest," remarked her husband. "Are you honest? Have you stolen anything lately?"

"Only when I was hungry, sir," I replied earnestly, certain tht he would understand."

He threw back his head and laughed loudly, making the locals stare. "Capital! I like your frankness. Well, come along now, give me your hand and I'll see if I can find the obligatory shilling."

Thus it was that I joined the Litton ménage. Lady Luck had smiled on me that day for they set me on the road which led to heights that exceeded my wildest dreams. Chance, fate, call it what you will, had ordained that they should be visiting Henrietta's sister at that time and, on the journey to London, I told them my history and far from making them regret their decision, it only seemed to engender further warmth. They, in turn, recounted their own story. Albert Linton came from a long line of actors and had, till a short time before, run his own touring company. He had met Henrietta twelve years back whilst playing in Bristol and, after a rather stormy courtship for she was a landowner's daughter and theatrical folk were frowned upon, they were eventually married. She had taken to the life like a duck to water, proving to be a talented actress.

By the time the train reached London, I was feeling almost drunk with delight, unable to believe my incredible luck. The capital took my breath away. It was the heart of England and, as everyone knew, the British empire ruled the world. I felt as if I had come home at last. The city was a challenge, and I responded to that intense energy illustrated by the milling crowds at the station, the bustle of departure, the travellers being greeted by loved ones. But as we went to the cab rank, just outside the depot, I became aware that perhaps city life was not quite as splendid as I had at first thought.

Beggars lurked there, imploring Albert to let them carry his luggage. He brushed them aside imperiously and as I walked along I saw a collection of women, their faces stamped with weariness and desperation. They were loud, vulgar sluts with hungry eyes, calling bawdy remarks to passing men and hurling abuse at a more fortunate colleague who had managed to snatch a customer.

"Take no notice, Rebecca," said Henrietta as Albert helped her into a cab. "They are nothing but low prostitutes. I can't think why it's allowed – disgraceful that such creatures haunt our stations."

I was fascinated. These were real, flesh and blood, Fallen Women, the kind Mrs Bowell had warned us about. It was rather disappointing for I had pictured such sinful creatures as being beautiful and superbly dressed. Wasn't London really a rich city, paved with gold? It was horrible to think that there existed grinding, degrading poverty which forced women to sell themselves to keep body and soul together. Was this what had happened to my mother? I pushed the thought from me. I didn't want to dwell on sad things and leaned from the cab window as we clattered off. Oh, London – it stirred my pulse with excitement, daring everything, promising much to the person courageous enough to accept the challenge. I'll take up the gauntlet, I whispered, test me all you like. I love you and I'll do my damnedest to make you respect me.

The Lintons owned a house in Soho, not far from Piccadilly Circus. It was a tall, narrow building in a surprisingly quiet square, and as well as its garden at the rear, there was a park complete with trees in the centre of the square, surrounded by spiked railings and reached by a gate to which every occupier had a key. The house was Henrietta's property, bequeathed by some distant relative. The front door was reached by a short flight of steps and there was a basement area below. Inside, it was shabby, cluttered and homely. I was at once introduced to Elsie, a harassed middle-aged woman with an eighteen-month-old child on her hip and a toddler tugging at her skirt. Three other children were hanging over the banisters, whooping with delight as their parents entered. Elsie's face lit up when she was told that I was the new help. She viewed me as a gift from heaven and lost no time in showing me the ropes, and handing over some of the responsibility for this family of healthy, high-spirited little Lintons.

I soon discovered that Henrietta ran a business from the house. She was a clever needlewoman and, driven by the constant need for money, had turned this skill to her advantage, touting for custom among the rich women she met whilst entertaining. She employed several seamstresses who worked in a room in the basement. Not only this, she also took in what she politely referred to as paying guests. There were two of them in residence. One was Gertie Brown, an exuberant dancer at the Gaiety Theatre, and the other was an elderly Italian musician called Maestro Angeleri. Gertie became my close friend whilst she took on the role of my teacher and mentor. So my life was punctuated by the continual purr of sewing machines, the sound of music as the Maestro drilled his pupils, and the laughter and cries of the children.

It was an amazing household where friends came and went at all hours, and no one was ever turned away, unless they were creditors. I was treated with the greatest kindness imaginable. There was never a dull or boring moment. It was exhausting but I loved it. The young Lintons were the apples of their parents' eyes. They could do no wrong, and I was surprised to find that they were given so much freedom and listened to as gravely as if they were adults. The eldest was Alfie, dark-haired and handsome, already on the stage; next came Archie, freckle-faced and jolly, forever in scrapes; Lilly was six, dark-haired, dark-eyed, with a sharp little face; Violet, a year younger, was chubby and placid, mother to a family of dolls; and lastly there was Rose, a fair-skinned elf with a strong will. She shrieked the place down if she didn't get what she wanted.

As Henrietta had predicted, the family was soon increased by the arrival of a tiny red creature who was called Hugh. He never screamed, he just lay and said "ah" to himself and sometimes he chuckled. He went from one person's arms to another with good-humoured tolerance. I was particularly fond of him, there from the start for he was born in Henrietta's bedroom amidst her clutter of stage photographs, posters, costumes and drapes.

Those were happy days, the nursery filled with warmth and that lovely baby smell. It seemed that I had a way with infants. I knew instinctively how to hold Hugh and what faces to pull to change his tears into gurgles of laughter, and the exact amount of pressure when I held him against my shoulder and patted his little back to bring up his wind and if, in the process, he was sick over me, I didn't mind at all.

"You're a great big softie, daft as a brush about that baby," said Gertie one day when I was ironing in the kitchen. I had just taken one of the flat-irons from the hob, wiping the soot away with a rag and spitting on it. The spittle bounced off and I knew it was hot enough. I applied myself to my work.

"He's a lovely little chap," I replied, smoothing the iron over the material.

Gertie helped herself to another cup of tea from the big brown earthenware pot. She was wearing a pink flowered wrapper, her brassy blonde hair straggling down her back. It was afternoon and she had only just got up after a late night. "You don't want to waste your time looking after nippers," she advised, lighting a cigarette. "With your looks, I could get you in the chorus easy as winking. All you've got to do is show a bit of leg. You're pretty as a picture, be blowed if you ain't."

I glanced at her, my rather loud friend who had not bothered to remove her stage make-up, before she crawled into bed. "I'm sure there's more to acting than that," I demurred, folding Hugh's nightgown and hanging it on the clothes-horse.

"Not much in my sort of game," she replied, blowing smoke rings and crossing one silk-stockinged leg over the other, a feathery, backless mule dangling from her toe. "I've been given a really good part in the new production, and soon I'll be a bloody star, but you can kiss my arse if I bloody well know how it come about!" She paused and then added: "Well, I do know, of course. That manager bloke fancies his chances. Gives me the gladdest of glad eyes, the cheeky bugger, and he's wasting his bloody time for he ain't getting nothing from me! Any road, my pay'll increase – yes, they're upping the spondulicks! Which suits yours truly down to the ground."

My lips twitched; conversations with Gertie were always amusing. She was twenty, an outgoing creature, a fund of wit and jollity. "Aren't you even going to let him take you out to supper?" I asked, replacing the iron and taking up the other one which had been standing on the hob to heat.

"You've got to be bloody joking!" Her plucked eyebrows shot up and her face was scornful. "Him! The cocky little jackass!"

I was pleased that Gertie was being promoted, for although she was in regular work, she hadn't risen higher than to kick her legs and sing as leader of the chorus. "It might pay off if you're nice to him," I suggested.

She shook her yellow curls. "No, deary. I've got this bloke what calls for me at the stage door. Ever such a masher – a real toff, and he waits there with a bunch of roses and a bloody great box of chocolates, then takes me to a posh restaurant, and drives me home in his car. It's one in the eye for the other girls, I can tell you."

Did I want to become a musical-comedy star? I wondered. Gertie had all the required attributes, wide blue eyes, red lips, dimples and masses of hair that shone like the sun. I had been to the Gaiety Theatre and seen her on the stage, but I can't say that I enjoyed it. Oh, the music was light, frothy, tuneful, but I hankered after something more, though I didn't know quite what it was. Yet her words fired my old ambitions, and I was once again sure of my destiny – a season at a big London theatre with every male in the audience crazy about me, followed by a meteor-like triumph across Europe with counts and princes waiting in a queue for my seductive emergence from the stage door.

I was awakened from the daydream abruptly. "You're scorching his nibs's shirt!" shouted Gertie.

Oh dear, sure enough there was the brownish imprint of the iron on Albert's shirt-tail. "That's what comes of listening to your silly chatter," I grumbled.

"He won't notice," she cried, tilting up her nose and prancing past me towards the door. "He's been at the bevy again."

I sighed. Albert Linton was one of the best men I had ever met. He had a rich, varied personality, talented and genial, lovable and kind, but unfortunately, he drank. This was the cause of their financial troubles as I had discovered after being there only a short time. Yet I'd never seen two people more devoted. She never blamed him for bringing them to their present pass. He was still her grand seigneur, and whatever his faults and shortcomings, she never ceased to look up to and admire him.

I had been so busy since my arrival, what with the children and the birth of Hugh, that I'd had no time to ask Maestro Angeleri to hear me sing. Now I made up my mind to do so, tapping on his door one day at the beginning of the year when snow crusted the jumbled rooftops of London. He was an energetic and fiery little man who occupied the Lintons' first-floor front room.

"Ah, yes," he said, ushering me in and listening as I shyly made my request. "So, *cara*, you think that you have a voice, eh? Very well, let us try."

He went to his upright piano and struck a note. For a moment I was too nervous to respond. Then I sharply reminded myself that this was the chance I'd been seeking and I sang it, very softly.

"Higher," he urged, striking a chord which went up and up, followed by another. I heard my own voice soaring in pursuit.

I stopped and stood there helplessly while he said nothing. The snow swished against the windowpane and the gas-jet popped. He suddenly leapt up from the piano and dashed from the room whilst I wondered what I had done wrong. The door flew open and he returned in a state of great excitement, dragging Henrietta with him and shouting: "Madame – listen to this! At last I have found a voice!" Then, turning to me, his face alight with a kind of exultation, he said: "If you are serious and study with me, I will make something extraordinary of you. You must apply yourself to your work assiduously. No half measures – practise, practise, practise – but we must be careful for you are still very young." He broke off, running to the gramophone and putting on a record. "Listen to this! Listen, *cara* – this is how a truly great singer sounds!"

So, for the first and never-to-be forgotten time, I was exposed to the magic of opera. It was a tenor voice, a marvellous, rich sound, the soaring phrases making me tingle. For days after I made a nuisance of myself by insisting on hearing Caruso sing again and again. This was the turning point for me and, very soon, the Maestro took me to the Royal Opera House at Covent Garden. We sat far up in the gods, those cheap seats made of bare wooden planks. It was cold and draughty, but I didn't mind, shivering with excitement as we waited for the red velvet curtain to lift.

"*La Bohème* is an opera for those who are in love or those, like myself, who have grown old but remember what it was like to be in love," he said, an elderly figure in a shabby brown overcoat, with twinkling dark eyes, greying hair and expressive hands. "It's a simple story about a collection of students living in poverty in a garret above the roofs of Paris. The poet meets a flower-maker – they fall in love, they quarrel and part, then are reunited as the girl dies of consumption in his arms, and the curtain falls. It doesn't sound much, I know, but just wait till you hear the masterly manner in which the composer, Puccini, makes his music tell the story."

We were in the front row and leaned over, staring at the bejewelled crowd of society ladies with their escorts in top hats and opera cloaks who were taking their places in the stalls, boxes and dress circle. One day, I vowed, I'll be up there on that stage to demand their acclamation! Then the house lights dimmed, the conductor raised his baton and the first notes surged through the auditorium as the curtain slowly rose.

I forgot everything, transported into a magical world where I laughed, loved and cried with the characters. Most of all, I remember the last act when the pathetic little heroine dies and, unable to find my handkerchief, I wept into my scarf. As the curtain fell to thunderous applause, it seemed that I stood at the nadir of an immense quiet, alone with my dreams, alone with this thing for which I had been created. It was something intangible, yet more solid, more real than any visible object. This was my purpose in being. For this I had been born, abandoned, orphanage raised, and brought to London. I felt that I had touched a perfect chord which rang out from the beginning of time to eternity. There I sat, a girl who in the eyes of the world was a misfit, a bastard, a charity brat, yet my voice was a gift from the creator. With me, surrounding me, streaming through my consciousness and passing beyond me into the music-charged atmosphere, was the force to which I would dedicate myself for ever.

Chapter 2

Every spare moment was now spent with Maestro Angeleri. He was a superb teacher whose passionate dedication to his art made me feel, even when singing scales, that I was producing something beautiful. He had given me the score of *La Bohème* and it was my most precious possession. With him as my *répétiteur*, I sat him down at the piano and learned the role of the heroine, Mimi. He was amazed at the speed with which I grasped the music. He gave me piano lessons too, and I found that I had no difficulty in mastering the technique of reading.

He would shake his head in wonder, saying: "*Cara*, it is almost as if you were born with music in your blood. Astonishing – remarkable."

It was as natural to me as breathing, and I wondered if my mother might have been a singer. I wished that I knew and sometimes looked at the baby clothes and her letter, thinking about this mysterious woman who had carried me in her body, given my life, and then left me. I must admit that curiosity about my father did not trouble me, and it was only later that it occurred to me that he might have been the one from whom I inherited this musical talent.

The Lintons were most impressed by my aptitude and tolerant if meals were not served on time or if I neglected to take Hugh out in his bassinet. We were accustomed to a daily stroll in the park, and I enjoyed pushing that huge, well-sprung, elegant baby carriage, with Violet on one side and Rose on the other. I met other nursemaids, usually accompanied by a smart young soldier. Soldiers and nurses were as inseparable as duck and green peas in those days. Gertie told me that so anxious were domestic servants to have an admirer in the army that they used to pay a fee, regulated by the rank of their escorts, to walk out with them. I refused to pander to this "promenade of convenience", and when I walked my charges, I had no lack of attention from the military. But my mind was too full of music, dreams and ambition to encourage any of them. I had no time for lovers. Maestro Angeleri was the only man with whom I wished to spend off-duty hours.

"Can't understand you liking that highbrow stuff," Gertie would grumble as she whisked past me on her way to the Gaiety Theatre, superb in violet silk with a trailing feather boa and an absurdly smart little hat on her golden curls. "I like something a bit more lively. You won't get the mashers hanging around an opera house, mark my words. Why don't you come along and let me introduce you to my gaffer?"

"The man you were telling me about?"

"No, not that common little squid – he only manages the box office. I'm talking about the star comedian, George Grossmith. Bloody hell, is that the time? I must dash." She was always in a terrible tear and would invariably have forgotten something. "Oh, damn and blast and bugger it! Where's my fan? Gord, I'd leave my bloody head behind if it wasn't screwed on tight! Run upstairs and get it for me, there's a love," and when I had obliged her, she would rush off in a cloud of perfume.

Sometimes I felt like Cinderella with everyone gone to the ball, particularly when the Lintons were performing too. Then there was an uproar and no mistake! It was "Run here – do that – where are my collar-studs? Who's hidden the curling tongs? Rebecca, fetch my white gloves – Rebecca, pack the music – " on and on till they finally whirled away in a hansom cab and the house fell into a silence more keenly felt after the hubbub.

My turn came, however, and I mustn't delay in writing about my own Big Night. It so happened that the Lintons had an important engagement at a house in Holland Park. Nothing else had been talked of for days. Henrietta was very excited at being invited to perform at the home of Lady Hermione Brinkworth. They told me that she was rather notorious, an eccentric patron of the arts who lived a bohemian existence, the subject of much gossip and speculation.

"Oh, she's a one, I can tell you," commented Gertie. "One of those rich bitches who can get away with bloody murder! Doing things that the likes of us would be stoned for. All manner of goings on going on, if you take my meaning."

I listened with interest but had no idea that I was soon to meet the famous Lady Brinkworth. I shouldn't have done so, I suppose, had it not been for Albert Linton's love of the bottle. By early evening of the day in question, Henrietta was ready, looking so lovely in bottle-green velvet that it was hard to believe she was the mother of six. But she had a worried expression when she came upstairs to the nursery. The girls shouted with delight on seeing her, smoothing her dress and trying to wrap her furs about themselves.

"Rebecca, have you seen Mr Linton?" she asked me, a hint of anxiety in her voice.

"No, ma'am, not since this morning," I replied, hushing Hugh who was wriggling in my arms, making a grab for his mother's necklace.

"Wherever can he be?" she fretted, biting her lower lip and patrolling the strip of carpet like a caged lioness. "He knows we're due to leave at seven-thirty. Lady Brinkworth's chauffeur will be coming to collect us."

It was getting dark and I put a match to the gas mantles. I could see that she was worried and a disturbing suspicion crossed my mind. Surely, he wouldn't let her down on such an important occasion? Not Albert Linton, who loved her so much, invariably referring to her as "my angel". But, sadly, it was proved to me that he loved something else too, and that was strong liquor. We hadn't been waiting long before we heard his key in the front door. Henrietta ran to meet him. I couldn't catch what was said down there in the hall, but his voice sounded thick and slurred. Presently she returned, and she was fighting to retain her self-control, close to tears.

"Rebecca – Mr Linton cannot come tonight. He is unwell," she lied bravely, loyal to the last. "Will you take his place, my dear?"

I was so astonished that I almost dropped Hugh. "Me?" I goggled at her stupidly. "You want me to sing?"

"Yes," she answered briskly, swinging into action. "Elsie will look after the children, so come along – get ready quickly."

Elsie took Hugh from me and I found myself being propelled towards Henrietta's room. "But I've nothing to wear," I protested when we came to rest inside.

"There's bound to be something in my wardrobe." She rummaged within, pulled out one or two gowns, shook her head and decided that they would be too large. Then she winged down to the workroom, now shrouded and quiet, the covers pulled over the machines, and came back with a dress spread over her arm. "I have it! The very thing! The girls have just finished it for Mrs Beauness's daughter. She's about the same build as you. Try it on."

Albert was stretched out on the chaise longue, the wrong way up with his feet high on the scrolled headrest. He was fast asleep. Henrietta covered him tenderly with a blanket. I hid behind the screen and changed into the gown. It was of white organza, frilly and lace-trimmed, a young lady's evening dress, the hem sweeping the floor and falling into a small train. She came round to fasten the back. "Oh, it's lovely," I breathed, seeing my reflection in the pier-glass. It transformed me. Henrietta became my fairy godmother.

She sat me down at the dressing table and commenced work on my hair. "You look most fetching, child. I knew you would. It suits you far better than Mrs Beauness's spotty offspring. We'll brush your hair up – so, and fix a comb just here – now, doesn't that look fine? My word, one would take you for a Spanish grandee's daughter – a little touch of rouge, I think – the faintest suspicion of carmine on your lips – and you'll be ready to brave the lion's den."

"But – but, I've never been to a posh house before," I mumbled, though my appearance was startling. I really did look aristocratic.

"Don't worry, pet. They're but human, like ourselves," she smiled, giving me a spray of perfume. "Thank goodness, you've controlled your West Country drawl, and the Maestro has worked wonders with your voice. I must go and tell him to get into his dress suit. He'll accompany you, of course."

In no time at all we were waiting in the hall where Angeleri and I decided what I was to sing, and he made sure that he had the music in his portfolio. The bell rang and a smart chauffeur conducted us to the Brinkworth limousine. It was dark when we arrived and though lamps hissed on either side of the wrought-iron gates, I couldn't see the exterior properly, just a quick impression of many windows ablaze with lights. We were driven round to the back where the butler showed us into an anteroom, there to wait until we were summoned to the music salon. I stared at the rather sparse furnishings. I was used to rooms too overcrowded for beauty, crammed to bursting point with occasional tables, chairs, footstools and carved bookcases. In the Linton establishment knickknacks abounded, making dusting a feat of endurance. Here, it was entirely different.

The furniture was delicate, ornamented with twisting

vines and flower carvings. There were no harsh crimsons or magentas on walls or fabrics, these had given way to soft blues and greys, giving a feeling of space and light. "It's rather bare, isn't it, dear," murmured Henrietta as we waited nervously. "Frightfully smart, of course. I think it's what is fashionably known as Art Nouveau."

I wished that I could emulate Henrietta's calm, and tried not to listen to the hum of voices, the laughter and chatter from the other side of the white door. The butler appeared and beckoned to her. She rose, straightened her shoulders and advanced imperiously, sweeping through as he held it open for her. I was trembling and Angeleri patted my gloved hand, his wise eyes smiling at me, an unfamiliar Maestro in his shiny evening suit, greying mane combed back, unusually neat and clean.

"Don't be frightened, *cara*," he said, eager to show off my talent. "Your voice is a luminous prayer – like a white candle burning. This is your debut, so make the most of the opportunity. It will go *pui che bonone* – more than swimmingly."

I could hear Henrietta playing, and then followed her sweet, true voice, singing a ballad. There was a scattering of applause. I stood up, feeling like a gladiator about to enter the arena. She returned, flushed with success. "Your turn, my love," she said gaily and gave me a little push towards the door. "On you go, and take them by storm!"

For an instant I hung back, unable to move, and then with my heart pounding fast, I held my head high and walked out on to a semi-circular stage with an arch like a huge shell curving above. This was at one end of the large room, and I stood there under the full blaze of the crystal chandeliers. I was too dazzled and far too nervous to observe my audience in detail. I knew that I had to announce my first song, so whilst Angeleri arranged his tails over the stool and set the music on the stand, I stepped forward and addressed that sea of faces.

"I would like to sing for you Gilda's aria, *Caro nome*,

from Verdi's opera *Rigoletto*," I said in a surprisingly strong, clear voice.

The Maestro played the introductory bars and, concentrating entirely on what I had been taught, I opened my mouth and sang. Gilda was a young, innocent girl, victim of an unscrupulous libertine, and I suppose I must have conveyed that quality of purity for when the last note died away, the acclamation told me that I had conquered. For the very first time, I heard the dizzying sound of "Brava! Brava!", that uplifting shout of approval which was to follow me round the world in the course of my career. There was another word too, ringing through the room – "Encore! Encore!"

I smiled at my dear teacher, who was beaming widely, clapping his hands and bowing to me over the keyboard. I didn't have to tell him what I wanted to sing next, he already knew and he led me into Mimi's first aria in Act One of *La Bohème*. There was a moment's silence, when I had finished and I had them in the palm of my hand. Thunderous applause broke out.

A lady seated in the front row of chairs leapt up and ran to me, taking my hands in hers. "My dear girl! That was truly wonderful," she enthused. "Where did you get that voice?"

Henrietta joined us on the stage. "You like her singing, Lady Brinkworth?"

"Like it? Like it! It's amazing. Mrs Linton, how can I thank you enough for bringing her tonight? What did you say her name was? Rebecca Costello? Good! That has a fine Continental feel to it. We must talk. Come, my dears, we simply must discuss the furtherance of Rebecca's career."

I was too overcome to say much, and Hermione Brinkworth was the kind of woman who swept all before her. Her single-mindedness, purpose and energy cleared every obstacle from her path when she had decided on a course of action. Her beauty was of a quality which can only be described as stunning. She was dressed in a green gown of a loose Eastern style, and her auburn hair was adorned by a turban. Amethysts glittered at her throat, ears and wrists, and she stalked through the throng with her head in the air, vibrant and vital.

I had but a fleeting glimpse of my audience, and this was enough to make my eyes widen. The men were bearded, very casual in trousers of tartan or crumpled velvet, and sporting Norfolk jackets, whilst cravats seemed to be the order of the day. The ladies were even more unconventional. Not for them the restrictions of corsets, upswept hair on tiaras. They favoured sacklike garments of Grecian origin, hair tumbling freely about their bare shoulders, garlanded with flowers of chiffon scarves. I remembered Gertie saying that Methley House was a meeting place for artists, writers and musicians.

Taking us to a smaller room, Hermione seated herself on a divan, poured wine for us and lit a cigarette in a long jade holder. "Now then," she commenced, her blue eyes going over me with interest. "This child has a unique gift. We must foster it. What is being done for her at the moment?"

"I teach her, madame," said Angeleri.

"Has she had any stage experience?"

"No, madame. She is very young, only sixteen."

"That doesn't matter. Adelina Patti was that age when she sang her first major role. I suggest that she does at least a year with the Carl Rosa Touring Company," Hermione said decisively. "I know the director and can get her into the chorus. She'll have to have an audition, of course."

"A fine company, madame," agreed Angeleri, then he turned to me. "This will be such good experience for you, *cara*. They have a first-class reputation. Why, the British première of *La Bohème* was given by them in Manchester in 1897. Puccini himself came from Italy for it."

"Then that is settled," said Hermione, giving me no chance to voice an opinion. She was like a steamroller;

she went into everything, hammer and tongs, seizing life by the collar and shaking it. Later I learned that she trampled on her enemies as if they were a bed of nettles, but she was equally fiery in her loyalty to her friends. She might act like an autocratic empress, but she had the kindest of hearts to those whom she took under her wing. Now she fixed me with those clear eyes and said: "I'll arrange an audition for you for next Monday morning. Signor Angeleri knows the address, and off you go touring England. Come back and see me in a year's time."

The interview was over. She bade us a gracious good-night and sailed off to join her guests. I recovered my powers of speech. "But I can't leave you, Mrs Linton. What about little Hugh?"

"My dear, this is a golden opportunity. She's a most influential lady."

"Don't worry about Hugh," she continued as we climbed into the car, settling our wraps about us. "Elsie's sister is thirteen now. She can come and look after Hugh."

It was out of my hands, and I allowed myself to be carried along by the tide of events. Although I cried into Hugh's fat little neck when the time came to say goodbye, I knew that I mustn't let sentiment, doubts or fears prevent me from seizing this chance and squeezing every drop of experience from it.

So, I toured the length and breadth of England, singing in the chorus at the start but gradually being given small parts, then working my way up to understudy the lead. The salary was minute, the experience without price. During those early days, I rejoiced in the life, despite its hand-to-mouth qualities, and I soon adjusted to the bewildering complications of an opera company on the road. I learned to deal with seedy lodgings, tiring travel, temperamental tenors, jealous sopranos and amorous baritones. The company consisted of a resolutely un-

Italian cast, though we performed the majority of the works in that tongue. It was exhilarating and exhausting, composed of work, work and more work – rehearsals in chilly, run-down theatres early in the morning after arriving in some small town late the night before, and shows in the evenings – we were lucky if we stayed a week in one place.

The year flashed by and I returned to the Lintons who had told me that I had a home with them whenever I needed it. It was a much more confident, young singer who went to visit Hermione, and she was delighted to see me. I was surprised to find that she'd not forgotten me. Far from it. She told me that she had been to Cardiff and heard me sing a tiny part in *Carmen*. "You're doing very well, dear child," she said, receiving me in the drawing room of Methley House.

"What happens now?" I asked, laying aside my muff and gloves and accepting a glass of sherry. It was a sunny autumn day, and London was glorious, its trees and parks copper-tinted. On this visit to Hermione, I had gone boldly to the front door, feeling my feet as a budding prima donna. There would be no servants' entrance for me! Henrietta had had a new walking-out costume ready and waiting, made of tobacco-coloured taffeta, trimmed with bands of black velvet. I wore a fur tippet and an incredibly fashionable hat with a close-fitting veil, convinced that I looked sophisticated, alluring and mysterious.

Hermione approved, her eyes dancing at me. "Well, my dear, talented and beautiful though you are, I don't think you're quite ready for Covent Garden yet," she remarked in that faintly sarcastic ways of hers. She reminded me a little of Nell. Then, seeing my obvious disappointment, for this is the acme of ambitions for every singer, she added kindly: "Never fear, your time will come. I promised that I would help you and I never disappoint friends. You have worked so hard. The Carl Rosa Company will be happy to keep you with them, if that's what you want. However, I have a little plan of my own which I intend to set in motion right away."

"A recital here?" I asked.

She shook her head, pendant jade earrings swinging. "Better than that. I'll say no more at present, but I want you to go home and rehearse *La Bohème* with Signor Angeleri."

I tried to question her, but she wouldn't tell me what she had in mind, teasing me and saying that Mrs Linton and my teacher knew all about it. Maddeningly, they too refused to tell, full of a secretive air of importance which intrigued me. I was treated like a royal prisoner, spoiled and pampered, given breakfast in bed and not allowed to lift a finger. I was permitted to see the children. Hugh was now a sturdy toddler and I snatched him to me and held him tight and he smiled, remembering me. Then Angeleri took me away, saying sternly: "We must work."

We studied the opera closely and, with his guidance, I began to understand it. "The idea that unifies the work is that of cold, associated with poverty, loneliness, illness and death. In each Act, cold is stressed," he explained, seated at the piano in his room. "Yet along with this are the contrasting feelings of warmth, spring, poetry and love. Have you ever been in love, Rebecca?" His black eyes peered at me shrewdly through his glasses.

I had not, and told him so firmly. Oh, there'd been plenty of chances with the male members of the company, but I wasn't interested. I didn't want to fall in love. Nothing must stand in the way of my career. "Does one have to have been in love to sing about it?" I replied tartly, seated beside him, following the score.

One grey eyebrow shot up and his mouth quirked. "No, one can sing of it with the lips, but until one is stirred by passion, one can't sing of it from the heart."

"Are you suggesting that I have a love affair just to improve my performance?" I was rather annoyed with him, feeling saint-like in my dedication.

"A grain of earthy passion would not go amiss," he countered with a mischievous grin.

"Let's get on and stop wasting time," I said sternly, making him laugh at such pomposity.

"Don't be angry, *bella* Rebecca. You can play Mimi without necessarily taking a lover. Now, were it Puccini's latest heroine, Tosca, this would be out of the question – a different lady indeed, full of fire and sensuality. I doubt very much whether a virgin could ever take that role successfully." His fingers moved over the keys as he spoke, picking out melodies.

Angeleri knew exactly what he wanted, leaping up sometimes and acting passages, singing in his quavering voice. Most of all, we worked on the difficult last Act. I had to suggest that Mimi was dying and he taught me how to do it movingly, delicately. I found that it was a matter of concentrating hard, of watching myself, never letting go of the character I was playing. Even the Maestro was moved, wiping his eyes, shaking his head and saying: "Ah, this music! I have loved many composers, *cara*, but there's no one can write for the operatic stage like Puccini. Such great sense of the theatre, speaking to the emotions – original and moving, penetrating and sincere. You feel this too – you interpret it to perfection, my dear, dear girl."

A month later we were invited to spend a weekend at Hermione's country house. Albert and Henrietta came, and Angeleri was hopping with excitement. I had a feeling that there was more to this than a mere party, and I was right. When we arrived I discovered that she had her own small theatre built in the grounds, and had planned a performance of *La Bohème* with myself as Mimi. I began rehearsals with the professional company she had engaged. I had been coached without being aware of this and it was just as well or I might have collapsed in a welter of nerves.

It was wonderful but terribly daunting. I was determined not to fail. I shall never forget waiting in the wings for my first entrance. "What in hell's name am I doing here?" I wondered. "Lord, how I wish Nancy and Nell could see me. I've done it! I'll make you proud of me, wherever you are!" Then I heard the tenor giving me my cue and, once on stage, I forgot everything. I became the ailing Mimi, borne along on the pathos and passion of the music and, when the curtain fell as I "died" at the end, I knew that I had won. The applause was tumultuous, and we had to do the "dying" bit all over again before they'd let us go. The tenor led me forward as the curtain lifted again and again, and someone handed me a huge bouquet of roses. I was crying in earnest by this time, still half Mimi and half myself.

In the dressing room, Henrietta flung her arms about me and Albert beamed proudly, as if I were one of his own daughters and, to honour me, he was sober. "Get changed quickly," ordered Hermione. "The lions of the artistic world are agog to meet you. The impresario Mario Pascarel is here, and two directors from the Théâtre de la Monnaie in Brussels. Mario came late, of course, and I had to leave my seat and greet him – such a nuisance – he's brilliant but erratic. We stayed in the foyer until the interval, and he listened in silence to the end of the first Act, then threw away his cigar and said: 'Hermione, I want that voice! I don't care whether she's short or tall, pretty or plain – I want her!' "

What a night that was! A night of champagne and congratulations when it seemed that my audience was truly at my feet. I was introduced to Pascarel, a small man in a dark overcoat with an astrakhan collar, cut in the latest extreme of fashion. He was very voluble, very Italian, and he wanted me for the Teatri Regio in Turin. I turned to Hermione for guidance.

"She needs more training, *signor*," she said immediately. "I suggest that she studies for a while under Madame Bellini and then we'll see."

It was agreed that I should prepare myself for a further three months and then go to Turin. "You must have experience in Italy before you attempt Covent Garden, *Signorina* Costello," Pascarel murmured, bringing me yet another glass of champagne.

"Rebecca will work, she has strength and courage. She's going to be great – greater even than Melba," said Hermione confidently. "And, by God, they'll have to pay for her!"

I met someone else of importance that night, and to have written so much and said nothing of Beville is indeed an omission on my part, for I owe him a great deal. But, looking back over events, it is difficult to remember times and places with precision and record with accuracy. However, there's no doubt that Sir Beville Treneman, owner of Pomphlet Mill on the Cornish border, came into my life then.

I was surrounded by gesticulating foreigners debating my future, when he rescued me. He was fair-haired, rather broad and stocky, and he reminded me of a large and kindly natured dog. His nose had been broken at some time and its thickened, slightly dented appearance gave character to a face which might otherwise have seemed simply amiable and handsome without this added touch of distinction.

"I say, Hermione, old girl, aren't you going to introduce me to your star?" he quipped, white teeth flashing as he grinned at me.

Within minutes, he had whisked me away to a quiet corner, fetched a loaded plate from the buffet table, commandeered a bottle of champagne and settled at my side on the couch. In no time we were talking as if we'd known each other for years. I was charmed by his healthily tanned cheeks and the sandy lashes hedging his deep blue eyes. He was good-humoured and bluff, as open as a book. There wasn't a shred of deviousness anywhere in his personality. Just over thirty years old, he was a typical country gentleman who would rather spend a moonlight night tramping the woods with his dog than indulging in town entertainments or amorous dalliance. The boudoir was not for him, though that isn't to say that he lacked interest in women – far from it – but his approach was direct and sincere, viewing the meeting of the sexes as a pleasant necessity rather than a preoccupation.

I had learned by now how easily my looks brought men to me and how quickly the demands made by my ambition sent them away again. I had known how hard it was to be wanted for myself as a real person and not just because of my body, my gypsy hair, my potential as a singer. It was not enough – not for me. Not that I didn't enjoy being chased and admired, of course I did, but now I had seen desire as well as admiration in Pascarel's eye. Oh, he would push me to the top because he considered that I had a fine voice, but there would be a price. I feared that I'd be prepared to pay it, driven by this urge to become a singer of international renown. I dreaded becoming hard, devoid of morals or feeling, utterly selfish. Meeting Beville prevented this. He protected me from the wolves and taught me so much about myself and the world.

In due course, we became lovers, and I like to remember the first time he kissed me, born as that kiss was of laughter and good-fellowship, a friendship warmed by passion, filled with fun and free from intensity. Hermione was delighted, saying that a woman in my position needed a wealthy protector. By the time I had made up my mind to become his mistress, she had moved me into a suite in her house; Holland Park was a much more impressive address for a rising diva than the crowded villa in Soho. Angeleri was pleased too, but for a totally different reason – I should be able to play Tosca now!

Beville had a secret hideaway where we used to meet. Outside of a select few, no one was familiar with the name of the street, although it was within a minute of

Sloane Square. "It was once a farmhouse," he explained when he took me to this strictly bachelor establishment where his valet, Dawkins, catered for his needs. "The story goes that more than two hundred years ago it was the haunt of highwaymen who held up coaches on Putney Heath."

It was a delightful place, filled with Elizabethan furniture under low, dark-beamed ceilings. I could picture a highwayman sitting there, unloading his pockets of the rings he had just plucked from the hand of some society belle. Behind the beams there were lights cunningly concealed and it had been skilfully modernised to give the utmost warmth and comfort. I lost my virginity to Beville in the quaint oak four-poster which graced his chamber.

At this period of my life I'm ashamed to record that so much fuss and attention went to my head. I became full of my own importance and was inclined to confuse bad temper with artistic temperament. Visits to the Lintons brought me to earth with a bump, and Beville's gentle teasing helped. My new teacher, Madame Bellini, cut me down to size. No one could remain conceited for long in her awesome presence. She would listen as I sang, with clasped hands and steeped, far-away eyes, and then tell me that I was croaking like a bullfrog in the mating season!

"No, no, no!" she would scold, dressed in black and of a forbidding appearance, thrusting out her arms with fiery, imperious gestures. "That is terrible – terrible! Have you no ear? Listen to yourself? Open your mouth and sing in the front of it, not at the back of your throat! I don't want to hear you pipe like a choirboy. I want fullness – warmth – depth!"

After three months of this dictatorial regime, I was considered ready to accept Pascarel's offer and go to Turin. Beville went with me, smoothing the path. He had acquaintances everywhere, and we stayed in the palatial villa of an Italian count. It was as well that I was young, strong and determined for I had to break down the barriers created by my foreign counterparts who positively refused to believe that an English woman could sing like an Italian, but I succeeded in winning them over, even receiving the approbation of the critical Turin audience. After this came Brussels, and minor engagements in other European capitals. Beville and I led a nomadic existence for two years and it was not until the summer of 1903, when I was almost twenty, that Hermione was able to fulfil the rest of her promise. I was engaged to perform at the Royal Opera House, Covent Garden.

Hermione had been beavering away for me behind the scenes, true to her word, but there was still much to be done. More than ever, I realised how lucky I had been to be taken up by her, for it was her influence which had obtained this coveted spot. Talented though I might be, I knew that there were many others as gifted who struggled on for years with little recognition. I was better known on the Continent than in England and still had a long haul before me, but was well on the way to the top, thanks to her. I met the other members of the cast and encountered a certain amount of resentment amongst the older, well-established singers who didn't take kindly to the sudden emergence of a comparative newcomer who threatened to steal their thunder.

The Lintons were ecstatic, and I was extremely nervous, taking myself off to Madame Bellini and working like a galley slave. Dear Beville displayed the patience of a saint, knowing that to be successful was the be-all and end-all of my existence. I'm afraid he took second place, though his love was a safety valve and I relaxed at the cottage, where we lived in companionable domesticity. We took an immense pleasure in doing the same things, the mere fact of being together adding a glow of happiness. We were glad to have a settled base after the hotels, travelling and hectic living of the Continent.

He had awakened me to passion and he was tender and considerate, as eager to give pleasure as to take it. I enjoyed sharing his bed, giving myself up to the luxury of sensuality, delighting in his kisses and caresses, the feel of his strong body lying next to mine at night. I knew that I wasn't in love with him, but thought that I might never experience this emotion, wedded to my art. I must have been difficult to live with at times, but we never quarrelled and, with hindsight, I can see that this was because that sweet man let me have my own way on almost every issue. He simply couldn't be bothered to argue and was so much in love with me that I could do no wrong in his eyes. He had asked me to marry him, but I hesitated. Not that the idea of being Lady Treneman didn't appeal to me, it most decidedly did, but there was something in me which delayed making such a final commitment. Maybe, in my secret heart, I still hoped to find that sweeping, all-powerful madness which would crush ambition so that I was prepared to give up everything for the sake of the beloved. So I put Beville off, saying that I was far too busy at the moment, but promising that if I married at all, it would be to him. I began rehearsals at the Royal Opera House.

At first, I sang important though secondary roles and I was understudying the prima donna. Then came that chance for which all aspiring actresses and singers rather unkindly pray. She fell ill and I stepped into her shoes. There was no likelihood of her returning to complete the season. I did rather well and became popular with the audiences. Those good fairies were still looking after me, it seemed. The critics were magnanimous and I was mentioned in the newspapers. Offers started to come in from America, Buenos Aires, Italy, France and Germany. Hermione began to employ the services of a theatrical agent to deal with this. Fortunately, I was working with such fine and experienced performers that it kept me humble.

One evening towards the close of the season I picked myself up from the mattress backstage on to which I had just fallen. As Tosca, that passionate Puccini heroine, I had just very dramatically committed suicide from the canvas and batten walls of a castle. It was always a fraught moment when I wondered if the stagehands had positioned it properly or if I risked a sprained ankle and bruises. All was well, and I took several curtain calls, listening to the rapturous shouts from the black auditorium. I could distinguish nothing beyond the footlights, only aware of that encouraging cheering.

I had that feeling of unreality which assailed me after an exacting role. Unlike some singers, I had been attending acting classes too. Puccini's operas were based on plays, demanding stagecraft as well as voice production. I tottered to my dressing room, wrung out and drained, longing to go home. Beville was waiting there, and my dresser fussed as she helped me out of the sumptuous, high-waisted gown of the Napoleonic era in which the opera was set, I sank on to a stool before the mirror and, as she unpinned the great swathe of false black ringlets which crowned my own hair, I begun to cream off the grease-paint.

Beville uncorked a bottle of wine. " '*E vin di Spagna.*' " he sang with a grin, using one of the villain's lines. " '*Un sorso per rincorarvi.*' "

Poor devil, he must have known the piece by heart for he had attended so many rehearsals and performances, ever supportive. I smiled back at him and rested my head against his shoulder. His bushy red-gold moustache tickled my cheek as he kissed me lightly. What a nice man he was. His kisses were always so soft, deep, warm and perfect. Kisses that seemed to be creations, suited to the time and the circumstances, entirely satisfying. Perhaps I should marry him after all. "Thank God it's Sunday tomorrow," I exclaimed. "Just imagine the luxury of lying in bed till late, with Dawkins bringing up breakfast."

"And the Sunday papers," he added, grinning and easing himself on to the stool beside me.

I unhooked the huge paste earrings from my lobes while my dresser unclasped the impressive, though fake, necklace. "Bliss! Sheer bliss, Beville – I can't wait," I said.

"Neither can I, my love." Then he leaned nearer to whisper. "I can't wait to have you, sleepy and warm, turning into my arms under the sheet. Perhaps you won't be too tired then, and will let me make love to you."

"Oh, dearling, I will," I promised, feeling guilty because bed, of late, had meant sleep to me.

I was still in my wrapper when there was a knock at the door. Hermione came swanning in, followed by a chattering, splendidly dressed group who wanted to meet me. My hopes of an early night died quietly, and I pasted a smile on my face and summoned up a final reserve of energy. Then, suddenly, my heart missed a beat before galloping on as I saw a woman at the back of the crowd. My God! It was Nell! I half rose but was arrested by the look in her eyes. I registered shocked surprise and a cold feeling of disappointment as she shook her head slightly. She didn't want me to acknowledge that I already knew her. Why was this? Was she ashamed of me? Didn't she want her smart friends to know that we were old acquaintances? It flashed through my mind that she might have hidden her orphanage background, as I had done, so I kept my mouth shut, waiting my moment to have a quiet word with her.

Hermione, in her customary juggernaut fashion, was presenting this bowing gentleman or that simpering lady. Then she came to the last of them, leading Nell forward. "Rebecca, darling – I want you to meet Mr and Mrs Charles de Grendon, and Miss Cordelia de Grendon."

He was kissing my hand and I was nodding at the

two women. Nell was a grown-up married lady now, beautifully dressed with jewels sparkling about her and a fur cape over her shoulders. Yet her eyes were so anxious, and though she murmured the appropriate compliments, she seemed like a puppet, her real feelings stultified. What was the matter with her? I wondered as I made automatic responses to the questions the public always ask performers. Why didn't she want it known that we were friends? Was it something to do with her husband? He was a tall, powerful man, immaculately dressed and handsome in a hard sort of way. His face was scarred, and this made him look like a brigand.

"We've recently returned from Egypt," he said, smiling into my eyes in such a way that I could tell he was used to making easy conquests. "Cordelia told us that you were a rising star and that we simply must come and hear you sing though, truth to tell, opera isn't really my forte. However, I'm deuced glad that I took her advice for you're quite ravishing." His down-sweeping glance took note of my carelessly fastened robe, reminding me sharply that I wore very little beneath it.

"Were you on holiday there?" I asked, giving him a look which plainly said: "Hands off, you bastard! You are married!"

He smiled and I noticed that he was glancing meaningfully at the half-empty wine bottle, but Beville did not offer him a drink. "Oh, yes, we were enjoying a vacation. My dear wife has been bereaved lately, and I thought a change of scene would do her good. I was right, it seems, for we're now expecting a child, aren't we, dearest?" His voice was low-pitched, with a cool, drawling sound.

Nell nodded, but it was his sister who burst into the conversation, an arrogant, handsome woman, rather flashily dressed, probably a member of the *demi-monde*. "It's going to be a boy – an heir for the de Grendons. What fun I'll have treaching him to hunt!"

"You live close to them?" I enquired levelly. There was something about Cordelia which inspired distrust.

"I spend most of my time at Combermere, yes," she answered with that brittle smile. I noticed that she was giving Beville the eye. "It's in Cheshire, you know. You must come and visit us – your friend too," this was delivered with a bold wink at Beville. "D'you like the country, sir? You look a sporting sort of chap. Of course, we all bet madly. It's so exciting. Don't you find it so? Why, Charles spends half his life at the gaming tables."

"Does he indeed," commented Beville drily, unimpressed.

Charles de Grendon, Nell's husband. I recognised the type. Handsome, yes – proud, cruel and pig-headed, most certainly. Our eyes met and his had a hard glint, like steel. I mentally saluted a fellow adventurer, and thanked God that I wasn't involved with him. Now I knew why the usually sharp-witted Nell was so subdued. How on earth did she get mixed up with him? And as for that sister of his – what a bitch!

"Rebecca is tired." Beville took up his post at my side like a protective St Bernard. "If you'll excuse her, it is time she went home."

Hermione looked annoyed, but Beville could be stubborn where my welfare was concerned, and people began to drift away. Amidst the hand-kissing and insincerity of the de Grendon departure, Nell paused to say goodnight and thank me for receiving them. I felt something drop into my lap and immediately rested my arm across it. As soon as the door closed behind them, I picked it up, seeing that it was a letter.

"Phew!" Beville exclaimed. "What a crew! I must say de Grendon strikes me as a bit of a bounder."

"And his sister?" I asked, running my thumbnail along the envelope. "Did you ever see such a low-cut gown?"

"Not since I was weaned!"

"You admire her?" I drew out the letter.

"God, no! She's impressive, I suppose. The sort of woman the chaps at the club joke about, but never marry."

I was not listening, absorbed in reading the brief note. It said: "My dearest friend, I must see you privately on an important matter concerning Nancy. I expect that you remember the vow we made before leaving the orphanage. Well, she needs help, most desperately. I will come to your dressing room alone, after the matinée on Wednesday. Yours always, Nell."

"What have you there? A love letter from de Grendon?" asked Beville with amusement. He was not a jealous man because I had never given him cause to doubt me. I didn't propose to start now, so handed it to him. He already knew my story, there were no secrets between us, and as we drove home we discussed what might be the nature of Nancy's trouble.

Nell was waiting for me when I came off stage on Wednesday. I sent my dresser away and, when we were alone, we embraced warmly. We both shed tears, I think, for it had been so long since we last met. Then I held her away and scanned her face. Yes, she was a woman now, soon to be a mother, and she had grown to be lovely, her skin of that delicate tint which went with the deep gold of her hair. But she didn't look well and I wondered if the pregnancy was to blame or if there was something else. We sat down together and she told me the whole story of what had happened in Alexandria. I was horrified at the despicable part her husband had played, bursting out: "You mean to sit there and tell me that he was willing to sell you to a sheik?"

"Yes, he was – but that doesn't matter," she said quickly, gripping my hands. "The important thing is that someone must go and help Nancy. I can't because Charles has forbidden me to interfere. He becomes violent if I disobey him, and I'm carrying my first baby. I can't risk being beaten."

"He hits you? The damned coward! Christ, I'd like

to get my hands on him!" I raged, remembering how he had leered at me. "What about Cordelia?"

She shuddered and her eyes were haunted. "Oh, no – I'd never mention it to her."

She's mortally terrified of both of them, I thought, fearful for her. If anyone needed help, then surely it was Nell, yet she kept insisting that it was Nancy who was in dire peril. "Are you quite certain about this?" I asked, struggling to be rational, wishing that Beville had been able to be present.

"Oh, Rebecca, I know it sounds far-fetched, but she was so desperate, and you know Nancy, she wasn't afraid of anything once, was she?"

Remembering her, I couldn't imagine Nancy intimidated or threatened. I made Nell repeat the story, wishing that I'd had the chance to read Nancy's journal, that controversial book which had caused so much aggravation. "So, this Quiller person has presumably delivered her diary to his boss, Sir Nicholas. Just why was he so anxious to have it?" I said at length.

"I don't know. I didn't have the chance to look at it properly, but I've this awful feeling that there's something bad going on. If ever there was a girl in fear of her life, it was Nancy. I dared not let Charles know that you and I were friends. He won't even let me write to her. Oh, you must help her – you must!" she repeated in tones of mingled rage and anguish. Then her troubled eyes searched my face and she struggled to control herself, making an apologetic gesture. "You must forgive me. I haven't congratulated you on reaching your goal. At least you have been successful, out of the three of us. When I heard about you. I knew there wouldn't be two Rebecca Costellos. It seemed like the answer to my prayers, and in the nick of time too, for we're returning to Cheshire very soon. Oh, you must do something! Nancy's in terrible danger – I'm sure of it!"

"The season here finishes on Saturday," I said. "My agent is arranging a visit to South America in the near future, but I could manage to get away for a few weeks before this. I'll speak to Beville about it. He wants to marry me, Nell, but I'm not certain."

"Marriage!" She pulled a wry face, her hands clasped about her stomach as if to protect her baby. "What is it they say? 'Marry in haste, repent at leisure.' "

I looked at her wan reflection in the mirror as I secured my hat with long pins. "Is that what you did?"

She bit her lip, confused, uncertain, no longer the cool, detached girl I had known. "I suppose so, but don't think that I didn't love him – I did, most passionately."

I threw my fur stole about my shoulders and picked up my gloves. "What is his trouble, Nell? Booze? Women? Gambling? Or a combination of the three?"

Her face was white and grim. "Would that were all! I could live with that. It's his sister – and much, much more besides. I'll tell you about it one day."

"Cordelia encourages his vices?"

She gave a twisted smile. "Cordelia *is* his vice."

I wanted to ask more, but she seemed thoroughly exhausted, though more with a malady of the spirit than the body. I longed to give her some of my own vitality and, as we paused at the door, she gripped me feverishly. "You'll go to Egypt? Promise me that you will! God knows what's been happening since we left three weeks ago. Can I rely on you? You mustn't try to get in touch with me." Her eyes, dilated in the dim gaslight of the passage, were like those of a wild animal, darkening with an expression of intense fear. "Charles wouldn't like that – he wouldn't like it at all."

I insisted on giving her Beville's address in case she needed it. "You must take care of yourself, Nell. Don't worry about Nancy. I'll go and Beville will help me. He may even know the Renshaws, he's a resourceful fellow, quite brilliant when it comes to organisation."

"Ah, how lucky you are to have someone like that," she said in a faltering voice. "I've been cruelly used and cruelly wronged. Perhaps one day we'll meet again and I can tell you of it."

Oh, Nell, what's happened to you? I wanted to cry. She had changed shockingly. I hated to see her cowed and broken. Rage against her damned bully of a husband swelled up in me. There was nothing I could do at the moment, but he'd better watch his step! I offered to drive her home in Beville's car, but she refused, saying that someone might see her and tell Charles.

It was drizzling outside, a grey, murky evening when the pavements gleamed like dirty pewter, the cabs and automobiles sending up showers of muddy water. The lamplighter were already at work, kindling the old gaslamps lining the street. Nell left me swiftly, lost in the crowd, and I stepped into the car, chauffeured by Dawkins who was waiting at the kerb. My mind was already streaking ahead, planning what I was going to tell Beville. I didn't doubt for a single second that he would agree to aid me in my quest. We would go to Egypt and find Nancy.

Chapter 3

When I reached the cottage, Beville wasn't there. By this time I could no longer control my emotions, throwing myself across the coverlet of the four-poster and bursting into a storm of weeping. My friends – my two dear friends! I had so hoped that they were happy wherever they happened to be, and now I found that one was in danger and the other desperately miserable. I couldn't bear it. Always subject to see-saw changes of mood, I felt on the knife edge of exhaustion. The season had tested me to the limit and I had a heavy schedule ahead. I needed a holiday. Fat chance of that! I told myself grimly, mopping up my tears, going to Alexandria to aid a friend in distress won't exactly be a joyride.

I had dispatched Dawkins to Beville's club with an urgent message and, very soon, I heard him running up the stairs. In an instant, I was in his arms, pouring out the whole story while he rocked me and made comforting noises. Then he said calmly: "We'll take the ferry to Calais and go by train to Italy, down to Brindisi where there's a regular steamboat service to Alexandria. We should be there in – let me think – under two weeks, so stop worrying, old girl. There, there, dry your eyes, get into something comfortable, and I'll tell Dawkins to serve dinner up here. We'll have a quiet evening making plans."

I suppose it was hardly fair for he'd never met Nancy, but it was such a relief to hand the problem over to him. We dined in front of the log fire which roared away on the hearth, a small table drawn up close. I had changed into a dressing gown, while he relaxed in a smoking jacket of a gaudy Oriental pattern. Dawkins, poker-faced, served us with his usual efficiency and discretion. I was far too disturbed to eat much; even the wine and warmth of the crackling flames failed to soothe me. I found Beville's calm rather infuriating. Brandy glass at his elbow, he sat back in the wing chair and lit a cigar.

"My God, how can you sit there smoking, as if nothing had happened? A woman's life may be at stake! Wouldn't it be quicker to take a boat all the way? It's urgent, Beville!"

I was in a ferment of impatience. I wanted to set out there and then. In answer, he held out his arms and I crept on to his lap, finding solace there. "I do understand, love, and we'll do whatever you want. But nothing can be done tonight, these things take time to arrange." His dark blue eyes grew serious. "Are you quite sure that Nancy is threatened? It sounds frightfully melodramatic. Naturally, I'll perform any feat of derring-do to save her but, dash it, Rebecca – I do hope that Nell wasn't imagining things. It's a hell of a long way to go to find out!" He touched my cheek with tender fingertips.

"I must see Nancy, if it's only to stop me worrying. They were like sisters to me – and it's not only Nancy – Nell's unhappy too." I tried to put my feelings into words, that instinct which was urging me to take action.

"Cluck, cluck, Mother Hen, you'll go grey fretting like this," he teased. "All right, I'll take a chance on it, though I'll be dashed annoyed with Nell for upsetting you if we arrive to find Nancy in fine fettle."

"You won't say a word to her!" I answered sharply. "Poor Nell! That damned husband of hers – refusing to help Nancy – willing to sell his own wife to settle his gambling debts! What a blackguard!"

"I'm sure you're right, m'dear. I didn't care for the way he was eyeing you in the dressing room. I've put out a few feelers at the club. Apparently, he's blacklisted in most respectable gaming houses. Gets himself deeply in debt, so I gather."

"That's what happened in Alexandria, and it was either Nell or Nancy's journal to redeem him. I wish I knew how Nell came to be mixed up with such a man. As for his sister – !"

"She has quite a nasty reputation. Not only that, she's very thick with her brother – the chaps made a joke of it, but they hinted at incest," he said crisply, then his voice softened as he felt the tension in my body. "First things first, my dear. It's Nancy we're determined to help, not Nell. We can sort her out when we return, if she wants sorting out, but from what I hear, she loves de Grendon, and probably wants to stay with him."

"What alternative has she?" I demanded indignantly. "She's expecting a child. Besides, you know how cruel and unjust the divorce law is."

"Funny you should mention that," he countered, his hand continuing its comforting caress. "Sir Nicholas Renshaw's sister-in-law was mixed up in a scandal some years back, and she was divorced because of it."

"You know the family?" This didn't really surprise me. Beville knew everyone.

"Well, vaguely. Pomphlet Mill is not far from the Renshaw estate. Let me think – yes, there were two brothers – Henry was the eldest, and then came Nicholas. Oddly enough, they married a pair of beautiful sisters – old Standish's girls – Dorothea and Emily. There was a great fuss when Dorothea ran off and left Henry. Later, he was killed when out hunting, and Nicholas inherited everything."

"Tell me more," I said, intrigued to learn of the man who had made such an impression on sensible Nancy. "D'you know him well enough to wangle an invitation to his house in Alexandria?"

"We were certainly on speaking terms, though his interests weren't mine," he replied thoughtfully, delving back into the past. "The country folk around our estates considered him to be a little eccentric. He's keen on archaeology, you see, and is also rather musical – plays the piano like a professional, and the local squires didn't consider either of these hobbies suitable for a gentleman."

I slid from his knee, curling up on the hearthrug, holding out my hands to the flames. "So, Sir Nicholas likes music, does he? This will be a fine reason for your renewing his acquaintance. Madame Bellini will insist that I practise whilst away, and I'll need someone to accompany me. That's it, Beville. You'll go and explain to him that you're on holiday with a singer who needs the help of a competent pianist. I think it will be wiser for me to pretend that I don't know Nancy."

Beville played with my curls. "What a clever little minx you are," he whispered admiringly. "Let's hope all this is nothing more than a storm in a teacup, then perhaps you'll give me a bit of attention for a change."

I flung my arms around his neck, pulling his face down to mine and kissing him passionately, gratefully. We went to bed then, but even while I responded to his lovemaking, my mind was elsewhere and when he was asleep, I lay wide awake, with scenes from my childhood moving across my inner vision. Nothing was of greater significance to me now than reaching Egypt without delay.

I told my agent that I was going away for a few weeks and he agreed that I needed a break to ensure that I was fresh for the trip to Argentina planned for the winter. Hermione wasn't pleased for she had wanted Beville and me to spend time at her country house, taking part in those interminable parties – days of playing golf, tennis or croquet, with boats on the lake and gentlemen showing off. In the evenings I should have been expected to perform in her theatre.

I said goodbye to the Lintons and my Maestro, kissing little Hugh while Henrietta confided that his place in the family crib would be taken by another in the spring. Dawkins was coming with us and he had found me a lady's maid. Till then I'd refused the services of a personal servant, liking to manage alone, but he said that I should find the heat taxing. So, Mary O'Dell entered my employ.

A furore of packing took place. Beville had been an officer in the British Army in Egypt until invalided home and retiring from active service, so he knew what was required. I equipped myself with lightweight dresses and shady hats for day wear, and gowns and warm wraps for the evenings which he warned me could be chilly. We left from Cannon Street station early one morning and soon arrived at Dover where, as the steamer left the dock, I watched the foam marking her way across the Channel. It was like an umbilical cord linking us with the mother country. I lingered at the rail, hearing the sad wails of the gulls and watching the white cliffs dwindling into the distance.

Perhaps this was a rash, ill-considered step I was taking. Nancy was a part of my past which I had thought left behind long ago, yet seeing Nell had brought it surging back. I sighed, chilled and depressed. Life always had some dirty little trick up its sleeve; just when one thought everything was going smoothly, along came the unexpected. If only it could have been different. How joyfully I would have greeted my old friends. I don't like alarmists and hated being one, but Nell had convinced me beyond all doubt that I was sorely needed in Alexandria. A tingle of apprehension ran along my nerves. The mysterious East! It had a powerful fascination. I wanted to go there, yet was frightened now of what I might find.

The first part of the journey was a repeat of our recent trip – careering along in the baking heat of trains, the nights spent in cramped little berths, jolting and shrieking through the midnight stations. Beville had booked rooms in the Great East India Hotel in Brindisi, and I need hardly say how wonderful it was to undress, bathe and sleep after that hot, sweaty train ride. The following evening, we boarded the P & O paddleboat, *Massilia*, moored alongside the quay, awaiting passengers for Alexandria. Beville was in a romantic mood. Bowing to convention, we had decorously occupied separate rooms in the hotel, but he had come to my bed in the small hours. We missed the privacy of our love nest in London, but all this stealing about after dark, added a bit of spice and, during the three-day voyage to Egypt, he continued to enter my cabin stealthily whilst I stifled my giggles, and made sure that he was gone by morning. It was ridiculous and I was thoroughly impatient with such hypocrisy. He and I were good friends, filled with affection and esteem for one another, far more so than many married couples I knew, yet we should be condemned for sleeping together. Providing that I didn't have a child, and this was unlikely for the down-to-earth Gertie had instructed me how to avoid such an occurrence, there was no reason why Beville and I should not enjoy the delights of the flesh.

In my journal, I find an entry which says: "Friday,

August 15th, 1905. 2.30 p.m. We are not far from land. Seagulls wheel overhead and the coast of Egypt is in sight. A hot wind blows from the desert. As we near the harbour, I can see minarets and the gilded domes of mosques, a feature which first strikes one's notice. We have taken a pilot on board and proceed at easy speed with him standing beside the captain on the bridge, and with an able-bodied British seaman on either paddlebox, heaving the lead (so Beville tells me), we have every assurance that the *Massilia* will not run on to a sandbank."

When the steamer had been brought to anchorage, it was visited by custom and quarantine officials and, being reported clear, we were at liberty to land. Beville knew it well, so we avoided some of the pitfalls of the ignorant tourists who were besieged by Arab boatmen, and we reached the landing stage with the minimum trouble and expense. Beville dealt equally firmly with a certain pompous person in the Custom House who demanded to see our passports. French seemed to be the language most in use, and the white-uniformed, pith-helmeted officer let us through without further parley when Beville exchanged a few brisk words with him. Our names were marked in the list, our passports returned, tickets to frank us through the gate were put into his hand, and we were bowed on our way.

"I thought he was going to keep us hanging about for hours," I said as we stood in the heat, dust and confusion outside his office. "Shouldn't he have gone through our baggage?"

Beville was eyeing the eager crowd of porters, dragomen and donkey-boys, choosing a strong-looking man to carry our luggage. "God, those bombastic officials!" he barked impatiently. "Power-crazy, most of 'em. I gave him *baksheesh* – money. None of 'em are above accepting a hefty bribe."

With my arm linked in his, Dawkins and Mary bringing up the rear, we managed to get through the crush. Our porter and his underlings were carrying the trunks on their backs, the loads supported against their foreheads by nooses, the running ends of which they held in their hands. Beggars plucked at me, boys clamoured for us to use their donkeys and, but for Beville with his stick and loud voice, I should have been in serious difficulties, beset on all sides by the dregs of humanity willing to do anything for a few coins. He dealt whacks and pokes upon boys and animals alike till, as if by magic, a space was cleared around a canopy-shaded victoria which awaited us.

We trotted away through the sounds and odours, past bazaars and temples and shuttered houses, while the sky shimmered overhead and so rapidly did one scene follow another that I didn't collect my thoughts until we came to the broad, clear avenue which ran along beside the sea, arriving at last at the Stanley Hotel. Beville said it was the best in Alexandria, and we agreed that Nell and her husband must have stayed there.

My stomach was churning with excitement – soon I would see Nancy! I had to wait a while though, for Beville said that we must proceed with caution, so he went out to reconnoitre, whilst I had to content myself with changing for dinner. Over the meal, he told me what he had been doing. "I went to El Tarifa, the Renshaw place, and left my card. I wrote a note on the back of it, reminding Sir Nicholas of who I was, and requesting that we might call on him tomorrow morning. How does that suit you, darling?"

I was disappointed, wanting to see Nancy at once. Delays and more delays. How frustrating it was. "Will she be there, d'you suppose? I don't quite know what I'll do when I see her, probably break down and cry."

"She's only a governess, don't forget – you must get the pecking order right," he reminded. "It's doubtful whether she'll be present. Get Renshaw talking about music. I shall say that I heard from the hotel manager that he was living here, and thought I'd look him up. Right?"

"Right!" I answered, feeling that we were about to embark on some secret military mission. Beville had that crisp air about him, and I realised that he was enjoying the challenge.

"I'll go and see a friend of mine who lives in the native quarter," Beville continued. "His name is Patrick Graham, although he prefers to be known by his Arabic title of Hoseyn Et-Taweel, which means 'The Tall'. We met in the Army and he had already studied the country and its people, fanatical about it. The double strain of work and study undermined his health, and a bout of fever which nearly killed him left him so depleted that it was impossible for him to continue his Army career – so he stayed here."

"He's never returned home?"

"He considers this to be his home. He's quite dotty about the place and wouldn't live anywhere else. He's adopted native costume and is generally taken for a Turk. He lives as one of the people, following their manners and customs – he may even have gone so far as to have become a Muslim. I've not seen him for years, but we've corresponded from time to time. I think a visit to him will be in order, after we've talked with Nancy. He may know something about the loss of the child. I want to see the old reprobate in any case – I think he has a beautiful wife or two tucked away in his harem."

I dressed with considerable care for my first appearance at El Tarifa. I much preferred strong colours, but white was best in the full blaze of the Egyptian summer. I noticed that the hotel was sparsely occupied as many Europeans went elsewhere during the hot season. Beville had ordered a carriage for ten o'clock, and the drive along the Corniche was pleasant and far removed from the squalid alleys of the dockside. Here were the enormous villas belonging to foreign embassies or state officials – rich, powerful people.

I couldn't wait to get there, longing to see Nancy. Beville was trying to interest me in famous landmarks and ruins but their ancient beauty was lost to me. One day I would appreciate them – one happy day when I'd satisfied myself that all was well. We came to some great gates and circled a white gravelled drive which wound through sweeping lawns and flowering bushes. Hidden amongst the olive trees, birds screamed and chattered, and the air was sickly sweet with perfumed blossoms. It was already very hot, an arid heat which hinted of the desert on the outskirts of the city. I alighted and shaded my eyes with my gloved hand, staring at that magnificent house which was like a sultan's palace, complete with turrets. We were ushered in by a fat major-domo. He salaamed and disappeared to announce our arrival to his master. There was no sound. This almost oppressive silence weighed on me, making me want to whisper.

Beville grinned, unaffected by the sombre grandeur. "Quite a place, what?" he said loudly. "Makes me want to clap my hands and order a slave to bring in the dancing girls."

The manservant reappeared and we were taken to a large drawing room, but I had no time to take in my surroundings, staring at the man who advanced towards us, his hand outstretched to shake Beville's. They greeted each other enthusiastically, as fellow-countrymen will, and Beville introduced me. I gave Sir Nicholas Renshaw my hand to kiss. My God, he was handsome! Every inch an aristocrat, and so tall, long-limbed and strongly built. The touch of his hand on mine as he raised it to his lips shot through me like an electric shock. I struggled not to be blinded by that lean, saturnine face or those dark, smouldering eyes. Keeping a tight grip on myself, I was very cool as we exchanged pleasantries.

"I must apologise for my casual attire," he said, conducting us to a couch, clapping his hands thrice and giving an order to the servant who appeared promptly. "You'd like some refreshments, no doubt – something cool to drink after your drive. I don't entertain often these days – usually away at daybreak, working at the catacombs which I'm excavating. That's why I'm dressed like this." He gave me the benefit of his charming smile, indicating his open-necked shirt and whipcord riding breeches.

"Sounds interesting. What exactly is it, Renshaw?" enquired Beville, taking a cigarette from the silver box which our host offered.

"I've disovered a rather fine example of Roman–Egyptian tombs on my land," he explained, his swarthy face filled with enthusiasm. "I must get the dig completed before I go back to England. You really must come and see it. What about it, Treneman? Shall we ride over there now?"

Beville was watching him through the curl of tobacco smoke, his eyes narrowed. We exchanged a glance. "Jolly decent of you to ask. There's no time like the present but, dash it all, I'm hardly dressed for riding."

"It's not far. I'll fix you up with a steady mount. I must get back there soon, for my workmen are an idle bunch and loaf around if I'm not present."

"Lazy beggars, the Arabs," agreed Beville as the servant returned with whisky and soda for the men and lemonade for me.

"To make matters worse, they think the place is cursed." Sir Nicholas expressed impatience, then he added more slowly: "Sometimes lately, I've begun to think there may be something in it."

Beville gave a snort of incredulity. "Oh, come – you know what they're like with their confounded superstitions. Can't take it seriously, surely?"

Sir Nicholas's expression flickered and changed. Under his calm exterior I suspected that he was seething with strong emotions. "I suppose you're right, and yet we've had nothing but disasters recently. My adopted nephew has vanished without a trace – and my wife committed suicide."

There was a second of silence. Then Beville broke it. "My dear chap – what can one say? You have my deepest sympathy."

Sir Nicholas was staring into his glass, his face unreadable. Was he keeping a stiff upper lip, I wondered, typically English? His thoughts seemed far away. At last he spoke, slowly, half to himself. "I don't know what's happened to the boy. We've searched everywhere. My wife was very ill, mentally disturbed."

"Is there anything we can do?" I asked, feeling guilty because I already knew this. My task wasn't going to be easy. I had come prepared to hate him and do battle, but now this fierce determination was slipping away.

"No, there's nothing," he cut me off, his face cold. "I have my work – my all-important work."

This selfishness stiffened my resolve. Could he, obsessed by relics of the dead, so easily dismiss those tragedies? A sense of urgency was driving me now. I could not shake off that terrible feeling of apprehension which had been with me ever since I entered the place. My intuition told me that something was wrong. I snuffed it in the air, that whiff of danger which had intensified when I saw this haughty, dark-visaged man.

"Have you anyone to help you?" questioned Beville cleverly, and I trembled inwardly for soon, if what Nell had told me was true, Sir Nicholas must mention Nancy's name.

"There was someone," he replied. "A girl who came from England as governess to my nephew. She shared my interest in antiquities, but now she's gone."

I almost dropped my glass, thanking God that my work had trained me in control. "Oh dear, how tiresome," I said.

"You dismissed her?" Beville was lighting up another cigarette, his voice casual.

"No, I didn't – though I could have done, with justification. She behaved very oddly after the child vanished, becoming almost demented when my wife died. Things got so bad that I had to take her to task one night and next day we couldn't find her. Her clothes had gone and I assumed that she'd decided to leave." Sir Nicholas's voice was clipped, his eyes stormy.

"So she went from Alexandria?" Beville was carrying on the conversation and I blessed him for it, unable to trust myself to speak.

"I don't know. My agent, Quiller, said that someone answering her description had taken the steamer for England that day."

Silence filled the sunny room. I sat there trying to convince myself that Nancy was probably safely back in England by now. Beville and I had come on a fools' errand – if what he said was true.

Sir Nicholas set his glass down on the table and changed the subject. "Enough of this. I mustn't weary you with my problems. What are you doing out here, Treneman? Taking a holiday? Your note was brief but intriguing, and I haven't yet thanked you for introducing me to Madame Costello. Oh, yes, your fame has reached Alexandria, madame. I've read about you in the newspapers."

He was either being incredibly brave in the face of such adversities or else they hadn't affected him. He was secretive and deep, there was no doubt about that. He fascinated me and I didn't trust him. "You are very kind, sir," I answered with a smile that matched his for insincerity. "And I have a favour to ask."

He gave an ironic bow, his black lashes shading his eyes. "Anything you desire."

I took a deep breath. "My singing teacher has commanded that I don't neglect my practice – she's such a dragon that I positively dare not disobey. Beville tells me that you play the piano. Would it be too much to ask that you accompany me sometimes – if you can spare a little of your valuable time?"

"It will be a pleasure," he answered gallantly. "I can't tell you how much I've missed the concert halls. Western culture is thin on the ground here." He went on to ask if I would consider singing if he arranged a musical evening at El Tarifa. I agreed of course, jumping at the chance of becoming a frequent visitor there, anxious about Nancy, and puzzled by the mental fencing which had been taking place between us. I was on my guard, determined to probe deeper. There seemed to be a brick wall a mile high around Sir Nicholas, which none could penetrate.

He suggested that Beville and he should go to the catacombs. They looked at me questioningly as Beville said: "What about you, Rebecca?"

"I'll come another day." I was being successful in sounding gay and light-hearted. "I hardly think white lace, complete with picture hat and parasol, is quite in order."

They laughingly agreed. "If you care to wait for Beville, I'm sure that Quiller will entertain you, Madam Costello," said Sir Nicholas. "Perhaps you'd like to see the gardens?"

When I met Quiller, my first reaction was: How suave he is – how bland. He had been instrumental in Nell's humiliation in the casino and I was ill-disposed towards him. He was a dapper man and his manners, though cold and unengaging, were impeccable. "You've not visited Egypt until now, madame?" he asked.

"No," I answered, cool as a cucumber, holding my parasol aloft as we went outside.

"I'm sure you will enjoy it. There's so much to see, and a most fashionable crowd," he continued, strolling along at my side. "Do you intend to stay long?"

"A week or two," I replied airily. "I've to sing in South America during the winter."

He was suitably impressed and we continued in this polite vein. But I kept thinking of Nell and it was as much as I could do to contain my fury, knowing what I did. What have you done with Nancy's journal? I wanted to scream. And where is she? You bloody, slimy upstart! I'd like to wring your neck! Outwardly, I expressed wide-eyed amazement at the splendour of the palace. "But it is so large! Far too big for Sir Nicholas, surely?"

"He's not entirely alone," he answered as we paused to gaze upwards at the ornate façade. "His daughter, Miss Fleur, is here too, and her governess, Miss Leigh. There's also old Miss Tranter, who was Lady Emily's nanny, years ago. She's getting rather senile, I fear. Lady Emily's tragic death has upset her greatly, and she's lost what little grasp she had on reality."

"So sad," I murmured, making my eyes big and sorrowful. "Sir Nicholas was telling us of his terrible bereavement, and about the mysterious disappearance of his little nephew. Oh, dear – the poor man does seem to have had a lot of trouble. So devoted to his work too, though having lost his assistant. Now – what did he say her name was? I'm such a scatterbrain – "

"Miss Nancy Gray," said Quiller helpfully.

"Ah, yes – that's it. Thank you." It was almost impossible to keep an impassive face. My cheeks ached with the strain of it. We continued our walk through the extensive grounds, returning to the house by a side path. "And do you find Alexandria entertaining?" I enquired sweetly.

"There's much of historical interest here, madame," he answered, pausing to unlock an iron gate, standing back so that I might enter yet another part of the garden. "And I have offered my services to Sir Nicholas in connection with the excavations."

"That isn't exactly what I meant, Mr Quiller," I simpered, giving him an arch, slanting glance. "I was told that it abounds in casinos and night life."

"I wouldn't know anything about that, madame. I never visit such places," he replied sanctimoniously.

I shall never know how I stopped myself from calling him a bare-faced liar. I suppose it was because I realised that I was dealing with a man who was as devious and dangerous as his master. We were now in a secluded area at the rear of the building. Pigeons cooed in the plane trees of that tranquil square with its antique pillars and carved gateway bearing fragments of Egyptian sculpture. Over the enclosing, sundrenched walls, a few small lizards flickered.

"What an enchanting spot!" I exclaimed.

"Lady Emily loved it very much," Quiller said. "She used to sit over there, on that stone bench, working at her sketches. It was here that she came to die. She hanged herself from the fig tree which stood beneath that balcony. It's gone now. Sir Nicholas had it chopped down."

Horror chilled me as I lifted my eyes to the balcony. That had been Nancy's room. From there she had stared down into Lady Emily's dead face. I shuddered and the garden no longer seem peaceful. "How terrible," I gasped.

"I often wonder if the unquiet spirits of the dead walk abroad." His voice was low, intimate. "The natives believe that they do. None of them want to work here now. The tree is gone, but they're convinced that Lady Emily's ghost still circles around the spot and writhes among the roots."

My skin was crawling. I couldn't take my eyes from that naked stump which rose two feet above the grass. The tufts grew longer there, adding to its forlorn, neglected look. No gardener would venture so close with his shears. The tone of Quiller's voice was disturbing, almost sexual in intensity. I became aware that he was watching me and gave him a swift glance. He looked away, but nevertheless the expression I had surprised on his face made the frank, good-natured lust of normal men seem endearing by comparison. The repugnance I had felt at our introduction came back, stronger than ever. What is there about this man? I thought. He's strange – strange and nasty.

Alone with him in that hushed garden, I experienced some of the terror which must have tormented Nancy.

On the surface, Quiller was far from a violent person, yet there was something violent lurking within his eyes. He was like a snake, waiting the chance to strike, patiently watching its victim for years, if need be. I didn't want him to know that he had succeeded in frightening me, and clenched my hands about the handle of my parasol. "What a dreadful thing for Sir Nicholas," I said without a tremor.

"It was most distressing for all of us." He had recovered himself, and I wondered if my imagination had been playing tricks. "Suicide is such a sad end – to be so despairing that one takes one's own life. What an extremity to have reached. She was mad, of course a very sick woman." He gave a cold smile. "I sometimes wonder if the natives are right when they say that the dust storms bring madness. I had begun to doubt Miss Gray's sanity too. She became most irrational after Master Jeffrey vanished, and it occurred to me that she might have done away with him herself."

"Mr Quiller, you can't be serious!" I exclaimed. Nancy mad! Mad to the point of killing someone she loved so dearly! It was impossible.

"Oh, I am, madame, I can assure you. Who knows what takes place in such a mind?"

It was a moment before I could move. A shiver was spreading downwards from the base of my skull. The heat fanned in thick waves over that silent garden of death. Everywhere the birds were singing, but not here. "Shouldn't you tell Sir Nicholas?" I managed at last.

"I have, madame," he said. "There's little we can do now, for she has gone."

"She left nothing behind? No letter – nothing?"

"Nothing," he answered firmly. "Her clothing, her personal belongings – all have gone." Then he gave me a glance from the tail of his eye. "You seem curious about her? May I ask why?"

Careful! Careful! I warned myself. I went into the attack. "Of course I'm interested, Mr Quiller. An

English woman, like myself – one is bound to wonder. I'm naturally concerned."

"Naturally – so kind of you to bother," he murmured, and we talked of it no more. I was convinced that he had taken me to the garden deliberately, wanting to alarm me, getting a peculiar thrill from it. I was angered, as if he had somehow taken an unfair advantage, dreading to think of what he might do if he knew I was associated with Nancy and Nell.

Beville soon returned with Sir Nicholas. We went back to the hotel and had much to discuss. I told him what had taken place in the garden whilst he pondered on Sir Nicholas's detached attitude to his wife's death, saying that it bordered on the callous. "He seems to care more about those bloody catacombs," he burst out indignantly. "Nothing else seems to touch him."

I took off my hat and lay on the couch, hot and tired. "I can't stand Quiller," I said.

"A rum sort of fellow, I'll agree." Beville strolled on to the balcony. "But let's look on the bright side. You must be relieved to know that Nancy's gone back to England."

"I suppose so," I replied doubtfully. "I wish I knew just where and when. Nell was so convinced that she didn't intend to leave until she'd found out what had happened to Jeffrey."

"There does seem to be something odd about it," he nodded. "Can't put my finger on it – just a kind of instinct for trouble. Used to have the same prickly feeling when I led my battalion into the desert. All quiet – not a sight of the enemy – place bare of everything save sand for miles and miles, and yet there was that sense of unseen eyes watching you. I get the same sensation at El Tarifa. I've found out a few things. There was a young doctor there too, Terence Armstrong – Renshaw says he's left them."

"Where is he?"

"Working in one of the hospitals."

"Can we see him?"

"We can try. You'll be practising with Renshaw tomorrow, won't you? I'll drive you there and then see Patrick. Perhaps he can get me an introduction to the doctor, and we'll invite him to dine here. I'm not saying that he'll be much help, but at least we can sound him out."

I nodded, tiredness forgotten now that he was forming a plan. Away from the palace, vitality came flooding back, that fighting feeling which had drained away from me during the morning. "Good idea, Beville. I'll try to meet this Miss Leigh whom Quiller mentioned and the old nanny."

Beville came across to join me and, though I enjoyed his kisses, my mind was not with him, and I was abstracted for the rest of the evening. Time and again, we pretended that we should discover nothing sinister at El Tarifa, joking about exploring the city, of becoming typical tourists, but I don't think either of us believed it. That night I dreamed of Nancy, and she was as I had seen her when we were caught in a skirmish at the orphanage. Her head was up defiantly, her red hair flaming in the flickering gaslight, green eyes glaring hatred at Mrs Bowell. Nancy – a hard, tough, sane girl who feared nothing. In my half-waking vision I heard the swish of the whip, as I had heard it that night, but when I looked, it wasn't that fat, loathsome woman who wielded it – it was Nicholas Renshaw, his lips curling contemptuously in a mocking smile.

Chapter 4

He was waiting for me in the music room. I heard him playing as I opened the door. I stood for a while listening and watching him. Utterly absorbed, he didn't hear me enter, his eyes fixed on his hands which moved with sure skill over the keys of the grand piano. Music thundered through the room like a passionate storm, and I let that tremendous sound bear me upwards, surrendering to the power of it. Somehow, the handsome man producing this thrilling magic became as one with the composer. I could no longer distinguish between them, only knowing that my every nerve was responding.

I burst into spontaneous applause when he had finished, and he came to greet me, accepting my approbation as if it were his right. I had brought an operatic score with me and he grimaced when he saw the difficulty of the key. It was *Madama Butterfly*, Puccini's latest masterpiece, and I was eager to add it to my repertoire. We worked solidly through the afternoon, and no one interrupted us. Nicholas was sight-reading, and making a very thorough job of it too. We started, stopped, argued and continued, aware of nothing but reproducing those wonderful notes. His grasp of the score was intelligent, his comments on my singing apt. Whatever he did, it seemed, was subjected to his intense, fiery scrutiny and came out molten with the heat of it. Eventually, after two hours of concentration, he mopped his forehead and smiled across at me.

"By Jove, it isn't easy," he remarked. "How the deuce do you manage to learn the whole thing? Besides the considerable acting skill required. I take my hat off to you, Rebecca, I really do."

Yes, by now we were calling each other by our first names. It had happened naturally, united as we were by the challenge of the music, neither of us aware of this breach of etiquette. I flushed with pleasure at his words, which was silly of me. Dukes and princes had complimented me and I hadn't reacted thus. But this man was different; strange feelings were surging in me, making me flustered. "It's entirely due to my stern teacher who's the best in the world, but old Maestro Angeleri, who taught me first, says that I'll never sing with true depth and meaning until I've been in love."

His eyes lifted to mine, and there was something glowing there which made me catch my breath. "Have you never fallen in love?" he asked slowly, doubtingly, his satanic face serious.

"No," I answered.

"What of the good Beville?" he said with forced lightness.

"We're the best of friends," I began, copying his flippant tone, but I couldn't keep it up, disconcerted by that hard gaze. "He's so kind – helping me, looking after me." I thought how empty and foolish the words sounded.

"But you are his mistress?" His voice was smooth as honey but the look on his face was terrifying.

Anger flared up in me. "What is that to do with you?"

"Absolutely nothing, thank God!" he shot back at me, rising from the piano stool and lighting a cigar, regardless of the effect it might have on my throat. There was fire blazing in his eyes before they narrowed haughtily. "But I don't like to see a good-natured fellow like him being used by you."

"Used! You've got a bloody sauce!" I shouted, forgetting two vital points; one that he was a titled gentleman, and two, that ladies were not allowed to swear. At that moment I reverted to a guttersnipe! "I don't use him any more than he uses me. He gets as good as he gives!"

The contemptuous look he gave me was withering. "No doubt you're an expert between the sheets," he sneered. "A skill born of long practice!"

I was trembling with rage. "How dare you! Beville is the only lover I've ever had!"

"Really?" His eyebrow went up and he studied my face closely, then his eyes softened and he smiled winningly. "D'you know, I think you're telling the truth. Damnit, I must be mad, but I believe you."

The fact that he was so surprised was insulting. I

controlled the sharp retort that trembled on my tongue, furious with myself for allowing him to upset me. He was staring at me with an expression of mingled puzzlement, admiration and something else which I couldn't fathom. "I expect an apology, sir," I said stiffly.

Before I could stop him, he took my hand in his, laughing with such candour that I was completely disarmed again. It was enough that my fingers responded to the feel of his strong ones, his touch making my arms and back tingle. "So be it," he said, smiling into my eyes. "Let there be peace between us, for the sake of your studies, if nothing else. I'm sorry, Rebecca. There, I've said it, and consider yourself honoured. I rarely, if ever, apologise to anyone. Admit that you've scored a point and say that I'm forgiven.'

I was rapidly finding that the situation was getting out of control, still angry at his audacity yet unable to still that trembling excitement. My heart was thumping and my hand remained in his. We were standing like that when the door burst open and a child ran in.

"Papa!" she wailed, her small, plain face streaked with tears. "Tell Miss Leigh to stop pestering me – you did say that I needn't practise any more, didn't you? She keeps forcing me and I hate it." She stamped her foot and burst into a fresh flood of tears.

"Miss Fleur, you naughty girl, bothering your Papa when he's busy," remonstrated the woman who had followed her. She turned her eyes to Nicholas. "I'm so sorry, sir, but you know what she's like. I couldn't prevent her coming in here."

He scowled at both of them. "Fleur! Stop that noise at once! Miss Leigh, it's a pity that you can't control her tantrums!" The child refused to listen and he seized her by the shoulders and shook her. She was shocked into silence, limp under his hands. "That's better. Now we can talk without that dreadful hullabaloo. Yes, I did say that you might give up music once I realised that it was hopeless." He turned to the governess. "From now on the subject is closed. Is that clear, Miss Leigh?"

"Yes, sir." Her face was very white.

So this was Veronica Leigh, and I struggled to recall what Nell had said of her. She was slender and pretty, like a dark-haired angel, with fine skin, big eyes and dimples. So pretty, so quietly spoken. Was this the woman who had plagued Nancy? I had seen enough of pink and white women, artless as children, who were really the deepest little baggages. It was probably true.

Now she looked at me with wonder. "Oh, pray excuse me, Sir Nicholas, I wouldn't have disturbed you for the world, but is this really Madame Costello? I know that I'm being frightfully rude, but I've read about you, madame."

God, such a show! She was most likely wild with jealousy. I inclined my head graciously. "Thank you so much. Very kind, I'm sure."

"This is Miss Leigh," rapped out Nicholas, his face like a thundercloud.

"I sing a little myself," she confessed shyly. "Sir Nicholas sometimes accompanies me – or he did – before Lady Emily . . . " she broke off, casting those pleading eyes at him. All right, I thought, you've made your point. I'm not the only one who has sung with Nicholas Renshaw.

He dismissed her coldly and she took the child away, but not without a backward glance at me. It was a long, hard stare. Her face was blank but her eyes spoke volumes. She hates me, I thought – she hates any young woman who swims into Nicholas's ken.

Later, Beville and I compared notes. He had not been idle and told me that we were going to see his friend, Patrick Graham. "What shall I wear?" I asked, panicking. "I've never been to an Arab house."

"Good God, woman, I don't know! You always look stunning." He laughed, and it was such a relief to be with him after the disturbing Nicholas. We stood at the window and watched the sun going down over the sea.

Several dhows were slowly creeping along the shore, their sales touched to deep salmon by the dying glories of the sun. A faint reiterated sound came from several points of the city. The calls of the *mueddins*, for it was the hour of Ula, the Islamic evening prayers, so Beville told me. Far away on the horizon was a tramp steamer, sending up a grey thread of smoke, moving along its route from one port to another.

"Could Nancy have taken a berth on one of those?" I asked him.

"I doubt it. A most unsuitable way for a young woman to travel alone. Their cargoes are often suspect – they're not above smuggling out drugs, arms, not to mention gems acquired in illegal ways."

I had been happier since leaving El Tarifa, but now a chill crept over my spirits, which shrank and drew together like a child craving shelter from some hidden danger. I was suddenly aware of the barrenness of the desert which girded Alexandria, yearning for a glimpse of the friendly green fields of home. I prayed that Nancy was already there. As Beville and I watched, the sun appeared to drown in the sea and darkness fell as though an unseen hand had drawn a velvet curtain over the sky – a curtain studded with diamond-sharp stars. They exercised a queer, compelling fascination, rousing vague, confused desires, unsealing a spring of emotion in my heart. Beville's arms were about me, his lips soft, and tender, yet I still felt lonely and frightened.

A victoria was waiting for us outside the hotel and we left the residential area, turning into the meandering, dimly lit Arab streets of Kom-el-Dik, running towards the crest of a hill. Behind us in the luminous darkness the lights of the port lay like a glittering necklace along the shore, and minarets thrust their needles into the purple sky. Now other lights began to twinkle, springing up till the streets on either side of us seemed inhabited by glow-worms, dancing from the open booths and café fronts, while a motley collection of humanity began its nocturnal activities.

"It's the hour of the prostitute," growled Beville, "And not only women – there are very young girls for sale, and boys too."

"D'you think that's what happened to Jeffrey?" I asked.

He didn't answer but his face was grim, and I stared into the crowd as we drove through, searching for I knew not what – a white child? A woman with red hair? I wanted to stop the carriage and go in search on foot, but he refused to let me. This was maddening and I was beginning to argue when we passed under an archway and came to a courtyard where an old man dozed under a palm, and half-naked children peeped at us from behind the pillars. "Here we are," said Beville. "This is the home of Et-Taweel."

He took me through a Moorish doorway and up a staircase whose pierced balustrade was worked in intricate, sinuous patterns. It looked like frozen hoar-frost, so light and fragile was its filigree. We came to a suite of rooms, opening out from one another, all built of white stone with tiles of turquoise and ochre. The sound of water permeated the central apartments as it filled a large basin in the middle of the mosaic floor. A tiny fountain flung up a cascade of silver drops, tinkling back with a cool splash. The room was furnished with Persian rugs, low tables and divans spread with embroidered silks which flashed and clashed and merged into renewed brilliance in the light of alabaster lamps which swung gently at the ends of long brass chains.

I was lulled and seduced by the fantasy of this romantic dwelling. How could I not yield to the enchantment of Alexandria? I was fated to be attracted to the unknown, to the night, to the smell of danger. I felt tinglingly alive, and this made me anxious. I'd come here with a purpose, seeking my friend, but where was she? I hadn't expected to be so intrigued by Nicholas Renshaw, but it was happening. Dreams and realities – illusions and disillusions – I knew them of old. With a sense of alarm, I realised that it would be all too easy for me to adopt the strange fatalism of the East, as Patrick Graham had done.

I met him then, and it was hard to believe that he was English. His Arabic name suited him for he was indeed tall and exceedingly lean. He wore a long black robe decorated with silver thread. A turban hid his hair, but I guessed it to be dark brown, like his beard and moustache. The only things which gave him away were his keen, light grey eyes – contrasting sharply with his sun-darkened features – and that he got down to business at once, without Eastern prevarication.

"Beville's already told me why you're here, madame. I'll do everything in my power to help. There's not much happening in the city which doesn't reach my ears in due course. I knew of the trouble at El Tarifa, and I've met Renshaw several times. I'll introduce you to Dr Armstrong. What is it you want?"

"Information," I replied.

"About the missing boy?"

"Yes – and the governess, Miss Gray. I came here to find her, but now they tell me that she's gone away. I don't want them to suspect that I'm connected with her."

"Quite. Beville put me in the picture." Those fearless eyes were kind and his lips curved into a smile. "You must trust me. I'm used to keeping secrets. I was in the British Intelligence Service, and still serve my country when I can."

"Then I've come to the right man," I beamed at him, more confident than I had been for hours. "It's such a relief to meet you. I'm terribly worried about my friend."

He pressed his lips together and shook his head, a benign man, possessing an inner calm which was contagious, although there was a steely quality there which made me glad to have him as an ally rather than an enemy. "She too has vanished, eh? I've made enquiries of a certain harbour-master who owes me a favour. It seems that there's no record of anyone of her name and description embarking within the past weeks."

My heart sank. "But Sir Nicholas thought she'd left for England," I began, my glance flying to Beville as if by seeing his square, honest face I might still that gnawing fear eating away at me. "Mr Quiller said the same."

"Quiller? Renshaw's agent?" Et-Taweel was combing his fingers through his beard thoughtfully.

"Do you know him?"

"I know of him," came the quiet reply.

"What sort of a chap is he?" put in Beville.

Et-Taweel hesitated, then said: "It's better if we discuss him when the lady is not present."

"I don't think Rebecca is easily shocked," averred Beville.

Those penetrating eyes were on me again, an amused quirk to his mouth. "In that case, I'll tell you what I know. He's over-fond of the gambling tables – "

'As my friend Nell de Grendon found out to her cost," I blurted angrily. "And the lying little weasel denied ever going to the casinos when I sounded him out!"

"Let Et-Taweel finish, my dear – he's been told about the de Grendons," said Beville.

"Play-fever is foolish, but not a crime," Et-Taweel went on. "But unfortunately it can lead to crime if money is owed. More damaging to Quiller is his tendency to pick up boys in the cafés along the rue Missala, a notorious area. There again, it's a common enough practice here, and each to his own taste, I say – but the danger to a man in his position is that he may become the victim of blackmail. I would hazard a guess that Quiller is constantly pressed for cash."

"So that's it – I knew there was something odd about him – he gives me the creeps." Beville's tone expressed the healthy heterosexual male's suspicion of anything that varied from the norm. "D'you think he knows what really happened to young Jeffrey?"

"I can't say yet, but I'm working on it. If anything comes to light you'll be the first to know."

Quiller's love life did not shock me. I knew several charming, intelligent men who preferred their own sex, but if money was involved along with treachery and deceit, then I found it sordid and sickening. My mind was clear now, helped by Et-Taweel's calm, and I asked: "The bodyguard – I can't remember his name – "

"He was called Hassan, and was found with his throat cut. I can't imagine that he was anything but honest for he was of a sect which believe they're descended from the Prophet. They're holy and wise, above corruption," he replied gravely.

"Quiller suggested to me that Nancy Gray was insane and may have murdered the child herself," I cried.

Beville took my hand in his comfortingly, still addressing his friend who was watching and listening, seated on the divan, his fingers laced in the lap of his caftan. "What about Sir Nicholas? What is said of him?"

"There's been much talk, of course, but there always is when a wealthy foreigner starts to disturb tombs. The natives think the catacombs to be accursed and that his subsequent misfortunes are the revenge of demons and angry ghosts. I've learned not to scoff at such beliefs. As for the man himself? He doesn't drink to excess, or gamble or run after whores, but it's rumoured that he has no need to do so, having his own private harem in the shape of Miss Leigh and the mysteriously absent Miss Gray."

"It isn't true." I shouted. "She couldn't have been his mistress! Not Nancy – it wasn't like her. Oh, it's all so confusing – I don't know what to believe!" I buried my face in my hands.

"Don't distress yourself, madame. This will serve no purpose. Leave the matter to me," he advised.

It was past midnight when we left. The streets were dark and deserted, and the rumble of the victoria's wheels, the drum of the horse's hoofs, seemed overloud. Emerging from the courtyard where the moonlight lay like a lake of silver, we drove through narrow passages between the houses. Their steep sides assumed the menacing shapes of great rocks, the split fingers of the moon running down among the inky blackness of fissures. The mingled beauty and loneliness of the night evoked a blend of fear and excitement.

"What a capital chap Et-Taweel is," murmured Beville close to my ear as we sat in the back of the carriage. "If there's villainy afoot, he'll get to the bottom of it. His spies are everywhere. Will you stop worrying, darling? It makes you pale and peaky."

I was about to tell a white lie to put his mind at rest when, all of a sudden, the victoria bounced horribly, flinging us from side to side. I heard shouts, having no time to think, everything running into a blur with events piling on top of one another. We stopped with a sickening jolt. There was a cry, quickly muffled, a sound of scuffing, and the door was wrenched open, the orange light of a lantern glowing like a fiery eye.

"What the hell's going on!" shouted Beville, leaping to his feet and pulling out a revolver.

Black faces surrounded us – the sheen of eyeballs and teeth the swathe of turbans, and the light running like yellow blood on the blade of a raised scimitar. There was a flash as Beville fired, an explosion that filled the carriage, hurting my eardrums. The man yelled and fell backwards out of the door. In an instant, Beville had pushed the limp body of our driver out of the way, taken the seat himself, and whipped up the horse so that we careered madly away. Driving as if the devil were in pursuit, he didn't slow down until we reached the Stanley Hotel. I was shaking so much that I could hardly stand but had to face the ensuing uproar when the manager came and the police were called.

Much later, when we were alone, Beville said to me sternly: "There's one thing that I didn't tell the police, Rebecca. I'd rather Et-Taweel deals with it. I recognised that brute with the scimitar. He was one of Nicholas Renshaw's servants."

I stood before the mirror in the small room set aside for the use of lady guests at El Tarifa. It was several days after Beville and I had been attacked and I still trembled when I thought of it. Now it was the night of the musical soirée, the first time that the handsome widower had entertained since the death of his wife. It was too soon really, he should have been in mourning still, but Nicholas didn't seem concerned, saying that he must seize the opportunity while I was in Alexandria.

I wore a dress of scarlet silk, a short-sleeved, low-necked creation, the skirt draped and slit at the sides, the waist girded by a jewelled belt. Over it I had added a black jacket exquisitely embroidered in native beadwork which I'd bought in the bazaar. Heavy jewels sparkled at my ears and throat, and the effect was decidedly Eastern.

I had visited the house every day to practise with Nicholas. He was sympathetic about my terrifying experience, shaking his head regretfully and telling me that the streets were badly patrolled and unsafe. I watched him and wondered, remembering Beville's instructions to keep a tight rein on my tongue. I met Nicholas now with increasingly mixed feelings. When alone with him, it was clear-cut enough: here was a good looking, sensitive musician with whom I was in total rapport. I felt intoxicated and it took every ounce of self-control to concentrate, so very aware was I of our peculiar intimacy, watching his hands as they moved over the piano keys, seeing his dark, absorbed face. I was supposed to be learning the role of *Madama Butterfly*, that dainty, submissive Japanese girl, but this was impossible when I stood so close to him, the music blurring before my eyes, longing to pull his handsome head against my breasts and run my fingers through his curling black hair. It was like a madness racing in my blood and I knew its insanity, fighting to quench this wild emotion, but finding it even harder to do.

When we were apart, it was quite different. Then, talking with Beville and Et-Taweel, I saw him as an unscrupulous individual, quite capable of removing a tiresome nephew, of driving his ailing wife to suicide and dismissing Nancy because she was asking too many questions. There was nothing concrete to support these suspicisons, but we'd decided that he was the one who stood to gain. We needed proof and I was seeking an opportunity to explore the room which had been Nancy's. We were puzzled as to why we had been attacked for, as far as we knew, no one could be aware of the purpose of our visit to Egypt. This remained a mystery, along with the others.

Through the intervention of Et-Taweel, Terence Armstrong had come to see us – a pleasant young man who made no secret of the fact that he had loved Lady Emily and hated Nicholas. "That brute," he repeated ever more frequently as Beville topped up his wineglass. "You should've heard the way he spoke to her and that poor child of his. It was as if he loathed them. I begged Emily to leave him, but she wouldn't. She was devoted to him – God knows why. His cruelty was appalling, and she was so ill. Then she died – I had to cut her down from the fig tree – she looked so pathetic." He had wept, there in the middle of the hotel dining room. I was moved by his sincerity, comforting him as best I could, confessing that Nancy was my friend and that I'd come with the express purpose of helping her.

"She's a good sort," he had replied when he was calmer. "Emily came to rely on her. She had asthma, you see, and Nancy's herb medicine helped. She was absolutely devoted to Master Jeffrey – couldn't do too much for him, but she'd taken a shine to Sir Nicholas.

God! Most women do – I can't understand it. Veronica is the same, mooning about after him."

"You are a doctor, sir – you would know about mental illness. Did it strike you at any time that Nancy might be going mad?" I had waited for his answer with bated breath.

Astonishment had crossed his face. "Nancy! Good God – no! She was distraught about Jeffrey's disappearance – but certainly not mad. Far from it."

Beville shot me warning stares but I ignored them, mentally crossing Terence off the list of suspects. Beville remained unconvinced, saying later that I shouldn't be swayed by a few crocodile tears. "Humph – he had no business falling in love with his patient. Shocking bad form. You told him a bit too much, Rebecca."

I thought about this as I lingered in the dressing room, trying to calm myself before performing for Nicholas's guests. I was jumpy, perhaps spending so much time at El Tarifa was having an effect on me, for I had begun to have the unnerving feeling that I was being followed, not only there but wherever I went in Alexandria. Had the person who now possessed Nancy's journal put two and two together and guessed that the Rebecca mentioned there and myself were one and the same person?

The door opened and Veronica came in. She was very lovely, clad in rose-pink with white lace, delicate and sensual with those gleaming brown curls swept up, the clearest of blue eyes and that little, pouting red mouth. She stared at me through her long lashes. "Are you nearly ready, madame? The guests are arriving. Are you terribly, terribly nervous? I don't suppose you are – I wouldn't imagine that someone as experienced as yourself suffers from stage fright."

"You're wrong, Miss Leigh," I said grittily. She put my teeth on edge, too sugary by half. She had the face of a prissy madonna, this woman who was Nicholas's mistress. "A professional artist always suffers from nerves. It wouldn't feel right otherwise. It's part of keying oneself up to give of one's best."

"Oh, really?" she murmured, prinking in the mirror. "You do surprise me. I stay perfectly calm myself. Of course, I'm not invited to sing tonight. How could I compete with someone as talented as yourself? Sir Nicholas hasn't asked me, though he usually does."

"What hasn't he asked you to do?" I said waspishly, knowing perfectly well but unable to resist this devilish impulse.

Her eyes snapped at me and, just for a moment, the mask slipped. She looked angry enough to knife me. "Why, to sing. What else?"

"Forgive me," I gushed. "I must be mistaken, but I thought – how silly of me – that you and Sir Nicholas were more than just – oh, dear – how embarrassing! I can't say 'friends' can I? But you do know what I mean, I'm sure."

She drew herself up, her fingers gripped about her fan as if she wanted to hit me with it. Her whole body was stiff with rage. "Are you suggesting that my relationship with him is the same as yours with Sir Beville Treneman?"

Thank God, I breathed inwardly, I've succeeded in cracking that doll mask. "I'm not suggesting anything," I replied blandly, adding a touch more carmine to my lips, staring at her in the glass. "But I could hardly fail to notice that he's the cherished object of your affections. It shows, my dear, and Lady Emily must've been aware of it too. In my experience, wives are extremely touchy about such things, and sense when someone covets something that belongs to them." Oh, I was enjoying myself. That's a smack in the eye for her, Nancy, I thought, imagining how she would have grinned in response.

"Lady Emily was ill. Contrary to what you may have heard, I didn't take him away from her. He had already withdrawn before I came," Veronica said shakily, her face ashen. "I didn't harm her. It was all right till Nancy came – then he began to despise me."

"He loved her?" I was watching her like a hawk. She was distraught, sagging against one of the chairs, on the point of collapse.

"Oh, no – not Nicholas – he loves no one," she said bitterly. "He never loved his wife – never loved me, only wanting me in his bed when it suited him. Nancy wormed her way in, pretending that she was interested in his work. That's the only damned thing he bothers about."

"Where has Nancy gone?" I hoped that she was too upset to notice my eagerness.

"I don't know. Back to England. Anywhere. I don't know and I don't care."

"You hated her so much?"

"Yes! Oh, yes, I hated her. I'd have killed her if I could."

"Miss Leigh, that is a dreadful thing to say," I hissed, and her hand flew to her mouth as if she knew that she had spoken rashly.

"You've no idea what it was like here when Lady Emily was alive," she said with a break in her voice. "Nicholas changed towards me – and now he acts as if he can't bear to look at me."

"A man in his position. How could you expect him to be serious about you?" I sneered, giving her no quarter.

"D'you imagine that you'll be more successful?" she shouted, her eyes wild, her ladylike image shattered. "A performer on the stage? Oh, I know you're an opera singer, all very highbrow and cultural, but gentlemen only make mistresses of women like you! I've seen the way he looks at you – I know of the hours you spend in the music room together, but don't be fooled. He knows what happened to Jeffrey! He's ruthless and he's a liar. I'm certain that he had Nancy silenced!"

"What do you mean?" I demanded, wanting to take her by the throat and shake the truth out of her.

Before she could reply, a manservant came to tell me that I was awaited in the salon and, from then on, my attention was entirely with the evening's entertainment. The audience was of mixed nationality and I was gratified that my performance brought tears to the eyes of the more unemotional Britishers, as well as those of homesick Europeans. But, when I paused between arias, Veronica's words hammered in my brain, though I bowed and smiled and blew kisses. Had she spoken the truth? Or was it just the malicious talk of a jealous woman?

At last the supper break was announced and I squeezed through the crowd, all eager to engage me in conversation. Quiller was there, irritatingly sycophantic, giving everyone the impression that we were on friendly terms. The expression of pleasure on Nicholas's face hurt me, for I wanted to be joyful at the success of his party, but suspicion clouded this. Well done, Veronica, I thought angrily, you've succeeded in spoiling it! Beville rescued me with his usual tact, finding an alcove where I might rest. Other musicians began to play and it was while Beville had gone to fetch me a drink that I realised I could slip away unobserved.

I glided up the finely carved staircase which, convoluted and serpentine, writhed into the dimness. Glass-shaded lamps gave off a pink light as I roamed the deserted corridors, my feet soundless on the thickly carpeted floors. I reached the door of the room which Nancy had occupied. It wasn't locked and I let myself in. Empty rooms have a weird atmosphere after dark. Even in the light of noon I don't like deserted apartments. It's as if they draw in on themselves, harbouring all the mysteries of the past, and the silence is strained, giving the impression that someone – something – is watching and listening.

I stood there, trying to buttress my courage whilst my eyes became used to the gloom. There was a movement by the windows as the white gauze curtains stirred in the breeze, billowing out, startling me. My heart was pounding and cold sweat trickled down my back. I opened my mouth, breathing hard. Don't be stupid, I said, giving myself a severe talking to, there's no one there. Go and look. So, shaming my craven cowardice, I marched towards the windows. They were ajar, tall French windows which led on to a balcony. I had difficulty in making my feet obey me but mastered them, stepping out there and looking down into the dark garden where Lady Emily had hanged herself. I could see the stump far below me shining like a gaping wound. The tree was gone, but it was almost as if it had left a luminous glow behind, like a skimming water beetle which indents a pond surface with a blinding dimple. How I wished that I didn't have such a vivid imagination! It was working furiously now, and I could see that dreadful, discoloured face turned up towards me, floating in space. I fled back into the room and made myself be quiet. Fine detective I was turning out to be, frightened of my own shadow!

Stilling my trembling, my ears attuned for any sound of an approaching servant, I forced myself to explore the room. Why should I fear it? Nancy had once made it her own and her presence seemed to haunt it still. The moonlight struck on gilt and marble, but the dressing table was bare, the bed neatly turned down beneath the netting, as if ready for her return. I crossed the floor, striped with silver bars of moonshine, and opened the wardrobe door. I felt around inside. Nothing. I could see my hands clearly, pale, with the sparkle of rings, but the wardrobe was empty, also the drawers of the tallboy. I noticed another door on the opposite wall and peered into the next room. A child-sized bed occupied its centre, Jeffrey's bed? The mosquito nets were tied back about the headboard. It had a forlorn, waiting air, everything as quiet as a tomb. A further door led into a passage and, curiosity getting the better of fear, I entered it. The corridor was long and dark. There was a great bay window at the far end and the moonlight streamed through it, cold, unfriendly moonlight. At the furthest point stood a small door which was unlatched, swinging creakily in the draught. It was then that I heard the music, faint, tenuous, coming from above my head, the notes of a waltz in a minor key.

Sometimes one performs an action already knowing what the next sequence of events will be, as if one had done it before and, locked in some weird quirk of time, will go on doing it, again and again, till the end of eternity. It was with this cognisance that I pushed open the door and found a flight of narrow stairs which screwed steeply upwards. The music was somewhere ahead, tantalising as a tune heard in a dream. I felt the sudden impact of an ominous intuition. My feet dragged but I had to go on. Up reeled the steps, turning in dangerous, dusty triangles, and up I climbed, holding my skirt high, my feet placed hesitantly on each tread. A faint light filtered down, touching the cobwebbed corners, and the air was stale as if this part of the building was kept shut and unused. I guessed it led to one of the several turrets.

I reached the top and drew a long breath, partly of relief, partly to satisfy the demands of my galloping heart. The music had faded, dying away as if, having done its work, it could return to its grave. Moonlight pierced the narrow windows and I saw that I was in a lumber room where unwanted articles were stored. I could make out shrouded furniture, a few chairs, discarded ornaments and, on an antique table, a candle in a brass holder. With a gasp of relief, I fumbled in my beaded bag, searching for my matches. I found them and struck the box and the sound seemed alarmingly loud. The sudden flicker of the flame was dazzling. I held it to the wick, feeling quite brave now that I had that friendly light.

As I had thought, it was a storeroom, and I cursed my folly at coming there alone; it would be a happy hunting ground for scorpions, snakes and nasty poisonous spiders. I held my candle high, peering around me, and could have sworn that I saw a swift scrawl of brown legs dart from one crooked shadow to another. Boxes, trunks, a pile of curtains, some paintings in dusty frames, the usual attic litter of objects which are too good to be thrown away, yet unneeded. I didn't know what I was looking for, allowing instinct to guide me, nerves at breaking point, moving onwards, step by step. It was nightmarish, morbidly enticing so that I couldn't tear myself away. I knew that I should be returning to the party. They'd be wondering where I was, but I had to go on searching. I found a broken spinning-wheel and an easel bearing a half-finished painting. I wondered if it was Lady Emily's work which would never be completed. Then I came to another trunk, hidden under a tapestry rug.

I stopped and pushed the rug aside. It slithered to the floor with a sound like a sigh. The lid of the trunk shone in the light of my solitary candle, and painted on it were the initials N.G. It was new and hadn't seen a lot of travel, its corners protected by brass triangles, its cane banding varnished. I knew that it was Nancy's. I set the candlestick down on the floor and tried the catch. It sprang up at my touch and I lifted the lid. It was filled with women's clothing, not packed but thrust in anyhow, as if someone had done it in a hurry. Everything was there which she would have needed in the tropics, personal effects too – a hairbrush and mirror, a comb in which a few red hairs were still entangled. Books lay at the bottom, and a small jewel case which contained, along with a few trinkets, a beautiful bracelet. I found some photographs in an envelope and it gave me a queer feeling to see pictures of Nancy in a country garden in the company of an elderly gentleman and a stout, kindly featured lady. I turned them over and read: "Myself with Dr Ridding and Miss Jenny at Sutton Compton.

September 1903." Why hadn't she taken these possessions when she left?

I sat down on the dusty floor, holding the photographs nearer to the candleflame, trying to read her expressions. She had changed but she looked very happy. "Oh, Nancy, where are you?" I whispered, filled with the dreadful conviction that she had never gone from Alexandria.

It was at that moment that a sudden wind, funnelling up, set the grey fluff on the boards into a whirling dance and extinguished my precious candle. I was plunged into darkness, unable to move for terror, and it was worse than the most horrible dream for I knew that I was awake. I felt around for the candle and couldn't find it. The moon, which had been shrouded by cloud, crept through the window slits, and the sight of it gave me the necessary stimulus to spring to my feet. Then it disappeared again, but the courage which had come to me didn't quite go, and I began to feel my way round the room. I was lost. I bumped into a chair and, recovering myself, stumbled against another object, hurting my shin. What felt like a table barred my way and, spinning round, I found myself up against a window. On the left of this had been the door by which I entered – or was it to the right?

I felt about me with groping, fluttering hands and came upon something soft and furry. My fingers curled away in revulsion until I remembered that I'd seen a lion skin, head and all, flung across an old sofa. Was it this I was touching? In the blackness my hand seemed to encounter a head and a back and feet. It was like a person, all covered in fur! I lost my wits completely, backing away, hearing someone whimpering and realising that it was me. I was trapped – trapped up there in the darkness, unable to find an escape. Caught up in sheer animal panic. I began to pray as I groped among the lumber, those odds and ends of ordinary life which had become so very terrible.

There came a sudden, unexpected answer to my prayers. Once more the clouds shifted from the face of the moon and the room started into life. I saw the trunk – saw the pattern made by the moonlight across the floor, and saw too another door which I'd not noticed before. The centre of the room was bare of furniture, and one swift burst of speed would take me to that possible avenue of freedom. The moon blacked out again, but I had my bearings now. I was still able to discern the gleam of the door handle, bright-brassed, luminous as a star. I would make straight for it – it was only a second away. I drew in a breath, awash with relief, but that breath was only half taken when I was stricken into immobility.

There came a whisper of sound – it was no more than that. I could see that the door was opening, a path of wavering reddish light inching into the darkness. Someone – something, stood in the opening, and then came towards me slowly, shufflingly.

My heart nearly stopped beating. I was paralysed with terror. Then, as the gap of light spread and the figure emerged fully, I realised that it wasn't some fearful apparition, but an old, bent woman who stood staring at me, moving her grey head this way and that, peering through rimless spectacles.

"I'm sorry, madam," she said in a polite English voice. "Lady Emily and Lady Dorothea are not at home. Would you care to leave your calling card?"

I was dumbfounded, goggling at that shapeless, untidy crone who was leaning on her cane and waiting attentively for my answer. The absurdity of the situation almost tumbled me over into hysterical laughter. "I do apologise for disturbing you at this late hour," I gasped, entering into the mad game. "I've neglected to bring my cards, so forgetful of me. May I know who you are?"

"I'm Miss Alice Tranter – the young ladies' nanny," she replied in that matter-of-fact tone.

"May I stay and talk to you?" My mind was

recovering from the shock. She was the only member of the household whom I hadn't met.

She gestured towards the door in a friendly way. "Certainly, madam. Come this way."

Useless to wish that Beville was with me. I'd brought this upon myself and must make the best of it. I stepped over the threshold into another crowded loft, but a space had been cleared at one end where someone, presumably Miss Tranter, had arranged the furniture so that it resembled a sitting room. There was an upright piano set at an angle – the source of that mysterious music. She saw me looking at it. "My young ladies like to play," she said proudly. "Just another of their many accomplishments."

Two kerosene lamps gave off a smoky flame and she invited me to sit on a dilapidated couch. I noticed a trunk with the lid thrown back. It was piled high with expensive-looking garments, while further gowns hung on a rail behind it. Shoes, hats, cloaks and furs gave the attic the appearance of a pawn shop. "Are those yours?" I asked.

"Oh, no – though she lets me wear them sometimes. They belong to Lady Emily. Sir Nicholas wanted them removed from the bedchamber. She's gone away, you see," she explained confidingly. "Gone on a long trip – rather unusual for her, as she's the quiet one, very sensitive, easily upset. Dorothea now, well – a very different kettle of fish! So restless and adventurous. 'I can't stay in one place long, Nanny,' she says to me, 'Ah, my dear,' I always tell her, 'you were born with itchy feet!' and she laughs, and goes rushing off on some prank or other."

It was uncanny to hear her speaking of them as if they were still alive. I changed the subject hurriedly. "D'you live here?"

She flung me an odd, veiled look and smiled slyly. "I've a room near the nursery. I have to be on hand in case Miss Fleur needs me, but I like it up here. No one knows. You mustn't tell them. Of course, it's impossible to make the servants clean properly, I've tried and tried, but they don't know the meaning of the words 'dust' and 'dirt'. Not that I want them here – no one must disturb Lady Emily's things. I look after them personally, just as I've always done. They rely on me, you see." There was pride in her voice, that wrinkled, pallid, mad face softening.

"Are Lady Dorothea's possessions here too?"

She looked at me questioningly, her lips puckered. "No. Why should they be?" She sounded so fierce that I was afraid again. Old she might be, but she was a big, gaunt creature and I'd heard that the insane have an unnatural strength. "I thought you said that you cared for their belongings," I said gently. "Is Lady Dorothea here too?"

"I don't know," she answered evasively, keeping her face averted. "Sometimes she is, sometimes she isn't."

"I thought you knew everything about them," I challenged.

"I do! They trust old Tranter with all their secrets," she answered pettishly. "Look – I'll show you pictures of us – here, take these." She had fallen on her knees at a box near the table, pulling out bundles of photographs and piling them into my lap. They were snaps of the same two girls, from curly-haired toddlers to strikingly lovely young women. "That's my dear Lady Emily," a gnarled finger with a clawed nail pointed to one of them. I recognised Fleur in that delicate face. "And this is Lady Dorothea." She was darker and bold-looking, her very posture a challenge to the world.

They had been photographed frequently, it seemed – playing tennis, taking tea on the lawn with a stately manor house in the background, romping with their dogs, posing formally in a studio, wearing their débutante gowns. Their clothes were those in vogue more than a decade before. Miss Tranter drew out two larger pictures – bridal photographs. There was Dorothea in white brocade with her hand resting on the arm of a dark, burly man who bore a resemblance to Nicholas. In the next, I saw Emily, the lace veil thrown back over her hair, flowers cascading down in a trailing bouquet, joy radiating from her face as she smiled up at her handsome bridegroom, Nicholas himself.

"I'll tell you a secret," whispered Miss Tranter, coming closer and gripping my arm, her eyes burning in their deep sockets, "Lady Dorothea has run away from Sir Henry. There! Doesn't that shock you? I knew she was going to do it. 'Nanny,' she said the other day, 'I can't bear it any more. He treats me like a slave. I can't have any fun. He won't let me go to balls and parties or receive gentlemen callers. It's just too tiresome of him, so I'm off.' I was worried because I knew that she was expecting her first child. 'Can't you wait until you've had your baby?' I said. Ah, you should have seen the look on her face – talk about wilful! 'I hate Henry!' she shouted and I knew that determined tone of voice. 'I'm going abroad till the divorce is over and he'll never get his hands on the child – never! I'll see him roast in hell first!' That's what she said, and that's what she's done."

She paused and there was a long silence. I looked at her closely, thinking that she'd fallen asleep, but saw that her eyes were open, though they were glazed as if she were dreaming. This was getting me nowhere, some old, forgotten scandal which interested no one any more. "Miss Tranter, do you remember Nancy Gray?" I asked suddenly.

"I don't know anyone of that name," she answered clearly, staring at me as if she had never seen me before. "Who are you? How did you get here?"

"You invited me. My name is Rebecca Costello."

Her eyes were suspicious slits. "Are you one of my young ladies' school friends?"

"No, I'm a visitor at El Tarifa. I want to find Nancy Gray."

She backed away from me, crouching among her scattered mementos. "I've never heard of her. Leave me alone! You'd better go before I call the servants and have you thrown out!"

She looked hideous, a sagging bag of bones, her grizzled hair a tangled bush about her head. So this was madness. Was it this state which had possessed Nancy, if what Quiller said was true? It was ghastly and I wanted to run, but the thought of my friend made me stay, asking her doggedly: "You must remember her. Please try, Miss Tranter. She came here several months ago, bringing a little boy from England – Jeffrey Standish – Lady Dorothea's adopted son."

The fierceness left her face and that cunning smile quirked her lips. She eyed me knowingly. "I remember what it suits me to remember. I know everything that happens in this house. There are grilles, you see, let into the walls. It was once the palace of a Turkish diplomat and the ladies of his harem were permitted to use these peepholes, spying on his guests though never seen themselves. Miss Gray? Yes, I remember Miss Gray. I could have managed the children. I always have – always will – that's my job. I was the nanny of my young ladies' own mother. I've always cared for the children. Who was it that Lady Emily turned to when she was in trouble? It was me – her faithful Nanny Tranter."

"What trouble was this?" I was desperately searching for any crumb of information that might make sense.

Again, that crafty smile. "She was engaged to Nicholas Renshaw, after her sister had married the heir. Very much in love, she was, determined to have him at all costs, but they quarrelled frequently even then – lovers' tiffs, I called them, of no importance. About three months before the date of their wedding, he went off to Paris alone. Something to do with music, I believe. Emily was furious, of a jealous, possessive nature, I'm afraid and, during his absence she was rather naughty, doing it out of spite. She encouraged the attentions of more than one gentleman. 'I can't bear Nicholas going away without me,' she told me when I advised her to be careful. 'Why did he go, Nanny? He doesn't consider my feelings. He loves music more than he loves me!' and she would cry, poor girl, making herself ill. Ah, she has shed a river of tears over Nicholas Renshaw."

Her voice quivered and she sat staring into space, lost in a reverie from which I roused her by asking: "What happened?"

"He arrived home shortly before the wedding, and she came to me, white and sick. She'd been ailing for some weeks but I had taken little heed for she was often ill. 'Oh, Nanny,' she sobbed. 'What am I to do? I fear that I'm pregnant.' I was shocked but not too alarmed. They were to be married at once and the lapse could be hidden, the early arrival of a baby explained as a premature birth. Then she said: 'It is not Nicholas's child. He's never touched me and thinks that I'm a virgin.' "

The full significance of this struck me with the force of a physical blow. Fleur had not been sired by Nicholas; this would explain his resentment of her and his unkindness to his wife. "What did she do?" I asked slowly.

Miss Tranter looked up at me, frowning. "Who are you?" she said crossly. "You're full of saucy questions, most ill-mannered. Well, if you must know, I warned her never to tell him, to let him think it was born before full term. But she made the mistake of confessing on their wedding night. This was foolish for although he acknowledged Miss Fleur as his own for the sake of the family honour, he never forgave Emily."

How typical of him, I thought, no, he'd never forgive such a blow to his pride, unable to accept that some of the blame lay with him for neglecting his fiancée. Time was running on and I must leave. "Thank you for receiving me, Miss Tranter," I said, "Have you any idea where Nancy Gray is now?"

There was a vague look in her eyes and she hardly heard me, drooping in her chair, an old, tired woman, bewildered by loss and sorrow. "They told me Master

Jeffrey was coming here – they said Lady Dorothea was dead, but they lied. She's not dead. I see her now. She's talking to me and so is her sister." She lowered her voice to a whisper. "Sir Nicholas is wicked. He plays tricks on me but I'm too clever for him. D'you know, he pretended that Lady Emily had killed herself? As if she'd do such a thing! I saw her. Her dear face was blue and there was a horrible mark around her throat. She was asleep. When everyone had gone, I crept in and talked to her. I brushed her lovely hair and we laughed together, the three of us. Oh, yes, Lady Dorothea was there too, wearing her best gown. My girls, aren't dead – it's a lie, a wicked, cruel lie! It was Miss Gray's fault. She did it to torment me because I didn't want her here, taking my place, looking after the children."

Her arms were clasped about her body and she rocked gently. She wasn't aware of me, conversing with invisible beings. I shuddered, staring back over my shoulder, half expecting to see the ghosts of the dead sisters, waxen and ghastly, like thick smoke in the wind or movement in a distorting mirror. Panic lent me wings and I fled the place. I longed to be back in the world of light and music and laughter, not darkness and insanity and death.

Chapter 5

Running from the attic, I found myself in the corridor by which I had come, hoping to slip back to the party undetected, but my heart flew up into my mouth when I saw Nicholas standing at a bend of the stairs. "What are you doing in this part of the house?" he demanded, his dark eyes snapping angrily.

A nimble lie sprang to my tongue. "I was looking for

the bathroom, but must have missed my way." I forced a laugh. "I bumped into the strangest old lady."

"Miss Tranter!" he bit off the name savagely. "I hope she didn't bother you."

"Not at all," I replied lightly and we went down to the music salon. There our progress was slow because we were delayed by so many people begging to be introduced to me. Eventually, we were able to escape to the terrace and I said to him as casually as I could: "The ancient nanny was most entertaining. She told me a lot about your family, and Lady Emily."

His reaction was explosive. "What's she been saying?" His hand shot out and gripped my arm painfully. "What else d'you think you know? You shouldn't listen to a word she says. She's off her head and I should have her committed to an institution."

That hated name was like a red rag to a bull. I glared at him. "How cruel! My God, you don't know what you're saying. Have you ever been into an institution? No, I don't suppose you have." There was scorn in my voice. "What would a gentleman like you know of asylums for the mad, the sick, the unwanted?"

He let me go. My arm hurt and I knew that I should bear the imprint of his fingers for days. Recovering his temper, he lit a cigarette, his eyes clouded and unfathomable. "You speak with conviction, Rebecca. How is it that the lovely and famous prima donna is so familiar with the subject?"

I bit my lip, my hands busy with my fan as I stirred the hot air between us. "I've lived in the poor areas of London and seen the hardships of the underprivileged," I replied.

"Indeed?" he murmured and his tone made me uneasy. "I find you difficult to pigeonhole, well aware that if I were to ask you about your background, you'd probably lie."

My heart was beating in a jumpy fashion and I was wondering where Beville was hiding himself. I needed to talk to him about finding Nancy's clothes and meeting Miss Tranter. "You must read the information given to the press by my agent," I answered flippantly. "He has stated that I'm the offspring of an Italian countess and a gypsy prince."

"How very romantic," he drawled, sounding almost amused. "And, I would say, a complete fabrication." He threw his cigarette away. "So convenient to have someone invent a past for one. I must confess that I'm intrigued. I wonder if, one day, I may be taken into your confidence and you'll tell me who you really are and where you come from. You sound like a lady, but I never forget that you're an actress by profession. This comes naturally to most women – actresses every damned one of 'em. What a comedy the world is, and what an ugly comedy! How sick I am of it all!"

His questions about my origins were deeply disturbing. I attempted to keep the tone of the conversation light. "I'm sorry that you find it so. It's not a bad old world really. I know that you've recently lost your wife, but haven't you the charming Miss Leigh to console you?"

"It's none of your damned business," he growled. "You ask far too many questions."

"I'm aware that it's nothing to do with me, yet though knowing you for so short a time, I am concerned about you," I stated boldly, wishing that I could tell him that I knew about his marriage and Fleur. I couldn't help myself. There was something about this tormented man that reached out to me.

His mouth twisted into a cynical smile. "How kind of you to care. I suppose it amuses you, whilst you dally here, killing time before setting off on your next tour – conquering the world."

"That isn't true, Nicholas. Whatever you think of me – call me ambitious, mercenary, what you will – there are certain things I care about."

"Then you are a bigger fool than I supposed," he said rudely.

"Is there nothing which touches your heart?"

"Oh, yes, but I don't waste emotion on people. I care for my work. I care for music – never for human beings with their lies and betrayals!" Moody, restless, he took to pacing the tessellated paving, his tall shadow flung by the lanterns. He suddenly stopped in front of me, his shoulders blocking out the light. "I care for beauty." His voice was soft and I couldn't see his expression, just the glitter of his eyes and the whiteness of his teeth. "You are beautiful – the most beautiful woman I've ever seen."

I was conscious of that feeling of controlled power which flowed from him. The wind sighed in the palm fronds; fireflies danced against the darkness, and in the indigo heavens the crescent moon was sailing serenely. Perfume drifted on the breeze, intoxicating the senses, but I was drunk not with wine or the enchantment of my surroundings, but by Nicholas. I could feel my suspicions melting away like snow before the heat of the sun. I made to move, but he caught me in his arms. I tried to push away the hand that cupped my face and his gentle touch turned to steel. Then his mouth closed over mine.

His breath was smoky, his lips hard. My senses were spinning as I stood stiffly in his embrace, willing him to release me. After what seemed like hours, his lips left my mouth and his hold slackened.

"What's wrong? Don't you like me or is Beville really the only one you sleep with?" he asked ironically.

Tightly, through clenched teeth, I rasped: "Why don't you ask him?"

There was the warning rumble of distant thunder in his tone. "Oh, I intend to, my dear. There are a number of questions I shall put to Beville."

"How very nasty you are!"

"Dearest Rebecca, you've really no notion of how nasty I can be if I put my mind to it."

What did he mean? Fear bolted through me as I tried to recall having done or said anything which might make him suspect my motive for being in Alexandria. Et-Taweel had his spies. Why shouldn't Nicholas have his? Particularly if he was involved in some shady business which he didn't want made public. He was an alarming man at the best of times. Now I pretended to be offended, not afraid. "You're extremely rude," I said coldly. "I'm a singer, not a whore!"

I felt the laughter in him, that mocking laughter which was so infuriating. "How spiky you are – how frigid, but your lips belie it."

Determined to break me down, he dragged me into his embrace again, forcing me to accept his kiss. I didn't fight or struggle, passive resistance was best, somehow coldly insulting, as if such sordid mauling bored me. When, baffled, he lifted his head, staring at me with angry bewilderment, I withdrew myself from his arms, coolly smoothing the front of my jacket as if put out to find that he'd creased it. "Really, Sir Nicholas – you're behaving like an uncouth schoolboy," I drawled. "Go and find someone else to pull about – Miss Leigh would no doubt faint with delight."

He was frowning, looking down at me. I was pleased to see that I had shaken him. "Will you ride out with me tomorrow and see the catacombs?" he asked, almost humbly.

"I might," I answered, though my pulse was jumping and I wished that he wasn't so handsome. "I've nothing suitable to wear."

I had seen riding clothes in Nancy's trunk. If he knew they were there, then he must suggest that I borrow them. He didn't and I was more confused than ever. Either he was ignorant of the fact or he hoped that I hadn't found them. "There are plenty of shops in town," he said.

"Then I'll buy something, if I decide to come," I answered and he led me back to the party. As we were about to enter, I could have sworn that I saw someone dart ahead of us. Inside, the brightness was dazzling, the upsurge of talk and music ringing in my ears, but I wasn't too occupied to notice that it was Veronica who disappeared among the throng. I was rather disconcerted by Beville's searching look as he took my hand, wondering if he minded my going outside with Nicholas.

I found the clothes I needed in the rue Cherif Pasha, a smart street where Mary and I went early in the morning. On returning, I breakfasted with a sleepy Beville and told him where I intended to go. We had discussed the latest developments last night, agreeing that it was becoming ever more complicated. I hadn't told him that Nicholas had tried to make love to me. I was far too mixed up about it and had lain awake long after Beville slept at my side, trying to sort out my bewildered feelings. This was difficult for I was still tingling with the memory of Nicholas's kisses.

I changed into a brown cotton blouse and divided skirt, complete with boots and a wide-brimmed hat while Beville sat in his dressing gown and lectured me. "Be careful. Et-Taweel has found out that it was Renshaw's men who ambushed us. It might have been attempted robbery, or they may have been acting under orders – so watch your step." Then he added, a shadow in his usually frank eyes: "You do seem to be getting rather involved with him, Rebecca."

"Don't be silly," I replied, my voice sharp with guilt. "If I appear to be so, it is only because I'm trying to find out all I can."

With that, I promised to be cautious, kissed him and went to find a horse. The hotel stable provided such a service and before long I was picking my way through the maze of alleys. Mules and horses passed me, and there was the slow, slippery pad-pad and gurgling of camels. Grey-bearded sheiks on gaily bedizen ambled along surrounded by their young sons wearing long braided locks, sitting proudly in their splendid saddles, a proud and ardent race. I was pleased with my sense of direction and reached El Tarifa without mishap. Nicholas was waiting for me.

"That nag isn't good enough for you," he said immediately, standing at my stirrup and looking up at me in that fierce, dominating way. "Get down at once. I'll give you one to match your beauty and grace."

He swung me up into the saddle of a bay mare, a lovely creature with a flowing mane and tail. "You'd better lodge a complaint with the Stanley Hotel," I answered tartly, piqued at his high-handed manner. "They supplied the animal." I was nervous for the bay was a mettlesome beast and I wasn't sure if I could handle her.

"Really?" he shot back as we rode out under the arch. "I should have thought that the daughter of a gypsy prince would have known horseflesh better than to be fobbed off with the likes of that!"

His eyes were slanting at me wickedly and he chuckled as if I were a child to be indulged. This angered me and I began to wonder again why he had asked me to go with him. I tried to repress thoughts of various unpleasant possibilities. We were riding through an avenue of trees and, in the distance, I could see the sand hills, rippled and ridged like a beach. The padding of our horses' hoofs changed to a slithering sound as the ground became looser, made up of sand. Overhead the sun shone brassily from a bright turquoise sky, and the humid heat was heavy with the inertia of the desert. We came to thorny scrubland where the straggling grasses fought a losing battle, and there was a clump of date trees and a well, in the midst of some adobe huts where a few goats and chickens wandered about and veiled women with dirty, naked children stared at us from doorways.

I asked Nicholas why each dwelling was marked with

of an outstretched hand, and he said it a spell against the evil eye. I think at that moment I truly realised just how far from England I was. I wondered if I would ever see it again. I felt an inward shrinking, and fought the spark of fear that glowed ever brighter. Yet this harsh land was beautiful, and the ground over which we travelled was dotted with flowers of every colour – tiny blue irises, yellow saffron, aromatic thyme – finding a precarious hold among the rocks and sand.

"You like my darling Gulnare?" Nicholas asked, nodding at my mount. "Arab steeds are the best in the world, and the Muslim rarely rides anything but the female of the species, be it camel, horse or mule, saying that they possess the greater endurance and tenacity."

I couldn't tell if he was teasing me for his face was partly concealed by a fold of his white headcloth, drawn across as a protection from the dust. He turned and looked at me, his eyes keen and fearless, compelling obedience and respect. I was angry because I shivered under their scrutiny, not with fear but with unwilling pleasure. "Your Islamic friends are wise!" I snapped.

"Touché!" he laughed and then, to punish me, he urged his own powerful animal into full career, a flight like a bird, easy, effortless, with that wonderful contact between rider and horse. Damn him! I muttered and gave a jerk on my reins. At once Gulnare followed her master and I had a job to stay in the saddle.

He slowed down, swivelling round to grin at me with taunting mockery. We had reached a small, neatly kept graveyard and our animals picked their way daintily between the headstones. "The Renshaw vault," he said, pointing to the mausoleum in the centre. I assumed that his wife lay there, but didn't like to ask. Soon we arrived at the catacombs, and he showed me round. I was fascinated by the Egyptian decor, but oppressed too. The atmosphere was claustrophobic, and I wondered how

Nancy had been able to work down there – but then, I reminded myself, she was in love with Nicholas.

By noon it was far too hot for further activity. There rose on the air the long, droning notes from distant minarets. The workmen spread their carpets under the thorn trees and everything was suspended for a while as the kneeling figures turned towards Mecca. Nicholas had told me to wait for him above ground, saying that he had something he wished to complete before lunch, so I clambered up the rough-hewn steps, blinking in the glare. The tombs lay beneath an outcrop of rocks which threw back the sun's rays like a mirror. I was attracted by a clump of brightly coloured flowers growing on a high, overhanging shelf above my head. I went up after them, gathering a bunch from the clefts between tumbled boulders, and watching the green lizards that flashed like fire from one bit of shade to another.

I rested on the narrow ledge, shading my eyes and staring out to that distant horizon where earth and sky met, shimmering in the heat. The terrible isolation, the lack of anything green, those shifting, rolling dunes had a depressing effect. How lonely it looks, how harsh and merciless, I thought. Men and camels must have died out there in their thousands. If Jeffrey had wandered off or been taken there, and Nancy had followed him, what chance of survival would they have had?

I was lost in thought, remembering Nancy and the promise made to help her, long, long ago at the orphanage. I wondered if Nell had been mistaken, yet there was the evidence of her things in the attic after I had been told that she had left and taken her possessions with her. I was troubled by the half answers and evasions I had received when asking about her. There was nothing to cling to – everything as slippery as the shifting sand of the desert – only my instinctive feeling that something was terribly wrong.

Suddenly I heard a sound above me and, without warning, a shower of scree rained down, followed by an avalanche of large boulders which went bouncing to the sand some twenty feet below. I took one horrified look up, shielding my head with my arms. I felt a staggering blow on my shoulder and lurched forward, missing my footing. I slipped over the edge and made a desperate grab at the scrub rooted in the steep slope. Thorns lacerated my hands. For an instant I thought I was supported, then the branch gave way and I only dimly remember a swift flight through the air into unconsciousness.

I drifted back into the world, finding that I was lying somewhere soft and warm. My head ached dreadfully and I felt bruised all over. I heard a voice close by, recognising it as Nicholas's. I opened my heavy lids. He was there, on his knees beside the rugs and cushions on which I rested. He was frowning, his eyes narrowed as I gazed up at him. "Rebecca! Thank God you're not seriously hurt."

Is he sincere? I wondered groggily, or just a damned good actor? I struggled to sit up but black flecks floated before my eyes and I sank back. "What happened?" I croaked.

"You fell. Why were you climbing those rocks? You might have broken your neck," he snapped angrily. He left me, pouring out a shot of whisky from a flask and lighting a cigarette. Then he stood staring at me for some time.

I was emotionally and physically spent, my head thumping relentlessly. I wished that I was dead. No, I thought drearily, I wish *he* was dead. I couldn't shake off the idea that he'd planned the rock fall, and had invited me to the catacombs with the intention of harming me. Anger gave me strength. "If you wanted to get rid of me so badly, you should have devised a more foolproof method!" I grated.

"What are you driving at? It was an accident – a landslide," he replied.

"Accident!" I spat out, wincing at the pain every

movement cost me. 'That was no bloody accident. And where am I now?"

Queer, kaleidoscopic impressions were rushing in on me. My sight was fuzzy but I saw what looked like silken tent-hangings and silver lamps which swung from the bellying blue and yellow canvas that formed the roof. There was a red-patterned Persian rug hanging to form a dividing wall behind one of the painted poles upholding the structure.

"This is my tent. I stay out here sometimes when I've been working late," he said, his face as inscrutable as the Sphinx. "There's peace to be found in the desert. A man may meditate and delve into the secrets of his own heart."

"Hah!" I barked. "And what do you find in your heart? I suspect it to be as black as pitch!"

He returned my angry stare imperviously, although one eyebrow rose as if he questioned the wisdom of my showing such antagonism so plainly in my vulnerable position. Quietly and efficiently, he stripped back the blanket which covered me and began to sponge my face, neck and hands. I was too weak to protest, waves of faintness breaking over me, the awning dipping and swaying. I forced myself not to flinch as his hand travelled lightly over my forehead. Gentle though it was, his touch hurt and he smiled in commiseration.

"No bones broken. You've been lucky. Now then, why do you accuse me? What makes you so sure that somebody set those bolders rolling?"

He was smiling at me so charmingly that it did seem ridiculous to suspect him. Yet he knew that Miss Tranter had been babbling and could not be sure how much she'd let slip. "I saw a figure on the crest of the hill, then the rocks started to fall."

"And who could possibly want to harm you?" he asked softly. "A rival soprano hiring an assassin? Myself, peeved because you prefer Beville's manly charms to my own?" He grinned wryly and spread some sweet-smelling ointment on my brow, remarking: "You're going to have a lump as big as an egg there."

"I don't know who it was," I mumbled. It hurt my head to think. I was sickly aware of an increasing sense of danger, though it could have been an accident, as he said, not an attempt on my life which had misfired. Yet I could have sworn that there had been a figure, half-seen, confused, above the ledge. When Nicholas had finished, he added a few drops of dark liquid to a tot of brandy and gave it to me with instructions to drink. "What is it?" I asked cagily.

"Laudanum."

'Oh, drugging me now, are you?" I didn't want it, terrified of what might happen if I slept.

"Yes I am, my vixen, and stop flashing those golden eyes at me. You need to rest after such a nasty tumble."

"I'm really all right now," I said rather feebly, fighting to maintain a haughty distance between us.

"I'll be the judge of that," he replied firmly, closing the first-aid box with a snap.

"You know about medicine?" I asked, wondering if there was anything he couldn't do.

"It's essential to have a smattering of knowledge, working out here. There are many dangers – snakebite, scorpion stings – things which could prove fatal if left unattended."

"You should have kept on the services of Dr Armstrong," I said without thinking.

He shot me a searching look. "What d'you know about him?"

"Miss Tranter mentioned his name," I lied, floundering in deep waters. "She said that he was Lady Emily's doctor."

"Did she also tell you that he was in love with her?" His mouth was grim. "Really, my dear, you do seem to be curious about the affairs of my household. I wonder why? Is it just female nosiness, or something else?"

I couldn't meet those savage hawk eyes. I'd never felt

more helpless. I should have asked Beville to accompany me, squashing my wilful desire to be alone with Nicholas. "Why don't we go back to El Tarifa?" I asked, struggling against ever increasing drowsiness.

"We'll return later – when you have rested," he said, moving quietly about the tent, tidying away the bowl and towels. I couldn't keep my eyes open, fighting against it but soon falling into a deep sleep which was like taking a plunge into a well of dark water. I didn't think that I slept, for, after a while, it seemed that I was gazing at the tent walls in a stupor of weariness and I remember thinking: I'm awake. The drug hasn't worked. It was odd, because the awning appeared to expand, changing shape and becoming the centre of a garden full of blooming shrubs and strange, exotic odours.

There were footsteps in the garden. I couldn't see anyone, but I could hear those light footfalls which, in spite of my dragging tiredness, I was compelled to investigate. I rose up from the couch, following the sound. Always the footsteps were round the next corner, and the path by which I climbed after them grew steeper and more difficult. Why do I go on, I thought resentfully, when I'm so weary? But the need to overtake urged me on and for what seemed hours I followed wherever they went. Eventually, they stopped, and I came to a door at which I beat with clenched fists, filled with a terrible urgency to get through. I could hear a woman's voice, weeping and imploring. Then the door creaked open. I glimpsed flame-red hair and green eyes which blazed in a dead-white face. A hand reached out and drew me slowly through the door into a swirling darkness which wrapped me like a shroud.

I sat bolt upright, bathed in a sweat, her name on my lips. "Nancy! Is that you? Where are you?"

I could see that one flap of the tent was rolled up showing the pure pink of the sinking sun lingering on the hills of sand. In the clefts and hollows it changed to blue and purple with touches of gold which were repeated on the hangings. I heard the sound of pigeons cooing and fluttering, and the rustle of palm leaves gently moving. The evening breeze had come. I remembered now – I'd fallen and hit my head. I'd been asleep and had a dream. I must go back to Alexandria and find Beville.

My temples throbbed persistently and I held my head in my hands. What a strange, vivid dream. It was Nancy I had seen – Nancy, standing in a doorway with a child at her side. That vision had not been a harbinger of peace and tranquillity – warning bells clanged in my brain. I was icy cold, long shudders racking me, that sense of dire foreboding filling every part of my being. I trembled with primitive terror, backing into a corner of the couch like a petrified animal. I, who had always fought shy of omens and portents, could not explain the dream or the sight of Nancy's dreadful face, so clear – so real!

I tottered to my feet, making for the tent flap. I had a heavy, drugged feeling and couldn't coordinate my thoughts. Where was Nicholas? I didn't want to be alone in this bare, stark desert of illimitable space. I was still enmeshed in my nightmare which had been so unlike a real dream – there was no sense of awakening from it. I felt inexpressibly lonely as daylight finally faded, and the moon, like a yellow scimitar, hung between the peaks of two hills. I could see that the tent lay at the edge of an oasis. A pool gleamed between reeds, the night wind stirred the great ragged fronds of the palms and the queer call of the little red grasshoppers sounded clearly. Far away, in the desert, came the eerie cry of a jackal.

Time seemed to stand still and I didn't know what to do. I had no idea how far I was from El Tarifa. I wanted someone to come and take care of me – I was so very tired. The unfamiliar night sounds mingled strangely with the echoing emptiness of the star-flecked universe

– an emptiness that hung above me, threatening and cold. Then I saw someone walking towards me from the pool. At first I thought it was an Arab until a deep voice spoke to me in English.

"Feeling better?" asked Nicholas. "I didn't disturb you for you were sleeping so soundly."

He looked comfortingly real and solid, remote from the sick miseries that ravaged my mind. I backed into the tent and he followed, striking a match and lighting the lamps. His appearance startled me, adding to the dreamlike quality of everything that came after. He no longer wore European riding breeches and shirt, but had changed into the caftan and over-robe of a bedouin, though his curling black hair was bare and wet. He was different. Gone were the quick, brisk movements of an English gentleman. Clothed as an Arab, he made gestures that were stately, dignified, even a trifle swaggering. He had just come from a dip in the pool; there was a subtle scent about him of oil and perfumed soap which somehow detracted nothing from his masculinity. "I went back to work and left you sleeping," he said, and gestured towards a picnic basket. "You haven't eaten anything all day. You must be famished."

The thought of food made my stomach heave, dizziness sweeping over me. My knees trembled under me in a most unpleasant way. "Oh, no – I couldn't eat – couldn't possibly – "

I could feel myself falling and he caught me, swinging me up in his arms and carrying me to the couch where he set me down, keeping his arms about me, my head resting against his shoulder. He felt the shudders which tore through my body and wrapped a blanket round me, his face concerned. "Don't try to get up. You're not recovered yet."

"I want to go back to Alexandria," I wailed, thoroughly demoralised. "I've had a dreadful dream. Oh God – I saw Nancy." Tact and caution had deserted me and I was hardly aware of what I was saying. I felt him stiffen and heard the tense quality in his voice.

"Nancy? D'you mean Miss Gray?"

I nodded, sobbing now, so glad to cling to someone warm, solid and human that I couldn't stop my tongue. "Yes – yes! I saw her – followed her. It was awful!"

He was silent for a moment, his hand passing soothingly over my hair. "But you've never met Miss Gray, have you Rebecca? How can you have seen her in a dream?"

Oh, dear, I thought despairingly, mentally apologising to Beville. I mustn't let the cat out of the bag! I gulped back my tears and tried to marshal my fleeing wits. "Miss Tranter showed me her photograph, taken with Jeffrey."

"Why are you so interested in her?" he asked quietly. "I don't believe you're telling the truth."

It was getting ever more difficult to keep him at a distance. I had the dreadful urge to tell him everything, but I mustn't – I daren't! "I'm just curious, that's all."

"You've been listening to too much idle gossip," he said sternly. "I suppose Veronica's been prattling. I'll dismiss the damned woman."

I pulled away from him. "Is that what you always do, Nicholas? Get rid of anyone who annoys you?"

"Certainly not!" He was glaring at me as he leapt to his feet. "I'm prepared to give anyone a chance, but she's gone too far."

"She's in love with you," I answered recklessly, forgetting my aching head.

"I've had my share of mistresses," he said brutally, "but never one as persistent as she. Why can't she accept that it's over?"

"Wouldn't Miss Gray recognise that you were tired of her too? Is that what happened? Is that why she left?" I challenged him loudly, to cover the angry pain in my heart.

He stood there with his legs spread and his hands resting on the sash girding his waist. He was seething with rage. "Miss Gray! Damn Miss Gray! I don't know why I'm wasting time talking to you but, if you must know, there never was anything between Nancy Gray and me. She helped me. That's all."

"What a heartless monster you are!" I countered, clutching the blanket about me with shaking hands. "Have you no pity for the women you've hurt so badly? What about your dead wife? I've never heard a single note of sorrow or regret in your voice when you speak of her. Didn't you love her?"

"Love her?" he snapped, then gave a mirthless laugh. "Oh, yes – I was fool enough to love her once, but it's hard to go on loving a woman who traps you into marriage when she's already carrying another man's child and breaks this news to you on your wedding night! She trapped me, and then turned into a pathetic invalid deserving of nothing but my contempt. After she'd had Fleur, the doctors told me there could be no more children, so I was denied a rightful heir. Fleur has no business inheriting my estates but there's damn all I can do about it now."

"You could marry again," I began but he cut me off.

"Bah! I'll not make that mistake twice!" There was a terrible bitterness in his voice as he stared out at the starry night. I saw his craggy profile outlined at the tent entrance.

"How did Jeffrey come into the picture?" I asked at last, breaking the fraught silence.

He swung round angrily. "Emily was a cheat and Dorothea an empty-headed flirt. My brother and I were both fooled by them. She left him when she was expecting his baby. Yes, it was his right enough, he'd made bloody sure of that, though he'd had to keep her under lock and key to do it! She came here and it was born dead – buried in the crypt, I believe. Yes, despite her flighty attitude, her loathing of pregnancy and all that motherhood entails, she apparently suffered acute depression after the stillbirth, and was advised to adopt to compensate for the loss of her baby. Then, true to form, she opted out of even this, dying suddenly, so that I had to assume the responsibility for Jeffrey."

"You resented him very much?"

He was as angry as a tormented panther. "No. How can one resent an innocent child? I did what I could for him, difficult though it was with the silly women pampering him. But I did resent it when Emily threatened to leave her money to him."

Now we were coming to the crux of the matter. "But you're rich, aren't you?"

He gave another snort of laughter. "Don't be deceived by appearances. When Henry died, Revelstoke Court was crippled by death duties. He'd mismanaged it, anyhow, and it is taking years to get it on a level keel again."

The lamps swayed gently, the shadows moving with them, planing deep grooves in his face. His eyes shone in the gloom and he seemed so large and formidable in his anger. I was trying desperately to communicate with him, to probe his mind and find some thread which might lead me to my missing friend. "The excavations must be draining your resources," I ventured.

"Of course they are!" he exploded. "But, don't you see, when completed they will be of enormous value. Nothing must stop this!"

"You wouldn't have hurt Jeffrey, would you, Nicholas?" I whispered. For good or ill, I had to ask him.

His eyes were narrowed slits, his hands hovering as if he wanted to choke the life out of me for such presumption. "What are you getting at? I might have smacked his arse if he didn't behave, but that's all. Christ knows why I bothered with him. What was he? Nothing but a snotty-nosed little bastard from a foundling home!"

My mind was trembling in a kind of bruised agony. What would he say if he knew that I too had been a foundling brat? Then pride kindled again – so, I had been born into poverty and humiliation but I'd clawed my way out of it. "He was a human soul, struggling to stay alive, as we all do," I said loudly and clearly, making him look at me.

His expression changed and he came over to sit by me, taking my reluctant hands in his. "I know. I didn't mean it. It's just that any mention of Emily makes me sick – and Veronica – the whole damned tribe! Oh, Rebecca, Rebecca – if you only knew – only understood."

"I'm trying, Nicholas, truly I am, but I can't make sense of anything tonight." I pressed my palm to my forehead, aware of that tender lump. Then I looked up at him. He was smiling at me with that disquieting preoccupation behind his eyes which had been there since the moment we met. "We should be starting back," I faltered.

"Not yet, Rebecca," he said slowly and there was an intensity in his face which riveted me to the spot. "Not until I've done what I brought you here to do."

My throat was dry, and I measured the distance between myself and the tent opening, realising that I had no hope of escape. "And what is that?" I whispered, my voice sounding hoarse and unnatural, thinking that my last hour had come.

"I'm going to make love to you," he said, and reached for me.

I have promised to make my chronicle as accurate as I can, so I make no excuse for retailing what happened next. I could lie and say that I was drugged, ill, not myself, but this would be a cowardly shirking of the truth. No, quite frankly, I was swept away by a passion which ousted every other consideration. I wanted him. We were miles from anywhere, surrounded by the magic of the night, the solitude of the desert, brought violently together by a need as old as time. Never in my life, no, not even when Beville initiated me, had I been so physically roused. It was like a raging storm, a madness roaring in my blood as I melted into the warm strength of his body, my lips parting under the demanding assault of my senses. It was a wild, savage emotion and I knew that he felt it too. His mouth found mine with a frightening urgency, and lost to coherent thought, we slowly sank back on the couch.

I was no shy virgin and knew what I wanted, recognising the desire that ran through me like fire, making me long for him to take me. At the welcoming touch of my arms about him, he lost control, dragging me against him, kissing me violently. Dear God, those kisses! They stirred me as I'd never been stirred before. Something seemed to fuse between us, transcending mere bodily sensation. Laxly, my body losing all rigidity, I surrendered myself, my head falling back against his arm while his mouth explored my face. I had a sense of emptiness as if he had drawn my soul from between my lips. Nothing mattered but this feeling of oneness, of belonging, and the passion of his mouth, passion told in his jerky breathing and the shaking of the hands that caressed me. I forgot Beville. I forgot Nancy. I was blinded, bewitched, only aware of the tingling of my skin and that aching, wounded sensation within me which I was very much afraid was the presage of love.

How can one measure such moments, let alone describe them? I think I went crazy as he tore away my clothing, finding my hot flesh beneath. The last remnant of sanity fled away, leaving only the need to get closer and closer to him. He took me swiftly and our bodies came together in a savage tempo, each rushing to meet the thrust and lunge of the other, oblivious to anything but the heedless desire which engulfed us. I clung to him, I recall, whimpering and babbling as aching pleasure washed through me, lying replete beneath him, feeling a queer stab of tenderness at his own eruption of fulfilment. For many moments we stayed there, joined together, our mouths gently mingling and tasting. Slowly, the tent righted itself and I became aware of the moths fluttering round the lamps. Passion faded and in its place came shame, yet it was shame mixed with a wry kind of triumph. How trite every other experience seemed, fading into the limbo of the unimportant. I was torn between the joy and agony of my own feelings, praying that I might find happiness with Nicholas, yet cynically certain that this could never be.

You fool, I sneered at myself. Fancy falling into such a trap! How d'you know that he hasn't deliberately set out to enslave you, so that you'll no longer question his actions, so blinded by love that you'll forget everything else? I didn't know – that was the awful part. I couldn't be sure – couldn't trust him. If this was what being in love meant, this destructive uncertainty, then I wanted no part in it. In retrospect, Beville's lovemaking had been so safe – pleasant, adoring, absolutely correct. There had been nothing about it to shake the very foundations of my being. I hadn't this silly desire to run away with him to some remote island where we could be quite alone for the rest of existence. Now I felt as battered as if I'd been caught up in a raging hurricane, yet it was a totally surrendered feeling that made me want to stay locked with Nicholas forever, shutting out the world and refusing to obey the call of cold, pale duty that beckoned me sombrely, reminding me of my purpose, and at whose dire summons I shuddered and turned my face away.

Eventually Nicholas moved slightly, lifted his body from mine and stared down into my face. There was a troubled, uncertain expression on his features as he said: "Rebecca, I – " but then, as if suddenly conscious of what we had just done, he jerked up abruptly and a strained silence yawned between us. He rearranged his clothing and then helped me to my feet, saying nothing further, his face once again masked.

I wanted to break through that barrier but couldn't find words to express my feelings. It was all so confused, even hysterical, and my head was spinning. The tent was plunged into darkness as he extinguished the lamps and then I followed him outside. I groped around and found his arm, clinging to it as he led me to the horses. Weakness assailed me and I leaned against the patient mare. I didn't have the strength to haul myself into the saddle, so Nicholas lifted me on to his own horse, mounted behind me and led the other. We rode in the direction of El Tarifa. The animals moved silently over the sand and we were bathed in the sapphire radiance of the night. The splendour, the silence, the blend of fear and excitement of Nicholas's arms holding me against his chest, played havoc with my nerves. England, my former life, even my stage career seemed banished from the universe, not so much forgotten as completely obliterated!

As we turned through the entrance to the palace, I was sharply aware of that sense of imprisonment which it gave out. The feeling of threat intensified, or perhaps it was just because I was so feverish, icy drops of sweat beading my face. I shuddered with chill although I was wrapped in a fold of Nicholas's burnous. I had never been wanted there. I was wanted even less now. This should have been the most wonderful night of my life, if I could have been certain that he wasn't using his charm to divert my attention from something he didn't want discovered. As he lifted me down, I gave him a slanting glance and saw him staring straight ahead. His face told me nothing. He had brought me safely back to El Tarifa, but for what purpose?

I don't know how I managed to reach the hall. I think he supported me. The light hurt my eyes, boring into them, a hot wave rising up over me and not stopping, flooding my head, beating in my ears, making me giddy. I felt a sudden tense wire of pain tear its way from the back of my neck into my temples. I stopped, my legs going weak and my head faint. Through a kind of red haze, I saw the hall shimmer and waver ahead of me. Then everything went black.

Chapter 6

Voices seemed to come from a great distance, approaching and receding, looming and fading like water. I was revolving on a giant horizontal wheel in slow and sweeping motion. The turning was making me feel sick. Someone was slapping my face gently. I jerked my head to one side to avoid the slaps and opened my eyes. Through a blur, I saw Nicholas's face hovering over me.

I tried to sit up, but it was no use, everything seemed to be swimming towards me and the sight of Nicholas, and several servants wavering at his shoulder, was dim compared with the figure of Nancy in the doorway, and my own awful realisation that there was something happening to me which I couldn't understand, something terrifying.

They told me later that I had fainted. I came to myself in a wide bed in a cool, marble-built room with an arched balcony and a staircase leading down to the garden. I must have been threshing in delirium for the sheet beneath me was soaked in perspiration. It was dark beyond the windows, and lamplight flickered and threw darting serpents of shadow across the walls. Beville materialised at the bedside.

"Hello there," he said brightly, though his face looked drawn with anxiety and lack of sleep. "Feeling better? No, don't try to talk."

"Where am I?" I murmured, and this was as much as I could manage.

"In one of the guest rooms at El Tarifa. Nicholas sent for me. We'll talk about it later. Sleep now, Rebecca."

He smoothed my pillow into a more comfortable shape, gave me a drink of lemonade, tucked the clothes round my shoulders and laid his hand on my restless fingers. His touch calmed me, bringing a measure of peace to my bewildered brain, so that I stopped my constant search for some thought or memory which was evading me. I fell into a fitful sleep, tormented by terrible dreams, none of which I can recall clearly, only knowing that they left me with a sense of dread and impending doom. I woke feeling very weak, as if every vestige of strength had been sucked out of me.

Sunlight made bright rectangles on the tiled floor. There were several people present and I peeked through my lashes, pretending that I still slept. I saw Beville and Terence Armstrong near the bed, talking in subdued voices. "What's your diagnosis, doctor?" Beville was saying, his kindly face extremely worried.

"Sir Nicholas tells me that she had a fall, but I don't think she's suffering from concussion. I would say it's a touch of malaria," Terence replied. "I've given her a dose of quinine. It seems to have quietened her, though she was raving last night."

"Malaria," said Nicholas, stepping from the balcony. "I disagree. She's not ill enough for malaria."

"In any case, it will be best if she isn't moved for a while," answered Terence stiffly, making no effort to hide his dislike.

"I'll have her things fetched from the hotel." Nicholas was taking command, obviously in a difficult mood, exuding a kind of dominating hostility.

"I'm sure she could be well looked after there. We don't want to trouble you," put in Beville quickly, and I could tell that he didn't like leaving me at El Tarifa.

"Nonsense. It will be a pleasure." Nicholas cut across objections. I sighed inwardly, wishing wistfully that I could be sure he wanted me to stay so that he might care for me, but his glance was so stern, his manner so cold, that it was as if our intimacy of the previous night had never happened.

Everyone tactfully withdrew, leaving me alone with Beville who was, after all, my acknowledged suitor. I was feeling better. Whatever it was that Terence had prescribed was taking effect. "What the devil went wrong yesterday?" Beville asked, sitting on the side of the bed.

I explained as well as I could, my mind skimming over the events. I heard my voice going on and on, while inside I was experiencing agonising qualms because I had allowed Nicholas to make love to me. The whole structure of my life had been devastated by it, but I couldn't tell Beville about it yet, perhaps I never would. Maybe it had meant nothing to Nicholas except physical satisfaction, easily done and just as easily forgotten. I don't care if that's all it was, I told myself defiantly – but deep in my heart I knew that I was lying.

"It wasn't an accident – I'm certain of it," I ended rather lamely. "There was someone up on the rocks, pushing the boulders."

"Another of Renshaw's minions?" Beville's mouth was tight.

"But why? What has he to hide?" I stirred restlessly, propped against the pillows. "If only we could find out what's been going on. Have you any news?"

His face was troubled as he told me that Dawkins, in whom he had confided, had come up with something interesting. That perfect model of a gentleman's gentleman had been making his own enquiries among the servants who came to Alexandria with their "families" year after year. "He mentioned Miss Tranter, and apparently was told that she was here with Lady Dorothea about six years ago."

"How odd. I had the impression that Lady Dorothea came alone. Miss Tranter didn't say anything about accompanying her, quite the contrary – she seemed annoyed at being left behind."

He shook his head. "Dawkins said it was remembered well because of the divorce scandal. She gave birth to a dead child here, then returned to England and nothing more was heard of her."

I couldn't see any connection between this unhappy event and the present mystery. "What has all this to do with Nancy?"

His tanned face was thoughtful though he flashed me his customary smile, so very likeable, this broad, quiet man. "I don't know yet, but I'd like to scout round the family vault."

"Oh, Beville, you couldn't! How macabre!" I shuddered. "It wouldn't be feasible, would it?"

"If I could get hold of the key, I could slip in there at night and take a look." He said it as calmly as if he were proposing to steal into the Renshaw wine cellar, not that dark place where the bones of their dead lay. The thought of it made me feel sick, but: "Where is the key?" I asked.

"Should imagine that it hangs with the other household ones, probably in Nicholas's study."

Silence crept across that magnificent, sun-filled room and I had to fight off a feeling of being compelled by an outside force to do something I hadn't reckoned on. "You want me to get it," I said at last.

There were little worried creases about his eyes, and his fingers tightened on mine. "I hate to ask you, darling, but your being here does seem a heaven-sent opportunity for a bit of spying. In fact, when they told me that you'd collapsed, I thought you were faking it as an excuse to stay here. It wasn't till I saw you, looking so damned ill, that I realised you weren't acting. You were really feverish and saying a lot of very weird things – "

"Good God, what was I saying?" Alarm shot through me as I suddenly remembered that Nancy had been part of my dreams. "Have I given the game away? Who was here?"

"They were gathered around the bed when I came in," he answered grimly, catching the drift of my terrified thoughts. "Nicholas and Quiller – and Veronica. You'd put them in a panic, you see, fainting away like that. I don't think they could've understood your ramblings – I certainly didn't make much sense of it all – "

I clung to the hope that I hadn't betrayed us, and knew that I had to do what Beville asked. I was much better, but could feign weakness which would confine me to the house. "Very well. I'll get the key. Make your arrangements for tomorrow night."

After kissing me and calling me his brave, lovely girl, he went away. I acted the delicate invalid convincingly. Veronica showed a completely insincere concern, insisting on attending to my needs. She brought in a great bunch of creamy-white flowers on long stems, arranging them in a vase, chattering lightly, telling me that those sprays of waxen blossom were thought by the Arabs to bring good fortune. All through the hot day I breathed in their heavy, sickly scent as I gathered my strength to do what had to be done.

Nicholas came to see me in the evening, and by that time I was out of bed and supping on the balcony, not yet dressed, wearing a white silk nightgown and peignoir. My clothes had been sent from the Stanley Hotel and Veronica had been determined to unpack them, though my maid had arrived with the baggage. I wanted to get rid of her, relieved when Nicholas asked her to leave. I had to remember to appear wan and listless, though in reality my heart was thumping madly. He was so tall and handsome, exuding charm, having recovered his temper, talking amiably of this and that, but not at all like a lover. I was baffled, nervously unsure of what to expect. Indeed, there had been more closeness before we made love; glances, meaningful words, the brushing of hands which had been so exciting. Now it was as if he'd never touched me, he was so cool and detached.

He stood on the balcony smoking while I watched him and speculated on those vast gulfs of silence and reticence between us. Perhaps I hadn't pleased him, or else the deep passion we'd experienced had been so fierce that it had burnt itself out. Worst of all, he might well have been using me for some dark plot of his own. I wished unhappily that I'd never met him.

"You're missing your singing practice, Rebecca," he was saying in his most conversational tone. "Madame Bellini will not be pleased with you, so, when you feel strong enough, we'll resume."

"Beville and I will be going back to England shortly. I've a series of rehearsals before we leave for Argentina."

I couldn't see his expression for the lamplight didn't reach the balcony, but was very aware of him, a large, powerful shape, his face turned towards me. "Must you go?" he asked quietly.

I kept my head, willing him to leave well alone. I couldn't bear it if he started another of those queer, unsettling conversations that seemed to lead nowhere. "I can't be on holiday forever," I exclaimed and tried to laugh. "I have my work to do – my career – "

"Ah, yes," he broke in roughly, striding into the room. "Nothing must interfere with your precious career!" He looked furious. "Nothing and no one must stand in the way of your glory! Just for a moment – last night – I forgot your ambition!"

A shiver danced over my skin and I let my gaze slide to his hands, those lean, sun-burned hands that had had such intimate knowledge of my body. But I checked myself, his tone making me equally angry. "I've been given this gift and I must use it," I declared, despising myself for bothering to try to make him understand. "It's not for self-glory." He flung me a sceptical smile but I pressed on. "Oh, I know what you're thinking, and I do enjoy the applause, the sense of achievement, but more than this is the urge to express beautiful music. Can't you comprehend this? You're a pianist, and a brilliant one. You too should be performing in public, bringing joy to your audience."

"How very noble," he jeered. "I wish I could believe you, but there's so much about you that mystifies me. You pretend to be honest with me, but I know you're holding something back. What is it? Why don't you tell me?"

Fear flamed through me at the intensity of his probing gaze. I sat rigid in my chair, my hands gripping the arms. "I came here to rest before a pretty arduous tour," I said stubbornly. "My God, for all the good it's done me, I'd have done better to spend a fortnight in Bournemouth!"

"I do apologise for disturbing you further, my dear prima donna. I'll leave you to your much needed rest," he answered sarcastically. With that, he stalked away, and I was close to tears, vowing to myself that I'd cut this dangerous love out of my heart if I had to do it with a knife!

I paced the room, thoroughly upset. I wished that Nell had never come to my dressing room, setting me on this journey which had robbed me of my peace of mind. Once, things had been simple; I knew where I was going, happy with my work, content with my affair with Beville. Nell, Nancy and I had made our vow so long ago, when we were little more than children. Now I was twenty, so many years older and so many years wiser. I laughed at that bitterly. Certainly not wiser, as I was discovering to my cost, but definitely learning caution. I made up my mind to make one final attempt to find a satisfactory answer to Nancy's disappearance and, if this failed, to book my passage home. I would reject my love for Nicholas, a love which was going to bring me nothing but sorrow. I would concentrate on bringing my voice to perfection and my career to the greatest possible heights and, if marriage was necessary, then I would accept Beville's proposal. So, on this high wave of resolution, I went to bed and tried to sleep, but sleep was a long time coming.

I didn't see Nicholas next day, but I was glad of this. I admitted being well enough to dress and by the afternoon suggested that I would wander down to the library and select a book to pass the time. I knew it was situated close to the study. My mind was cool and clear and determined with that desperation which drives the individual to take the most appalling risks. There was no one about; most people retired for a siesta during the grilling heat of afternoon. I passed down long corridors that I couldn't recall having seen before, through carved marble doorways hidden in unexpected corners, turning and twisting through a maze of dim, shuttered rooms. My footsteps echoed upon the tiled floors in the shadowed emptiness of the beautifully vaulted apartments.

My heart was thumping as I glanced up and down the passage before turning the brass handle of the study door. It opened on well-oiled hinges. I had never been invited into this sanctum. It was a small room with a businesslike atmosphere where accounts were tallied and detailed reports on the catacombs carried out. Nancy must have spent much time working here with Nicholas. The walls were lined with shelves; there were filing cabinets and ledgers, windows which opened towards the garden, and a massive writing desk with carved legs ending in lions' claws, and a leather top with gilt embossing. A gold inkwell squatted on it beside a pen tray and a collection of papers. On the wall behind it were hooks from which dangled bunches of labelled keys. One in particular caught my eye. An iron key, bigger than the rest. The key of the vault. Its coldness seemed to burn my hand as I lifted it carefully down, the accidental brushing of a nearby bunch reverberating through the silence like a peal of bells. I was sweating by now.

I slipped it into the pocket of my skirt and was about

to leave when, my mind sharpened by tension, I looked again at the drawers of the desk. What capital hiding places for secret documents, even for compromising journals. I began to rummage through them, hurriedly passing over letters and the odds and ends which such compartments collect. Much of it was Nicholas's reports on his finds, with answering correspondence from colleagues in Cairo. I was about to give up, admitting defeat, when I chanced upon a little inlaid box, pushed to the back. It was locked, but this didn't deter me. I had dealt with locks at the orphanage and, with the aid of a hairpin, soon heard that satisfying click which announced that it would now yield up its contents. There, under some loose papers, I found Nancy's journal.

I held it to the window, turning the pages, becoming oblivious to anything save that which my friend had written. The early entries were not unusual, a young girl's accounts of her travels, but in the later ones a sense of alarm and urgency began to creep through to me, so that I read them several times, and with each reading that smouldering quality grew stronger No wonder that lackey Quiller had been so anxious to get hold of it on his master's behalf! There were no outright accusations, but even so, if it fell into the hands of the police it could raise some awkward questions, setting into operation investigations which might prove very damaging to Nicholas.

I was so totally involved in it, losing all sense of time, place and danger, that my heart leaped with shock when a voice spoke just behind me. "Can I help you, madame?"

I spun round, the diary held behind my back, horrified as my eyes met those of Quiller. He was smiling his usual bland smile, but there was a baneful expression on his face. My pulse was jumping madly. At best, I had no business prying into Nicholas's personal papers, and at worst? It didn't bear dwelling on.

"Thank you, Mr Quiller, but Sir Nicholas gave me permission to look for a musical thesis on which he's been working," I replied, thanking God for my orphanage grounding in quick, face-saving lies.

Our eyes remained locked as he said, smooth as silk: "You won't find it in that old box, I can assure you, madame. I'll show you where it is kept."

"That will be most helpful." I had decided to be brash about it. After all, I was a guest in the house, whilst he, for all his airs, was nothing but a servant. "I found this journal whilst I was searching. It's most entertaining. D'you suppose I could take it to my room and finish reading it? It belongs to Miss Gray – the runaway governess! She appears to be a young woman of spirit and intelligence."

"A diary, madame?" Really, I thought, he's missed his vocation. He should have been an actor. Had I not heard Nell's story of his behaviour in the casino, I would have accepted his puzzled expression as genuine.

"Yes – Miss Gray's diary. She kept a day by day account of everything that happened to her."

Oh, he was foxy all right. Not by the merest twitch of an eyebrow did he reveal that he knew anything about it. "If it belongs to her, then I can't let you have it," he replied. "It wouldn't be right. She may send for it, and it is her private property. I expect Sir Nicholas is keeping it until she sends a forwarding address. I think we should replace it, don't you?"

God, but he's a cool customer, I thought, subtle as a serpent, the man ideally suited to carry out Nicholas's dirty work. He held out his hand and I gave him the journal. He made no comment about the forced lock, though I didn't doubt that he'd noticed it. Then, still in the role of impeccably mannered agent, he found me the music manuscript and stood back politely so that I might precede him into the corridor. It was an absurd charade; we had crossed swords at last, taking each other's measure. The very air seemed to crackle about us. I hadn't had time to read the journal thoroughly but had seen enough written about me there to convince even a fool that Nancy and I were old friends, and Quiller was no fool – neither was Nicholas. All I could be grateful for was the fact that Quiller had been so intent on wresting it from me that he hadn't noticed the missing key.

Beville came at sundown and I was able to give it to him and tell him about the journal. "Good girl," he murmured as we strolled in the garden, hand in hand, supposedly admiring the rainbow hues which swathed the sky. The walls of the palace glowed like blood; the rose-red light was reflected by the broom-like flowers of the juniper bushes that gave off their perfume only after dark.

Dear Beville. How immensely comforting it was to have him there. "Don't leave me for long," I begged, hating to be alone. "Come back when you've explored the crypt. I'm frightened, so very frightened."

"Stick it out for a short while more. Tomorrow you can return to the hotel. Who knows what we may discover tonight? Everything, or perhaps nothing at all," he replied and I knew that I had to let him go. "Lock the door of your room and wait for me."

I was torn in two and had never been in a more horrible situation, conniving to bring about the exposure of the man I loved. I had suffered acute misery at the dinner table with Nicholas there, the most considerate of hosts, lavishing attention on us whilst he and Beville held forth on a variety of themes. I hated every moment of it, wanting to leap to my feet, crying: "Tell me the truth, Nicholas. Why are you hiding Nancy's journal? Where is she? Where is your nephew? What have you done, you wicked man?"

I didn't say it, of course, answering the politely interested questions about my future plans, concealing my fear and anguish. But where was the intimacy and understanding, the quick glances meant for me alone, the whispered exchange of confidences, all the silly trifles which existed between lovers? Gone, all gone, since the night I surrendered to him.

When Beville left me, I didn't go inside, walking restlessly up and down, my soul tossed in a never-ending search for a moment's relief from the sick confusion of my mind. I could have refused to give Beville the key and kept silent about the diary, but how could I do that? My conscience demanded that I aid my friend and now there was more than this; I wanted the mystery solved, one way or the other, either damning Nicholas or clearing him. Then there was Beville – I had been rehearsing a cold little monologue, telling him of my lapse with Nicholas, but when I saw him, I didn't have the courage to speak. I loved his warm smile, and that was half the trouble – I loved his smile, his hair, his looks, but I didn't really love him. Not deeply, irrevocably, as I knew I was capable of loving Nicholas, even if he proved to be the most ruthless scoundrel under the sun.

Hardly knowing where I walked, I followed a path leading to the garden and came round some bushes to the side of a small pool. The drops of water falling like smoke from the fountain were dyed red with the sunset. The pool looked like blood and the surrounding shadows were deep purple-blue. I sank on to a corner of the marble basin and started to cry, passionately at first, with great tearing sobs that shook me from head to foot, then more quietly, appalled at my own emotion but unable to quell it.

Maestro Angeleri would be proud of me, I thought wryly. This cruel experience must surely improve my operatic performance. I was learning the dreadful agony of thwarted love, understanding how it was that people under its influence committed murder or suicide, did the maddest, most despicable things. Many had paid with their lives for such folly. And I too would pay all my life for mine. Loving Nicholas was so hopeless, so wearying, and I was very much afraid of him.

I was disturbed by a rustling in the bushes, but it was not some bloodthirsty assassin who came out, but the shabby figure of Miss Tranter. She stopped on seeing me, her head on one side like an inquisitive bird. "Young lady, you shouldn't be here unchaperoned," she admonished sternly. "Who are you?" She came closer, her glasses glistening in the fast-fading light. She was clutching a reticule in one hand and a walking stick in the other. "Have you been crying? Well-bred ladies mustn't cry – only servants show such lack of control. Pull yourself together at once! I don't know what things are coming to these days – there are always ladies weeping in this garden. I hear them – their laments reach my window like the sighing of the wind. I had to come down and see what was the matter, Miss Gray. You are Miss Gray, aren't you?"

It was useless to argue; she was mad as a hatter. So I dried my eyes and listened to her mumbling vague, meaningless phrases. I thought she had forgotten my presence but when I rose to leave, she dropped her stick and her bony fingers clamped round my arm. "You're in danger, young lady," she hissed, glancing furtively around. "There's nothing you can do for Master Jeffrey. Such a pretty child. Lady Emily often goes into his room at night and stands looking at him while he sleeps. She wanted a son, you see, but something went wrong when Fleur was born – she nearly lost her life, and now there can be no more babies. They should have let me look after him – but no!' 'You've done enough, Nanny,' she said. 'You must go back to Cornwall and take care of Miss Fleur.' "

I couldn't understand what she was talking about, it was so muddled. Did she refer to Lady Dorothea or Lady Emily? I wanted to get away and tugged at my arm. "Please, Miss Tranter, let me go. It's chilly out here and I'm recovering from a fever."

"I know about that," she said in a firm, natural voice, her eyes no longer misted by visions of the past. "I've watched you from the spyholes. You were hit by a rock. They want to get rid of you, as they did Miss Gray. Leave El Tarifa at once. You are in grave danger."

" 'They'? Who are 'they'?" I asked, curbing my desire to fly for the safety of my room.

Lucidity left her again and, by the time I'd finished speaking, her thoughts were confused. "What are you talking about?" she said crossly. "Who invited you? You don't sound like a lady. I can't let a nobody walk in here without a by-your-leave. Oh dear, no, that wouldn't do at all!" and she marched off down the path, still shaking her head and grumbling.

Mary was in my room and she'd laid out my nightgown on the bed, but it was too early to retire. I knew that a long, worrying night lay ahead and wished that Beville had let me go with him to the burial ground. Anything, even that nastiness, would have been better than this nerve-racking waiting. I dismissed Mary and sank down on the bed, my eyes wandering the room, noting the graceful carved garlands and the text from the Koran in Arabic script cut deep into the plinth above the doorway. Oh, Nicholas, I grieved, how wonderful it would have been if this were our nuptial chamber, so lovely when night fell. It was filled with perfume, a mingling of roses and spices, yet stabbed across with the sharp odour of citrus as if to remind me that such beauty was a façade, hiding corruption, danger and fear.

I was weeping again. How horrible it was to fall in love with a man I suspected of dark, shifty dealings. Life was a bitter, cruel joke, as Nicholas had said not long ago. I clung to the thought of my work. I must go home and prepare for the important tour ahead. I would get over it. That's what people always said, wasn't it? Or was this too one of those lies told by those who refused to remember the pain, the wild frenzy, the insane feeling of futility and failure which tortured me now?

Lecturing myself firmly, I took up the score of *Madama Butterfly*, intending to have a stab at concentrating on it, when Mary tapped at the door. She told me that an Arab boy had brought a message for me. She handed over a folded letter. It said: "Madame Costello. Vital information has come to light. It is imperative that I see you at once. The bearer knows the address." It was signed "Patrick Graham, Et-Taweel."

My first reaction was that he and Beville had found something in the vault. They must have worked exceedingly quickly. I didn't hesitate. Mary said that the boy was waiting in the stable. Nicholas was nowhere about, in fact the house seemed curiously deserted, but I didn't stop to think about it, giving orders that the gig should be prepared. The Arab was an engaging street urchin who had, no doubt, been promised a few shekels to fetch me. He was ragged and dirty, but grinned at me in a friendly way, his teeth gleaming in his dusky face. He assured me that he could drive, hopping up on to the seat and taking the reins. I was amused by his cheeky confidence. In no time at all we were heading towards the native quarter.

I was impatient to reach our destination, hungry for any news which would clear away these dark uncertainties, hoping against all hope that Nicholas might be proved innocent of any crime. Turbanned men and veiled women streamed past us, illumined by flares, for this area was populated by small traders, moneylenders, coffee shops and bazaars. Through the open arcades came sounds of revelry, a shrill piping, the beating of drums, singing, shouts and yells. At any other time I would have told my driver to stop, wishing to linger and absorb this exciting conglomeration of exotic images, but I dared not delay. It was as if Nancy herself was seated beside me, urging me on, her face white and grim as I'd seen it in my dream.

We emerged once more into a main street and the boy drew up at a brightly lit confectioner's stall, filled with sticky sweetmeats, biscuits and sherbet. We left the gig, and my guide conducted me into a courtyard which was completely dark, smelling vaguely of camel dung and jasmine. A house loomed up. I could see its silhouette against the star-flecked sky. My heart missed a beat as I stumbled along, following the darting, luminous shape of the urchin's dingy caftan. An arched door stood ajar, and we plunged into a darkness even more dense.

"Wait for me," I commanded, my voice echoing thinly as I stood there for a second, trying to get my bearings.

"Come, *sitt* – follow me. Don't be afraid," came the boy's reply from ahead, and there was something disembodied in the sound.

It was then that I became really frightened. I had been a fool to come, obeying a message that could have been sent by anyone. I should have demanded proof that it was sent by Et-Taweel. Too late to turn back now – too late to do anything but meet that which awaited me. I strained my eyes into the darkness but could see little. The walls presented an impenetrable blackness, except for a staircase. I felt my way up, knocking my feet against old, worm-eaten risers. The stairs were so rotten that they rocked and swayed. I could hear the lad a step or so above me, and I shuddered as I caught the squeaks and scramble of rats on the upper floors. The air smelled bad, with undertones of decay. I suddenly froze, listening, staring back down into that Stygian well, certain that we were being followed. There was something creeping up the stairs, its form mingling with the darkness as if it were part of it. But when I stopped, so did it; there was no sound but the house creaking about us.

My laboured breathing rose above the thudding of my heart and, tripping in panicky fright, I collided with the boy who had paused at the head of the stairs. I clutched at him, shaking him in my scared anger. "Where are you taking me? Haven't you a light?"

"We're nearly there, *sitt* – don't be alarmed," he said,

and I felt his fingers on my wrist, leading me down a black passageway.

The darkness was so thick that the light, when it did come, nearly blinded me. I found myself in a gaunt, high chamber lit by a twist of rope floating in a dish of oil. This threw spiky shadows across the crumbling ceiling and dilapidated walls. It contained nothing but a rickety bed and an iron washstand flanked by wicker chairs from which two men rose as we came in.

One was an Arab, a big, thickset man wearing robes and a headcloth. His face looked villainous in that smoky light, two incisive streaks running from his broad nostrils to his mouth, a black beard streaked with silver forming a sharp wedge on his chin. I backed against the door. This was not Et-Taweel.

He spoke to the boy in a swift spate of Arabic and tossed a few coins which the lad caught expertly before running from the room, then the man turned to me. "Madame Costello, is it not?"

"Who are you? Where is Et-Taweel?" I shouted, groping for the door handle, but he moved quickly, his hand clamping over it.

He chuckled, his dark eyes shining in the gloom. "Now, madame, be sensible. If you struggle or scream, no one will hear you. I have to take you on a journey," he said smoothly in very precise English. "A thousand pities, for I see that you are a jewel of a woman, and it would be Allah's blessing if I could take you as my bride."

"Get on with it, El Darim." The other occupant of the room stirred impatiently, the red tip of his cigarette like a spark in the shadows. There was a vicious ring to his voice. I stared at him, seeing a handsome fop in a check coat that must have cost a mint of money, and a black velour hat with a broad brim. "Tie her up and let's get out of here."

"Patience, my dear Osman, patience," counselled the sheik, with a wolfish smile. "Spare me a few moments with this ravishingly lovely vision." The mixed contempt and humility of his speech and the way he gloated on me gave me a sickening sensation of dread.

Osman and El-Darim! I heard Nell's trembling voice speaking those names! It was they who had witnessed her humiliation in the casino. So it was true. She hadn't been suffering from delusions. I had feared it – had *known* it – but now that the blow fell it was terrible in its finality. "If Et-Taweel isn't here, as I expected, then I shall leave," I said coldly, giving them my haughtiest look. "Get out of my way."

This fell on stony ground. El-Darim did not budge. His throaty laugh held no humour. "So beautiful," he purred. "So proud! Is she not splendid, Osman?"

"Don't waste time!" exclaimed Osman with a curse. He suddenly came towards me. "He's waiting for her."

"I'm not going anywhere with you," I yelled, dodging away to a corner of the room. "I don't know you. Who is it that waits for me?"

Osman moved like lightning, catching me before I had time to run. I tried to scream, but the scream was locked in my throat as he pushed me backwards into El-Darim's embrace. The sheik's breath was hot on my face, the scent of musk oil quite overpowering. "No – no," he crooned. "No use to scream, my turtle dove." One hand caught me about the neck, nearly throttling me, and even as I tried to beat at him with my fists, I felt a sharp, searing pain on the soft inner flesh of my arm. It jolted me with agony, my body arching convulsively under the restraining hands.

"Are you coming quietly or do you want more – more – more?" hissed Osman, his face contorted, each word implemented by jabs of his smouldering cigarette tip against my tortured skin.

Resistance was hopeless, though I writhed and cried out in rage, feeling my wrists grabbed and held while El-Darim chuckled devilishly. There was the bite of cord about my hands as they were yanked behind my back.

A foul-tasting gag was thrust into my mouth as I opened it to scream again. Then I was enveloped in smothering darkness when they flung something over my head. I was lifted bodily and heard Osman say: "We'd better hurry and do what has to be done," and his voice came from a distance, drowned by the drumming of blood in my ears.

"Such a pity," answered El-Darim. "I would have taken her out of his way. No need for such drastic measures, but he's too vicious and powerful to quarrel with over the life of a mere woman."

I was hoisted up, feeling myself dangling, head-down, over a broad shoulder. I couldn't breathe properly, my chest constricted, nose blocked by the evil-smelling blanket, the gag tearing at my mouth. I dimly remember being flung across a saddle, and a terrible pounding jarring right through me as we moved, before unconsciousness swallowed me, a merciful release from pain.

Chapter 7

There was hardness and coldness beneath me. I didn't want to wake. My body hurt too much, my arms burning areas of agony. I touched them and could feel that blisters had formed. I could breathe again, cold damp air, not fresh and sweet, but fetid. The gag had gone. I passed my tongue over my bruised lips, tasting blood, still not daring to open my eyes. I was reluctant to know where I was, instinct telling me that it wouldn't be anywhere pleasant. My hands were free and I felt around blindly, my fingertips encountering sand – a thin layer of sand on rock. I lifted my lids but it was as dark as when they were shut. For one awful moment, I wondered if I had lost my sight – totally disoriented, feeling about me, babbling half-remembered prayers to some deity in whom I no longer believed. I lost control, raving, screaming, yelling for help. My voice bounced off thick walls and when I stopped there was nothing, an oppressive silence shutting me in.

I willed myself to be calm. I couldn't see, but I had other senses, my ears for example, but I couldn't detect the slightest sound. It was far too quiet, with a stillness that was unearthly, seeming to press in on the cavities of my skull, making me shockingly aware of its fragility. Such dreadful silence held all the agony of a soundless, protracted scream. Where were Osman and El-Darim? I tried calling them, but was answered only by the echoes of my own trembling voice.

Very well then, I said to myself, it's a waste of time being hysterical. Stop it at once. I was denied the use of eyes and ears, so must rely on touch and smell. There seemed to be no draughts of air, just dank, musty coldness, so I must be below ground. The grains of sand under my searching fingers indicated that I wasn't far from the desert. Where? Had I been buried alive? Panic seized me, my nostrils inhaling putrefaction – the smell of death and decay. I was afraid to move lest my hands encounter something horrible. There are no words to describe my terror. I had been so silly, walking into a trap cunningly devised by the man I loved. I struggled to my knees and clawed at the stone walls at my back, blood wetting my hands as I tore my nails. This was no dream, no creepy story which I could read with a pleasurable thrill before flinging the book aside and emerging into the light. This was really happening! I was going to die here in the darkness. How long would it take, this dreadful death of starvation and thirst? I would never know for I'd be driven mad before the end.

I sank to the floor, my head buried in my arms, and I must have lost consciousness for a while, because when I looked up at last, the darkness was less dense. I had the illusion of something shining very far away, in the sky. Thank God, I wasn't blind – but where was I? The chamber was like those in the catacombs. There were hieroglyphics on the walls and stone statues, weirdly threatening, gods with animal heads, guardians of the dead. I could make out the shapes of several sarcophagi. I had been right in thinking that I was in a tomb. I got up on weak, trembling legs, supporting myself against the wall. One thought obsessed me – Nicholas had shut me up here. How could he have done such an evil thing? How cruel – how monstrously cruel!

There was a sound associated with the tiny shaft of light which fell from an aperture in the low roof. Fascinated, I watched it widening, hearing the scrape of stone as a heavy slab was dragged back Now I could see a flight of rough steps carved into one wall, directly beneath the opening. "Nicholas!" I rasped out, rushing to the foot of the steps, my dark-blinded eyes dazzled by that blessed glow of light. "Nicholas! Is that you? Let me out, for God's sake!"

A dark silhouette partially blocked the way. I could see him towering above me, then he began to descend slowly. I couldn't see his face. Nearer he came and nearer. When he was two steps from me, I saw who it was. "What's the trouble, Becky Smale? Are you frightened of the dark?" said Quiller.

The chamber was spinning – that name, that hated name that I'd not heard since orphanage days! I was a charity child again, without hope, without dignity. "How did you know?" I gasped.

He laughed, a light, mocking sound which contained no joy. "It wasn't difficult. I had read Nancy's graphic journal, you see, and when you turned up in Alexandria, as I thought you would, the name of Rebecca Costello gave you away. I'd already met the other member of the trio, Nell de Grendon."

"I know. She told me of your despicable treatment of her." There was no longer any need to pretend, and I was glad. Now I could tell him exactly what I thought of him. "Your behaviour was disgusting! You dirty bastard!"

Again, that mocking, sinister laugh. He was enjoying himself hugely. "Not only *my* behaviour, Becky – her husband was to blame."

"And who engineered it? Who encouraged his gambling?"

He shrugged. "He needed little encouragement – dissipated, amoral, an utterly useless individual, prey to his own particular devils. I had Nancy followed constantly and knew that she'd met Nell. I guessed that she'd try to give her the journal. It was a simple matter to organise events so that I got hold of it."

"When you stopped her helping Nancy, did you also guess that she would try to find me?"

"I suspected that she might, though de Grendon is a hard man and ready with his fists, keeping her in order. I waited, planning for such an emergency."

"Sir Nicholas must have rewarded you handsomely for such loyalty," I shouted, and all the time, I was slowly edging round him. Keep him talking, said a cool corner of my brain. One stroke of luck, one burst of speed, and I might reach the steps and freedom.

Quiller stepped into my path. "Don't try to run," he advised softly. "Osman and El-Darim are keeping guard above." His taunting smile deepened the lines each side of his mouth. "Sir Nicholas Renshaw? Ah, so you think he's the brain behind this? Oh, no – the man's a fool, so easily blinded by a pretty face, so wrapped up in his desire to make his mark as an archaeologist, that it's easy to deceive him, making him do as I wish without him realising it."

I couldn't believe it – my ears refusing to credit what I was hearing. Nicholas wasn't at the bottom of the trouble! "Then why was the journal in his study?" I breathed.

"I put it there to implicate him, if the need arose.

These titled gentlemen are all the same – fair game for a clever man."

"Or an unscrupulous lackey!" I retorted recklessly.

"An accident of birth, Becky," he answered, a sneer twisting his features. "You, of all people, should understand this. Didn't you ever feel when you were living in that orphanage that you were destined for higher things? Didn't the injustice of it burn and rankle? You've got out of the gutter and so have I. Oh, yes – I was supposed to be a butler's son, but my mother had gone to bed with the master and I'm sure that he was my father. I was forced to watch others, less able than me, rule the roost simply because they were got on the right side of the blanket!"

"You've done well for yourself. One could almost take you for a gentleman." I no longer cared what he did to me and didn't bother to hide my loathing.

"They owe it to me, those bloody aristocrats!" His eyes were wild, his face white as he continued boastfully: "It was like taking sweets from a baby. They didn't suspect – so full of themselves that they couldn't see what I was doing. It was 'do this, Quiller, do that', they never realised how much they relied on me, and that I knew all their nasty little secrets."

"It was you who sent that message to me – " I could see it all now.

"Yes, and didn't you fall for it? I'm a bit disappointed in you, Becky. I would have thought your backstreet training would've made you more canny. Did you hope to find Sir Nicholas had summoned you for an assignation? You women! How easily you fall for a handsome face and a title. Veronica is the same, the stupid slut! And so was Nancy."

"Where is she? Where is Nancy?" The man was mad, envy and resentment festering in him like an unhealed wound.

"She's quite safe. You'll see her soon," he promised.

"Take me to her. Let's leave here – go above and talk about it?" I begged.

A sly expression crept into his eyes. "No, Becky, I haven't finished telling you the story. You'll find it most interesting. I was a young man when I first went into service with the Renshaws. I worked for Sir Henry, or so he thought, but in reality I was Lady Dorothea's man. She was charming, gay, irresistible to the opposite sex, and she knew it. She trusted me. I ran errands of a delicate nature for her, and arranged trysts with her lovers, right under her husband's nose. He was insanely jealous, but we neatly pulled the wool over his eyes. She was generous in her appreciation of my help. Then Sir Henry decided that he wanted an heir. She was most reluctant, complaining that she didn't want to lose her figure, and suffer the pangs of childbirth, but he was insistent. He could be brutal – many's the time I've seen her bruised – so a child was conceived. She sulked and stormed and they quarrelled violently. Then she told me that she was leaving him. It was done secretly, giving him no chance to stop her, and I attended to the organisation. We sailed for Alexandria. Lady Dorothea was determined that her husband should never have the child!"

His face was working feverishly, losing that bland, polished look. Now I saw the real man beneath the surface and I shuddered. He was evil. "Miss Tranter told me of the scandal," I said, watching his hands clenching and unclenching. I hadn't realised that they were so wiry and strong.

He stared at me, eyes ablaze with fury. "That old hag! She'll be the next to go. She knows too much. She was with us – Lady Dorothea's faithful nanny; even then she was unbalanced, but her Ladyship doted on her. Tranter forgets what happened most of the time, but she sometimes remembers and that's dangerous."

"The baby died, so Nicholas said," I whispered, not

daring to move. Quiller was a maniac. I was looking the Grim Reaper in the face.

His laughter rang eerily round the tomb, the lamp throwing spectral shadows. "It didn't die! It was a strong, healthy boy – Henry Renshaw's son that he'd wanted so much! Lady Dorothea made Tranter and me swear to say that it had died at birth. We arranged a so-called funeral, but the body in the coffin was a baby goat. We fooled everyone. Lady Dorothea was delighted and she made it worth my while. My silence cost her dear."

I couldn't breathe; the walls seemed to be closing in on me. "And the child? What became of him?"

Quiller was impatient with my dull wits. "My dear Becky, haven't you guessed? How slow of you. Her Ladyship went home to England and settled down quietly in her old home in Devon. It amused her to think of Henry Renshaw fuming because his heir had been stillborn whilst, in reality, he was thriving and well in Egypt. Tranter and I stayed here to look after him, then we heard that Sir Henry had been killed and Lady Dorothea ordered us to bring the child to her. Her sister, Lady Emily, met us off the boat. Yes, she was a party to the secret. Tranter went to Cornwall to live with her, and I arranged for a nurse to take Master Jeffrey to Devon. The ground had been prepared. For some time Lady Dorothea had let it be known that she had been so distressed by the loss of her infant that she had arranged to adopt one in his place. It worked like a charm. No one suspected that the foundling, living over the border in Devon and bearing her Ladyship's maiden name, was in reality the rightful heir to Revelstoke Court. What a joke! Don't you relish the irony of it, Becky?"

"How remarkably clever," I replied, but my sarcasm was lost on him. "And how did you manage to wriggle into Sir Nicholas's service?"

"The new owner of Revelstoke Court was seeking an

agent, and it seemed an opportune moment for me to enter his household." He was watching my face like an actor playing to an appreciate audience. For the moment I was safe. He needed me.

"The new owner? D'you mean Sir Nicholas? But surely, Jeffrey should have been the legal heir?" My head was pounding, my thoughts whirling madly.

"Oh, no," he frowned, blond hair shining in the dimness. "Lady Dorothea wouldn't hear of it. She was determined that her husband should be cheated – such was her hatred, unmitigated even by his death."

"So Nicholas was believed to be the only heir. Why didn't his wife make the truth known?"

"She loved him to distraction, Becky. A feeling that you should be able to appreciate," he jeered, assured of his triumph. "He hated her. No doubt that old blab-mouth Tranter has already told you why. Lady Emily was desperately anxious for him to have the estate, hoping that with money and position he might be happy and love her. He didn't of course, but that's by the by. Also, it meant that her own bastard daughter would become the owner one day."

"But that was wicked, grossly unjust. It belonged to Jeffrey!" I was disgusted by their behaviour, yet there was a tiny spark of hope in this web of lies and intrigue – Nicholas had known nothing about it.

"What did it matter? Jeffrey was well provided for. Lady Dorothea had made him her sole heir. Then everything was thrown out of balance when she died suddenly. There was no one else, so it was decided that he should live with his adopted uncle and aunt. I was instructed to find a governess and I hired Nancy Gray. We brought him out here."

He paused for dramatic effect, sickeningly full of his own importance. I knew there was more to come and I didn't want to hear it, but his face told me that I must. "And then?" I asked, so very cold, with a chill creeping up through my shoes like the chill of death.

"Then, my dear, I decided that as I had lost my benefactress, Lady Emily should take her place. Oh, I've other business interests, but I'm the sort of person who needs to live expensively. I've such excellent taste, don't you agree? I enjoy the good things of life which only money can buy. So Lady Emily paid me to hold my tongue, just like her sister. Unfortunately, her husband was also after her money, asking awkward questions about why she needed such large sums. Then I had this quite brilliant idea – I'm sure that when I tell you, you'll think it a stroke of genius. I would arrange for Jeffrey to vanish, then I could blackmail Nicholas Renshaw, saying that if he refused to pay I would alert the authorities, telling them that he'd had him killed, knowing who he really was – the heir to Revelstoke Court."

"You fiend!" I shouted.

This delighted him. "Yes, I am. But you must admit that I'm an extremely clever one."

"So Nancy was right all along. What have you done with Jeffrey and where is she?" I cried in anguish.

"Nancy was a nuisance, always probing and prying. I had to stop her or she'd have given the game away eventually. From the beginning I knew that she'd come from an orphanage, thinking that she'd be useful to me, but I didn't tell Sir Nicholas, not till later when I wanted him to suspect her of harming the child. I said that she had inherited insanity from her mother who had died in a madhouse, all quite untrue, of course, but he believed me." He was scowling, then he brightened. "Lady Emily's suicide was quite providential, another black mark against Renshaw. She felt dreadfully guilty about Jeffrey, having grown very fond of him – dangerously so. I had to act quickly. She was tortured by remorse, such a tiresome emotion, and I added to it a trifle, rubbing salt into the wound."

"You enjoy torturing people, don't you?" I couldn't contain my contempt.

"One of life's simple pleasures, and I'm really rather

subtle about it," he answered, then his expression changed – malignant, demonic. "I like to have people in my power – to see them squirm. I wanted mastery over Sir Nicholas. I'll have it yet. Oh, yes, I've plans for him. He's going to pay whatever I demand. He'll give me the greater part of Revelstoke Court, to keep my lips sealed. If not, I'll blow this affair sky-high and see him swing for murder."

"Murder!"

He stood there, smiling at me. "Yes, murder, Becky."

My mind refused to accept it. It must be a horrible dream. I would wake from it soon. "What d'you mean? Where's the boy? Where's Nancy?"

"I'm coming to that. You'd like to see them now? Come along, then – come and see your friend and her little charge – they are here, waiting for you." He took my arm and dragged me across the floor. A huge stone sarcophagus yawned in front of me and he raised the lantern high. He was grinning, pitiless and insane. "Take a look, Becky!"

He forced my head down, and then I saw them. A charnel-house stink invaded my nostrils as I stared at the contents of that cold coffin. I had found Nancy at last. Long red hair crowned the gruesome thing within. By her side lay the decomposing body of a child. Quiller was laughing – that cold, ruthless killer.

I clung to the rim with fingers colder than the stone, convulsed by violent retching, hearing his voice droning on relentlessly. "The boy was simple to kill, once I got rid of that fool Hassan. I strangled her but it wasn't easy for she was a strong girl and fought furiously. Now, I shall have to kill you too. Such a shame to silence that golden voice. I've enjoyed listening to you singing, but you were too curious – like your friend."

"You can't do it," I whispered, struggling against his grip but he merely went on smiling, anxious that I should realise how cunning and skilful he was.

"Oh, but I can. See this cord?" He held up a slender

length of twine. "You won't feel much pain – just a few seconds, a quick twist to send you into eternity, then you'll be in there with them. Won't that be nice? Unwise of you to be so inquisitive. You came here to find out what happened to Nancy, didn't you? Now you know.

"You won't get away with it," I cried, stabbing around desperately for a way to delay him. "Beville has gone to the vault. He'll have alerted Nicholas."

"I know he's gone there. You stole the key," he said scornfully. "My men were sent to wait for him. I expect he's dead by now. You and he weren't very cautious. I've had you followed ever since you arrived in Alexandria. Everything you've said or done has been reported to me. Spies and assassins are cheap here, but there are some jobs I prefer to do myself."

The lamp was on the sandy floor now. Quiller had the rope in both hands, turning it slowly. One swift movement and it was round my neck, choking me. I fought, kicked and clawed, agonised by the pressure on my throat. My chest was bursting. I was going to die. Fear gave me a savage strength, my arms flailed and I heard him curse as my nails struck home. But it was useless, that killing pressure increased. Nothing would stop it now. Sparks and spirals danced against a crimson glare. I could feel my energy ebbing, my tortured lungs bursting for air.

For an instant I didn't register relief as he suddenly released me. Fiery pain filled my chest; circles and stars swirled madly. Someone pulled the ligature from my throat. I stood there gasping. Quiller had backed into a corner. He had a gun in his hand. The tomb seemed to explode as he fired. There was an answering report, and his face split asunder, spattering the wall with brains and blood.

Strong arms caught me as I fell. Nicholas was holding me, and I heard him say: "Rebecca, it's all over now. You are safe. Quiller is dead."

I felt myself lifted and carried up into the night air. I

could still see Nancy's decaying face and the pathetic remains of Jeffrey. The cold seemed to have penetrated my bones and paralysed my brain. I could do nothing but cling to Nicholas, shuddering uncontrollably. There were further men at the catacomb entrance. I saw the white uniforms of policemen. They were fully armed and there was a guard around the handcuffed sheik and Osman. Nicholas put me down and I took a stumbling step towards Beville. "Well done, Rebecca," he whispered, holding me tightly. "You've been so brave." He rocked me like a hurt child, but I was unable to cry.

"I'm sorry to have put you through such an ordeal," Et-Taweel said, still carrying the gun with which he had shot Quiller. "We had to get a full confession and have been listening to everything that took place. Although Quiller is dead, there are enough witnesses to vouch for his guilt and see that El-Darim and Osman face the death penalty for their part in the business.

"No time for talking now." Nicholas sounded angry. "We must get Rebecca back to the house. She's in a state of shock."

I felt Beville stiffen. "I'll take her to the hotel."

"No," snapped Nicholas. "She stays with me. Don't be an idiot, Treneman – El Tarifa is closer."

I couldn't speak, closing my eyes and giving myself up to his care, dimly aware that Beville was annoyed, but floating on a cloud of relief as Nicholas took complete control. There followed the ride through the night, the arrival at the palace with lights springing to life in every window and Nicholas carrying me upstairs, barking orders to astonished servants en route. Soon I lay in the guest room – there was comfort and warmth – the most wonderful warmth I had ever known. I was not dead. A miracle had happened – but Nancy – oh, Nancy! Tears crawled between my lashes. Someone was holding a cup to my lips. It contained a hot, sweetish liquid that burned my throat and settled like fire in my stomach, the fumes rising to make me drowsy so that I forgot the horror in deep slumber.

When I awoke, Nicholas's arms were still holding me. Feeling me stir, he stared down at me. Semi-conscious still, I couldn't believe the look in his eyes. There was a new quality there which made hope soar. "Oh, Nicholas, is that really you?" I murmured, then terror took control. I saw the tomb – Quiller's mad eyes – the bodies in the sarcophagus. "Nancy!" I shrieked, struggling to sit up. "God, she's been murdered!"

"Hush, darling – I'm here – try not to think about it." His lips were against my brow and the nightmare receded. Cradled close to him, I cried heart-brokenly, mourning Nancy, feeling that I had somehow betrayed her. Then, when my tears were spent, I obeyed his command to sleep.

Explanations came later, though they were clouded by grief. I couldn't get Nancy out of my mind, unable to eat, unable to rest. Every time I closed my eyes I saw her dead face. It was impossible to keep morbid thoughts at bay. It was making me ill. Nicholas, sensitive to my feelings, was rarely away from me, and he told me what had happened on that fateful night. Beville had arrived at the palace, accompanied by Et-Taweel, with news of the startling revelation in the family vault. They had had a skirmish with a gang of Arabs who were El-Darim's private army. Some they had killed; the others ran away. Et-Taweel set a guard of his own men to keep watch whilst he and Beville investigated the tomb. They found the skeleton of an animal in the tiny coffin which was thought to be that of Lady Dorothea's dead son. Although, at that time, they didn't realise the connection with this and Jeffrey, they considered it to be significant enough to report their find to Nicholas. I think they intended to confront him, possibly forcing an admission of guilt, I don't exactly know. However, when they entered the study it was to find one of Nicholas's spies there. He had come to say that I had been kidnapped. He had followed me from El Tarifa to the Arab quarters. It was he whom I had heard on the stairs of that rotting building.

"But why did you engage him to follow me?" I asked on the day after these dreadful events.

"I thought you were up to something and I wasn't sure what. I no longer trusted anyone, you see. I had this feeling that I was being tricked, yet couldn't get to grips with it. I'd suspected Quiller of chicanery for some time, before we left London even. I thought he was an embezzler, unsatisfied by his handling of the estate money, yet he was clever and I couldn't catch him out," Nicholas replied, seated beside me on the balcony, holding my hand. "I wasn't surprised when I heard him telling you that he'd been blackmailing Emily, though I had thought it was to do with her romance with Armstrong, but it was a bombshell to discover that Jeffrey was really my nephew. When Beville told me about the body in the vault, we tackled Miss Tranter and she confessed everything, including trying to scare Nancy by encouraging Emily to hover about in the boy's room at night, while she played ghostly tunes on the piano. She was the woman who had spirited my brother's heir away to the desert, and later brought him to England as the supposed foundling. It was El-Darim's tribe who had sheltered them."

"So, El-Darim got a cut of Quiller's profits?"

"More than that – with such a hold over him, he was able to force him to take an active part in his own shady dealings."

"And Osman?" I could hardly bear to mention his name, my arms bandaged over the burns.

"He was Quiller's lover – a vile brute who enjoys causing pain." I'd never seen such anger on his face before and I hoped that he would never look at me like that!

There was still a piece of the puzzle which didn't quite

fit. "I can't understand why Quiller hid the bodies in the catacombs. Surely they would have been found at some time?"

"Not necessarily." He sat back, resting his arm along the chair behind me so that we were still touching. "The place is honeycombed with galleries and passages. El-Darim, coming from a long line of tomb-robbers, knew a secret entrance. It must have given Quiller a perverted satisfaction to know that he was carrying out his murderous activities right under my nose. Oh, we'd searched everywhere, but he'd always led us away from the actual spot. What you did was invaluable, Rebecca."

"You didn't know who I was? Had no idea that I was a friend of Nancy's?" I breathed, drinking in every detail of that handsome face and those dark eyes watching me so intently. "You hadn't read her journal?"

"I knew nothing about it, except that she'd kicked up a rumpus when someone forced it open. It was Quiller who was so anxious to get hold of it."

"Then why were you so unpleasant to me sometimes?" I said, smarting under the remembrance of some of the cutting things he had said.

He looked a trifle shamefaced, and cross too. "God damnit, Rebecca – you do drive a fellow hard! I thought you were a scheming butterfly, intent on furthering your ambitions by any means, including having an affair with whoever would help you."

"That was unjust!" I cried, moving away from him, still so weak from my ordeal that I couldn't prevent the hot tears prickling my eyes.

Then he told me that Emily had destroyed his faith in women. His experiences with Veronica and a variety of mistresses had done nothing to alter his low opinion of females. He had been badly hurt, bearing scars that were still raw. He had sought to place me on a pedestal because of my musical gift, but this image had been tarnished because I proved to be a sensual, physical woman, not a pure goddess. Every time he'd seen me with Beville, this had been brought painfully home.

This was the moment for confessions and I told him about my past, explaining why I had needed Beville. It was humiliating, but I was frank about the orphanage so that he might understand my love for Nancy and Nell. When I had finished, he put out his hand and gently turned my head to look at him, for I had been speaking low, my face averted. "Oh, darling – you amazing creature. To have achieved so much from such a beginning. You've the sort of courage which humbles me. If only you'd told me at the start."

"How could I? I suspected you," I whispered, ashamed now of my doubts.

"And yet, despite thinking me a villain, you did forget it for a while, that night in the tent," he said in dusky undertones which rocked my slender hold on common sense. His hand was caressing that tender spot at the nape of my neck, sending shivers down my spine. "How would you react now – knowing that I'm innocent – if I were to make love to you?"

Dear reader, there is no need to tell you what that reaction was. I was hot-blooded and desperately in love, unsure of how long this bliss would last, grabbing what I could whilst it was offered. I had had a close brush with death, and this gave life an added urgency.

Oh, those early days of confusion, passion and great sorrow. There were cold practicalities to attend to – visits from the police, questions I had to answer, so much to endure and it was only Nicholas's strength that gave me the courage to do it. Of course, my involvement with him could not be concealed, bringing the inevitable clash with Beville. He kept urging me to return to the Stanley Hotel, baffled by my refusal, his anger and pain exploding on the day of Nancy's funeral.

It was a sad little procession of mourners which wound its way to the El Tarifa graveyard. There was only a handful present, and I was stunned as I watched the internment. Jeffrey's corpse had already been placed in the crypt and she was laid to rest not far from him. After the brief ceremony, Beville walked with me to the gate. We were both dressed in black, swwltering under the brazen Alexandrian sun. My face was shrouded by a thick veil and I was thankful that he could not see my expression when he came straight to the point.

"Look here, Rebecca – what's going on between you and Renshaw?" he demanded as we stood in the shade of a spreading tree, the rest offthe party some distance behind. Nicholas was glancing in our direction, probably guessing what was taking place.

"Oh, Beville, what a moment to choose! I can't speak of it now – please," I protested, feeling dizzy and sick, the tears running unchecked down my face. "Not with Nancy just buried!"

"I'm sorry, but I've got to know. It's driving me crazy. Why haven't you come back to the hotel?" he persisted stubbornly and I saw that there were new fine lines etched around his eyes. The light sparkled on his bright, curly hair and glanced off the ridge of his broken, sunburned nose. He had never been angry with me before and it hurt. Sadly, I realised that I'd taken him for granted, behaving despicably. I couldn't speak, shaking my head weakly. His mouth tightened and he stared at me hard. "You're his mistress, aren't you? Are you in love with him?"

I nodded dumbly, fumbling for a handkerchief. "Think what you will of me – I can't help myself."

His face was grim – he looked suddenly ten years older. "And he? Does he love you too?"

"I don't know," I whispered. "I don't think so."

"God, what a mess!" he grated, glaring at the distant figure of Nicholas "I'd like to knock his bloody block off! What the hell's got into you? I thought you cared for me."

"I do – oh, I do – but not in the same way." I wished he'd leave me alone – I didn't want anyone at that moment, not even Nicholas. I wanted a quiet corner where I could pray for Nancy's soul.

"Oh, Rebecca – " he almost groaned. "This is madness. You don't need the emotional upset of love. Forget him, come home and marry me. I still love you – damnit, I wish I didn't."

I tried to withdraw my imprisoned hand without offending him. I was too tired to think properly. "I can't marry you, Beville. Please don't ask me again."

"Are you going back to England with him?" His shoulders sagged but he was simmering with anger still. Helplessly, I shook my head. "D'you mean to say that you haven't sorted it out? What about your tour?"

I hadn't thought about my work, too absorbed with Nicholas and miserable about Nancy, but: "I shall carry on with that," I said rather stiffly, afraid to admit that I hadn't pressed Nicholas because I dreaded his answer.

"Very well, Rebecca, but don't think I'll give you up easily." His voice was stilted with emotion, then he softened, giving a crooked grin and smoothing my fingers in his. "I'm a stubborn old mule, you should know that by now. I shall be around, if ever you need me, waiting my chance to catch you on the rebound. Wherever you are, I'll come to you and, by God, Renshaw had better be good to you, or he'll have me to reckon with!"

I wasn't at all proud of myself, ashamed because I had hurt this generous man. He did not lose control again, very civil to Nicholas when he joined us at the gate. Had I been a more calculating woman I suppose I would not have been so honest, hedging my bets. For all I knew Nicholas might take himself off to Cornwall as soon as we docked, leaving me high and dry. He'd not mentioned future plans and I was too proud to ask him.

As the days passed, I began to recover, though Nancy was never far from my thoughts. I went often to kneel on the sandy soil by her grave, taking armfuls of flowers, thinking of our youth together. I felt guilty too because

I had obtained love at her expense. She had wanted Nicholas, as study of her journal clearly showed, and it was I who now had him, for a while at least. Reading her diary had brought her very close and I felt that I knew her now much better than I had in Bristol. Gradually, those solitary visits to the cemetery where the beige stones threw back the heat and the breeze stirred the olive trees, brought a measure of peace to my tormented spirit.

It turned out that Quiller had had a finger in any number of illegal pies – drug trafficking, slave trading, smuggling and espionage – anything, no matter how unsavoury, which would yield a quick profit. Once the lid came off this cesspool of crime, many notable persons in Alexandria were highly embarrassed and heads rolled. Et-Taweel was more than pleased; he had been trying to break the ring for years. Veronica, rather more deeply involved in Quiller's plots than was at first supposed, made good her escape and was never heard of again. Terence Armstrong came to say goodbye and then disappeared into the interior, serving in a leper colony. Nicholas was planning to return to England, leaving the excavations in the capable hands of a colleague. Beville and I were to travel with him, Fleur, a temporary governess, and Miss Tranter.

Nicholas and I found joy in each other's arms, for I stayed on at El Tarifa, closing my mind to the impropriety of it. They were healing days and magical nights when nothing disturbed us but the whispering palms lifting their graceful heads to the moon and the scent of flowers drifting in at the open windows of the bedroom. But, of course, this had to end, life intruded no matter how I strove to shut it out. Nicholas had not spoken of any permanence in our love affair and this was difficult to accept. Why was everything so complex? I wondered. One had to pay for happiness with a corresponding amount of pain. Pleasure and sadness, joy and agony – I knew them all now, but also knew that I'd rather pay the price than travel along a dull, calm road, with tomorrow a repetition of today.

When the time came to leave Alexandria, Nicholas stood beside me as we looked our last on that strange port which held so many dark secrets behind its shutters. I was happy and sad all at once, my heart breaking because my search for Nancy had ended in tragedy, yet so crazily in love that merely looking at Nicholas made me feel giddy. We lingered on deck, drinking in the breathtaking Egyptian sunset, nearly blinded by the band of scarlet light which lay across the water. Soon the sun would disappear, leaving a peacock trail across the dark clouds of night. It was as if we stood alone in an emptied world.

"Well, Rebecca, and what have you to say for yourself? Is your head brimming with visions of operatic triumphs?" he asked caustically, a shadow in his dark eyes.

"I'm looking forward to getting back to work," I answered truthfully. "I've been away from it too long."

"Ah, so eager for the glare of the footlights – the cheers of the crowd," he observed cynically, his manner coldly aloof.

His changes of mood were exasperating, but I was determined not to be ruffled, saying calmly: "You know perfectly well that it's the music that's important, not I. Haven't we been over this ground before?" I paused, uncertain of how to continue, then took a deep breath and plunged on recklessly. "I've found someone who matters to me far more than anything – even my singing. Yes, I want to go to Buenos Aires and yes, I'm ambitious, but it would be all the more wonderful if you were coming with me."

"You can't be serious, can you?" He was staring at me with a half hopeful, half doubting expression on his thin, tanned face. "I'm sorry, my dear, but I've learned to distrust pretty speeches and fancy promises." His voice was unsure. Nicholas, who always gave the impression of supreme confidence, was hesitant.

I had to say it no matter what transpired, voicing the words which had trembled on my lips for ages. "I love you, Nicholas. I'll follow you to the ends of the earth, if need be. I'll give up my career. We'll do whatever you want."

There was a second's pause, then: "Rebecca, my darling, you mustn't make such a sacrifice for me – you'd end up hating me. I forbid you to mention giving up the stage – and, if you'll have me, I'll marry you as soon as we set foot in England."

I was struck dumb with wonder as he pulled me into his embrace. Recovering my powers of speech, I remonstrated with him. "Marriage? You can't be serious. I don't expect marriage. I'm happy to be your mistress. You can't possibly marry me – I'm a bastard – a charity child – it wouldn't look at all well on your family tree! I know nothing about running a great house or handling servants. My God! You'd be the laughing stock of society if you made me your wife."

"Damn society! I want you! I want us to be married! I may be mad, but I'll take another chance in the matrimonial stakes, but if you're ever unfaithful, I'll kill you! D'you understand?" he said fiercely.

I nodded, dazed with happiness, nudging my head against his chest. Let him be as tyrannical as he willed with me, I didn't care. It was his way of showing how much I meant to him, and yet: "Oh, I'll marry you, Nicholas, if you are quite, quite sure. I love you with all my heart and soul – but you've never actually said it."

He frowned, impatient with the things that bother women. "Said what? Oh, I see – those three damning words, eh? I've told you that I love you on many a night, and showed you how much too."

I placed my fingers over his lips, feeling the brush of his black moustache. "You've said it in the heat of passion, but never in the cold light of day," I reminded gently.

"Damn it all, Rebecca," he protested, kissing my hand and holding me close. "I'm wild about you. I love you and you know it! I love your laughter, your tears, your courage – even your damnable temper! I love you!" he shouted, making one or two strolling passengers look round. Then he kissed my lips, a long, deep kiss.

I watched the fading light from the circle of his arms. Soon the ship's lanterns would pierce the dark wall of night. I thought of Nancy. Darkness had closed her eyes forever, and yet she had come to me on that evening when I had first surrendered to Nicholas. I was convinced of it. I don't know how, but she had brushed aside the veil of death, warning me of danger, demanding retribution. I shivered as I saw in my mind's eye the dead body of Quiller. What horrible pit of hell did his evil soul now inhabit?

Nicholas felt me tremble and, thinking that I was cold, drew my wrap more closely about me. It was a simple, loving gesture and it filled me with contentment. I was in his care now, belonging to him, dependent on him. I could look forward to the future with confidence, and gradually forget the terrors of the past. I was soon to be his wife and, with his arms holding me, I could feel myself shedding layer upon layer of tiresome, inessential things. Any trace of self-importance, greed and vanity melted away. I felt so good, transformed into a woman at peace in the presence of her mate, and this healing sense of tranquillity was powerful enough to banish the dark nightmares for all time.

Epilogue

Seated in my study during quiet moments snatched from my full, busy life, I sometimes find it hard to believe that my adventures in Egypt really happened. It now seems far away and remote, and yet sometimes as vivid as if it happened yesterday. What am I doing here? I ask myself. What right have I to be living in this gracious manor in the heart of Cornwall? Once I was Becky Smale – now I'm Rebecca Costello, opera singer, and Lady Renshaw, mistress of Revelstoke Court. The workings of fate are inscrutable. Who are we to question chance, destiny, Karma? Call it what you will, there seems to have been some mysterious force which linked Nancy, Nell and myself.

I was given little opportunity to brood about Nancy and for years had pushed it to the back of my mind. Then something happened to bring memories of Alexandria back again. Ten years after making that binding vow under the clock tower, I met Nell there. I had tried to find her when Nicholas and I returned to England but was unable to do so, then I was swept up in the whirl of preparations for the South American tour. I was newly married to the man I adored and life galloped ahead, bearing me with it. I was totally fulfilled. I had my career and, above all, I had Nicholas. I gave him the son he wanted and, a little later, we had a daughter. There was no happier woman anywhere in the world.

Of course the pathway to success is a stony one and I had met setbacks but had overcome them, with the help of hard work, dedication and good friends. Life had been good to me. I had this home and another in London, beside a villa in Italy and El Tarifa. My voice had matured and I was now well known, the pinnacle being reached when I had starred in productions supervised by Giacomo Puccini himself, who said that I was his ideal Madama Butterfly. I hadn't forgotten my old friends. The Lintons often came to stay and it was a joy to have their children (nine by now) romping on the sands and rioting in the orchards with mine. Henrietta's business was booming and she made most of my clothes. Albert had joined the Temperance Society and was acting again. Gertie had married a titled gentleman, like many another Gaiety Girl, though it was difficult to understand how they achieved it with so many taboos in upper-class society. Dear old Maestro Angeleri, frail now but young in heart, was still imparting his knowledge to a new generation of musicians.

So the years slipped past and I suddenly realised that it was 1910, and time for me to return to the orphanage as promised. On the anniversary of the day of the vow, I waited there under the clock tower. I had the strange sensation that Nancy's ghost would keep the tryst. The sun was hot, making the playground shimmer and I could have sworn that I saw her – that tall figure striding out boldly. I could hear her quick step, see those challenging green eyes and that mantle of shining red hair. I wasn't afraid to meet her shade, filled with tremendous joy.

"Nancy!" I cried, running forward. "Nancy, I'm here!"

"It's not Nancy – it's Nell," said a voice, waking me to reality, and I felt her hands gripping mine.

My eyes cleared and I saw her, yet I'm certain that the other presence was there too – there were three of us. Yes, it was Nell, but dowdy and careworn, old before her time. A small boy clung to her hand and he was looking at me questioningly, the child she had been carrying on the last occasion that we met. There was so much to say, so much to tell and first of all I had to explain about Nancy. She wept, and so did I. Then, when we had recovered, she recounted what had happened to her. It was a sad story. Things had gone from bad to worse. They had lost Combermere. Henford Grange had been mortgaged to the hilt and the bank had foreclosed. Then, Charles de Grendon was found dead in a London back street. It was drink that had killed him and Nell had watched his deterioration through agonising years. She and her son had gone to the Dower House, living with her aunts on the small allowance wisely invested for her by her grandfather. She had steadfastly refused to let Charles touch it, withstanding his rages and bullying. Even after his death, she lived in constant fear of Cordelia turning up, demanding money. The aunts were failing in health and Nell acted as housekeeper and nurse, an exhausting round of toil.

We talked for a long while, ignoring the stares of the orphans who had come out to play. At last I managed to convince her that I needed her assistance. I was having trouble with Fleur, a difficult, sulky girl who had always resented me. Miss Tranter had been the only one who could do anything with her and she had died two years before. Since then, governesses had come and gone, unable to cope with her. I had done my best to love her, but her position rankled and she had a chip on her shoulder as big as a house. We had treated her as our own, though she was Emily's daughter with no true connection with Nicholas and we had made our male heir, my own lad. I frequently lost patience with her. There was only room for one prima donna – and that was me!

Nell was reluctant to leave her aunts, but I was very worried about her own health. She looked as if a puff of wind might blow her away, so thin and pale. My heart was heavy with dread. I certainly wasn't going to risk losing her too! When I assured her that I would personally engage a competent body to care for them, she smiled for the first time, hope lighting up her sunken eyes. Before we left, I honoured the other part of our pledge, going to see the matron of the Home – not Mrs Bowell, I'm glad to say, she had been sacked long ago for gross mismanagement, but a motherly woman who was grateful for the substantial sum I donated, promising faithfully to use it for the benefit of the children.

Nell's coming has been a great blessing to me, but her presence has also brought back the past. It is with a sense of relief that I now allow the floodgates of memory to open, my mind spanning the years, seeing those terrifying events in Egypt flickering across the screen of my brain like a picture show. Nicholas agrees with Nell, saying that we should get it down on paper. She has changed so much lately, the roses have returned to her cheeks, the youthful spring to her step, and her child loves it here. So, between engagements, I work with her. We have more than just recollection to guide us, for there are the three journals. I have kept Nancy's safely all these years.

"Oh, Nell," I cry, as the fears, the horrors rise up like grisly spectres. "I don't think I can go on with this!"

"Of course you can," she replies crisply, stabbing her pen into the inkwell. "God, if I can bear to dwell on Charles and his bitch of a sister, you can do your bit too!"

She is right, and I try to gather my thoughts. I go to the window looking out across the lawn enclosed by flower beds. There are lupins spearing the cress-green foliage with spikes of mauve, pink and blue, with delphiniums nodding behind them. Hollyhocks stand boldly against the soft grey walls, drowsing under the afternoon sun. My eye travels beyond to the circular patches of burnt-umber soil where damask roses breathe out their perfume as they did in the gardens of El Tarifa. There are pines too, as there were on that exotic shore, twisted into grotesque shapes by the wind from the sea. I hear the gulls crying and, in memory, another sound mingles with this lament – the eerie call to prayer chanted by blind *mueddins*. That sound had wailed over

Alexandria – we three had heard it. I had thought I would never be able to go to El Tarifa again, but I had done so, laying flowers on Nancy's grave, begging that she would pardon me for marrying the man she had loved so hopelessly.

"Come along, Rebecca – stop trying to avoid the issue," scolds Nell, writing away industriously. I'm afraid she does most of the work, while I supply the information. I shiver, even now when the manor lies dreaming under the somnolence of a summer heatwave. That tomb, I'll never forget its deathly chill, but we plod on, Nell and I, making some small recompense to Nancy for all that she suffered. The afternoon is wearing on and I sit at the window, hearing the squeak of Nell's pen, answering her as best I can. How blessed is the peace of my home. I smell the tang of the sea mingled with the delicious odour of sun-warmed strawberries. Voices disturb my meditations and, leaning out, I see two men coming across the lawn from the stables.

"Put your work away, Nell," I call gaily. "Here come Nicholas and Beville."

Nell loses her composure, quite flustered, and I'm amused to see that she is blushing. Nicholas has been humorously accusing me of matchmaking, but really I've only meddled a very little, for Beville has had eyes for no one but Nell ever since she arrived. This makes me happy for they're well suited. I hurt him once and can't forgive myself for it, whilst she deserves a kindly, considerate husband after that brute she married. Then, all other things are forgotten as, my heart thumping as it always does when Nicholas is near, I rise to greet him.

I can hear him shouting greetings to the children as they rush to meet him. Nanny is ordering them to make less noise because we are busy in the study and must not be disturbed, but I smile across at Nell. My husband's footsteps are coming along the passage, impatient and eager, knowing that whatever I'm doing, I shall put it aside for him.